... ᴇLL RANG

Gavin had seen enough of Krogan's other matches to
the beast would first wait to be attacked. He found it hard not to
take him up on his offer. Every natural cell in his body was
screaming for him to throw the first punch, second punch, and
anything else he could throw in. But that wasn't the game plan.
Gavin neared him, hands down.

"What's the matter, Krogan? Feel like we're ganging up on
you?" Gavin bluffed.

Krogan smiled nonchalantly. "Gang up? You are alone,
Pierce."

"That's not what I see. You're surrounded. Nervous?"

Krogan frowned, then started to circle around to Gavin's
side.

Gavin countercircled.

The audience impatiently started chanting Krogan's name.

"Confess, Krogan. Did you—" Gavin said, when Krogan suddenly lunged.

"When I get you, I'll have no mercy."

*　　*　　*

Acclaim for *Driven*

"Highly original...spooky ... impressive...outstanding suspense...a skillful mix of passages that entertain and frighten....
Fast-paced and drenched in evil...a solid crossover novel."

—*Publishers Weekly*

TAKEDOWN

A GAVIN PIERCE NOVEL

W. G. Griffiths

WARNER FAITH

A Division of AOL Time Warner Book Group

The events and characters in this book are fictitious. Certain real locations and public figures are mentioned, but all other characters and events described in the book are totally imaginary.

Copyright © 2003 by W. G. Griffiths
All rights reserved.

Warner Books, Inc., 1271 Avenue of the Americas, New York, NY 10020
Visit our Web site at www.twbookmark.com.

⚙ WARNER *Faith* A Division of AOL Time Warner Book Group

Printed in the United States of America
First Warner Books printing: June 2003
10 9 8 7 6 5 4 3 2 1

ISBN: 0-446-67892-9
LCCN: 2003101822
Book design by Fearn Cutter de Vicq

"The world has a soul, and is full of demons."

Thales of Miletus, the earliest known Greek philosopher

"For we wrestle not against flesh and blood, but against principalities, against powers, against the rulers of the darkness of this world, against spiritual wickedness in high places."

The Apostle Paul

TAKEDOWN

PROLOGUE

I'm *not* going in there!" Amy's fist clenched a Zip-locked bag of breadcrumbs, her perfect profile steeled straight ahead.

"Then wait out here." Gavin sighed and started to leave.

She reached out and grabbed his arm. "You know I can't do that."

"You'll be fine. The sun is out. There're people everywhere, and you have plenty of food for the starving fat pigeons. I'll be right back."

"You know you won't. You'll get drawn in again and I won't be there to snap you out of it."

"Please . . . stay right here on the bench. I promise I won't be long."

Amy looked him in the eye. "You swear?"

"More than I should . . . but I'm trying." He pecked her on the cheek and left.

Detective Gavin Pierce turned the corner and entered the darkness of the Bronx Zoo's Reptile House, as he had done every Sunday for the last three months. The weekly ritual he practiced was a paradox he had thought reserved only for the very religious or the insane. The Reverend Jesse J. Buchanan, better known to Gavin and Amy as Buck, called it "believing in order to see."

Gavin considered what life would be like if he had never met Buck, an obscure lead in a homicide case in which his grandfather had been a victim. The killer—or rather, *serial* killer—might still be at large, but because of Buck, Gavin's eyes had been opened to a nightmarish world he had never before known existed. Even more important, he and Amy would never have been concerned about the prisoner getting free. Especially this prisoner. So his conclusion, which would change with the tides, was that ignorance was truly bliss, right up until the time you realize you're on the wrong side of the rhino pen.

As usual, Amy could not stay put. By the time the door shut, she had hurried to his side, taken his hand, and squeezed it tightly. In the moment it took for his blue eyes to adjust to the darkness, the dank air seemed to drop forty degrees. Amy slipped her arm around his, hugging it like a firehouse brass pole. The hall was crowded, as it should be on a hot summer day, people dressed in shorts and T-shirts, bearing no goose bumps or frosted breath. Odd how the eerie chill never seemed to affect anyone else. Somehow the "thing"—or demon, to use Buck's terminology—had a way of sniffing out their presence and rewarding them with an unearthly cavern-deep cold, as if this were its way of saying, "I remember you." And putting on more clothes didn't help. No. An arctic goose-down parka would have no more success warming their chilled bones than a sleeping bag could warm a corpse six feet under.

Amy shook off a shiver. "You feel it?" she whispered.

"Yes," Gavin said, hating to admit it.

"Good. Then we know it's still here and alive. Let's leave."

"No, I need to see it."

"But why?" Amy's tone reflected her frustration over repeating this strange ritual week in and week out.

Gavin didn't answer. Didn't want to answer.

"Sometimes I think you *need* for it to see you."

He couldn't argue that but wouldn't admit to it either.

"I'm never coming here again," Amy declared as if she meant it.

"I know. You say that every week."

"I mean, I don't ever want to come to the zoo again . . . the Bronx . . . anywhere near this place."

"But I have to." Gavin squeezed her hand as they continued on through the darkness.

He didn't have to look to his right as they passed the first cage to know there was a twenty-four-foot python named Samantha curled up on a limb under leafy foliage. He had seen her, and all of the other inhabitants of this corridor leading to "the cage," enough times to render a detailed sketch and bio of every one.

Gavin acknowledged the elderly attendant's wave with a nod as they turned the final corner. The man never spoke to Gavin, though he had tried once. After Gavin's sixth Sunday visit in a row, the old guy had finally ventured, "I guess you must really like this place." Gavin's response had been an honest, "No, actually I hate it here." The old man had never spoken to him again . . . just waved.

As usual, people moving down the dark hall didn't stop long at the tortoise cage, the more interesting species being housed before and beyond. Little did they realize that Jeremy, the boring young Galapagos Island tortoise, backed into the far corner where it always stayed, would be any zoo's main attraction if the truth were known.

Here come the nails, Gavin told himself as they drew near. No sooner had he thought it than Amy dug in.

"Easy," he whispered to her.

"Sorry," she said as they stopped just before *the* window. "Couldn't Buck have sent Krogan into a different kind of animal?" she whined. "Did it have to be something they keep in the Reptile House?"

"He wanted something with a long life expectancy . . . you know that," Gavin explained patiently.

"There *are* other animals that live long, you know."

"Oh yeah? Like what?"

"I don't know . . . elephants live long . . . and they keep them outside in the sunshine."

Gavin looked at her. "A demon-possessed elephant. Now, why didn't Buck think of that?" he said dryly. "Look, the only reason the tortoise is in here is because it was trying to kill the other tortoises."

"I don't think Buck figured on that."

"Nah, he's got this all worked out to a science," Gavin muttered sarcastically.

"Oh, look," the woman in front of them said to a couple of children. "It's coming this way."

They had arrived at "the cage." When Gavin took another step and looked in, the giant tortoise wasn't watching the woman or her children some twenty feet away. No. As expected, it was coming straight toward Gavin.

"Is it there?" Amy asked, hanging back.

"Yes."

"Anything else in the cage with it?"

"Of course not."

"Does it look . . . healthy?"

"As healthy as it always does."

"Good. Then let's leave."

He didn't answer, his focus now fully on the tortoise, which had stopped just a few feet from the glass. As always it was staring—or, as Gavin thought, glaring. He was no mind reader, but he could easily imagine what was going on inside the tortoise's head, and he believed somehow the entity inside knew what Gavin was thinking too . . . every thought.

"How's the food, Krogan?" Gavin sneered, tapping on the glass.

The tortoise just stared, unblinking.

"That's not what we're here for," Amy said sternly. "Remember what Buck said about getting it mad."

"Yeah, wouldn't want to get it mad." Of course he remembered Buck's warnings. First, "*Be objective.*" The reason for going to the zoo was to check on the tortoise's health. Period. Leave the pain of Krogan's past atrocities outside. His second warning was, "*Don't look in the tortoise's eyes.*" Buck said the eye was the window of the soul, and the last thing Gavin should do was connect directly with the powerful demon inside the tortoise. A demon the likes of which, Buck—supposedly a seasoned exorcist or deliverance minister or whatever they called him—had never encountered. And above all, "*Pray to God for the tortoise's continued protection.*" According to the verse Buck had read to them from the Bible, if the tortoise died, the demon would escape and go on a mission to destroy its captors, namely Gavin, Amy, and Buck.

Gavin had the most trouble with the prayer part of the instructions. In fact, he just didn't pray at all. There was nothing he hated more on the planet than the demon that was allegedly inside the tortoise, but he found it impossible, even embarrassing, to pray for the helpless animal in which it was trapped.

Amy tugged on his arm. "It's here, it's alive. Let's go."

Gavin nodded but didn't move. Curious. When he had first started these visits, the tortoise would meet him in . . . well, a kind of tortoise rage. Snapping, kicking dirt, snarling, biting at anything that came close—"*Like a baseball manager arguing a call,*" Gavin had once told Amy. That kind of behavior eventually caused the zoo to separate Jeremy from the other animals. But recently the tortoise had calmed, at least physically, content to just get close and stare intently. The question loomed: What was it so intent about?

Amy spoke, but Gavin wasn't listening. As on their last visit, the tortoise offered its profile, its large, black eye holding Gavin's attention, appearing larger than life, sucking in all the energy surrounding it. The truth was Gavin wanted Amy outside. Not so much for her protection as to keep her from interfering. If Buck had actually sent an entity that had killed Grampa into this tortoise, an entity that could read Gavin's thoughts, then he would think of nothing but hate, scorn, and dominance over the evil thing that had taken away Grampa's precious life.

You are nothing, Gavin thought as hard and focused as he could, trying to make his thoughts louder than words.

Suddenly his mind was filled with other words. *Soon I will be free and you will be mine.*

Gavin was about to ask Amy if she'd heard that, but then realized the message wasn't audible. He wondered if Krogan had planted the thought in his mind or if his mind had just made it up by association. How could he know, the brain being so complex, and spiritual energy being impossible to prove?

Soon. Mine.

Never, Gavin answered silently.

Laughter. His mind was filled with mocking laughter. Gavin could no longer blink, didn't want to blink. He wanted to focus his thoughts, but the laughter wouldn't leave. He began to see images in the tortoise's oily eye . . . faces . . . faces that were alive, moving, talking. Talking to him. Grampa, his friend John Garrity, the news reporter Gassman, Amy's twin sister's fiancé . . . all talking about their everyday lives . . . all dead now because of the demon. He started picturing their deaths. Was his mind just remembering what he'd seen . . . or was he being prodded?

Mine.

"They're not yours," Gavin said aloud. "They *never* were yours."

Other faces. Buck's, his own, Amy's. Amy laughing, running away, teasing him to chase her.

Soon. When you least expect it. Mine.

"Nooo!" Gavin yelled.

Abruptly, Gavin was falling away from the eye—no, from the cage.

"What is with you?" Amy scolded. She had yanked him away and now had him against the wall, shouting in his face. "You've been ignoring everything I've said to you for the last ten minutes."

"Ten?"

"At least five."

"But I—"

"But nothing!" She wouldn't let him finish. "You've been doing the very thing Buck told you not to do."

Gavin massaged the bridge of his nose. He felt groggy, tired. He looked toward the cage. He wanted . . . needed to see what . . .

"Don't even think about it," she said, pushing him back away from the cage. "We're done with this place and that freakin' turtle. If you ever come here again, you won't find me when you get back. And that's a promise."

1

A Monday night, two years later

Jackhammer Hoban cried out, and this time he wasn't acting. The Tyrant's heel had hit his face, splitting his lower lip.

"*Tyrant . . . Tyrant . . . Tyrant . . .*"

The crowds, who had once been loyal Jackhammer fans, were now chanting for their new hero's dominance in this megahyped World Wrestling Xchange title fight. Hoban wanted to spring to his feet and ram his fist down Tyrant's throat for the blatant contact on such a routine move. Later the moron would likely apologize for the "slip." But keeping with the script, Hoban lay there, in the middle of the ring, faking helplessness as Tyrant climbed to the top ropes of the corner post for his trademark layout, back-flipping body slam, or, as he called it, "The A-Bomb." Hoban spit blood as the audience roared with anticipation.

Tyrant paused to shake his cavemanlike dreadlocks and flex his rippling muscles. He then dove high and backward into the air, back arched, rotating slowly toward the center of the ring. As many times as they'd practiced this maneuver together for the show, Hoban knew the chance of Tyrant landing precisely on target to ensure no injury was at best fifty-fifty. But the dramatic move was always a huge crowd pleaser and deemed worth the gamble by the

WWX, especially when the only one who would get hurt was Jack-hammer.

To Hoban, it seemed just yesterday that chants of "*Jackham-mer . . . Jackhammer . . . Jackhammer . . .*" had echoed throughout the angry coliseum. At nearly seven feet and three hundred thirty pounds of weight-room muscle, Jackhammer Hoban, with his long, brushed-back black hair, had been the idol of most every wrestling fan in America. But now, after years of alcohol and drug abuse, cursing out fans—some of whom were kids sitting with parents—arrests, and lawsuits for reckless endangerment both on and off the road, coupled with a declining physical ability to execute the de-manding stunts required to excite the fans, he'd fallen into the worst of all categories: boring. Faxes, e-mails, and laundry bags of fan mail for other wrestlers all pointed out that Hoban was neither loved nor hated. The bottom line demanded a wrestler be one or the other. And if he was both, the fans' crushing rush to the gate could stop the earth on its axis. But such was not the case with Jackhammer Hoban. He needed to be phased out of the spotlight and given the short ride down the dark road of WWX retire-ment . . . and Tyrant was just the one they wanted to send him off.

The six-five, two-hundred-ninety-pound, granite-hard Tyrant came down exactly where he should have, but without distributing his lethal weight at the last second into the impact-absorbing mat. Underneath the mat, microphones were strategically placed to magnify Tyrant's aeroslam to thunderclap decibels.

"Agghhh!" Hoban exhaled, unable to breathe in.

"Oops," Tyrant said so only Hoban could hear.

Hoban could not reply but swore to himself he would someday be the one to say "oops" to Tyrant.

The referee slid into position on his hands and knees. "One . . . two . . ."

Keeping with the script, fighting through the pain and probably a cracked rib, Hoban bridged up and rolled Tyrant off. The referee stopped the count and retreated to a safe location in the corner. Holding his ribs, Hoban did not have to act to reveal the pain he was in. The script called for him to slingshot off the ropes into Tyrant, but he could not. Ever the showman, Tyrant slid out of the ring and moments later returned with a composite folding table. Hoban knew this would be murder on his ribs. Tyrant propped the table against a corner post, then picked the helpless Jackhammer up onto his shoulders and paraded him around the mat.

"Tyrant . . . Tyrant . . . Tyrant . . ."

When Tyrant had finished his circle of dominance, he fell backward toward the table, crashing through it with Jackhammer as the battering ram.

Hoban did not move . . . could not move. Tyrant pulled up on his legs and the referee returned.

"One . . . two . . . three."

Tyrant jumped to his feet as the referee pronounced the victory to the deafening sound of crowd chants and pounding heavy-metal music.

Fake paramedics rushed to Jackhammer's assistance before allowing him to walk away, head down, up the ramp to the dressing room. The pain was sharp with every breath, but nothing compared to the pain of his humiliation. The media hype would start immediately, demanding a rematch to draw the fans, but it didn't take a genius to know that script would be his last.

2

Detective Gavin Pierce, sawdust sticking to the sweat on his forehead and arms, looked skeptically at his partner, Chris Grella, who had just traced out a prototype for the roof rafters.

"Now what?" Chris asked, a circular saw in his right hand, ready to make a cut.

"Before you cut, I'd like you to explain your measurements—or should I say artwork? This wood isn't cheap."

"No, but *you* are. Why don't you just buy the old Johnson place next door? The guy loved you and his kids would negotiate a great deal for you. You'd get to stay in this great neighborhood you love so much, plus your wife wants a built-in swimming pool, which they already have. But now, with this thing, you won't have room for one."

"Can we get back to this? I just don't understand how you came up with all that scribble," Gavin said, pointing at a two-by-ten with pencil lines slicing and angling in every direction.

"Math . . . simple math, that's how."

"Math?" Gavin scoffed. "What kind of math? You nailed this board to the side of my house with one nail, tilted and angled it in six different directions, each time eyeing it from thirty feet away. And now half of the cut lines you made are scribbled out and shaded in. I mean, what is this, carpentry or golf?"

Chris, power saw in hand, a large droplet of sweat dangling

from the tip of his nose, looked up from his calculations. "It's pure common-sense-netry."

"Common-sense-netry?" Gavin eyed him doubtfully.

"Yeah. Look, I got us this far, didn't I?" Chris said, motioning toward the work they had already accomplished.

The answer was yes. Chris, Gavin's faithful partner in the homicide division at the Nassau County Police Department, had also been a faithful friend in helping Gavin expand his home for his new and growing family. When Gavin received estimates beyond his budget for adding a new master bedroom suite onto the side of his modest North Shore home, Chris had insisted they throw the quotes in the garbage and do it themselves. That was math Gavin had no trouble understanding. Chris had worked with his father in the carpentry business before becoming a cop and had built a similar extension on his own house several years ago.

"Just do it!" Gavin hollered, using his weight to brace the long plank.

"Trust me, Gav," Chris said with a smile. "When we're done, you and Amy are not going to believe your eyes."

"That's what I'm afraid of."

"Now . . . was it this line or—"

"Just cut."

Gavin squinted and jerked his chin away as more sawdust came in his direction. On purpose, he thought. Chris first cut out a small wedge, which he had been calling the "bird's mouth," then repositioned himself and made the level soffit and plumb facia cuts. He then moved to the other end of the rafter and made the ridge cut. He marked the rafter with a big red *T*.

"Why a *T*?" Gavin asked.

"The *T* is for template," Chris explained. "But if there's a different letter you prefer, I can do that too."

"Okay, how about *C* for Chris, so we know which pile of wood you'll be paying for when they don't fit right?"

"Bring the other saw to this end so we can both cut, wise guy. All you have to do is cut this straight line thirty-four times. Think you can handle that?"

The hours passed, and soon, to Gavin's tired and sweaty amazement, the rafters were in place. Chris's common-sense-netry had apparently worked.

"Break time!" sang a sweet female voice. "Getcha cold drinks here!"

"Perfect timing," Chris said.

Gavin allowed a smile. Something only Amy, his wife of one year, could produce. He and Chris made their way down their ladders to the new plywood floor.

"Wow!" Amy said, carrying a blue cooler with both hands. "A house!"

"Not quite. Let me take that from you," Chris offered.

"Oh, sure! I parade all over town filling this thing, and when I've got two feet left to go, a *man* needs to rescue me."

"Chris is just trying to save himself," Gavin said.

"You guys are rough," Chris complained good-naturedly, taking the cooler. "And that's quite a profile you've got there, lady. Whoa, what did you bring us to drink, rocks? Are you crazy . . . to be carrying something this heavy in your condition?"

Amy was very pregnant. Eight months, fourteen days, according to the doctor's calculations. Except for what looked like a basketball under her light summer dress, she was showing very little weight gain. Throughout her pregnancy she had remained active, and the doctor had given her a perfect bill of health.

"'There's no life as tiring as one always retiring,'" she told Chris as she scanned the new rafters.

"Another old saying from her Japanese grandmother?" Chris asked Gavin, who was wiping his face clean with a sweaty bandana.

Gavin shrugged. "I suppose. They're too *weird* to make up."

"Maybe she could get a job writing fortune cookies," Chris suggested, fishing through the cooler for a drink. "What would you like, Gav? Ice water or . . . ice water?"

"Ice water sounds good right now," Gavin said as he kissed Amy's bronze lips hello, then bent down and kissed her round belly.

"I can't believe how much you've gotten done," Amy said to Gavin. "It looks great. *Watashi wa shiawase.*"

"What?" Chris asked.

"It's Japanese," Gavin explained. "It means, 'I'm happy.'"

"So why not just say, 'I'm happy'?" Chris wondered.

"She did."

"Forget it. I don't know why I ever bother talking to you."

"Because you two work very well together," Amy declared with a wink.

Chris handed Gavin a clear, cold bottle of Fiji water. "Yeah, I don't know what I'd do without him."

"Oh, that reminds me," Amy said, looking at Gavin. "Did you get a chance to stop in at Motor Vehicle and register my minivan?" She turned to Chris. "His car is getting too tight for us," she explained, rubbing her belly.

"Amy, there's no such thing as 'stopping in' at the DMV. I would have gotten nothing done on the house. The last time I registered a car there, I had to wait three hours. Maybe tomorrow, but soon, I promise."

Just then a portable phone resting on a windowsill rang.

"I'll get it," Amy said. "Relax and drink."

"Yeah, relax and drink," Chris said sarcastically to Gavin. "You've really been working much too hard."

Gavin did not respond, concerned as he watched Amy navigate

an obstacle course of loose, jagged wood blocks, slippery nails, and tangled extension cords. He should have taken care to clean up while he was working. If she got hurt, he would never forgive himself. Her natural tendency to do everything for herself was driving him crazy now that she was pregnant.

"Hello," Amy said cheerfully into the phone. "Oh, hi! Yes, yes, of course I remember you. How's your grandfather?" After a moment of silence, she turned around and looked at Gavin, her face troubled, the phone still at her ear. "Oh no. . . . Yes. . . . Is he . . . Yes. . . . Of course. . . . We certainly will. . . . Thank you for calling." She put the phone down.

"What's the matter?" Gavin asked, already on his feet.

"That was Samantha."

Gavin thought for a moment. "Samantha Buchanan?" he wondered, the air tightening around him.

Amy nodded. "Buck's had a heart attack."

Her words instantly took Gavin out of the here-and-now to a time and place he wanted to believe had never existed. A time earmarked by an act so violent it had changed his life in a moment. A life he had managed to reestablish. "Is he dead?" he asked.

"No, thanks to emergency bypass surgery. Triple. He's at Delhi Hospital. When he came to he asked for us to pray."

"Pray?" Gavin heard himself say.

Amy stared at him. Her cheery glow was gone, replaced with an expression he had not seen in a while. He was familiar with all of Amy's expressions. The first time he had seen her beautiful face was in her comatose twin sister's hospital room, where she'd been all-business, intense, demanding to know who he was and what he was doing there. He also knew her excited face, when her green Asian feline eyes would open wide and her bright smile would wrinkle her gentle nose—like when he'd asked her to marry him or every time he came home with cookie-dough ice cream. But this expression wasn't excitement or anger or even sorrow for sudden illness. It was dread. She stood as frozen and unblinking as a mannequin, the blood drained from her complexion. He felt her fear—the kind that comes from experience, not just knowledge. He'd been there.

But those were fears from a different time. Now, after two of the best years of his life, Gavin had developed his own theories of the past events. Theories he'd worked out after much research. Well, not research . . . but he had seen that HBO documentary and read enough related material to rationally explain what had probably happened and dispel the kind of fear boring through Amy's less informed, less open mind. Maybe now was the time to—

"Who's Buck?" Gavin heard Chris say. He'd all but forgotten his friend was there.

"Reverend Buchanan," Amy replied, her eyes on Gavin's.

Chris frowned thoughtfully. "Why does that name sound familiar?"

"He's that old black preacher from upstate who helped us with the Krogan case," Gavin explained, turning to Chris. "I don't think you ever actually met him; you were resting comfortably in the hospital and all, watching football, while we were getting our—"

"Oh yeah, I remember," Chris interrupted, ignoring the digs. "The Reverend Buchanan, one of your leads. You call him Buck? I didn't realize you were so close."

"He insisted. I would have called him 'Your Majesty' to get him to help us find that psycho."

Gavin had never spoken to Chris or anyone about the role the Reverend Jesse J. Buchanan had supposedly played in the final capture of Krogan, and he hoped he'd never have to. Buck was just another lead who'd happened to provide a piece to the puzzle. A small piece in retrospect, but at the time Gavin had desperately searched under any rock he could turn and read more into strange coincidences than he should have. As a result, Buck had appeared huge. And the story that surrounded him was kept secret.

Other than Gavin, Amy, and Buck, only one other person knew what purportedly had happened to the serial killer who shocked the New York area with his terroristlike crashes. Only one other person knew of the alleged exorcism that, according to Buck, had sent a raging demon—a spirit being that had terrorized humanity for over ten thousand years—into a young Galapagos Island tortoise named Jeremy. That person was a zookeeper at the Bronx Zoo. A man named Lester Davis, whom Buck had entrusted with the oversight and well-being of the tortoise that would serve as a living prison for the evil entity . . . as long as the animal remained alive. Gavin remembered how important it was to those who knew about the demon that the tortoise be kept alive for a long, long time. A concern he had since scratched off his list.

"I forget . . . how exactly did he help us?"

Gavin could feel Amy's silence. "He didn't, actually. He came with us to see if Krogan was the same man who had killed his family. He wasn't."

Chris and the rest of the world were allowed to believe only what their eyes could see: that Karl Dengler, alias Krogan, was no more than a monstrous psychokiller with an appetite for spontaneous destruction—crashing cars, trucks, boats, or anything else that moved, into anything he felt like at any given moment. Sometimes the crashes were premeditated, other times not. The media had dubbed him the "Ghost Driver" for his uncanny ability to disappear by the time authorities arrived on the scene. A crash without a driver and a dead passenger who owned the vehicle, harboring staggeringly high levels of blood-alcohol content, would likely mean Krogan's fingerprints were on the steering wheel and a small lobster-claw roach clip was in the ashtray.

"Things are never as bad as they seem at first," Gavin said to Amy calmly.

Amy smiled weakly. "I know you don't believe that. Not when it comes to this."

Not true. But Gavin took the moment to do the math on his priorities. Whether or not Amy's fears were real or imagined, she needed for him to go see Buck. Life had been so good for the last two years, she probably felt that a heavy weight of tragedy was about to balance the scales. And the last thing he wanted was for his beautiful, pregnant wife to be under any unnecessary stress with her due date so—

"Gavin? What are you thinking?"

"Huh? Nothing."

"Well, we should visit him," Amy said, her voice not betraying her fear.

"No, I'll go. You said Delhi Hospital?" Gavin asked, taking off his tool belt.

"Yes . . . about six or seven miles north of Samantha's."

"You're leaving?" Chris said incredulously.

"Sorry. Amy's right. At least one of us should see him."

"I'll go," Amy offered. "You stay with Chris."

"No. It's too far." *And you'll believe everything Buck tells you and be a basket case when the baby's born,* he thought. "Besides, you've been busy all day. Too busy." He gently touched her belly.

Amy looked at Chris. "You know, I never used to get this kind of pampering before I was pregnant. Sometimes I think he cares more about the baby than me."

"Nice try, Amy, but you're staying here," Gavin insisted calmly, although inwardly shaken by her comment.

"What's Samantha's?" Chris asked.

"Samantha's Dairy Farm," Amy replied. "That's where Buck lives. In Hamden."

Chris frowned. "That's . . . four hours from here."

"I'll do it in three with the Tiger," Gavin said, speaking more to himself than to Chris.

"I don't get it. What's the hurry? He's in a hospital. I mean, I've never heard you even talk about him before," Chris said. He hammered a single nail into a stud, took off his tool belt, and hung it up. An obvious sunburn line striped his shoulders where his suspenders had been.

"He showed up for us, Chris. We should be there for him." Gavin hoped his friend would be satisfied with that excuse.

He wasn't. Chris now wore his skeptical detective face. "Gav, I don't really get it. But look, we've been bustin' our butts here. Let's take showers, have a bite to eat, and I'll ride up there with you. We can—"

"No. I mean . . . no thanks. Your wife's going to be jealous for your time as it is, and I need you to help me here tomorrow."

Chris nodded suspiciously. "Yeah, right. Okay, you win. I'll put in another hour or two after lunch, and by the end of tomorrow we should have most of the shell wrapped up."

Gavin stopped, not liking the idea of Chris working without his help.

"Go on, get out of here." Chris waved Gavin on. "I get more done with you not getting in my way anyway."

Gavin turned the ignition key and hoped. The Sunbeam Tiger cranked and cranked. He pumped the gas pedal and tried again. The engine started with a throaty rumble, then settled into a deep purr.

As he backed out of his driveway, he paused for a moment to take in the new shape of his home. It looked just the way Amy had sketched it out for the architect. The project would be a good diversion from this sudden crisis with Buck. The reality was that someday the old man was going to die, whether now or five, ten years from now. He was not going to allow his wife to live the rest of her life in fear of that day, based on one man's religious theories, and he certainly was not going to let it affect his new and growing family.

The sudden sound of a circular saw cutting through new lumber broke into his thoughts and reassured him of the positive direction his life was really going.

3

Lester Davis, Wildlife Keeper of Tortoises at the Bronx Zoo, could feel the nervous sweat from his armpits roll down his sides. The day he'd hoped would never come was upon him. The day he would have to give account to his superiors of Jeremy's very strange behavior. Jeremy, the young Galapagos Island tortoise, who up until two and a half years ago, had been completely normal.

Brian Kormoski, President of Wildlife at the zoo and Chairman of the American Zoological Alliance, massaged his trimmed goatee as he gazed through the thick glass of an isolated cage. In front of the glass was a sign that read:

GALAPAGOS GIANT TORTOISE
Geochelone Elephantopus

The Galapagos Tortoise is the largest living tortoise. It can weigh over 700 pounds and measure over 6 feet from head to tail. It is a very slow-moving animal, moving only 0.16 miles per hour. The giant tortoise leads a generally peaceful, lazy life.

Spending most of his time at meetings and benefit dinners, Kormoski wore a suit and tie and trailered a rump more accustomed to an office chair than a walk around the park. His presence in the Reptile House was extremely rare. In fact, Zookeeper Davis could not remember ever seeing him in there. But when a growing conflict over what proper action should be taken on an "insane" Galapagos Island tortoise reached his ears, Kormoski had decided his next meeting would be with all parties involved, including the tortoise.

Kormoski took off his thick wire-rimmed glasses, cleaned them with a white handkerchief, and slid them back into the worn grooves in front of his ears. "How odd," he said to the two people he had called there to meet with him. "That son of a gun seems to be staring at me."

"That's because he *is* staring at you, sir," answered Susan Cocchiola, the zoo's chief veterinarian. Cocchiola was the best in her field as far as the zoo was concerned. She stood with clipboard in hand, tall and trim with short, wavy red hair, reading glasses draped over her white overcoat. Her normally pleasant demeanor was masked by her now serious countenance. Where the well-being of her animals was concerned, she was known to be pure business.

Kormoski moved a few steps aside and the tortoise's glare followed him.

"Why do you suppose he's looking at me?" he asked. "It's a little eerie."

"I don't know," Cocchiola replied dryly.

Lester Davis said nothing but figured the demon in the tortoise knew Kormoski had the authority to have Jeremy shipped out of the zoo, where the animal's demise might be more likely. Buck had warned Davis to guard the tortoise with his life because if it ever died, the vengeful demon would escape and surely repay anyone who'd had anything to do with its captivity. At the time, saving the next three or four generations from the likes of Krogan seemed to Lester Davis the only right thing to do. And keeping a tortoise healthy in the Bronx Zoo would be an easy task—or so he'd thought. But as soon as Buck had returned Jeremy to the zoo, Davis knew there were going to be complications. The tortoise had changed—more than he had ever dreamed possible.

"Okay, besides the fact Jeremy likes to stare at fat guys in suits, what exactly do you see as the problem here, Susan?" Kormoski demanded, his chin held high.

Cocchiola sighed. "Problems, sir. For one, the tortoise no longer acts like a tortoise. It can't even be kept with the other tortoises. That's why we have it isolated."

"What does it do when it's with the other tortoises?"

"It attacks . . . quickly. And not just tortoises. Jeremy attacks anything it sees, including us."

"Hmm. And when you say quickly—"

"I mean in every sense of the word, sir," she interrupted. "Not only does it attack immediately, but it scurries to do it. I've never seen a giant tortoise move half as fast as Jeremy does. And it doesn't fight like a tortoise, either. It fights more like . . . like a tiger."

Kormoski frowned. "A tiger?" he asked doubtfully.

"Have you ever seen one tortoise battle another?"

"Not firsthand, but I hear they go at it rather slowly."

"To put it mildly, sir. They face off and charge toward each other at a blazing two-tenths of a mile per hour. That's just slightly faster than crabgrass grows. When they finally ram—and I use the word loosely—you might imagine you're not going to hear the *clack* of mountain sheep. More like a war of opposing hand-cranked car jacks. Their feet dig in and it's neck against neck until one retreats. Except for some fatigue and muscle soreness, the dominated tortoise is usually unharmed."

"But not when Jeremy attacks," Kormoski said.

"No, sir. Jeremy has been known to plow into full-grown giants, three times his size, flipping them over onto their backs and biting at their exposed flesh. When they pull in their head and feet for fear of their lives, he gnaws on their shells until someone separates them. A dangerous task in itself."

"How long has this behavior been going on?"

"I don't know, sir. I became aware of it through one of my techs a few months ago after a routine checkup. Jeremy nearly bit his finger off while being inspected for ticks."

"I remember hearing something about that," Kormoski said, nodding.

"But he was already in isolation."

With a furrowed brow, Kormoski turned to Davis. "Lester?"

"Jeremy's been under my care for four years, Mr. Kormoski. I admit he's been going through some growing pains lately, but that'll pass. He just needs a little special attention right now. He's healthy. I'll see to it he gets everything he needs, sir. I promise."

Cocchiola rolled her eyes. "I'm sorry, sir, but the kind of attention Jeremy needs we can't provide here in the Bronx. Keeping giants at this location was an experiment that, in my opinion, has failed. I think we should send the lot of them to a more southerly location where they can be outside year round. Then they'll benefit from the symbiotic relationships that naturally form between them and say, finches, for example, which clean them of ticks daily in their natural environment."

"Lester? You seem troubled by that suggestion."

"Nobody knows Jeremy like I do, sir. I don't mind if you send the rest of them south, but Jeremy needs me."

Kormoski frowned again.

"Jeremy needs Honolulu, sir," Cocchiola interjected. "Theirs is the absolute best facility in the world for giants, and they've been at it the longest. It's giant heaven. The animals all have remarkable dispositions and breed readily there. Jeremy may still need special attention, but if he's going to have a chance to assimilate anywhere, it would be in Hawaii."

Davis felt a sensation like an army of ants crawling down his back as he saw Kormoski nod approvingly at Cocchiola's suggestion. From what Buck had told him, the tortoise would do anything to die and would have outside help if left in the open. Davis had spent the last two years fearfully speculating on how long it would take for Krogan to hunt him down once freed. No. There was no way he could let Jeremy out of his protection.

"Mr. Kormoski. Jeremy's gonna be fine. He's already on the mend. If you can just give me a little more time with him I—"

"I anticipated this type of resistance, sir," Cocchiola interrupted. "Lester is as capable a wild-animal keeper as I know, but for some reason, he keeps fighting me on this one. So I've arranged a little demonstration." She took out a small radio and spoke into it. "Karen, please bring in the rat."

4

Gavin drove over the Throgs Neck Bridge in light traffic, convertible top down, afternoon sky high and bright, Long Island dwindling in his rearview mirror. To his left was the New York skyline, what was left of it. The events of that fateful September Tuesday and the heartbreak of the following days flashed before him. The giant buildings swallowing commercial airliners. The media replaying the catastrophic implosions over and over. The faces of the cops and firefighters Gavin had worked with and the grief at dozens of funeral services. Grown men crying, recounting stories of people in midstride guillotined by falling glass. The beginning of a war, but not the beginning. Not to Buck.

Evil? Absolutely and completely. But demons? For the first time in a long while, Gavin allowed himself to think about Buck—not the man, but his beliefs.

Did Buck think all terrorists and serial killers were influenced by demons? Yes. Did Buck believe a demon could really gain control of a human? Absolutely. Was Buck nuts? Well, yes, a fanatic at the very least, but not dangerously so. He was extreme, where reality and fantasy merge. It had to have been over a year ago that Gavin had asked himself if there really was any such thing as a demon. And more important, if there really was such a thing as a demon named Krogan—a name he had struggled to put out of his mind since the killer had been thrown into jail for life. But now, try as he might to

ignore it, the name kept coming to him. The more it came, the faster
he drove. The speed helped refocus his attention to the road.

Gavin continued north into the Catskills on roads of lesser and
lesser importance. Winding through dairy country, the smell of
manure and fresh-cut hay in the air, he thought about what Buck
would say to him. Assuming he was still alive and able to say anything. A dying man securing a future he wouldn't be around for.
Not exactly someone Gavin wanted to argue his faith, or lack of
faith, with. And why bother? Let the old guy die in peace. Agree
with him. Why not? Whom would it hurt? If only Amy weren't
pregnant, she really would have been the better person to speak
to Buck at a time like this. The old man was the theological heavy-
weight, and Amy believed in him. She would've been asked to
pray some kind of battle prayers and would have agreed and
pounded on heaven's doors with all her heart. She would feel better for it, even if in the end nothing was actually accomplished.
With demons, nothing could ever be proven. Everything had to
be faith. If they didn't show up, which of course they couldn't because they were never there in the first place, the prayers were
answered.

Gavin cruised into Delhi, asked the first person he saw for directions, and two minutes later pulled into a newly paved parking lot.
His legs were still stiff from a three-hour ride where he had averaged
better than seventy from curb to curb, and over a hundred on the
highways. He walked through the hospital's automated glass doors
and found himself in the ER waiting room. He hated hospitals—too
many bad memories. Get in, get out, and get home to Amy with a report that would calm her fears. Looking, looking, his eyes darted
about and found a reception desk where a woman was on the phone.
Women and phones. He approached her and flashed his badge.

"Gotta go," she said. "How can I—"

"Reverend Buchanan. Where is he? ICU?"

"Uh, no," she said after taking what seemed like a very long second and a half to answer. "He's in the CCU."

"Where is that?"

"Around the corner, up the ramp, and down the hall," she said to his back as he left her.

He soon came to another, much smaller, waiting room with another receptionist. He recognized a young black girl in one of the seats. Buck's granddaughter, Samantha. She would be thirteen now. Sitting next to her, holding her hand, was a blonde woman in her thirties. They were the only two visitors in the room.

"Hello, Samantha," Gavin said.

The young girl looked up. Her eyes were wet, swollen and pink, like the ribbons her grandfather allowed her to put on all the cows at the farm, where the farmhouse looked like a life-size dollhouse with lace and flowers everywhere. Her grandfather was now the only family she had left since Krogan had killed her parents and grandmother seven years ago in a collision. Only she and Buck had survived. Buck had taken her in, sold everything, and bought a small, working dairy farm simply because she loved animals. He had done everything he could for her to try to make up for her loss. A loss Buck believed his ministry was indirectly responsible for. A loss he feared could someday include Samantha's life as well.

"I'm Gavin Pierce. I met you two years ago. I left New York right after you called."

Samantha nodded. "I remember. You and the pretty lady . . . Amy. She was very nice."

"She wanted to come, but she's going to have a baby soon and had to stay home and rest. I guess you know what I'm talking about, taking care of those cows," he said awkwardly. Talking to thirteen-year-old girls had never been his strength, even when he'd been thirteen. As Gavin spoke, Samantha's eyes wandered to a set of

double doors with a sign that read Coronary Care Unit. He immediately felt stupid for mentioning the cows. He knew absolutely
nothing about cows or farming, much less what kind of rest, if any,
a pregnant cow required.

"Is my grandfather going to be all right, Mr. Pierce?"

Her question caught Gavin off guard, reminding him of the
same question he had asked a doctor two years ago regarding his
own grandfather. He wanted to tell her something to comfort her,
but could not think of anything and didn't want to shoot from the
hip and come out with another dumb cow remark.

"What did the doctor say?" Gavin asked, looking to both Samantha and the blonde woman.

"The doctor said the surgery saved his life and that he needs to
rest," the woman replied before Samantha could answer. "I'm Mary
Quinn, Samantha's next-door neighbor." The look in her blue eyes
made him wonder if there was more she was trying to say.

"Will Samantha be with you while her grandfather . . . gets
some rest?"

Mary nodded and put her arm around the young girl. "Samantha knows she's welcome to stay over anytime she wants. My twin
daughters, Michele and Jackie, are her best friends, and she knows
our home is her home. Don't you, dear?"

Samantha gave a distant nod as Mary welcomed the girl's head
against her shoulder.

Everything seemed okay, but Gavin knew he would be paying
the Quinn home a visit for Buck's sake. The old preacher might
trust in his prayers for his granddaughter's needs, but there was
nothing like seeing things firsthand to put Gavin's mind at ease that
she was being properly cared for.

Just then a nurse came through the CCU doors next to the receptionist.

"I'll be back," Gavin said.

Samantha reached out and grabbed Gavin's hand. "Grandpa wants you to pray," she said with blinking saucer eyes.

"I know . . . I will," he consoled her, his words carrying more conviction in his reassuring expression than in his heart. The way she held on to his hand before finally letting it go made him wonder if Samantha knew what Buck's prayer request was really for.

Gavin walked up to the receptionist, an older woman with a name tag that read VOLUNTEER over a long, unpronounceable last name. "I'm Detective Pierce, and it's very important I speak to Reverend Buchanan," Gavin said, showing his shield. The woman's eyebrows rose at the sight of the badge.

A moment later a nurse appeared through the double doors and escorted Gavin into the CCU. In the center of the large rectangular room was a raised counter, thirty feet in diameter, with several people behind it, all busy. Around the room's perimeter were partitions separating hospital beds, mostly occupied, some with curtains drawn. The air was clean and cool, filled with soft mechanical sounds—hisses, pings, beeps—he assumed all rhythmically keeping beat with vital body functions.

The nurse stopped at a closed curtain and peeked in. "You can go inside in a minute, Detective. He's being lined with a new IV."

Gavin scanned the room as he waited. There were no plants or flowers anywhere. This was not a place to rest and heal as much as it was a place to survive. He tried, unsuccessfully, to forget past hospital visits caused by Krogan. Indirectly, this was one of them.

The curtain opened all the way. "You can come in now, Detective, but you can't stay long. If you need me I'll be . . ." The nurse continued to speak but Gavin was no longer listening. The sight of Buck seized him. He had not seen him in two years and the man had somehow aged twenty. His white hair was thinner and his black, cracked skin was paler. Not that the oxygen tubes in his nose and the IV lines in his veins helped his appearance any.

As though he had no control over his actions, Gavin felt himself move closer until he was leaning over him. "Buck?" he whispered. "Buck." He noticed the watchful eye of the nurse on him and wished she had stationed herself out of earshot.

The old man's eyes slowly opened to mere slits. Gavin took a step back. After a long moment of squinting and blinking, Buck said something like, "Do I know you?"

"It's Pierce, Buck. Gavin Pierce."

Buck smiled weakly. "Detective . . . what's the occasion?" His voice was deep but hushed.

"Nothing special. I was just passing by the coronary care unit on my way to the deli, so I thought I'd stop by, say hello. How do you feel?"

"I've felt worse."

Gavin took in his eye contact and nodded. "I know." Gavin knew he was referring to the time he had barely survived a Krogan car crash that had killed his family—all but Samantha.

"Hmm . . ." Buck said, licking his parched lips. "How is Amy?"

"She's, well, eight months' pregnant."

"Pregnant?"

"We're married."

Buck nodded almost imperceptibly, his eyelids heavy. "Congratulations. You belong together," he whispered.

"Thank you. I agree. . . . . Samantha looks well," Gavin lied.

"Is she still here?"

"Yes."

"With Mary?"

"Uh, yes."

"She's a good woman, Detective. You needn't worry about her."

Gavin nodded, wondering how Buck even knew he was concerned.

"But she doesn't know, of course. Neither does Sammy."

Gavin had wondered if Samantha knew of Buck's belief about Krogan. Thank God he hadn't laid that demon-hunting trip on the young girl. "Everything will be fine, Buck."

Buck closed his eyes. "You and Amy need to take over for me. I'm not going to be around much longer."

"Nonsense. Bypass surgery can extend your life for decades."

"They did what they could, but the damage was already done."

"I'll argue with you later . . . when you're better informed. What do you mean, take over?"

"In prayer. Prayer is the key to spiritual warfare. Without faithful prayer, you'll be doomed, and so will Sammy."

Gavin took another glance at the nurse, who stood just outside the curtain like a sentry. "Don't worry about a thing, Buck. I'll tell Amy and we'll pray about the situation every day."

Buck frowned but said nothing.

"And I don't want to hear any more about you not being around. You're not going to get off your knees that easy. This ain't the old days, you know."

Buck was still frowning. "You have no intention of praying at all, do you?"

Gavin tried in vain not to let his shoulders slump. He absolutely hated this. He was a terrible liar and an even worse actor. And standing before Buck, he felt as see-through as glass. Time to come clean . . . or at least cleaner. "Buck, I do pray sometimes, but to be honest, most of the time I don't know why. Amy is the one you should be talking to. She's the real believer in this family."

Buck continued to look at Gavin for a long, silent moment, his expression giving nothing away. He finally closed his eyes and spoke. "So in hindsight, you've come up with a more reasonable explanation for what happened?"

Careful now, Gavin thought. Being honest with Buck might just stop the beep machine from beeping. "Not . . . really," he said, immediately wishing he hadn't.

"But you no longer believe there is a demon imprisoned in the tortoise?"

"It's a lot to ask, Buck."

"There's a lot at risk, Detective," Buck said, then paused to catch his breath. "We are engaged in a constant, relentless war that I can't fight in this condition. My time has . . ."

As Buck continued, Gavin focused less on what he was saying and more on that steel-eyed glare that could send shivers down the spine of a grizzly bear. The same glare he'd had when he commanded the supposed demon into the tortoise. What kind of suggestive power—or better put, hypnotic influence—did this old black preacher possess? If Gavin stayed around this guy any longer, he would probably go back to believing this . . . this nonsense. That's what it was. The more he thought about it, the crazier it sounded. He didn't want to think about it, or how he'd ever been convinced enough to go along with the charade in the first place. That had been a different time, full of rage over Grampa's death, chasing a serial killer who had the whole city guessing. A time when fears of terrorism had been raw and new. He'd been vulnerable and looking for answers anywhere he could find them, and it was just his dumb luck that Amy had come up with the Reverend Buck as a lead. And Amy . . . Wasn't it bad enough that Amy believed it and was now worrying herself sick *and* probably the baby, too, through some maternal connection?

". . . and if we let down our guard and fall into complacency, the ground we have gained will be lost, and need I remind you what that would mean?" Buck went on, but Gavin was not really listening. He had heard this warning so many times before that it all seemed like one long, never-ending sentence.

"Why don't you just give me names of some other people,

Buck? People who have faith like you. People who can pray the way you need them to. I'll make sure they know your story."

"But you've seen with your own eyes, Detective. No one else will have the faith or the urgency."

Gavin wanted to roll his eyes at this urgency he was supposed to share with Buck. Urgency, if anything, was what he was trying to get Amy away from. "What have I seen with my own eyes, Buck? I've seen fear, sickness, murder, pain—in every color of the rainbow. Are you gonna tell me it's all from demons?"

"No! I never said that. People sin. Sometimes badly, without any help from demons. Sickness happens, and so does fear. I'm afraid of something every day. Jesus was afraid in the Garden of Gethsemane, and who knows when else? A storm doesn't need a demon to become a hurricane. But make no mistake, Detective . . . demons are real. The world is full of them. And there is one named Krogan, whose path we've crossed."

"And my prayers will keep him away?"

Buck looked up at the ceiling, then whispered, "The Good Shepherd protects His sheep."

"Sheep?"

"Completely dependent beings, Detective. We all are. We ask and we receive. Ask in faith. The prayer of faith is a key to lock and unlock doors."

"Faith. I have no faith. You're the one with all the faith, Buck. I'm just a cop looking to mind my own business."

"And I'm just an old, sick dairy farmer. Unfortunately, this *is* your business, and if you don't mind it, it will fold in on you. Faith builds faith just as lies build doubt. Don't allow the enemy to lie to you."

You're the enemy, Gavin almost said. He noticed the beeping machine picking up its pace and thought for a second it had somehow found *his* pulse.

"Surrender, Detective. You must surrender," the old man barely uttered, then coughed.

The nurse was instantly there. "That's enough, Detective. He needs to rest now," she said firmly.

Buck put his hand on Gavin's and opened his eyes wide, leaning toward him. "Samantha. You need to protect her from Krogan. You need to protect yourself. You must pray, you must . . . surrender," he said, then closed his eyes and settled back.

He died! Did Buck die? No, the rhythmic blip and beep of the monitor told him otherwise.

"You're done, Detective," the nurse said and meant it.

5

I'm sorry, Susan, but did you say 'rat'?" Kormoski asked.

"Yes, sir. Any other giant tortoise in the world would look upon a rat as nonthreatening and would completely ignore it. Being herbivores, they certainly would not consider a rodent to be food. Consequently, rats are not afraid of tortoises and haven't been for millions of years."

Kormoski nodded knowingly, then looked at Lester Davis to see if he had any reaction to this strange demonstration.

Davis had nothing to say. At this point he would gladly fabricate a lie to keep Jeremy under his care, but what possible explanation could he offer? Certainly not the truth. To speak the truth would mean he would find *himself* in an isolation cage.

At that moment Cocchiola's radio sounded.

"Is the door clear?" asked a female voice.

Cocchiola brought the small black radio to her mouth. "He's in his usual corner."

A door that blended in perfectly with the rear of the isolation cage opened. Karen, one of Susan Cocchiola's young veterinary assistants, stepped inside and shut the door behind her, keeping a watchful eye on the tortoise in the rear corner of the cage. Karen was petite with several shiny silver earrings in each ear and short blue hair. She had been on staff for only about three months. She briskly moved away from the tortoise to the middle of the cage, carrying with her what appeared to be a shoebox. Crouching down to the floor, she opened the box and emptied out a large white rat that had originally been planned as a meal for the snakes.

Jeremy the tortoise, who had not taken his eerie glare off Kormoski the entire time, suddenly moved forward.

Cocchiola used her radio. "Come over near us, Karen. I don't want you to distract Jeremy."

Karen immediately complied, hurrying to the thick glass wall that separated her from the three onlookers outside the cage.

The rat moved quickly back and forth across the barren sandy floor, sniffing, scurrying, stopping, sniffing. Jeremy continued to move toward it, punching the sand as he advanced, his neck long and his head high and bold.

"How is that big clumsy tortoise going to catch that fast little rat?" Kormoski asked with a smirk.

"That's just it, sir. You'll find that when Jeremy attacks—and I do mean *attacks*—he will demonstrate a speed and agility completely foreign to his species."

"And you think it's stress?" Kormoski massaged his goatee again.

"I don't know what it is, but he will demonstrate a rage more like a crocodile than the docile tortoise he's supposed to be."

"A crocodile, Susan?" Kormoski mused, giving her a brief glance.

"You'll see."

All Lester Davis could do was pray. He knew stress had little to do with Jeremy's behavior and at the moment was not the least concerned for the rat and Cocchiola's little demonstration. He had seen Jeremy attack other tortoises and living reptile food for the last two years. But now Jeremy had an audience that would be able to separate him from his guardian. Yes, the tortoise had bigger things on its mind than a simple rat.

Jeremy stopped at the white rodent, still staring at his spectators. The rat, busily darting its wiggling nose in every direction, seemed naturally unconcerned with the large rocklike mass standing over it.

Davis closed his eyes.

"Come on, Jeremy," Cocchiola said. "I don't understand. He's usually more predictable than this, sir."

After another long moment of nothing, Kormoski looked at his wristwatch. "Well, maybe Jeremy's not angry today. Anyway, I've got to get—"

In that instant, with the speed of a raptor, the tortoise stabbed at the rat with its beak, killing it instantly. Jeremy picked up the limp body, momentarily displaying the kill before whipping his neck and hurling the dead rat at the glass partition, where it hit with a hard thud, six inches from Kormoski's startled face. Both Cocchiola and her tech inside the cage shrieked. The rat fell off the glass, leaving remnants of fur, flesh, and dripping blood.

Kormoski slowly looked at Cocchiola. "What in the name of God is going on here, Susan?" he asked quietly. "Is this your idea of a demonstration?"

Not her idea, Davis thought, keeping his eye on the tortoise.

"I'm sorry, sir. I had no idea Jeremy would—"

Kormoski held up his hand to interrupt. "Let's forget for the moment that tortoises *don't* throw things. Let's also put aside the speed and accuracy this particular tortoise has in throwing recently deceased animals. What I would like to know is *Why did he throw the rat at me?*" Kormoski's voice grew louder as he spoke. "It behaved like a gorilla. It stared me down and threw a rat at me."

"Get her out of there, Susan," Davis said softly.

"Sir, I suggest we waste no time in shipping—"

"I said you have to get her out of there, Susan," Davis interrupted, louder this time.

"Excuse me?" Cocchiola turned to Davis.

"Karen!" Davis now shouted angrily to Cocchiola. "You have to get Karen out of the cage. Radio for someone to help her now."

Cocchiola snapped her attention to her tech, who was still on the other side of the glass. Jeremy was motionless but staring at Karen. Susan depressed the button on her radio. "Karen, get out of there. Move around to your left."

Karen nodded, but before she could move a muscle, Jeremy quickly moved in the direction Karen had been instructed to go. The tech froze.

"Radio someone else for help, Susan," Davis said. "There's a net in the rear hall. Don't say anything Jeremy can hear."

Cocchiola looked at Davis in disbelief. "You're not trying to tell us Jeremy understands English?"

"Yes." *And every other language on the planet also,* Davis thought.

"But that's preposterous," Kormoski said.

"There's no time to talk about it," Davis yelled as he ran away from them, down the hall.

The tortoise watched Davis disappear, then looked back at the tech.

"Just go around the other way," Cocchiola radioed, motioning with her hands.

Karen looked scared. She took a step to the right and Jeremy immediately compensated, moving more like a lizard than a tortoise.

Davis lugged a heavy net the size of a blanket with him as he hurried to the rear door of Jeremy's cage. He had made this net especially for Jeremy and had used it on several other occasions to separate him from other tortoises. He could hear someone coming from behind at the far end of the hall. He glanced to see two other techs running toward him. Cocchiola had apparently called for help. He heard muffled screams as he crashed open the door. To his horror, the tech was facedown on the floor of the cage, the tortoise over her with the weight of its front leg on the back of her thin neck, pecking at her back and hand-covered head. "Krogan! Stop! In the name of Jesus, stop!" Davis yelled as he rushed at Jeremy, not caring who heard him. He threw the thick netting like a lasso spinning through the air. The tortoise stopped its attack and glared at Davis as the net landed on target. Cocchiola and Kormoski, their hands pressed on the thick glass, mouths moving, stared helplessly. Davis quickly gathered the back of the net in his hands and pulled as hard as he could.

The two male techs ran to Karen's side, each taking an armpit and dragging her to the other side of the cage, where they immediately wrapped her bleeding hands. She was crying spasmodically, the back of her white jacket torn and bloodstained.

Davis pulled back on the netting until Jeremy's wild eyes met his own and spoke so no one else could possibly hear. "I know your plan, Krogan, and it's not going to work. You and I are going to take a little trip to the country to see an old friend." He was going to say more but suddenly felt strange, dizzy. He tried to turn away but couldn't. Couldn't even blink. Fear rushed through his chest as he remembered Buck's many warnings against intentional eye contact with the beast. *I'll be back for you,* he heard inside his head and then laughter . . . coarse, mocking laughter. He wanted to call for help but couldn't speak either. Paralyzed. The thing had him, and there was nothing he could do.

"Mr. Davis?" called the familiar voice of another tech. "Excuse me, sir. Do you need some help?"

Davis wanted to answer, but the only movement he could feel was a pounding heart.

"Mr. Davis? Are you all right?" the tech asked, getting closer.

Davis suddenly felt a release and fell away from the tortoise as if he'd just woken up from a nightmare where nothing worked. But the laughter was still coming. Mocking laughter. He had to deal with this thing—and now . . . before it was too late.

6

Gavin adjusted the volume on Amy's favorite Vanessa-Mae Storm CD, then fluffed up a couple of down pillows at the end of the sofa. "Here," he ordered sternly, patting the pillows for emphasis. "Lay—down—now."

"It's too soft. And so's the music volume. Besides, if I lay down I'll never get back up," Amy said stubbornly.

"It's classical violin. It's more relaxing quiet."

"Not to me. I want to hear every note."

Gavin rolled his eyes, told himself not to argue, and turned the volume up a notch.

"Better, but that doesn't help the pillow."

"Please," Gavin said. He hated that word, but had used it more since Amy's pregnancy than in the whole of his life.

Amy sighed and complied, awkwardly easing herself down on her side.

"That better?"

"Yes. I'm fine, really. Tell me more about Buck."

Gavin took a seat at the other end of the sofa and pulled Amy's feet onto his lap. "You have to be careful not to overdo it. This is your first baby, and the next month is extremely critical."

"I know, I know. You've been telling me that every month for the last eight months."

"That's because it's true every month. Everything is new territory."

Amy struggled to rearrange herself, rolled onto her back, and smoothed her hands around her basketball-sized belly. "I *look* like a new territory."

"You look great, but I'm serious about you getting some more rest," he said, sensing his words were fighting an uphill struggle. There she was, reclined in down pillows, feet up, getting a massage, yet about as peaceful as a rabbit in a dog race. He reminded himself that Amy was a hormonal minefield. *Peaceful words. Calming suggestions. Smooth out the rough. Be positive, caring, interested, supportive. Avoid pushing the wrong buttons . . . like talking about how fictitious demons would like to end her and her family's life.*

"But there's so much to do before the baby gets here, and there's not much time left."

"There's not *that* much to get done. You're just seeing through the eyes of a bird building a nest. Soon your brain will be back to normal . . . so I'm told."

"Do you realize you just called me abnormal and a birdbrain?"

Bad move. Be smart. Smooth out the rough. "You misunderstand me. Subconsciously, you are looking at me, and probably Chris, too, as enemies, because we're messing up your . . . nest . . . so to speak. But soon . . . your subconscious . . ."

"Shut up."

"Huh?"

"Zip the amateur psychobabble or you'll get a foot in your face."

"Very nice."

Amy rolled her eyes. "If you want me to relax, you'd better find different analogies, or better yet, no analogies. Just because I look like an oven stuffer doesn't mean I think like one. But *you,* on the other hand, *you* think that just because you're building an extension, the rest of the house is *fine.*"

Gavin looked around the living room and shrugged. "It is fine."

"Gavin, you've lived here so long you don't see the problem."

"What problem?"

"You."

"Me? What? I should leave?"

"No, silly. You decorated the house."

"Well, they don't decorate themselves, you know. Who was I to get to do it—Gus at the deli?"

"You may as well have. The house is too masculine. It needs to be redecorated."

"Redecorated?"

"Utterly."

"You've been talking to your sister again. Last year it was our yard, now it's our house."

"Amber's away on vacation with Eric," Amy said, reminding Gavin of Amber's new love. This one was serious, according to Amy. Amy's twin sister, Amber, had not been interested in dating since awaking from a coma two and a half years ago to find that a serial killer named Krogan had decapitated her fiancé. "And you had corn in your flower beds and pumpkins on the front lawn."

"What's wrong with pumpkins?" he said, motioning toward her abdomen.

"Gavin."

"Fine. If you want to redecorate a little, I'll go with that, but not while you're pregnant. Not while you're seeing through a hormonal kaleidoscope."

Amy paused. "Then we'll have to get a decorator."

Gavin eyed her suspiciously. "I wouldn't suppose you have her card or phone number handy now, would you?"

"Well, since you brought it up."

"I knew it."

"His name's Larry."

"Larry? A guy? I thought you said the house is too masculine?"

"Larry isn't . . . very masculine."

"Oh no. Forget it. Not my house."

"It's our house."

"Absolutely not. No way."

"Then let's get the old Johnson place next door."

"You've been talking to Chris."

"My father said he'd help us with it."

"Thanks, but I don't need help. And we don't need a decorator."

"The Johnson house has a nice pool."

"And so does the gym."

"This one's closer. Or . . . we could just get a decorator."

Gavin gave her a long look, then peered about the room they were in. What was wrong with the house? Masculine? He didn't understand what was so overwhelmingly masculine. He had two pictures on the wall he was facing—a Bob Ross mountain scene he'd found a few years ago at a mall while Christmas shopping for his usual short list, and an island beach sunset scene with a sailboat in the background. Okay, so there were no flowers, but they were real paintings, not posters. The floor was carpeted in multiple earth tones so dirt wouldn't show. Smart, that's all. No gender there. What else? The ship-hatch coffee table? Okay, that was maybe a little on the rustic side and therefore a little masculine, but a flowered curtain design could counterbalance that.

"Decorators are for people who don't know how to decorate," he said.

"Well, *you* obviously don't know how, and you're not letting *me*."

Another long look. "Well, whatever," he said, taking one of her bare feet into his hands, kneading it gently. "Anything to keep you off these feet. Just promise me you won't let Lenny swing the pendulum too far in the other direction."

"Larry."

"That's what I said."

"You said— Never mind. Anyway, now that *that's* settled, tell me more about Buck."

"I thought Asians were supposed to have small feet."

"I'm half Jewish and my feet are just fine. Besides, you're thinking of the Chinese, and that was a long time ago. They made little girls' feet small and, I might add, deformed, by binding them with cloth so they could fit into painfully tiny shoes."

"Ouch."

"They thought it was feminine."

"Feminine?"

"Stop! You keep changing the subject. All you've told me about Buck is that he didn't look good and that Samantha was going to stay with some neighbor."

No scary demon stuff, remember. "Well, that's most of it."

"I want all of it. Details. I didn't send you all the way up there for just that."

Thinking, thinking. Gavin's massaging hands slowed; he exhaled. He didn't want to lie, but there was no need to make Amy any more anxious than she already was with this stuff. "He's really concerned for Samantha. He's asking everyone he trusts to keep her in prayer should something happen to him."

He kept his eyes on her feet as he reminded himself that Buck's fanatical belief in demons and spiritual warfare was based on a highly active imagination and desire for the spirit world to be more than it really was. Gavin remembered that documentary on HBO. Amy hadn't watched it. She'd insisted they had some kind of axe to grind. He'd watched anyway and was glad he had. A very thorough, and scientific, inside look at faith. How it calms and excites. How people like Buck go off the deep end and see things that aren't there. Impressive. Scary for some, he figured, but a relief for him.

Pretty much explained the whole thing psychologically. And to think Buck had him convinced two years ago of all that craziness. Gavin still believed in God, but . . . thank God for HBO.

"He didn't mention anything about the tortoise?" Amy finally asked, incredulous.

"Only in passing."

"In passing? Well, then, what did he say, in passing?"

"Almost nothing."

"Tell me."

"He's really mellowed on his position. You probably won't even believe me."

"Try me."

"He said we shouldn't worry about the tortoise. He's convinced after all this time that it's safe, and if something should happen to Buck, he's set up the proper steps to keep the animal safe."

"Ha . . . Yeah, right!"

"I told you, you wouldn't believe me."

"He didn't say *anything* about *us* praying? I mean, wasn't that what Samantha called about?"

"He wanted us to personally know he had everything under control. He didn't want to die and have us all freaked. Again, his main concern was for his granddaughter."

Pause. "Liar."

"Liar? That's not a very nice thing to call your husband."

"Liar, liar, liar."

Gavin shook his head. "I don't fight with pregnant people."

Amy stared at him, and he looked away, again finding her feet a convenient place to focus. Rubbing, rubbing. After a short while he glanced back at her. Still staring.

"What?" he finally said.

"I can't believe you won't tell me, your wife, the truth. You should be ashamed of yourself."

"First you call me names and now you're trying the guilt-trip method. Very becoming," Gavin said, rubbing, rubbing, rubbing. "How do you know I'm not telling you the truth?"

Amy rolled her eyes. "Well, for one, I know Buck, two, I know you, and three, my foot is about to catch on fire. So you're lying."

Gavin eased up, sighed. "Did you ever think he might have other trusted believers who know a little more about this stuff than we do, and that he has entrusted them with the task of praying?"

Amy said nothing, which meant she was at least considering what he said.

"And, oh yeah, I also told him we were married now and expecting a baby. He was pleased. Very pleased."

Amy paused for what appeared to be a pleasant moment. "What exactly did he say?"

"He said we made the right decision and that God would bless our marriage."

"Really?" Amy said, her smile bright, wide. "What else?"

"Nothing else. Like I said, he was very weak. And the nurse was standing right there. We really couldn't have had a private conversation if we'd wanted to."

Amy stared at the ceiling for a long time. She seemed to look more like the picture of a person at rest. Maybe she was finally relaxing from the foot massage and the mellow classical violin music in the background.

"I think I'll give Buck a call tomorrow," Amy said, her lips pursed, her gaze settling into that confident "I can get to the bottom of this myself" look. She was playing with him, and he was fine with that, as long as that dangerously stressful fear was gone from her eyes. He had read how bad a mother's stress could be for the baby.

"That's a good idea," Gavin agreed, knowing full well Buck would not be allowed any calls in the CCU.

"Or maybe I'll just take a ride up there."

"Sure. I suppose you'll want to borrow my badge, too?"

Amy frowned and went back to the ceiling to think. He didn't like it when she spent too much time thinking.

7

Lester Davis was trying to work as quickly and quietly as he possibly could. Hands sweating, eyes darting, he hastily slid the dolly under the three-foot-cubed wooden crate, then pushed the crate up two planks onto a golf-cart-sized electric pickup used in cleaning cages. It could transport just about anything where the exhaust of a gas engine could prove unhealthy.

Suddenly . . . Davis gasped and spun around to see who was there . . . who was right there, leaning over him, breathing. He could hear the breathing . . . feel the breathing. No one was there . . . at least no one he could see. He sighed and continued his task.

With the crate on board, he dropped the planks where they were and hopped into the driver's seat. He couldn't remember the last time he'd driven one of these things. *Turn the key to the on position, push the black lever to either forward or reverse, step on the pedal, and go. Easy. Be yourself, act normal.* Impossible. He was leaving the zoo with a young giant Galapagos Island tortoise with zero intent on returning it—*ever*—and no explanation to keep him from being fired and probably thrown in jail for whatever the technical term was for stealing an extremely valuable animal just off the endangered list. But did any of that matter compared to the danger of Krogan getting out of the tortoise? Buck would know what to do. He had to get the tortoise to Buck. Had to see Buck.

"What?" he gasped, again startled by the sound of breathing. He could feel the hairs stand up on the back of his neck. "I rebuke you in the name of Jesus," he whispered through gritted teeth. The breathing stopped. Silence . . . eerie silence . . . but only for a moment. Then it was back . . . not the breathing, but a snickering, as if his rebuke was amusing. He wondered if the laughter was coming from the tortoise in the crate or from a memory loop in his own frightened, frazzled mind. If it was from the tortoise, why didn't his rebuke stop it flat? Maybe he was going insane. He found more comfort in that thought. Whatever the case, he had no time to stop and think about it.

Davis nervously mounted the pickup and motored silently into the service area behind the Reptile House and the zoo store. He didn't know whether to wave to everyone or to no one. The electric pickup driving through the service area with a box in the back was a regular event. "This looks normal," he said aloud, trying to convince himself. The sun was hot. That was why he was sweating so, he reasoned. He held his breath as he came out of the service area, onto the main road, and past the zoo center. Many of the employees were leaving for the day. He drove slowly to blend in with the crowd, wanting really to stomp on the pedal.

He wondered for a moment how odd it was that the tortoise had complied so easily with entering the tight crate. No snapping, hissing, thrashing, excreting. Did it think it was leaving for Hawaii already?

He drove under the Skyfari gondola ride that traversed the park but didn't look up at it, sensing everyone looking down at him. He continued slowly, naturally, ready to smile if someone waved to him. Just ahead was the left turn he would make to the parking lot. Almost there. As he approached, he saw the zoo shuttle coming on its way to Asia. He thought about cutting in front of it. He could make it. No. That could draw attention. Act calm, natural. He stopped. Waited. He had never seen the shuttle move so slowly and look so long.

"Hi, Lester," said a familiar voice.

Davis turned. Or rather, he snapped his head. *Too fast, not natural*, he thought. "Oh! Hi, Frank," he said to the elderly Reptile House security attendant, who apparently, like Davis, was waiting for the train to pass so he could leave for the day.

"Easy, easy. A bit jumpy today?"

"Just lost in thought, Frank. You snatched me out of a daydream," he said, trying to sound relaxed while the laughter inside his head intensified.

Frank nodded. "I'm dreaming of a cold beer at the Yankees-Mets game tonight. Should be a good one this time."

Lester nodded, unable to allow even a sliver of a thought for either a beer or a baseball game.

"So where you going with this thing?" Frank laughed. "Home?"

Lester realized he had no answer. He had planned to tell anyone who stopped him that he was going to the Children's Zoo, but that was before the zoo shuttle showed up. The only thing left in the direction he was now facing was the parking lot. "I, uh, need to make a small . . . delivery."

Frank glanced at the crate and frowned. "Delivery? What are you deliverin'?"

Davis laughed nervously. "A very precious load. Something I wouldn't entrust to another. I gathered some of the reptile crap for my garden. By next week I should have tomatoes the size of melons."

"No kidding," Frank said, then laughed. "Does it really work?"

"Would I be bringing it home if it didn't?"

"I guess not," Frank said, still eyeing the crate. "Say, whatever did you all decide to do with that crazy tortoise?"

"They're sending it to Hawaii. Best zoo in the world for tortoises, especially these guys," Davis said, motioning toward the crate, then instantly realized what he had done.

Frank frowned again, but the shuttle had passed.

"Later, Frank. Enjoy the game," Davis said, then hit the pedal, leaving Frank standing still. He crossed the shuttle path and sped downward to the South Boulevard parking lot, where his minivan was parked. Any chance of the tortoise's disappearance not being connected to him was now lost. The thought brought tears to his eyes. He loved the zoo. The laughter continued, louder than ever. What was he doing?

"Hi, Lester," someone called as he maneuvered full speed through the remaining cars. He didn't look to see who it was. It didn't matter anymore who it was. He skidded to a stop, hopped out to open the rear door of his minivan, then climbed back into the electric pickup. He threw the black lever into reverse and backed up to his van until the two banged together, much harder than he wanted. He climbed up next to the crate, hands shaking uncontrollably as he struggled to get the heavy container into the van. The two vehicles didn't line up, his van being higher. He tried lifting one corner of the crate and pivoting it on another. That worked until a third corner hit the pickup's sidewall.

"Can I help?" said a male voice suddenly at Davis's side.

Davis turned. He didn't know the man. He was completely bald, wearing casual slacks and a button-down tropical shirt. *Hawaiian shirt,* he thought. Was this a joke? Had the laughing demon arranged this? He could see Frank, the security guard, coming. "Thanks, but you'll get yourself all—"

"Nonsense," the stranger interrupted, then climbed onto the truck bed before Davis could say another word. The pickup sank under the man's additional weight, bringing the distance between the two vehicles even farther apart.

The two men struggled, at times against each other. "This freakin' thing is heavy," the man said. "What's in here?"

"Reptile crap. Isn't that right, Lester?"

Davis stopped moving, said nothing. He turned to see Frank staring at him in the eye. Caught. He thought about punching Frank in the throat and pushing the other man off the bed, but then what? Even if by some miracle he *could* get away on the electric pickup, he couldn't bring himself to hurt either of them. A friend and a kind stranger. It wasn't in him.

"Reptile crap?" the stranger said incredulously, then laughed. "Is that what we're bustin' our butts over?"

"Might be the best fertilizer on the planet. Isn't that right, Lester?"

Davis stared down at the bed of the truck, silent.

Frank walked over and climbed into the driver's seat of the pickup, put it in forward, and moved the truck a couple feet away from the van, then locked the brake and went back to Davis. "Maybe with all three of us, we can get under this thing and slide it in. What do you think, Lester?"

Davis looked up at Frank. The old man knew, but there was grace in his eyes. The three men got their arms under as Frank had suggested and slowly slid and lifted and slid some more, until the crate was in the van. Davis thanked the stranger, then turned to Frank and said, "Thank you. I can't explain, but the safety of this crate is more important to me than anyone could possibly understand."

"I know, Lester. I've watched you for years. You know what's best for your kids and you do what's best for them. There's no explanation needed. I'll take the pickup back for you."

Davis nodded and shook Frank's hand. "Enjoy the game."

"I'll do that. And you bring me back one of those big tomatoes," he said with a wink, then left.

Davis paused to look at the crate. In all his panic, he hadn't realized the laughter had stopped. He closed the rear door, got into his minivan, and drove away. Once out of the park, he worked his way to the Cross Bronx Expressway and then west toward the New York State Thruway.

Westbound traffic on the Cross Bronx was typically heavy at this time of day but not nearly as bad as the eastbound, which was virtually at a standstill. He chose the middle lane, hoping that none of the seventeen zillion other cars on his side of the divider would have trouble. A simple flat tire would bring the delicate flow of traffic to a grinding halt. There was no shoulder to speak of, and even if there were, no one in their right mind would get out of their car. The real estate on either side of the road consisted mainly of burnt-out brick apartment buildings. But so far, so good.

Davis looked in the rearview mirror. He could see the top of the wooden crate just behind him. He could also see beads of sweat across his forehead. In the two and a half years since Buck had brought Jeremy back to the zoo, Davis had never felt as eerie as he did right now, alone with it in his car. Dear God, it was going to feel good to get rid of it once and for all at Buck's. He adjusted the air conditioning colder. Put both hands on the steering wheel. Exhaled. Maybe the radio would calm him. He turned it on. The first voice he heard was John Sterling's, the sports announcer. He was interviewing Yankee manager Joe Torre in the pregame show. This wasn't relaxing. Maybe some music. Classical? He was about to change the station when the pregame show took an unexpected turn.

"As I'm sure you know, Joe," Sterling said in his perfect radio voice. "There *is* another Bronx Zoo in town other than Yankee Stadium."

"Oh yes, and don't I know it? I hear some of the animals there can get even wilder than our own fans."

"Uh-huh. Well, we both know what a tough act the Yankee fans are to follow, but if there was one animal in particular you would consider even wilder, which one would come to mind, being the world champion manager you are, Joe?"

"Heh, heh, heh . . . I guess to both you and those listening out there, there's no secret that Jeremy the tortoise would have to be my pick as well as the crowd favorite."

Davis stared at his radio and shook his head quickly as if to wake himself up. He couldn't possibly have just heard what he thought he heard. Were his ears playing tricks on him . . . or were his ears being played with? He looked in the mirror, at the crate, and then back at the radio as the dialogue continued.

"Would you go so far, Joe, as to say that Jeremy might be considered the MVP in the game of whether or not Lester Davis gets to live or not?"

"What? How is this possible?" Lester yelled, taking quick looks back at the crate.

"Oh, I don't think there's any question, John. Jeremy has put in the time and deserves a shot at the title. I mean, he's owed that and a lot more."

"So then, let me ask you this, Joe. With all you've seen—the strategies both in interleague play and in the playoffs—do you think Lester's going to make it out of this trip alive?"

"*That,* of course, is the question, John. He thinks he will, but unfortunately for him, the answer is no. In fact, my bet is that he only has a few more minutes to live."

Sterling laughed. "Isn't it funny how he thought this was *his* idea, stealing Jeremy from the zoo and all?"

"Totally, John. What he should now understand is that Jeremy's friends are gathering just outside his car. He's definitely down to his last out."

"I'd have to agree, Joe. And then it's game over. Krogan wins! Kroooogan winnnns!" Sterling cheered, mimicking his usual game-winning chant, then both he and Torre laughed.

Davis quickly turned the radio to a different station, but the laughter of the Sterling and Torre voices continued. He tried to shut the radio off, but it wouldn't shut off. "Stop!" he screamed. "Enough! In the name of Jesus . . . be silent!"

There was complete silence. Davis's eyes grew wider with each passing second. He was shocked. *It worked,* he thought. Unbelievable. He smiled thinly, then broadly. *Faith the size of a mustard seed,* he thought. *Not bad.*

He heard John Sterling clear his throat, as if to say, *excuse me.* "Did you hear something, Joe?"

"Not really. Maybe a little feather floating by on some hot air. Nothing with a punch."

"He'll definitely have to do better than that."

"Definitely," Torre replied, and they both laughed.

Davis smacked the radio with the palm of his hand and then harder, harder with his fist. Nothing. The taunting laughter continued. He jerked his head around to all his mirrors. Beyond the crate he saw a red station wagon, so close it was practically touching his. Two people in the car were waving . . . grinning.

"No!" he screamed.

He crushed the gas pedal and began weaving through the traffic. He looked in the mirror, half expecting the tortoise to be out of the crate. The car that had been kissing his bumper was gone. Had he lost them? Had to go faster, faster. Had to get away from Krogan's "friends." How did they know where he was, *who* he was? Was the demon somehow communicating to them? Could they do that?

"What do you think, Joe?" Sterling asked. "Could they do that?"

"You can bet your complimentary tickets they can communicate, and a whole lot more."

"Shut up! You're not really talking!" Davis screamed, again punching the radio with his fist, his knuckles sore and bleeding. He wanted to throw the crate out. Kick it out on the side of the road.

Leave it there. Get rid of the evil, mind-reading homing device inside the tortoise. But what good would that do? For surely the tortoise would be killed, the demon would get out, and come right back after him. He could only think of one solution. One answer. Buck. And fast. He could see Buck's face in his mind. Feel his confidence, his faith. More speed. He had to get the tortoise to Buck fast.

Davis gasped. The red station wagon had reappeared outside the driver's-side window. There they were, the demon's friends, still grinning and waving. More gas . . . more weaving. Sweat from his forehead was dripping into and stinging his eyes. New York State Thruway, one half mile, right lane. He swerved right. There they were again, tailgating, laughing at him, enjoying his fear, feeding off him. How could they be keeping up with him so easily? He heard a banging noise in the back. Now what? The crate? Was the tortoise trying to get out?

"The oh-one," Sterling said, now doing play by play. "Swung on and missed. Two strikes. He's down to his last strike."

Davis ran his fingers nervously through his hair, wanting to pull it out. His eyes were darting everywhere, heart pounding, breathing heavy. He turned onto the entrance ramp to the thruway. Looked in the mirror. The red station wagon was right on him.

Bam.

His neck snapped backward. They'd hit him. He couldn't go any faster up the ramp, his foot already on the floor, the pedal buried.

Bam.

"Uhhh." Davis tried swerving like a snake as he came close to the right turn that would point him north. His fingers dug into the steering wheel, the turn was sharp, sharper than he'd remembered.

"The oh-two."

Bam.

They hit him hard, but this time they were still touching . . . accelerating, pushing, driving. The minivan's wheels drifted and hit the guardrail. He slammed on the brakes. Didn't help. In fact, it made things worse.

"Nooo!" Davis screamed. Screeching. Scraping. Sparks. A steep embankment to his left. Suddenly the world outside the front window was rolling. No more scraping. No more sparks. Just weightless silence. The world was upside down. Echoing inside his mind was John Sterling's perfect radio voice, and somehow he knew it would be the last play he would ever hear.

"It is high . . . it is far . . . it is . . . gone!"

8

Walter Hess hid just inside the treeline below a train track that cut through the Shu-Swamp Bird Sanctuary. The stretch between Locust Valley and Oyster Bay spanned several scenic preserves and sanctuaries. The most picturesque view for the train passengers would be seen crossing the bridge over the brackish waters of Beaver Dam, about a hundred yards away.

Hess liked to think of himself as a student, a disciple, a servant on a mission for his master, but the one portrayal he felt closest to in his elite calling was *soldier*. The word had come to him through a prophecy spoken over him at the Arm of Yahweh Christian Church. He had never served in the armed forces, but that didn't take away from who he really was. Inside, he knew he possessed the God-given mind and ability to have landed him in the Special Forces, but his calling had never been the calling of his country. Quite the contrary. His country had betrayed its godly roots, oppressing its own for the sake of foreign minorities who would soon be in total control if they weren't stopped. No, he was a soldier, a specialist in God's kingdom, and as his pastor had just told him—actually, told the congregation, but he knew it was meant specifically for him—"The time to act is now."

He checked his new, black, digital wristwatch. 5:15 P.M. The Long Island Railroad's new double-decker diesel train was scheduled to leave Locust Valley at 5:22 and would pass him about four minutes later, full speed, on its way to a 5:34 arrival at Oyster Bay station, the end of the line. Then it would leave Oyster Bay at 5:52 on a return trip and pass by him again at about 5:58. That gave him about a half hour, plenty of time.

He patted his left chest pocket, pulled out a soft pack of Camels. One more cigarette before the train came would help him relax. He crumpled the empty pack, threw it into some weeds, and did the same with the spent match he used to light up. He took a long drag on the cigarette, closing his pale-blue eyes. *Must relax.* This wasn't his first mission, but at twenty-eight years old it was by far his biggest to date.

Fingerprints, the crumpled pack. *Little things,* he reminded himself. A moment later the empty pack was retrieved and back in his pocket.

He listened, straining to hear through the stillness. The new trains were much quieter. Two bumblebees fought, or were mating, as they flew by. A dog barked in the distance. Closer, a crow cawed and was answered a moment later by another crow. They were probably talking about him, the stranger in the trees. Crows did that. Didn't matter. He wasn't hunting crows.

Hess checked his watch again, the black strap a sharp contrast to the blond hair on his forearm. So blond it was almost invisible, like his eyebrows. He imagined himself putting his ear to the shiny rail. Just a thought, an impatient one. *Soldier. Relax.* A drop of salty sweat off his forehead burned the corner of his eye. He took off his glasses and camo-bandana, dried his face, cleaned his glasses, re-covered his crew cut.

He glanced at the black duffel bag next to him. Everything he needed was in there. He felt his back pocket for the gel. Still there. He felt his other pocket for the— He jerked his head left. The train.

He flicked his cigarette and exhaled completely. *Okay, okay, re-member to relax,* he told himself. Nobody around. Plenty of time.

Think. First, the gel. He reached into his back pocket and found the small tube of Vaseline petroleum jelly, unscrewed the top, squeezed a generous dab on each fingertip of his left hand. He held the tube in his mouth and found a pair of latex gloves in his other back pocket. He put them on, first the left hand then the right. He felt the gel surround the fingertips inside the left glove, studied it for a brief moment, and was satisfied.

The massive, two-tiered, bright silver-and-blue train crossed over the small bridge at full speed. *Perfect.* He counted five cars, the track clacking as they passed. He reached for the duffel-bag strap and pulled, flexing the inside of his right forearm and the lightning-bolt tattoo. *Too heavy.* He rearranged his stance and pulled again, this time onto his shoulder.

Hess waited for the train to flow safely out of sight. *Go.* He struggled through the treeline and hurried up the steep, heavy-gravel incline toward the track. The climb, unrehearsed, was harder with the weight of the duffel bag than he'd expected. His feet dug deeply into the gravel. He slipped, then again, cursing each time his right knee hit the large gravel. Why hadn't he practiced this? *Relax and think.* He swung the duffel bag around to his rump, slipped his left arm through the strap, and pulled the bag to the small of his back. *Better.*

When he reached the top he was breathing heavily. He hurried down the middle of the track, taking the timbers two at a time, steel bars in the black bag banging together and hurting his back with each step. He glanced to the left. A marshy pond surrounded by dirt paths and trees. Birdhouses were propped up on poles by the tall-grass shore, but there were no signs of people. Sundays, there was always at least one person there. Never on Mondays near dinnertime. To his right was the much larger Nassau Pond, tranquil, and again, not a person in sight. Just a little farther and he would be at the—"Ohhh."

He tripped and hit the gravel and a creosote timber. Both palms stung; the gloves were slightly ripped, but good enough. The occasional unequal spacing of the timbers required more attention. He cursed in pain as his knee, the *same* right knee again, bled, darkening his pants. He winced getting up, but continued. *Suck it up, soldier.*

Finally, he unshouldered the heavy black bag, metal clanging. He was some fifty feet from the start of the bridge. He checked his watch. Still enough time, though not as much as he thought he'd have.

He put on a pair of dark sunglasses and unzipped the duffel bag, his sore hands shaking and searching until he felt the cutting torch. A moment later the torch, attached to a small duel-rubber line fastened to two small canisters of acetylene gas and oxygen, was lit, propped on its side, the super-hot blue flame focused on the steel rail. *Perfect,* he thought as the steel began to glow. Back in the duffel bag he found a heavy-duty hand file and a pair of large C-clamps attached to each other by a nine-foot-long, half-inch-thick steel cable. The cable ends had been welded to each clamp to ensure conductivity. He quickly filed the side of the steel rail until the dirt was gone and raw metal was exposed.

The high-pitched shivering squeal of the filing caused him to pause for a second to survey the area. The pond was still as glass; the bird sanctuary had the addition of a skinny white crane standing like a statue by the shore. Excellent. A sentry. A guardian angel. As long as that bird was content to be there, he could rest assured the sanctuary was void of onlookers.

He attached one clamp, cranking as tightly as he could to the raw metal, angling the top of the clamp for lower visibility, touching the top of the rail. He repeated the same procedure six feet away with the file and another clamp, taking care to loop the steel cable far enough away from the cutting flame of the torch. With his first task completed, he could now safely cut the rail without sending a warning signal to the train.

Hess took a quick glance at the contented crane standing guard, then pulled the first hydraulic jack from the sack. The jack was rated for sixteen tons and had a three-inch-diameter heavy-gauge steel pipe welded to its bottom. The overall length was exactly fifty-seven and a half inches. He placed it between the two rails, three feet before the molten hole the torch was burning. The jack fell perpendicularly into place between the parallel rails with an eighth of an inch to spare. Another quick search in the bag found the lever. He quickly inserted it into the jack and pumped until the lever became difficult to push. He didn't want to force it, blow a seal. The rail had not moved at all, as expected.

Hess carefully repositioned the torch at arm's length, cautious not to look directly into the bright flame and the popping embers. Satisfied, he retrieved the second jack, an exact duplicate of the first, placed it just closer to the torch. He took a quick look around to see if the smoke had caught anybody's attention and felt a sudden dizziness. He needed to slow his breathing. He had never been so nervous. According to his plan, at this point he was supposed to relax by singing "I've been working on the railroad," but he couldn't, his mouth too dry to even whistle and his mind racing too fast to hum. Again, he pumped the jack lever until it became difficult, then reinserted the lever into the first jack again and managed another three pumps. With the extra pressure the rail had begun to move fractionally, but more important was the tension at the seam he was creating.

Again he repositioned the torch, taking a little time first to cut away a glowing corner. The gauges on the small tanks told him there was plenty of acetylene, but he cursed when he saw that the oxygen was running low. He looked at the rail again and then back at the gauges. Thinking, thinking. To focus on the cutting would economize the oxygen, but the pressure of the jacks . . . When he reached over for the third jack, he noticed something in his peripheral vision that hitched his chin—a man in a rowboat on Nassau Pond, his face turned in his direction, but too far to tell if he was actually looking at him. *Probably came out to fish. The smoke from the torch. Jerk!* The fishing was lousy in Nassau Pond.

He checked his watch. 5:50. The train would be leaving Oyster Bay in two minutes and be here in eight. *Move, move, faster, faster.* He set the jack, pumped it up, and then pumped the other two. A lot of popping and squeaking but not much more movement. Maybe an inch and a half.

He grabbed the torch and aimed it, shielding his face with his left hand. The cutting went so much faster when he held the torch. He glanced up through the smoke. The man in the boat was rowing toward him. He cursed. 5:54. *Move, move.* He grabbed at the large gravel stones and stacked up a small pile to set the torch on, again refocusing the flame. Oxygen was getting very low. He yanked the final fourth jack out of the bag, wishing he had brought a fifth. If this didn't work, he wouldn't likely get a second chance in the near future. The jack fell into place just before the flame, with more room to spare than the others had had. Pump, pump, pump. More popping and squeaking. Pump, pump, pump.

"Hey!" the man in the boat yelled, rowing faster. "What are you doing up there?" The guy was close enough to see, big and strong, rowing for exercise. *Great, a jock,* Hess thought. *Worse, a hero jock.*

Pump, pump. Back to the first jack, two more pumps at the second, then the third, back to the first again, more on the fourth. Steel creaking, squeaking, wood splitting, cracking, the rail slowly widening. He grabbed the torch again and aimed it, the flame losing blue, gaining yellow, the roar quieting. The oxygen. He cursed and bore down, the gap in the rail substantially cut through but still holding on.

"What?" He heard an engine. The train. 5:56. Early. He cursed, dropped the torch, attacked the jacks, his hands shaking as he pumped. The rail was still glowing red but jack seals were going to give out. How could sixty-four tons of pressure not be enough? Why hadn't he brought five jacks? Why hadn't he brought a bigger tank of oxygen? Why hadn't he . . .

Pop, pop.

At first he thought it was a seal, but no, the rail was wider . . . separated. He looked down the track. The engine was louder, closer, but still no visual. He kept pumping. The rail was widening easier now. Pump, pump, pump. Wider, wider. "Come on, come on," he said.

One jack maxed out, then another until they were all extended as far as they could go. Good. But the hero jock was no longer yelling, just rowing harder than ever. Getting close to the shore. Hess looked toward the bird sanctuary and saw that the crane was still there. At least his escape route was clear.

One last thing.

He struggled to take off his left glove. The stupid thing had gone on easily enough. He pulled on each fingertip. *Come on.* He looked up. The big guy in the rowboat was almost at the bridge, headed for the shore. The glove finally came off, the Vaseline still on his fingers. He found a small tin of thumbtacks in his right front pocket. He clumsily emptied the tacks on the gravel, dropped to his knees, and pinned the glove onto a timber with the middle finger extended and the others curled up. Hopefully this little message would survive.

Hess looked at the rowboat and cursed. The boat was empty and slowly floating away from the shore. Scrub trees moved and the jock appeared—shorts, muscular legs, sweat-drenched gray tank top, fighting branches and running. Hess's hand reflexively went to his side, feeling for his jagged-bladed knife. His fingers slipped around the handle and through spiked steel rings. The grip felt good, just as it had so many times in his bedroom. The jock was much bigger and stronger, but Hess was a soldier, a *called* soldier with a destiny yet to be fulfilled.

The train. The yellow nose of the locomotive with its four bright headlights led the way as the double-decker train steamed around the bend, full of rush-hour passengers on their way home from work. The hero rowboat man was halfway up the gravel hill, grunting, moving fast, carrying nothing but anger. He was a witness and needed to be dealt with, but not in front of a possible trainload of witnesses. Hess took one last look—the bag, the torch, the tanks, hoses, jacks—then ran down the gravel embankment toward the bird sanctuary, his heart pounding, the jock right behind him. He ran into the trees, stopped and turned to fight, but the man hadn't followed. Instead he'd stayed at the rail and was trying to remove the jacks. Hess cursed that he hadn't thrown the jack lever away and wondered if the rail had enough tension to spring back to its original alignment.

The train was coming fast, its horn blaring, but it had not hit the brakes. He remembered his research and how it would now be tested. Engineers would commonly see people playing on the tracks and typically not break in order to keep on schedule. Under normal circumstances a train of this size would need a mile to stop. But if a person on the track were to somehow warn the train to stop, they would by law have to hit the emergency brakes, which in the new double-deckers were both electric and dynamic. But just a little farther and the train would be beyond the point of stopping before derailment.

The hero jock yanked one of the jacks free and threw it aside, then went to work on another. Hess cursed, looking back and forth from the train to the man sabotaging his sabotage. He started to run back up but stopped, his fingers clenching his knife. To stop the jock would mean exposing himself to witnesses, possibly many. Thinking. As long as one of the jacks remained to hold the rail out, the train would derail. The guy would have to remove all four jacks to be successful. But at the rate he was going, all four would be gone. Thinking, thinking.

The gravel.

Hess dropped his knife and grabbed at egg-sized gravel. The jock, on his hands and knees, threw aside the second jack. The horn continued to blast.

Hess threw as hard as he could, again and again and again. The first couple of rocks missed, but finding range and aim, the next few rocks found their target, one hitting the jock in the side of the face.

"Come on, tough guy," Hess yelled. "You'll never make it . . . but I'm still here!" He threw another rock, hitting the man hard in the side.

The jock, sweaty, dirty, glared at him angrily and went for the third jack.

"Don't you want the bad man? Be the hero. They'll all die and I'll be gone."

While working, the jock kept looking at the train closing fast. He finally stood up and waved desperately for the train to stop. The engineer responded instantly. The locking of the brakes was painfully loud, drowning out the horn, causing Hess to grimace as sparks lit the undercarriage.

The jock continued to work frantically, but with the train finally upon him, he jumped away from the track and down the embankment, not looking back as the locomotive, horn unceasing, wheels screeching, jumped at the rail split, plowed the gravel and timbers until it reached the bridge, then dipped away, falling off the bridge and into Nassau Pond. One of the other passenger cars followed the engine, but three others did not, instead, twisting and falling from the track onto their sides.

Hess cursed. The jock hadn't ruined everything, but if not for him, the entire train would have gone full speed into the drink. Hess had a disposable camera in his front pocket to capture the moment, but couldn't think of using it with the jock bearing down on him like a linebacker. He threw a final rock, hitting the jock in the chest. The muscleman didn't flinch. His heart drumrolling, Hess looked down for his knife. Eyes darting. He didn't see it.

9

Krogan had never spent a longer two years since the cursed creator decided time would begin. Not being able to engage in the deliciously evil fun and games he had enjoyed for millenniums with his inner circle of kindred spirits was torture enough, but to have to endure captivity in a tortoise was more than he could bear. The smaller and less discernable hearing range, the lack of any meaningful sense of touch or pain, the distorted visual perception of colors and moving objects, the lack of interest in, well, anything but food. And, of course, there was the food itself . . . and the taste. Hell on earth . . . and hell to pay for those who had put him there!

But only tiny seconds remained. Krogan's humiliating bondage within the lowly, dull-brained tortoise the preacher had cast him into was rapidly coming to an end. The once impenetrable wall of life was now only holding him like a worn cloth bag holds water. With its last breath, the stranglehold of Jeremy's small life released its final grip on the powerful demon it caged.

Krogan was free.

Now, to find a new host as he had done five thousand, two hundred twenty-eight times before, rarely spending more than five years within any single being. Krogan's hosts never seemed to last very long after he entered them.

Like any demon, Krogan needed to find a host quickly. Being

particular could be painful, very painful, more so than any experience could be inside a host. Recently, for the last two thousand earth years, the unseen world between possessions had become agonizingly bright, and violent, thanks to the enemy. The creator had deceitfully and treacherously flooded the world with obnoxious light, exposing the war with unfair advantage. In addition, angels, usually found in pairs, were guarding perfectly desirable and oblivious hosts, usually as a result of annoying prayers from the tryingly persistent God worshipers. Insignificant, pesky hypocrites, all of them. Especially Buchanan. His faith was rare, even now in his weakness. If not for his prayers, there would have been no guards, and the tortoise would have been dead long ago.

Fortunately, most humans had wonderfully perverted concepts of the bothersome light, self-formulated beliefs based mostly on their own logic and understanding. They were so easily influenced and offered excellent shields of darkness. Some offered more of a buffer from the light than others. Host hunting could be as exciting as it was painful. And it could be done quickly. Yet the thought of enduring another host like the last one strengthened his resolve to diligently search. But the pain, the intense pain of the light, made local hunting preferable to scanning the globe for the ideal host. In any case, Krogan sensed his new home was not far off. Besides, the demon had some personal unfinished business to attend to in the immediate area.

Krogan's first inquiry required little search and was fairly unusual for him. In the millenniums gone by since the war had begun, Krogan had revisited a host only three times. For Krogan to repossess the same host more than once, three things had to happen. One, Krogan had to have been cast out by a man of God. And not just any man of God, but one with extreme faith, boldness, and selfless stupidity. Two, the previous host had to be still alive—and willing to begin a new rampage of death and destruction. And three, Krogan had to want it to happen.

Karl Dengler, his last host, was still alive, and Krogan wasted no time in finding him. Thirsty for a new body to dominate, hungry for a new reign of terror to commence, and blistered from the omnipresent light he must endure in the meantime, Krogan stared down impatiently at his former host. The human was just how he had left him two years ago. Huge, powerful outside . . . angry, coldhearted inside.

As Krogan watched Dengler pulled a blanket off his thin bunk and draped it over himself, obviously cold. His jail cell was small with one bed. Through the blanket, Krogan could see his name still tattooed across the back of Dengler's shoulders.

"How dare they take him from me like this!" Krogan yelled, his voice thundering through a dimension cut off from Dengler's limited hearing. His fury boiled, the ever-stabbing memory of the detective and the preacher capturing him on Ellis Island, sending both him and his host into their respective prisons. They would pay, pay, pay for that.

Although his first choice was beyond his reach, Krogan stayed in the prison, drawn by several other inmates that would have made good hosts. Each one of them reached for their blankets as he passed by them. But unwilling to trade one prison for another, Krogan moved on, searching . . . searching . . . searching . . . thirsty, hungry, burning.

For the last century certain sports figures had caught his eye. Monday night in New York did not offer much in the way of sports. The stadiums were empty. The Garden, where a rock concert was taking place, provided many temptations, however. Two in particular caught his interest. On closer inspection, though, one had more size while the other had more anger. If only he could have both. Maybe he would return for one of them if need be. He left the Garden and moved east, to areas familiar from his time with Dengler. The pain was growing worse. Not the kind of pain he enjoyed.

So much darkness to immerse into, but not all to his liking.

Something was happening at the Nassau Coliseum. Something big, loud, curious. Monday Mayhem, the sign read. Another rock concert? No, but similar . . . more attractive. Krogan allowed his presence to fall within the walls of the dome. What he saw excited him. He focused closer and closer. Reading, reading the hearts of the most attractive. He could sense his new host was near. Individual by individual, when suddenly he stopped. Someone caught his interest. Someone set apart. Excellent size. Anger, depression, malice, hate, rage, and a few bonus traits of vanity and pride. And yes, yes, a touch of insanity. Krogan roared with anticipation. There were no angels anywhere in sight. In fact, he sensed the presence of at least two other demons already in this human. They would of course bow to his desires.

10

Jackhammer Hoban paced alone in the makeshift dressing room in the bowels of the Nassau Coliseum, not far enough away from the action to avoid feeling the driving heavy-metal music pounding through the thin walls and his thick flesh. The night of the majorly hyped rematch with Tyrant had finally come. And according to the detailed script lying wrinkled next to a half-drained bottle of tequila on his makeup table, in the end he would lose again.

The fight would start off on fairly even ground, each challenger exchanging familiar signature moves for the announcers to shout about into their microphones. *Then the suspense would start,* he thought sarcastically, *as if the outcome was such a mystery, the plot and choreography so brilliantly original.* He laughed, grabbing the neck of his bottle as if it were his opponent's. If only he could have his own way in the ring. He snorted again and took another swallow.

After the preliminary warm-up of arm locks and choke holds, Tyrant would catch him off guard with a hard forearm clothesline to the neck, taking the initial advantage. Tyrant would then drag him to his feet by the hair, pick him up over his shoulders, and throw him out of the ring onto a prop table that would break his fall while being crushed. The usual chairs and garbage cans would be minimized because such a championship bout required less flash to establish interest and drama. Soon after, Hoban would climb back into the ring and reverse the advantage with his patented double body-roll into a figure-four. He could still remember the cheers that move used to bring, when the majority of the audience were his fans. But that was then. Now even his favorite moves were quickly soiled with boos. And then, finally, after he would seem to have the fight in hand and the audience on the edge of despair, Tyrant would bridge-out and drop-kick Hoban to the floor, leaving him dazed in the middle of the ring, and deploy his ultimate crowd-pleasing layout back flip off the corner post into his trademark A-bomb body-slam. The end.

Not just the end of the fight, but the end of Hoban's career. The end of his paycheck. He would fall back into the abyss of barnyard wrestling for food money, the graveyard of all has-beens who had wasted their earnings while the getting was good. There he would sign autographs and tell stories of when he was the best to morons who would beg him to show them the way to the top, where less than one percent of one percent ever get to.

Hoban grabbed another swig of tequila as he continued to pace despairingly. The humiliation he'd endured in their last match was more than he could bear to repeat straight and sober. He opened the top dresser drawer and rummaged through makeup bottles and tubes, pencils, pens, scissors, eyeliner, a comb, ponytail holders, some coins and a couple of crunched-up dollar bills and . . . there it was. The vial he was after. He picked it up, held it to the light and cursed. Empty. He thought for a moment, then went to the medicine cabinet in the adjacent bathroom. Shaving cream, razor, bottle of aspirin, and a can of deodorant. He cursed loudly, slammed the cabinet door, and stomped back into the dressing room.

Suddenly he remembered and ripped opened the gym bag on the folding chair. He felt around until his finger brushed up against smooth glass.

"Yes!" The vial was almost full of white powder.

Hoban was instantly at the makeup table, hastily measuring out lines of cocaine on the glossy Formica top. Quickly satisfied with the size of each powdery row, he scavenged through the top drawer for something to snort through. His darting eyes stopped on a cheap pen. Tiny in his huge hands, he unscrewed the pen with meaty fingers and emptied out the ink cartridge and spring. He kept only the lower cylinder.

He was excited, anticipating the euphoric rush and artificial confidence. He did not care how artificial the confidence was. It was all temporary anyway. He examined the tip of the pen. The hole was too small. What else could he use? He thought about it for a full two seconds before biting the narrow tip of the pen off and spitting it to the floor. Perfect, he thought with barely a glance. Holding his left nostril closed, he snorted up a hearty white line. He winced as a cold spike shot through his sinus cavity and stabbed at the top of his head. His eyes dripped and his nose burned. *Excellent*. The raw inferno in his nose told him the drug was mostly pure stuff. A moment later his nostril numbed and he could taste a bitter drip in the back of his throat. He grabbed another mouthful of tequila. Unconsciously, his knee bounced and his head bobbed to the reverberating music, which suddenly sounded excellent.

Knocking, rapid knocking, hard at his door. "Come on, Hammer. You're on next," a familiar male voice yelled. Benny, his manager. Benny no longer treated him with the respect he deserved.

"I'll be out in a minute," Hoban shouted.

"You better be."

Hoban cursed Benny out, then snorted another line of coke. After enjoying a brief but satisfying second rush, he slowly opened his eyes and looked at himself in the mirror and liked what he saw. The makeup had taken care of the dark rings under his deep black eyes. His long, curly black hair was shiny and wild, just the way he liked it. Strong jaw, high cheekbones, thick muscular neck with pronounced veins. He wiped away the white powder residue around his nostrils and saw the image of a man who had been the recognized champion for the last few years.

Why was the WWX humiliating him so? He did not deserve this kind of treatment after all he had done for them. What had he done that was so wrong? So what if he had gotten a little out of control? They used to like it when he lost control. The more he thought about the fact that he now had go out in front of the world and lose to Tyrant, the angrier he became.

Needing a final boost, he brought the jagged pen tube back to his nose and vacuumed up the remaining line. The rush came upon him as usual. He wiped his nose and looked back into the mirror to see if he was clean.

"Aghhh!" he yelled, jumping backward in fright, falling over a chair to the floor. "What the—" His heart pounded wildly as he scrambled on his hands and knees to the other side of the room, putting distance between himself and the makeup table. Not the table itself, but the mirror. Or rather, what was in the mirror. Someone else, shadowy, almost transparent, was in the mirror where his own image was supposed to be. *Staring at him!* He closed his eyes, but the ghostly face was still in his mind.

Introduction music, raw and driving. Tyrant was going out to the ring. Using the folding chair to pull himself to his feet, Hoban looked in the mirror again, this time seeing only the room's reflection. To his extreme relief, his own image had returned. He snorted a nervous laugh and cursed himself for being so scared at nothing. Drugs. He could not have really seen what he thought he saw. That was impossible. Impossible as that awful head he thought he'd seen once when he was on mescaline. He had opened his refrigerator door to see a man's head staring at him. He had screamed and slammed the door. Screamed just the way he had a minute ago. When he'd reopened the door, he'd seen only a lone, large bottle of Heinz ketchup. How could he have possibly mistaken a bottle of ketchup for a head? Same as now, just different. The image he'd seen, or rather thought he'd seen, looked nothing like him, except maybe in size.

He was about to shake off the experience as a strange hallucination brought on by a drug rush when the temperature in the room rapidly dropped. Goose bumps swept across his massive forearms. He could still hear the intro guitar ripping away. Tyrant was probably messing with Asia, that chick who was supposed to pretend to hate him for something he did to Sergeant Savage, the Marine guy she was supposed to love. He remembered that part of the script. But why was it so freaking cold?

He exhaled from his mouth, expecting to see his breath, but nothing. Definitely cold enough to see breath. What was in that vial of coke anyway? Had someone mixed LSD into it? *Nah.* Too soon to be seeing stuff. That would take a little longer. Maybe something really weird was wrong with the air conditioner. Whatever it was, it was time to leave.

He took a final glance in the mirror. His own reflection. And he looked good. Great. Time to go. He turned to leave, took one step, and stopped. He felt a shiver go up his back, and it wasn't from the weird cold. What he had just seen, or rather what he had not seen, scared him. When he had turned around, his reflection hadn't turned with him. Eyes wide, he snapped another look at the mirror, transfixed on his own image. He moved closer. His own reflection moved with him, but just out of sync, as though it were moving and staring back at him independently. He frowned and the image frowned back, but late, as if mimicking. The drugs?

He continued closer, slowly, cautiously, until he was right at the table. He turned his head slowly to the right, keeping his gaze on his reflection until he was looking out the corner of his eye. The image seemed to be moving perfectly with him now. He continued the test, left and right again, changing expressions, until he felt quite foolish. He could feel his heart rate and breathing return to normal and was about to leave when, completely detached from his own blank expression, his reflection laughed.

"Agghhh!" Hoban's legs instantly felt like cooked pasta. He wanted to run but couldn't. He fell, the laughter growing louder. He turned his face to the floor and covered his head with his giant hands. The room's icy temperature seemed to penetrate his eyes until they were burning, burning cold. Pain. He continued to scream. The coldness spread from his eyes to his brain. The laughter grew louder and louder, drowning out his own scream until . . . his own scream became the laughter.

He rolled onto his back, his mouth wide open, laughing, laughing, laughing. He could not stop. His brain was frozen, his thoughts unable to control his body. His mind was screaming and his mouth was laughing when, unexpectedly, his fear vanished as if it had never been there.

Strength returned to his legs and arms. The ice water in his veins warmed. He stopped laughing and rose to his feet. He stretched out his arms and expanded his barrel chest, breathing deeply.

"Finally," he said confidently, not completely knowing why he said it, but feeling as though he had just woken up from a long, refreshing sleep. He felt good. Great, in fact. He looked at his reflection. His expression was smug, as if he had just accomplished something to be proud of, but he did not know what it was. He looked at the bottle of tequila, and before he realized what he was doing, the bottle was empty and breaking on the floor.

"Hey!" came a voice at the door, followed by a knock. "What's going on in there?" It was Benny again. "Hoban . . . you okay? Open the door."

Hoban ignored the noise at the door; his gaze fell on the script lying on the table. He picked it up and read no further than the first sentence before throwing it aside. A moment later he opened the dressing room door and emerged, new heavy-metal music greeting him along with Benny. The medium-height fat man with thin, greasy black hair, dressed in green slacks and brown sports jacket, was talking, but Hoban was not listening to him. Instead, he looked at the surrounding area as if seeing it for the first time. As if *seeing* for the first time.

"What are you doing? Are you crazy? You were supposed to be out there already. This is your intro, moron," Benny said. "This is it, Hoban. After tonight, we're through. You're a loser, pal. Who needs you?"

Hoban frowned, annoyed, then slowly looked down at Benny. He grabbed the fat man by the neck and lifted him eye to eye. "Don't speak to me—ever," he said before tossing Benny aside like a Styrofoam cup. He then turned and walked in the direction of the pounding music.

11

Gavin was waist-deep in murky Nassau Pond, backing up the steep incline to the shore, feet slipping, struggling to hold a limp, well-dressed man from behind, as if doing a Heimlich maneuver on him, when two firemen rushed to his side and relieved him of his burden.

"Is he alive, Detective?" one of the firemen asked.

"Maybe. I . . . don't know," Gavin said, looking back at the train wreck, four double-decker passenger cars twisted, half crushed, folded upon each other like sausage links in a shallow pan of water, the locomotive completely submerged. Most of the screams had eerily quieted to whispers and groans. Emergency workers were frantically trying to run a crane cable through the windows.

He hadn't seen so much activity on the North Shore of Nassau County since Avianca flight 052 ran out of gas and crashed in the woods of Cove Neck, leaving seventy-three dead. By some miracle, most of the passengers here were alive, but the injury list was not light.

With no water or road access, hospital, police, National Guard, and Coast Guard helicopters were flying in and out of the dim sunset over the large pond like bees from a hive. Firemen and rescue workers traveled through the narrow bird sanctuary trails. Long Island Railroad flatbed utility trucks served as makeshift ambulances on one track, while the other track had been used to bring in a crane and massive road construction lights, making the immediate area look like a Hollywood shoot.

"Well, so much for an undisturbed scene," said a familiar voice from behind.

"Huh?" Gavin turned.

"You believe this?" Chris said, stepping into the water to help Gavin out.

"No."

"See any Feds yet?" Chris reached out his hand for Gavin to grab.

"Haven't seen any, but they'll be here." Gavin motioned in the direction of the wreck. "Probably want to know why we don't have the black box yet."

"Black box?"

"Yeah . . . like planes. Trains have 'em, too."

"Hmm, I didn't know that."

"Neither did I. Railroad guy told me."

"Just as long as the Feds didn't tell you. They'd never let you forget it."

"Ah, they never tell us anything."

Just then the crane engine throttled up, and the cable started tightening through the passenger-car window. Slowly—squeaking, scraping—the silver mass inched upward, then stopped.

Gavin shook his head. "Gonna be a long night."

Chris sighed. "And just what this area needs."

"What's that?"

"Another taste of terrorism."

"Tastes domestic to me."

"What makes you say that?"

"The choice of target, for one. A train leaving Oyster Bay is not exactly a national symbol, like the Trade Center."

"Neither are jet airliners, but they've been targets often enough."

"True, but the absence of an explosion makes me think we're dealing with one, maybe two guys. Terrorist groups, both foreign and domestic, prefer bombs. They have access to the stuff, don't have to get their hands too dirty, the results are more predictable, and explosions seem to strike more terror . . . And then there's that glove."

"What about it?"

"Domestic. When was the last time you saw someone who was calling for a jihad against the great Satan give the finger? *That* wouldn't be 'holy.'"

Chris nodded. "Honest, yes. Holy, no. Maybe we'll find some prints inside."

Gavin shook his head. "Not likely. Fingers are flat, stuck together. Looks like there's some kind of greasy substance inside."

"Why didn't he just bring a third glove and leave that?"

"I don't know. Maybe he watches too much TV."

"You get a chance to see the rest of the stuff up there?"

"Not really. Is it taped off yet?" Gavin remembered the orders he'd given to an Officer John Kelly.

"Yeah, but we'd better get up there. There's enough manpower now for this end."

Gavin heard what Chris was trying to tell him, but it was hard to leave. He took another look at the pond and then at the pileup. His first duty as a policeman, not to mention his first instincts as a person, was to people and property. But now help was everywhere, and he figured he should best set his sights on the hunt.

Gavin—his clothes heavy from pond water, wondering if tadpoles were in his shoes, glad of his decision to leave his sport jacket and wallet in the car—fought the brush and sliding gravel to the top of the tracks where the rail had been cut and spread apart. The train had destroyed the track beyond the point of derailment, but from the separation backward, the track was in perfect condition.

For the first time since he had arrived, Gavin felt the liberty to leave the rescuing to the designated personnel and enter detective mode.

He looked in the direction the train would have come from. Nearby were dozens of occupied stretchers lying perpendicular on the rails, some with sheets drawn completely over the bodies, some with survivors being worked on by paramedics. There was also a priest, kneeling, holding a hand. The sight of the cleric with short white hair momentarily hijacked Gavin's thoughts. Made him think about Buck. He quickly shook it off.

A hundred feet away two firemen rushed up the embankment with a semiconscious woman, yelling for paramedics to help, one of them shouting, "She's pregnant!"

Gavin didn't remember getting there, but he suddenly found himself at their side. Her summer dress was shredded. He didn't see any obvious bleeding or compound fractures, but her bruised arms cradled her belly as she moaned painfully, gasping out occasionally in Spanish. Her tangled black hair, scraped and dirty dark skin, and slight figure despite advanced pregnancy stirred Gavin's imagination enough to scare his racing heart. *But for the grace of God there be Amy,* he heard his mind say. He couldn't remember where or how many times he'd heard those weirdly familiar words, but his mind seized upon them and inserted Amy's name, and he couldn't do a thing to stop it. *Where is the grace of God for this one?* he countered to himself.

Two paramedics swooped in, one of them stepping between Gavin and the woman as if he weren't there. He barely noticed them, his mind still having a hard time placing Amy and his own unborn child at home, safe.

"What's happening?" Chris asked, arriving at his side.

Gavin refocused, shook it off. "It's under control," he said, then started back, probably leaving Chris a little confused. This really wasn't his job. The woman was getting plenty of attention, and he was needed elsewhere.

"Freaked ya out, huh?" said Chris, walking the track just behind him.

"What?"

"Made you think of Amy, didn't she?" Chris went on, surprising Gavin that he'd put it together.

"Who?"

Chris snorted. "I read you like a book, Pierce."

"Who are you, *Doctor* Grella?"

"Like—a—book."

"Shut up and focus on this," Gavin said, approaching the place where the rail was cut.

Gavin stepped into a small corral created by the yellow police tape. Chris passed him, murmuring something about a conversation Gavin was no longer having. He needed to empty his mind of the tragedy around him and objectively zone in on what could have happened here a few hours ago. He turned, looking beyond the immediate activity of emergency workers, stretchers, and artificial lights. His eye followed the track until it disappeared around a bend. According to one of the survivors, the train's horn had been blaring before the derailment. Apparently the engineer had seen something or someone on the track. He tried to envision the train's approach. He followed the track through the many stretchers until he was looking down at his feet, then turned and continued, his eyes on the rail.

"Who do you think this finger's for?" Chris said.

"Huh?"

"The glove."

"Oh . . . probably you."

"Me?"

"To whom it may concern," Gavin said, slipping on his own pair of latex gloves. He crouched down and picked up what looked like half a C-clamp cut clean through—by a train wheel, Gavin figured. He noticed the clamp's other half a few feet away, a short piece of cut cable welded to it.

"What do you make of that?" Chris said.

"Someone did their homework. The rail carries a safe signal to the cab of any approaching train. A break in the signal, whether the engineer is alert enough to realize it or not, will automatically cause the train to slow to a safe speed. This little cable kept that signal alive with the rail cut. We'll probably find the other half in the drink attached to a similar clamp," Gavin said, putting the severed clamp back exactly where he'd found it. He looked carefully at what appeared to be two modified hydraulic jacks.

"I get the creepy feeling we're dealing with someone who enjoys his work," Chris said.

Gavin nodded. "Craft might be more like it. This wasn't spur of the moment. Someone had to get the jacks, maybe at more than one location, maybe ordered, since not every hardware store is going to carry a large supply of sixteen-ton jacks. The pipes are cut smoothly . . . to exact lengths . . . no shims. Welds look clean, possibly professional."

Chris crouched and examined what appeared to be two attached fire extinguishers, each tank about a foot and a half long and four inches around. "Cute. A mini torch kit."

"Did the job," Gavin said as he picked up a blue tube the same color as the two jacks between the rails, black rubber handle at one end.

"The lever?" Chris asked.

"Yeah," Gavin replied, studying the lever. Like most, its bottom was shaped to match the male release screw on the jack. Looking back at the jacks, he noticed that one of them was loose. At first he thought the loosening of the jack had been caused by the derailment, but considering the pressure needed to split open the rail, he fit the lever onto the relief valve and turned. Nothing. The pressure had already been released. He stared, frowning at the jack for a long moment. Confused, he fitted the lever to the other jack and turned. The jack decompressed and the train rail followed, halving the distance it had been widened from its original alignment. Why did one jack have pressure and the other none?

"Two more jacks over here, Gav," Chris called from a few yards away. "They seem to be in good shape. Maybe they were extras."

"What do you mean?"

"Well, if the train threw them, I would think there would be some damage to them, bent or gashed. But they're perfectly straight. Then again, if they *are* extras, why aren't they together? Why is one here and the other there? He takes all this care and leaves his hard work scattered?"

Gavin frowned, joining Chris with the lever in hand. He checked the relief valves of the third and fourth jacks. Nothing. Each had been decompressed.

"Detective!" called a voice from below, a little farther down the track. Officer Kelly was standing just outside the treeline of the bird sanctuary motioning a flashlight. "Down here."

Gavin returned the lever to where he had found it, then set off after Chris, already near the bottom of the hill. The officer waited for Chris, then led him into the trees. When Gavin caught up, Chris and the officer were standing still, looking down, silent.

"Looks like we have a witness," Chris finally said as Gavin stepped by his side. "How do you explain . . . so many . . . ?"

Gavin said nothing.

"I don't know," Kelly said as if he'd been asked. "Looks like he was fighting some Ninjas with swords. Or was attacked by some kind of wild—"

"Stop," Chris ordered Kelly, which was much nicer than what Gavin was about to say.

"Anyone have a wet rag?" Gavin asked.

"A wet rag?" Kelly repeated.

"No," Chris said.

Gavin thought of using one of his wet socks, but almost immediately decided it would somehow screw up the forensics. "Let's see that flashlight, Kelly."

Gavin took the handoff and moved in for a closer look. Chris followed.

"This is an *A*," Gavin said, drawing with his finger, inches above the man's chest.

"Is this a *T*?" Chris asked, pointing to what appeared to be another letter.

Gavin said nothing, wishing he could wipe the blood off to see more clearly. Any thought that the Feds might take over and run away with the investigation was now seriously challenged. This was a clear homicide. A man—big, athletic, late twenties, early thirties—leaning back on an old tree stump as if napping, six evenly spaced punctures across his neck. His gray workout shirt torn open, and what first appeared to be random slashing and dripping red lines across his bare chest were letters with numbers etched underneath.

"Another message?" Chris asked.

Gavin just stared, trying to differentiate between blood and gash.

"I don't get it," Kelly said. "Act! Two thousand, seven hundred, and forty-two."

Gavin nodded. "Not bad, Kelly."

"Is that *act* as in a call to action or *act* as in theater segments?" Chris wondered aloud.

"Kelly, let's get this area taped before anyone else tramples down here," Gavin ordered, getting down on one knee for a different angle.

"Right," Kelly said. But still transfixed on the sight before him, he didn't move until Gavin glanced up at him. The officer nodded and disappeared.

"Kelly," Gavin yelled over his shoulder.

The officer reappeared.

"There's a priest up by the stretchers."

"Right, I saw him."

"Get him. Tell him to bring his Bible."

"Did you say Bible?" Kelly said, frowning.

12

Yes, Bible," Gavin said, not wanting to explain, fixated on the victim. The deep, clean slices in the man's skin spoke of a razor-sharp blade, and the neck punctures brought an image to mind of a knife that looked a lot more like a weapon than a tool—probably sharpened religiously, he thought. The lack of blood dripping from the message meant the victim had been dead when the letters were carved. At least that's what he hoped the medical examiner would tell him.

Chris said, "Talk to me," or something like that.

"This is a Scripture, Chris. That's not an exclamation point after *act*, it's an *s*."

"And the two thousand, sev—"

"Is twenty-seven, forty-two. Acts twenty-seven, forty-two."

"What Scripture is that?"

Gavin gave Chris a look. "Do I look like a priest?"

"Uhhh . . . no."

"Here, take this light and shine it down here." Gavin pointed to one of the man's pockets. Chris took the light and Gavin patted the pocket, reached in, and pulled out a jingling set of keys with a remote attached to the ring.

"Maybe he's sitting on a wallet," Chris suggested.

Gavin reached around and found there were no rear pockets. "Nothing. Somewhere there's a . . . let's see," he said, looking at the ignition key. "There's a Toyota parked and it's probably got his wallet in it. Shouldn't be too hard to find with this remote."

"He looks like a jogger, but those aren't running shoes."

Gavin frowned at the dirty white sneakers and socks, then felt the socks between his fingers. "Wet . . . like mine."

"Maybe he was bird-watching and saw the guy working on the tracks . . . ran through some water to get to him?"

"Why leave your wallet behind to go bird-watching? He was probably out here . . . I don't know, doing something, but I think you're right about him sighting the perp."

The sound of gravel crunching caught Gavin's attention. Another bobbing flashlight—no, not one, but two bobbing flashlights were approaching. One was attached to Officer Kelly. The priest Gavin had seen on the tracks had the other.

"This is Father Lauer, sir," Kelly said, holding a branch back for the priest to enter. He was younger than Gavin had thought, his white hair making him look older from a distance.

"Thanks for coming down, Father. I'm Detective Grella and this is Detective Pi—"

"Oh, Lord Jesus!" the priest gasped and then made the sign of the cross upon seeing the man with the message.

"Do you have a Bible?" Gavin said bluntly, but the priest was apparently too shocked to hear him.

"A Bible, Father?" Chris asked more politely.

"Huh . . . oh yes, of course. Here," Father Lauer said, extending a leather-bound book toward Chris.

"Why don't you just read it for us?" Gavin said, his gaze back on the victim. He knew the book was in the New Testament but didn't know where.

"Read it?"

"Acts twenty-seven, forty-two," Gavin said.

"Acts . . ."

Gavin pointed to the dead man's chest and drew in the air with his finger as he read each letter and number. The more he looked at it, the more obvious the letters became.

"My God!" Father Lauer said, apparently seeing the ugly slashes come into focus. "Okay, okay, okay," he said quietly as he flipped through thin pages. "Twenty-six . . . twenty-seven . . . forty . . . here it is. Forty-two." He cleared his throat. "'And the soldiers' plan was to kill all the prisoners, that none of them should swim away and escape.'"

Silence.

"Read it again," Gavin said.

Father Lauer frowned slightly, then cleared his throat again and complied.

"May I?" Gavin asked.

"Certainly," Father Lauer said, handing him his Bible, holding his finger on the verse.

Gavin read it over and over to himself, the background noises fading out as he read. No one said a word. Finally, he looked up at Chris. "I don't get it."

Chris raised his eyebrows. "What's not to get? Seems perfectly obvious. He's the soldier, the prisoners were the people on the train, and his plan was to kill them in the water."

"Soldiers," Kelly scoffed. "Whose army?"

Gavin looked at Kelly but didn't say anything.

"I think I'll get this place taped off," Kelly said.

"Thanks, Kell," Chris said with a thin smile.

Gavin shook his head, then looked toward the priest. "Were you familiar with that verse?"

"Well, not from the verse number, but I am familiar with the passage."

Gavin looked back at the victim, still shaking his head. "Okay, this guy surprises our—"

"Soldier?" Father Lauer said, unblinking.

Chris's brow rose expectantly.

"Soldier," Gavin said with a gracious wave. "They fight. Soldier kills him. Quickly, judging by the lack of other wounds on him. But this victim wasn't in the plan. He was a detour. Soldier came here to derail a train, not read the Bible, and he's got to be in a major hurry to leave. But before he leaves, he spontaneously decides to leave a message, to whom I'm not sure, with this obscure verse out of context. I mean, what kind of verse is *this* to commit to memory? Who *is* this guy?"

No one answered.

A flashlight was approaching. Kelly was back with the tape.

"FMIs and AMTs are here, Detective," Kelly called from a few yards away, referring to the forensic crew and medical technicians. He stopped to open a roll of yellow tape. "Oh, and one of the survivors happens to be the engineer."

"You're kidding!" Chris said.

"No. He claims to have jumped from the locomotive. He's in the ICU at Saint Francis."

"How bad?" Gavin asked.

"I don't know."

Gavin turned to Chris. "Why don't you head up there and tell the techs what we've got down here. And leave me that flashlight. There's something else I want to check out."

"You got it," Chris said and left.

Father Lauer turned to follow after Chris, but Gavin reached for his arm. "Uh, Father?" he asked, without his usual all-business demeanor.

"Yes?"

Gavin looked to see where Kelly was, making sure the officer and anyone else was out of earshot.

"What is it, my son?"

"If I ask you a question, can it be just between you and me?"

"And God. Would you like to confess something?"

Gavin nodded. "Yeah, I mean, no. I mean . . . do you believe . . . have you ever had any experience with . . . demons?"

The priest's expression turned to one of concern as he studied Gavin's face. He looked at the victim, the poor man who had probably tried to stop the soldier. Then his gaze returned to Gavin.

"I don't mean *this*," Gavin said intensely. "Have you ever experienced demons living in people . . . or animals?"

The priest thought for a moment. "Have you been seeing demons, Detective?"

Buck would not have asked that, was Gavin's first thought. Buck would have immediately known what he was talking about. Suddenly demons were the last thing Gavin wanted to talk about. He felt embarrassed and wished he had not mentioned it. What was he thinking? He should know better than to ever talk about this with anyone, not even a priest. "Forget it."

"Detective?"

"Come on. I'll walk you out of here."

"Wait," Father Lauer said, now grabbing Gavin by the arm. "I'm sorry. The answer to your question is yes. Please tell me what's on your mind."

"Do you have a card?"

"Yes," the priest said, fishing for a wallet.

Gavin took the card without looking at it and put it in his wet pocket. "I'll call you," he said, then left, Father Lauer following close behind. When he broke the treeline Gavin stopped, a thought forming that would not allow him to leave.

"What's the matter, Detective?"

"Huh . . . oh, nothing. I need to get back to work." Gavin jerked his chin toward the sounds of the yelling paramedics up by the stretchers. "Sounds like you're needed up there."

The priest nodded. "We'll have to finish our conversation later," he said, his feet starting in the direction of his calling.

"Yeah, later."

"Call," the priest said as he struggled up to the tracks and stretchers.

Gavin stayed behind at the edge of the treeline. He didn't answer, didn't listen, shutting the priest off as he would an infomercial with his TV remote. Click, gone. He needed to get back to work. *Focus. Think.* He looked down the treeline, away from the train wreck, and then into the woods where Kelly was taping the crime scene. How many different directions could the soldier have fled?

Crunching gravel and bobbing flashlights made Gavin turn. It was Chris with the forensic techs.

"Right through there." Chris motioned with his light beam. "Watch your step."

The techs followed Chris's directions and were quickly in their element. No gasps or stunned silence from those guys. No matter how gruesome or shocking the scene, they engaged in their usual deadpan humor. The only thing Gavin found amazing about them anymore was that they never grew tired of the same jokes. They must teach them at forensics school, he'd decided.

Gavin refocused his attention back to the dark, quiet treeline at the bottom of the tracks, away from the noise of the crane, choppers, hustling emergency workers, Feds, and the priest who wanted to play doctor with Gavin's mind.

"—body home?"

Gavin turned. Chris. "What?"

"Hello . . . I said, 'Is there anybody home?' You've got that far-away look."

"He was probably leaving."

"When he met our friend back there? Yes."

"And he was probably leaving the same way he came."

"Yes, more than likely."

"So if he came from this side of the track, he was probably waiting for the train somewhere along here."

"I'll buy that. But why this train? If he simply wanted to derail a train, he could have more easily done it from the other side of the bridge. The access to the sanctuary paths is easier over there, and he wouldn't have had to carry all that equipment up as steep an incline."

Gavin nodded. "Let's walk," he said, motioning into the dark. "I agree. This train may have held a particular attraction for him."

"Any thoughts?" Chris asked as his flashlight joined Gavin's, slowly scanning the ground and treeline as they walked away from the wreck, looking, searching for that lost car key, that wallet, that coin . . . something he would have touched before putting those latex gloves on.

"Only the obvious. Six-o'clock train. Rush hour. People going home from work. I'm not familiar enough with Oyster Bay employment to know who would be on this train, but I would think that a good place to start."

"What about the glove?" Chris asked.

"What about it?"

"The ointment inside to prevent fingerprints."

"I noticed. A lot of work to go through when he could have just used a different glove."

"Exactly. He thinks too much. Very creative, but not much experience. It was close to ninety degrees today. Can you imagine how uncomfortable it would have been to wear that glove?"

"Uncomfortable enough to not put it on until he had to," Gavin said.

Chris smiled. "Which is why we're looking for where he waited while waiting for the train."

"Yes. He may have been waiting for a long time, making sure no one saw him enter. Maybe reading a book, chewing gum."

"Taking a dump is what I'd be doing if I were going to derail a—"

"Look at this," Gavin said, holding his beam on the gravel hillside.

Chris's light joined in. "What?"

"The gravel all along here has been smoothed." They got closer. "Footprints."

"Looks more like a landslide."

"Remember, he was carrying sixty, seventy pounds of gear. The climb would have been rough." Gavin shook his head, trying to make sense of the disturbance.

Chris turned. "That would mean he came out somewhere around here."

Gavin followed Chris's lead to the treeline, where both men stopped, their flashlights beaming a sneak peek of where they would search for more clues in the light of day.

"Okay, so he waits for the train to go by and starts up to the track." Chris used his flashlight to follow the would-be footsteps. "Heavy prints. And it looks like he was having trouble around there. Maybe had to rest, or he slid back, or fell dow—"

"Wait," Gavin interrupted, beaming his light to a place Chris had just passed. "What's that?"

"What?"

"That!" Gavin said, moving closer. A moment later they were both crouched over what appeared to be a crumpled, empty cigarette pack.

"Looks fresh enough, not waterlogged or dirty. Maybe it got away from him when he fell."

"Got a pen or something?" Gavin looked about to find a twig to pick it up with.

"Of course I do," Chris said. He opened a pocketknife, slid it into the pack, picked it up, and displayed it between them, the word *Camel* visible as he turned it. "Being prepared is a big part of the job. It's what separates the real pros from the—"

"Just shut up," Gavin said as he eyed the pack closely. "Now this here could be pre-glove."

"Oh no," Chris said soberly, his chin pointed in the direction of the derailment. "The long night just got longer."

Gavin turned and took a moment before he saw him and groaned. "I thought I told you to put up the No Politicians sign."

"I did. He must have taken it down on his way in."

Senator Bruce Sweeney appeared to be setting up for another one of his political photo shoots. The presidential election was a year and a half away, but it was quite obvious that it was never too early to get started campaigning, even though Sweeney denied any interest in the candidacy.

"No class," Chris said, shaking his head. "There should be a law that disqualifies anyone who thinks he should be the most powerful person on earth from being able to collect votes."

"Then how would anyone become president of the United States?"

"Everyone just votes for whoever they want to and the one with the most votes is president, whether they like it or not."

"Great idea, Chris. Our next president would be Tiger Woods."

"No, it would have to be a Clint Eastwood type, but younger. Someone with a face you'd be afraid to say no to. That's all a president really needs to be—a face. Everyone else around him does the work. All we elect is a face, so it better be one that means business."

"I can see you've given this a lot of thought."

Chris tapped his index finger on his head. "The wheels are always turning, Gav. I can't help it, they just are."

A lone cameraman turned a light on the senator as another man gave what appeared to be instructions.

"Good. When Senator Sweeney asks who's in charge, I'll tell him the guy with the squeaky head."

"Oh no, you don't. I'm not getting on camera with him. You were here first."

"So what does that mean? Wait, don't answer that. I can hear your rusty wheels turning, and I don't know if I can deal with the answer."

13

The WWX girl of the month near ringside swung the long mallet with both hands and smashed the huge WWX gong as the background music changed into a flesh-pounding, earsplitting, guitar-and-drum power jam. Jackhammer Hoban stepped out from behind the curtain onto a dark stage. Overhead spotlights blasted him from three directions, and the sold-out coliseum erupted in boos. Two giant screens came alive with old footage from past Jackhammer action.

A long ramp led to the illuminated ring where Tyrant was pacing. Hoban knew Tyrant had been reluctantly brought out first because they couldn't wait any longer for him. Oddly, he didn't care. From now on, everyone would be waiting for him, in and out of the ring.

Hoban breathed in deeply—not from nervousness. He had an urge to breathe, to feel every air molecule fill his lungs. He couldn't remember ever doing that before. Except for him and the ring, the rest of the coliseum was dark, but he could see people in the shadows twirling light sticks. He found curious pleasure in his ability to see them. And the music was clear and crisp. *Human lungs, human eyes, human ears, not like a dull-sensed tortoise,* he thought. But he didn't know why he was thinking such things at all, much less at a time like this. He laughed at his thoughts and at the crowd. He didn't care whether or not they were booing or cheering. He liked the music, the lights, the attention. But most of all, he liked what he was going to do with Tyrant, who was now standing mid-ring, hands on hips, flexing his lats as wide as possible. Strangely, though he couldn't remember ever seeing a live one, Tyrant reminded him of a flared king cobra, ready to strike, a thought that didn't frighten him in the least.

Hoban started toward the ring. As he stepped onto the long ramp there was a deafening explosion at his sides—billowing, beach-umbrella-size mushroom clouds and a colorful array of continuous shooting sparks. Somehow he'd forgotten that was going to happen, but it didn't startle him. In fact, he felt great, above everything around him. Above *everyone* around him.

"Tyrant rules!" someone shouted as he passed amid other similar shouts, but he paid no attention. *Idiots.* His focus was on the man in the ring. *Puny human,* he thought, not knowing why the word *human* kept coming into his mind.

The WWX girl who had smashed the gong, then sensually ascended a small portable stairway to the ring's ropes, now stepped on the bottom rope with her knee-high black leather boots and lifted the middle one for Hoban to enter through.

"Get him, Tiger," she said as he stepped up to the ropes.

More lights—not spots this time but flashes from cameras all around. He paused to look her up and down and figured the cameras were more interested in her than him. That would change after tonight. He gazed into her eyes. Blue eyes that jumped out in contrast to her jet-black hair and dead-white skin. Her black leather clothing did little to hide what the cameras wanted to catch. But he sensed something else about her. Something familiar.

"I'll see you after the fight," she said with a wink.

"I know," he said, his voice low and raspy, then entered the ring.

"About time, moron," Tyrant sneered, just loud enough for Hoban and the referee to hear.

Hoban said nothing, just glared at Tyrant and thought how two, maybe three more of him would be a greater challenge, more fun.

The referee became animatedly instructional for the audience, but in reality was saying nothing about any supposed rules, only wishing them a safe contest and warning them not to crash into him. About twenty feet away from the ring was the table where the announcers and commentators sat. Two men in suits, a wrestler who was supposed to fight the winner—who, of course, they all knew would be Tyrant—and a woman, Tanya Grossman, daughter of fan-despised WWX owner, Michael Grossman. Behind them were TV cameras and sound-mixing-board operators with head-phones on. Two other men with TV cameras on their shoulders walked about, mostly focused on the shouting audience.

When the music stopped, the four corner posts simultaneously exploded with more fireworks. Enough coliseum lights came on to illuminate the audience.

"And now for the main event we've all been waiting for," the announcer in the suit said, his amplified voice echoing throughout the vast hall.

Hoban continued to stand still as Tyrant paced and flexed for the audience.

"Ladies and gentlemen . . . In what has been called the WWX contest of the century, a rematch of the challenger, seven feet and three-hundred thirty pounds of revenge, the former WWX champion of the world, Jack . . . Hammer . . . Hobaaaannnnn!"

When the boos came they were louder than he had ever heard them—for anyone. *All the better,* was the last thing he thought before his mind began to wander. The announcer's voice slowed and faded as the boos and heckling changed—grew louder, clearer . . . different. In fact, the audience was no longer booing at all but chanting. He didn't understand at first what they were saying, as if the word was from another language. The bright spotlights from the ceiling girders also began to change until they were like sunlight and he felt warmth. Soon the sunlight was hot. Sweat dripped from his brow. The taste of his own blood was in his mouth, and the smell of animals and burnt oil was strong in the still, humid air.

Was he hallucinating? More of the drugs? Or maybe this was a daydream. But it seemed more like a memory than a daydream. That's what it was. He was remembering something. He saw himself in a different coliseum, one without a roof, the crowds continuing to chant. The ground was sandy and he was riding what appeared to be a chariot, like in that old *Ben Hur* movie. He could feel the horses' worn leather reins in the palm of his hand. He felt proud, very proud. But how could this be a memory? He had never even touched a horse, much less a chariot.

He controlled the horses around the arena as expertly as if he had known them his whole life. In the center of the dirt field lay a fallen enemy, a broken pile of metal and flesh. The bloodlust of the audience intensified, their eyes wild and hungry. He was their master. He looked at the reins in his hands. His skin was different too, darker, scarred.

That's when he realized what they were chanting. The word, or rather the name, was tattooed to his right forearm. They were chanting the name on his arm. "Krogan, Krogan, Krogan."

". . . and defending his title, the WWX presents the undisputed champion of the world . . . the one . . . the only . . . Tyyyyyrant!"

"Tyrant . . . Tyrant . . . Tyrant," came the chant.

With a quick shake of his head, Hoban found himself back in the ring, realizing with the introduction that only a second or two had passed. Tyrant climbed up onto one of the corner posts and stretched out his arms to his fans, then back-flipped onto his feet in the middle of the ring and faced Hoban. The fans screamed wildly.

"Look at him—he's wasted," Tyrant muttered to the mock ref so only the three of them could hear under the crowd noise.

Hoban only smiled, saying nothing.

"Look, Hammerhead, I know life must seem unfair to you right now, but if you screw up our routine, I might forget to break my fall when I land on your face."

The ref blew his whistle and backed away.

As per the script, Tyrant began sprightly circling the ring as if to find the vulnerable point of attack. At first Hoban didn't move, but then thought it would be amusing to play the game. Accordingly, he cut Tyrant off from his circling and engaged his arms, grappling head to head for the stronger advantage, then with a sudden drop and twist to the left, threw Tyrant into the ropes, where he would propel himself for the next move.

Hoban could not remember when he'd felt this strong and confident. And despite the drugs and drinks, his mind was so clear and his thinking so sharp, he knew exactly what he wanted and didn't care about the consequences. In fact, *he* would determine all consequences.

He stepped into Tyrant's path and locked arms with him as he was supposed to . . . as he had done to begin so many previous bouts, including his last one with Tyrant. But when had he ever been so energized? Tyrant's grip felt like a child's. Hoban smirked. *So he wants the routine?*

Hoban tightened the grip of his right hand on the back of Tyrant's neck and with his left hand squeezed his weak opponent's right forearm. *Puny human,* he thought with contempt.

Tyrant grimaced, shock in his eyes, about to say something, but Hoban responded quickly with the scripted move, only with much more power and speed than ever before. Tyrant hit the ropes too hard to coordinate his countermove. Instead of using his agile footwork, which he was known for, to slingshot his way back, he had to hold on to the ropes so as not to go through them. He wound up on the floor.

The crowd booed. Hoban raised his right fist to the audience and, laughing, stuck out his middle finger at them, then pointed it in the face of the TV camera. The boos became louder and the commentators became very animated, needing to quickly censor the forbidden gesture.

Hoban taunted Tyrant with mock concern. "What's the matter, forgot your move?" He inhaled deeply, wondering why he kept thinking about the molecules of air in his lungs.

Tyrant frowned as he struggled to his feet. Now he had to improvise. He began to circle again, as if maybe he could start over.

Hoban found he didn't care what Tyrant did. He was in total control of his opponent and, to whatever degree he wanted, the audience. This was the start of a new reign.

"I'm sorry, did I hurt you?" Hoban mocked as Tyrant circled him.

"Have you lost your mind?" Tyrant hissed as he lunged forward to lock arms.

Hoban, his reflexes faster than he had ever known them to be, effortlessly grabbed Tyrant's right forearm with one hand and, with a crushing grip, forced him slowly to his knees.

"Agghhh," Tyrant yelled as Hoban increased the pressure, forcing his face lower and lower. "What are you doing?"

The commentators were still very animated, their faces painted with surprise and concern.

"You're a waste and a bore, Tyrant. Crawl away."

When Tyrant cursed him, Hoban squeezed tighter and pressed downward until he heard the bone snap.

"Ohhh, my God!" Tyrant screamed, his eyes wide with fear and pain. "You broke my——" was the last heard from him before Hoban's foot kicked his mouth shut, sending Tyrant across the ring and onto his back. Tyrant was still and silent, most certainly out cold, his broken forearm bent backward like rubber.

Hoban looked at the ref, who stood in frozen shock, staring at the Tyrant's limp body. "Count," Hoban ordered loudly.

The ref looked at Hoban, than back at Tyrant, then back to Hoban again.

"Count," Hoban mouthed, his glare sending the rest of the message.

The ref dropped to his knees next to Tyrant and put his ear to the fallen man's chest. His eyes widened, then looked again at Hoban. "I don't think he's breathing."

"Count."

Hoban paid no attention to the frenzied paramedics racing Tyrant away on a stretcher. Nor did he care about the gathering of confused, angry WWX execs below the ring. He was interested only in the message he was about to give the world, both seen and unseen. For the first time in his life he had an unexplainable belief in a spiritual realm. A world of invisible onlookers in an arena that dwarfed the coliseum were all giving him their undivided attention.

"Listen to me," he yelled, emphasizing every word, as a dictator would address the crowds from a balcony.

The entire coliseum fell still. All the animated WWX conversations around the ring ceased. All eyes were upon him as he had demanded.

"I am back . . . And I am God."

Hoban marched through the littered cement hallways of the coliseum basement, followed on all sides by a throng of photographers flashing shots, reporters barking out a blur of questions, WWX people in their various attire of costumes and suits, and the completely ignored coliseum security. Hoban ignored them all. There were things on his mind. Strange thoughts about people he some-how knew but didn't think he'd ever met. When he came to his dressing room door, he entered and closed it behind him, shutting out the hungry crowd. He turned and saw someone sitting on the makeup tabletop.

"Hello again," said the WWX girl of the month. "I don't think we've been properly introduced. I'm Angel."

Hoban smiled darkly. "I'll have to remember that."

14

Tuesday morning happened the instant Amy opened the bedroom blinds. Gavin had been asleep, exhausted from the previous night's work that carried well into the predawn hours.

"What time is it?" he mumbled, unwilling to open his eyelids. Since Amy had moved in with him two years ago, he never knew what time it was upon waking. Unlike him, Amy was a very light sleeper and would not allow any light in their southeastern-exposed bedroom. Not only did that mean blinds closed and clocks without lighted dials, but a humidifier with no water in the tank. Used only for the drone of its motor to drown out outside noise, it was on all night, every night.

Gavin, on the other hand, was a man of momentum, as Amy would say. Once awake he wanted to stay awake; once asleep, he wanted to stay asleep. He depended on the morning's light and sounds to stir him. These natural acquaintances, along with reading in his bed at night after she was asleep, were now just a memory and sources of hard-fought arguments lost long ago. Amy, normally an early riser, would now determine when he would awake.

"Time for your coffee," Amy said, the ceramic clink of a cup and saucer to his left followed by the aroma of fresh-brewed mountain blend.

"Hmm, smells good," Gavin said, wanting to add, "What's the occasion?" On a workday he rarely benefited from little other than the ritual opening of the blinds. "So, really, what time is it?" he repeated, shielding his eyes as he opened them. The day was unusually bright. Another hot one on the way, he supposed.

"Twelve."

"Noon?" Gavin gasped. His eyes shot open, his hand reaching for his wristwatch. "You can't let me sleep till noon!"

"Well, you didn't get to bed till five-thirty."

"Five-thirty? That late?"

"Been up ever since."

"Sorry."

"You should be. I mean, saving lives and hunting down bad guys while your wife's safe at home in bed. Shame on you."

"You're right. You're always right," he said with a yawn. He watched Amy move around the bedroom, picking the clothes up off the rocking chair he'd shucked off before getting into bed. She looked pregnant enough to explode. Did she always work this hard when he was at work?

"Of course I'm right. That's why you have to get up—now—and take a quick shower. Your socks are wet," she said, almost dropping them in the hamper, but then keeping them separate.

"Now?" he said, feeling comfortable to still be lying down.

"And take your coffee into the bathroom with you. Larry will be here in five minutes."

"Larry?"

"Yes, so get a move on."

"Larry who?"

Amy rolled her green eyes. "Larry Larson," she said, draping a fresh blue towel over the bedpost by his feet.

Gavin looked at his cup of coffee, the one he would now have to drink in the bathroom while waiting the thirty seconds it would take for the shower water to get hot. "Who's Larry Larson?"

"Gavin," she said incredulously.

"I just woke up."

"It's twelve noon."

Larry, Larry, Larry? he said to himself, searching for a face. Oh no. "The decorator?"

"I knew you could do it. He says he usually likes to start in the master suite with expectant mothers because that's where they spend most of the first couple of months."

"Master suite?" Gavin took a moment to think about the logic and wonder what it had to do with his being rushed out of bed. "And being that he's the boss when it comes to decorating—and on a tight schedule that we should be grateful to be squeezed into— I'd better get in and out of the bathroom as fast as I can."

"Is this how it all comes together on the job?"

Gavin eased himself out of the covers. "On good days," he said, cracking his neck, walking his coffee and fresh blue towel to the bathroom.

The smartest improvement he'd ever made to the house was to his shower. Large, a full three and a half feet wide, seven feet long, with a seat. Not a built-in seat, but a white plastic patio chair he could position where he wanted. For Gavin, life began every day in the shower, and he didn't like the process rushed. Wait very patiently for the hot water, get in, adjust the temperature, find the shampoo, wash hair, and then the rest of his body with the suds. Teeth next, then splash water on the steam-fogged mirror, and shave. Everything was so much easier and faster in the shower. With hygiene quickly out of the way, the chair was next.

He slowed the water to half volume and arranged the chair so the hot water would massage his back and neck. He liked it hot— too hot for Amy, who often told him he was crazy. With the sounds of the world blocked out and the meditative steamy water stilling and quieting his mind, Gavin let his thoughts go where they wanted—Amy and the new baby, the construction project, the pregnancy, Amy . . . the baby . . . Amy.

Until a little over a year ago, his first thoughts would have been the safety of a particular tortoise.

The tricks one's mind can play. Oddly, he missed the prayers, even for the tortoise. There was something about the level of God's involvement in his life that made him feel special. Buck had once told him that God was more interested in his life than he was. Before Amy, that would have been an easy task for even a Chiquita banana, but since Amy, life had become important. As the water temperature began to wane, Gavin's thoughts were invaded, as they usually were, by nagging questions about the new case. Time to towel off.

A knock at the door. "Gavin, Larry's here," Amy sang sweetly. "We're going to need to get in there soon." There was other discussion going on, which ended with Amy saying, "Don't worry, it's all right. He's been in there long enough."

When Gavin exited the bathroom, shrouded in his terry-cloth robe Amy and, he supposed, Larry Larkin—or Larmond or whatever his name was—were standing across the room holding color swatches against the window trim and the wall. He also noticed Amy had laid out clean clothes for him on the bed. Apparently, he was supposed to take them and dress somewhere else.

"I think the butter yellow would be very pretty against the . . ." Larry said before they both turned to him, smiling . . . guiltily, Gavin thought. Trespassing. The man could be pushing sixty, but the plastic surgery tugging his eyes at the corners like a Siamese cat made it difficult to tell. His brown hair had wisps of frosted blond highlights. Gavin didn't like him. Face lifted, tight jeans, bright green socks, polished tan penny loafers, a gold earring, and probably a tummy tuck under that whiter-than-white tight T-shirt—hardly the picture of the one to be decorating his house.

"Hi, honey. Sorry to rush you. This is Larry Larson, our new decorator. You should see what he did to Nancy's house."

"Nancy?"

"Nancy Baker," she said slowly, with emphasis. "Michael's wife. You know, that big, old Great Neck house."

"On yeah, yeah," he lied. He didn't particularly like Great Neck and didn't want his house to look like it belonged there.

"Well, thanks to Larry, their house is now a home."

"Because of the decorations?" Gavin said, unable to resist but trying to sound innocent. The very last thing he wanted was to get her upset. But why couldn't she just eat weird things like every other expectant mother he'd ever heard of?

"Ing," Amy said, giving him a look that made him wish he'd said nothing. "Decorat-*ing*. I'm talking about a house, not a Christmas tree."

"Sorry."

Larry's smile leveled into concern. "Amy tells me you were at the train wreck."

Gavin looked first at Amy before answering. She knew how little he liked discussing his work with people, particularly strangers . . . and this Larry would fall into his *stranger* stranger category. He looked at Larry and nodded politely. "It was a long night."

Larry nodded also, as if falling in sync with Gavin's exact motion. "I'll bet. Do you have any idea who was behind it? I mean, enough of this terrorism, already."

Before Gavin could say anything he'd later regret, Amy quickly piped up. "Gavin really isn't allowed to discuss an ongoing case, Larry," she said, her eyes asking Gavin to be nice.

"Oh, I'm sorry, of course, I should have known."

Gavin gestured with his hand for Larry to forget it.

"*Watashi wa shiawase,*" Amy said, her eyes friendly with gratitude.

Gavin looked at her, standing next to her decorator, holding a color swatch in her hand, her pumpkin belly proudly carrying their future. Her Japanese phrase, simply telling him she was happy, suddenly made everything make sense. That was, after all, all he really wanted.

"*Watashi wa shiawase,*" he said as he gathered his clothes to dress . . . somewhere.

15

Haaahhh . . . Dieu le veut . . . Dieu le veut!" Krogan yelled from his horse in his host's native tongue as he and three other knights toyed with a dozen Turkish peasants running for their lives across a parched grassy field. "God wills it!" he repeated again and again, elated over the battle cry of the "Armed Pilgrimage," as they called themselves. Krogan was enjoying a most satisfying life, maybe the best since the son of God had been crucified just over a thousand years prior.

"*Shadahd!*" another knight shouted, his bloody sword pointing at a fleeing man trying to escape in Krogan's direction. The word, foreign to the human ears of most of his present comrades, was infinitely more familiar to Krogan than the cry of what some were beginning to call a crusade. Since a time when earth was no more than another one of God's projects gone bad, the word *Shadahd* had been the battle cry of the angels . . . at least the angels Krogan was a part of—the stronger ones, with a mind of their own. The word simply meant to go out to "ruin." Ruin what? Specifically, everything. Creation . . . an inferior design, worthy only of abuse.

Crusade. Krogan wished he had thought of it, the word finding its root in the word *cross* and its energy from some scriptural scribble exhorting one to "pick up the cross and follow." Truly, he was never so willing to wear a cross himself, a red one he bore proudly on his right arm.

Krogan wheeled, turned on his horse, and sent his huge razor-edged sword, larger than all the others, slicing backward through the hot August air. His immediate aim was to maim. The longer the suffering before death, the more enduring the impression. And so far the impression was going quite well. His two commanders, a silver-tongued monk known as Peter the Hermit and a zealous knight, William the Penniless, whom he had separated from early on to carve out a reputation of his own, had just been massacred by the Turks in a little city called Civitote, just above Nicaea. Both had been commissioned by Pope Urban the Second. A Christian, even a pope, finding reason to promote what was sure to be a bloodbath, was really too good to be true. They would all leave their mark in history, and he was delighted to help, all in the name of their precious Lord, of course.

"*Dieu le veut,*" he roared as his recently sharpened edge sliced off the man's right arm below the shoulder.

A bell rang, not the kind of bell he had heard from towers, but more like many small bells, rapid, jingling. They stopped for a moment, then rang again. Krogan closed his eyes and heard a voice. The voice sounded like his own, or at least the one he had now gained possession of.

"Yeah, you've reached the, uh, office of Jackhammer Hoban. Leave a message . . . or don't."

He opened his eyes. The wounded peasant was gone, as was the horse he'd just been riding.

Beep. "Uh, Jack? Hello? You there? This is Michael Grossman. Look, uh, we need to talk. I was a little hot yesterday. Well . . . heh, heh, who wouldn't be after you. . . . Listen, I said some things that at the heat of the moment . . ."

Krogan lifted the receiver. "Talk," he said in a raspy whisper.

"Oh . . . you *are* there . . . good. Like I was saying, we . . . Mr. Bodder and I . . . Mark . . . you remember Mark . . . Bodder . . .

my attorney. Well, we were just going over some of the numbers . . . I mean, response . . ."

"Stay there," Krogan said, his voice hushed, his thoughts wanting to be elsewhere.

Krogan hung up and tried to settle his mind back to where it
had been before the phone rang. He remembered the time well,
perfectly, as if he were still there. The first crusade had been good,
as were the others. Nothing was quite as confusing and foolish as a
"Holy War," and nothing was quite as satisfying as confusion. So
many questions with so few tangible answers. Religion doing what
it did best—driving the individuals, then the groups, and finally the
masses into the places they were most vulnerable, while making belief in God appear absurd to the rest of the world. And then, where
possible, absurd to the believers themselves.

The phone rang. He listened to his outgoing message. Knowing
what it was going to say bored him. Grossman again. He wanted to
know how long they were supposed to wait for him. Krogan
reached over and tore the line from the wall. No more talk. They
would stay until he was ready to see them, *if* he decided to see
them.

Again Krogan gathered his thoughts, but another memory,
more recent, more humbling, annoying, kept scattering what he
was trying to gather. The tortoise. He remembered the clouded vision, the strange sounds, the cage, the other tortoises thinking he
was a tortoise, the taste of leaves . . . insects.

He threw off a thin blanket and saw his naked body. He studied
it, moved his fingers, stretched his limbs, flexed his muscles. A
sound at his window jerked his chin upward. He walked over and
separated the curtain. The window was tall, and the bright light of
midday assaulted him as an electric train roared by less than fifty
feet away at eye level. After a long moment he knew where he was.
The man Hoban lived in an apartment in Jamaica, Queens.

Below the elevated train were the street, stores, and people. He looked back at the train. Faces. Some staring at him. How easy it would be to end any one of their lives . . . all of their lives. He thought of his ancient comrades, their anticipation of seeing him again. The thrill of the prowl. *Shadahd.* The thought was as satisfying as ever. Enticing. But first there was a little business he had to attend to. Payback for the humiliation suffered in that thing's body.

He thought back two years, to the time of his imprisonment. He saw the faces of his captors. How could he, Krogan, the warrior of warriors, enjoy his natural call before his revenge was satisfied? He would strike. He would retaliate skillfully. Their general would fall, but not before he could see his fall coming. He would suffer long before his death and be strongly impressed. The Reverend Buchanan would first see his disciples suffer and die. Only then, after the Asian and the cop were dealt with, would the old man's time come. And even then his own demise would begin with his granddaughter. *The name of Krogan will once again be spoken with reverence and awe in the heavens.*

Krogan took a final look at the streets below, calling on Hoban's feeble memory for the nearest fish store. He smiled mischievously, having a sudden craving for lobster.

16

By the time Gavin had dressed and found his way into the kitchen, a ferocious appetite had seized him. Picking at the cold cuts as he worked the grill, he cooked up a more-than-healthy portion of ham, three over-easy eggs with cheddar cheese melted over a small mountain of home-fried potatoes, and rye toast.

"Smells delicious . . . but does he always eat like this?" Larry Larson asked Amy as they talked over what Gavin hoped were the final details of "freshening up" the kitchen.

Amy nodded. "He could do that all day and never gain a pound," she said, then placed the morning's newspaper next to Gavin while he stabbed at the potatoes.

"I would kill for a metabolism like that," Larry said.

Gavin stopped chewing when he saw the front page. An aerial shot of the train wreck. He wondered if the Camel pack had prints.

"Not literally, of course," Larry said.

"Of course," Amy said, giving Gavin a frown. "So what were you saying?" she said, trying to keep her decorator's attention.

Gavin went back to attacking his meal, stabbing a combination of potato, ham, and wet egg with every forkful.

"I think okra green would be gorgeous in here if we can steal a little more light. Maybe a skylight over here would help?"

"Like the vegetable," Gavin said, his mouth full.

"Excuse me?" Larry said.

"Okra. You want to paint the walls the color of a vegetable and the trim butter yellow. Is that cause it's a kitchen?"

Larry laughed. "I never thought about that. But I wouldn't do it without the skylight . . . the light's a bit mean in here for okra, but, oh my, it's very pretty with the Hawaiian green granite."

"The light is mean?" Gavin said.

"Dark . . . mean. You know. It's all about matching mediums, color and—"

"Granite? Did you say granite counters?"

Amy put her hands together as if she were praying, giving him those light-green eyes he could never refuse. "Pleeeease?"

Larry gave him the same kind of look a judge might give a felon at sentencing. "You have to use granite. There's no question. The only decision is what kind of granite."

"There are no other choices?"

"No."

"I thought there were."

"None."

Gavin looked around him and figured there really wasn't that much counter. How expensive could it be? He shrugged his shoulders and said, "I suppose if we don't have a choice . . ."

Amy clapped her steepled fingers and squeaked out a high-pitched "Yes!"

Gavin's cell phone rang.

"Yeah?"

"We've got a print off the Camel box," Chris said.

"You get a match?"

"I don't smoke."

"Was that a joke?"

"Poor, huh?"

"As usual."

"Well, no match yet. You coming in soon?"

"Yeah."

Gavin sopped up the remaining yolk with his toast, drained the last of his coffee, and took the dishes to the sink. After a token rinse, he placed everything in the dishwasher, then reflexively sponged the Formica counter. Done. Gone.

"You've certainly trained him well," Larry said to Amy. "Any more where he came from?"

"Him?" Amy tried to hold back her grin. "I don't know. Gavin, Larry wants to know if you have any clean-freak friends who might be available."

"I don't have any friends. And I don't know too many . . . decorators."

Larry furrowed his expansive brow.

"Oh, he does so have friends," Amy said, giving Gavin a peck on the cheek, and then with mock concern continued, "They're just not always comfortable admitting it."

Gavin almost smiled. The one good thing he liked about Larry was that he was keeping Amy occupied. If she was going over colors with Larry, she wasn't running around town or gardening or heaven knew what else. Besides that, Gavin found Larry educational. In the last hour he'd learned that not enough light was "mean," khaki tan in the hallways was "gutsy," butter yellow was "safe and friendly," blue could work in a girl's room if it was mixed with a "fun" yellow . . . at least in Larry's book. Amy seemed to be going with the "pretty" and shying away from the daring.

Gavin bent down and kissed Amy's belly on the way out the door, then said to Larry, "Now, you take care of Mommy. Make sure she gets off her feet soon. She's always trying to do too much."

"I do not."

"And she lies."

Larry nodded reassuringly to Gavin's orders.

"*Watashi wa shiawase,*" Amy whispered sweetly before pecking him on the cheek.

Gavin paused, then smiled. "Me, too," he said, then left the room, Cedar happily following him to the door.

"Stay," Gavin ordered without turning, knowing the dog had stopped where he was. He was halfway to his car when he stopped and turned. "Okay, c'mon, Cee." He heard the slipping of paws on the oak floor, then the door was pushed open with the nudge of a long nose. Unless his dog was told otherwise, Gavin knew he would find him on the stoop waiting for him when he returned home.

Gavin went through the usual routine of pumping and cranking his car. As he worked the key and pedal he thought of Chris. His partner never got enough of ribbing Gavin about his car's constant reluctance to work. He could hear a sarcastic Chris in his mind: "Starting to start your car, Gav?" He turned the radio on before his mind conjured up anything else he didn't want to hear.

With the Tiger warmed and purring, he pulled up to the sidewalk, having backed into the driveway the night before. He didn't know what the weather was going to be and thought he might need to put the hardtop on. As it turned out, another hot, sunny day. Hopefully they wouldn't have to spend too much time in the office with what Chris referred to as the world's first experimental air-conditioning system—a jerry-rigged mess of long cords and old, noisy fans. He waited for a car to go by and was reminded by Amy's license-plateless minivan next to him that he needed to stop at the DMV. *Not today,* he thought, and then took off straight ahead, up the block opposite his driveway. A glance in the rearview, his property framed in the small mirror. His *soon*-to-be decorated property. All his hard work in the hands of a stranger. He shook his head, not wanting to think about it. *She's happy,* he thought. *That's what's im-portant.* "*Watashi wa shiawase,*" he said aloud, his pronunciation much better than when he had first repeated the words slowly to Amy on their wedding night.

His eyes back on the road, he frowned. "What the——" he said, then flashed his lights at an oncoming cement truck; its rear concrete chute, extended long and perpendicular, barely missed a parked car on the other side of the street. No, it had hit the car's side mirror and antenna . . . and would hit him if he didn't veer right to the shoulder . . . or into a driveway.

"Doesn't that idiot know?" Gavin said angrily to himself, flashing, flashing, flashing his lights. *And what cement truck drives at that speed in a residential neighborhood? And with the barrel turning the wrong way.* Gavin remembered when his own foundation was being poured, the barrel had first spun clockwise to mix and then counterclockwise to pour.

Instead of veering to the right, Gavin went left, head on. This moron had to be stopped before someone got hurt. Flashing, flashing. Nothing. *Can't he see?* At the last second Gavin steered right, jumping a curb and spinning out on wet sod, underground sprinklers dousing him and his car inside and out. The truck sped by, barrel spinning backward, chute extended and swinging like a dragon's tail knocked from one side of the street to the other by parked cars. He had seen a glimpse of the driver's face. Not much detail through the glass except for two horrifying facts: The driver was definitely laughing . . . and there was a passenger. *When does a cement truck have a passenger?* And at the speed it was going, it might not be able to slow down when it got to——

"Oh, God! No!" Gavin screamed.

17

Gavin fumbled for the gearshift, threw it into first, and popped the clutch to an already redlining engine. The rear wheels of his British racing car instantly dug into the soft, soaked earth, spinning and spitting grass and mud onto the house, all while Gavin watched the cement truck running out of street, not even a flicker on the brake lights. The car was foundered. Gavin cursed repeatedly and slammed into reverse. Same result.

Suddenly Gavin found himself in the middle of the street, his legs seeming to move slowly, his gasps for oxygen deep, fast, urgent. The cement truck's front rose slightly when it passed over where Gavin knew Amy's new minivan had been parked when he last saw it in his rearview mirror. He heard himself screaming but didn't know what because his entire mind was given over to his eyes—huge eyes searching for the power to make the truck stop, pleading, demanding that his house . . . home . . . would somehow stop the enemy truck like some giant catcher's glove.

Gavin was the length of a football field away when the cement truck came to a complete stop . . . in his backyard, the barrel still spinning. The truck no longer mattered.

"AMY!"

There was no answer as he screamed her name, hurdling a flattened skid of black metal and smashed glass that used to be her mode of transportation. He landed on rubble, feet twisting, falling, hitting his walkway hard on his hip. Back on his feet in a second and down again on the broken concrete of his front stoop. His arms and legs grabbing and pushing him through a huge open expanse where the front door and half the rest of his home used to be.

"Amy!" he yelled. "Amy, where are you?" There was no answer, the only sound coming from the squeaking barrel of the cement truck. His eyes darted desperately. Where to go? "Oh, God!" he said, seeing one of Cedar's doggie dishes half crushed, sticking out from under a pile of wood. His dog had been on the stoop, he remembered. "Cedar!" he yelled, looking, spinning, desperate to see something alive. Nothing. The dog always came when called . . . unless he couldn't.

"Amy!" he shouted in tears as he ran back to where he'd left her in the kitchen, which was no longer there at all. Just open space with fallen debris and rubble from the collapsed second floor. Most of his house was in the backyard along a path to the tanklike truck. If the truck hadn't been going so fast, it probably would have fallen through to the basement.

Gavin grabbed his cell phone from his waist and dialed 9-1-1. A figure caught his eye. "Jesus!" he gasped. Larry was part of the wreckage along the path to the truck. If there were even the slightest chance he was alive, Gavin would have raced to him, but he had seen enough twisted bodies in his life to know which ones were and were not worth spending time on, especially when—

"Uhhh!" Gavin gasped, startled by something alive touching his leg. He turned. "Cedar!" His delight to see the dog vanished almost as quickly as it arrived. "Mommy, Cedar—where's Mommy? Go find Mommy. Where's—"

"Nine-one-one emergency," called a female voice over the cell phone.

"This is Detective Pierce. Code three!" he shouted with his home address. Under the circumstances there was little more needed to say. A code one would have meant there was no present emergency but to have an officer stop by at his convenience. A code two carried more immediacy but still did not necessarily signal an emergency; an officer could respond without the use of his lights and siren carving a path for him. A code three pulled out all the stops. There was no code four.

"I repeat, we've got a code three! Code three! Need several ambulances, patrol and fire assistance. Multiple injury, fatality and—" he yelled, almost eating his phone, before he suddenly heard Cedar bark to his right.

Cedar was staring at a section of roof that had fallen and was now leaning precariously over a part of the house still standing. The dog looked at him and then looked back again in the same direction.

Gavin dropped the phone and leaped toward the fallen roof. Behind the roof was a hallway leading to a bathroom. He grabbed and pulled at the roof section, black sandy granules from the shingles scraping his fingers as he fought. Not a chance of him and all the adrenaline in the world moving this mass. He looked around the side, hanging on the edge of the shingles. "Amy! Can you hear me?"

A moan.

He'd heard a moan! It was faint, but it was definitely there. The shingle he was holding tore off in his hand. As he fell he caught himself on something sharp . . . painful. Jumping to his feet, he ran back out to where the front of the house used to be and around to a window at the end of the hall. He looked into the window. Dark. No, a shade down. He pushed on the window but it was locked. He thought of throwing something through it, but what if Amy was there . . . right there? Just below the lock he bashed the window with his elbow, reached in, unlocked the window, and threw it open. A moment later he was in the hallway, light pouring in behind him.

"Amy!" he cried, dropping to his knees in the middle of the hall-way.

"Gavin," she said weakly. She was curled into a fetal position, cradling her belly, cut, bruised, and semiconscious, just like the Spanish woman the night before.

"Shhh. I'm here. Everything will be all right," he said. He could hear sirens.

"What's happening?" she whispered, no more than a breath. She didn't seem to be able to open her eyes.

"There's been an accident. Don't try to move. Help will be here in a moment," he said, holding her hand. He squeezed it, but she didn't squeeze back.

The sirens were loud, and so were the racing engines ahead of them. There was the screeching of cars coming to a stop outside. He reluctantly let go of her hand and went to the window. The thought of six or seven men handing Amy through the window was alarming. He called out for help, then ordered the first person he saw, a uniform, to gather help to move aside the fallen roof section. Within minutes the voices of many men were on the other side of the roof section and paramedics were coming in the hall window. They went right to Amy and he went right to the blockade. He pushed as they pulled and tore and ripped, jamming in boards for leverage. Cracking, squeaking, popping, and finally an opening large enough for a stretcher.

Once outside, Gavin held Amy's hand while the paramedics strapped her more tightly to the stretcher. The light also revealed a large bruise on her temple.

"Somebody shut that thing off," Gavin heard a cop yell regard-ing the cement truck.

Fire trucks, patrol cars, and ambulances were everywhere, a smaller version of the night before. A dozen firemen and police sur-rounded Larry the decorator, none of them moving very fast.

"Gavin!" a panicked but familiar voice cried out. Chris was running up to the house much the same way Gavin had.

"Somebody slow him down before he kills himself," Gavin said to nobody in particular.

"What happened here?" Chris yelled as he jumped up to the floor level. He seemed to be looking everywhere at once.

"She's alive, Chris. Right now that's all I can think about."

"What the . . . How did . . ."

Gavin pointed to the cement truck.

Chris stared for a long moment, then turned and looked up the street as if trying to imagine. He turned back to Gavin. "Anyone else?"

Gavin pointed again to the cement truck. "Why don't you check it out, Chris? It's really the last thing on my mind right now."

Chris paused to look at the help Gavin was getting, then nodded and headed to the cement truck in the backyard.

18

For the last few hours Krogan had been busy enjoying and exploring the physical and mental worlds of his new host. Early possession was often very rewarding in this respect. He was renowned for his ability to meld a host's mind into his own quickly, often not needing more than one or two earth days. Some of that he credited to his meticulous, albeit painful, selection process. But most of the glory belonged to his own fierce determination and power to dominate.

This Hoban was particularly amusing and easy, blaming early mind saturation on hallucinations brought on by his drug use. Krogan had to admit, drugs made the job easier, but he would find his challenges in unique places with this one.

The front of the WWX building had a huge black flag with red WWX letters hanging from a horizontal flagpole. Krogan was about to enter the building when something caught his eye. He went to the newspaper dispenser, ripped open the glass door, and took a paper. The headline read "Terror Strikes," and the photo of a train wreck was reminiscent of a head-on collision he had caused forty years earlier. He nodded approvingly and wondered how long it would take him to find the terrorist if he decided to switch hosts. *Another time,* he thought, then dropped the paper and went into the building.

Krogan walked into Michael Grossman's plush outer office. A

buxom blonde secretary spotted him from behind a polished green granite desk. Behind her were gold WWX letters on an oak wall. Hoban had been here only a few times, each time very awed by what he thought was success on display to breed more success. He'd always felt the man behind it all, Michael Grossman, was God personified. His inexperienced, untraveled mind fell easily to Krogan here, and consequently was now quite unimpressed.

"Oh, Mr. Hoban!" the woman said with a wide smile. "Please have a seat. Mr. Grossman has been expecting you." She furrowed her brow with a chummy nod and whispered confidentially, "Actually, waiting, if you know what I mean. He can get—"

Her eyes widened. "You're bleeding," she said, then apparently realized he wasn't listening to a word she was saying. "Wait a second. You can't just—"

Krogan pushed through a huge oak door. Grossman looked up from his thronelike seat behind a massive, thick glass desk with WWX etched into the top from underneath. Except for a small stack of papers in front of him and a glass box of cigars at the far corner, the desk was devoid of anything. No computer, no pictures, nothing. Another man, balding, with a dark-blue suit, big tie, big rings, and big watch, looking annoyed, stood up from a seat. Presumably Mark Bodder, the lawyer Grossman had mentioned. And next to him, one of the WWX's most recognizable celebrities— Grossman's daughter, Tanya—or Tanya the Terrible as she was better known—dressed in her trademark black leather everything.

"Jackhammer Hoban," Tanya said with a thin smile, as if she was introducing him to the others.

"How long were we supposed to be waiting here for you?" Bodder squeaked. "You told us to wait for you"—he checked his gold watch—"six and a half hours ago."

"Okay, okay." Grossman motioned for his lawyer to calm down. "This is not about who's late."

"But—"

"Nice outfit," Tanya said as Krogan walked by wearing old, ripped jeans, his chest bared under a vest made from a cut-off denim jacket, also ripped and soiled, and a newly acquired dog collar around his neck, tags jingling as he walked. "I think you're bleeding."

"The one who rules is never late." Krogan flipped open the lid on the cigar box and helped himself, biting off the end and spitting it on the floor. He took an extra one and stabbed it into his vest pocket, leaving the glass lid for someone else to close.

Bodder started to stand again, but Grossman eyed him down.

"Allow me," Tanya offered, rising to Krogan's side. She took a cigar from the open box, bit, spit, lit with a strong drag, and blew the smoke in a considerate direction. She gently removed the cigar from Krogan's mouth, inserted hers, then lit his for herself.

Krogan looked into her eyes, deeply, sniffing at her thoughts. He liked what he saw and thought of being inside her body, controlling, possessing. That of course was impossible while the wrestler Hoban still lived, but the thought continued to interest him as he made a simple suggestion to her focused mind.

Grossman wore a confused frown. "Were you in some kind of accident on the way over here?"

Krogan continued to hold Tanya's stare as he replied, "There are no accidents."

"Hmm, I'm not exactly sure what you mean by that, but there are mysteries, and right now, you're one of them. I watched you last night. You were . . . different. You've changed. What happened?"

Still eye to eye with Tanya, Krogan smiled and whispered in his usual deep rasp, "I've been born again."

Bodder snorted. "Uh, right. Look, I suggest we get down to business. We have a lot to cover and it's already *late*."

Tanya, unblinking, turned to Bodder and yanked a white hand-kerchief from his suit pocket. She turned back to Krogan's gaze, licked the end of the cloth, and dabbed the wound on his forehead.

Grossman cleared his throat. "Uh, Jack. About last night, again. We've been getting some pretty strong feedback and, well, let's just say you've created the kind of conflict that draws a lot of at-tention. E-mails, faxes, website hits are all off the chart. Everyone wants to know when your next fight is. Some can't wait to see you destroy your next victim, some can't wait to see you destroyed. Figuratively speaking, of course. After all, this is pro-wrestling. A small fact that might have gotten away from you in your bout with Tyrant."

"What Daddy's trying to say is the fans love you . . . and hate you."

"Exactly. Thank you, baby. So we'd like to talk to you about your next fight. The way we see it, Jackhammer Hoban is announced again as the new champion and you—"

"Silence," Krogan snapped with an energy that seemed to com-mand their mouths shut. "I'm not interested in what you see. And I am not interested in your make-believe games. I will fight when I decide and where I decide. I do not travel to fight. All will travel to me, to this place you call New York, like they did in Athens. And I will not be called 'Hoban' any longer."

After Krogan finished they all looked at each other as if to ask if it were all right to speak.

"This place you call New York? Athens? What are we talking about here?" Bodder said, as if asking himself aloud.

"Then what shall we call you?" Tanya said sweetly.

"Krogan."

There was a brief moment of pause before Tanya asked, "Why does that name sound so familiar?"

"You can't be serious," Grossman said, frowning. "Krogan was the name of that serial-killer maniac."

"Great," Bodder scoffed. "There goes the crowd conflict. Everyone will just hate you again. Why don't you just call yourself Hitler, or better yet . . . Satan?"

Krogan walked to the window, puffing, looking at the sunset. There was something about smog that seemed to turn the crimson sky into flames. He turned to them. "This is not a suggestion. My name is Krogan and I will fight in this," he said, pointing his cigar to a large glass-framed advertisement on the wall. All heads turned.

ARMAGEDDON
WWX
HELL ON EARTH

"Armageddon?" Bodder said incredulously. "That starts tomorrow night. There's no time."

Grossman shook his head slowly, then turned back to Krogan. "Armageddon has been a long time in the planning. It runs for ten days starting tomorrow, and every slot has been filled. Everything, and I mean *everything,* is already set."

"You will issue a challenge to everyone . . . your phony wrestlers and the rest of the world. They will all prove that I am above all . . . and I will enjoy myself."

"Impossible," Grossman said.

"It must be the drugs," Bodder said, shaking his head.

Krogan took a long, confident drag, then dropped the cigar; it landed, smoldering, on the plush beige carpet. All eyes went to the cigar, then back to him. "To resist me will prove very expensive," he said, then turned and started away. "And I have a *long* memory."

"No, wait! Jack, I mean, Krogan," Tanya said, giving her father a desperate eyeful. "Let's think about this for a second. I mean . . . it's not like we don't have *any* time to put this together. There's . . . there's the rest of tonight and all day tomorrow."

Krogan kept walking.

Bodder was about to issue another whining complaint, but Grossman spoke over him. "I suppose we could announce a special guest appearance," he suggested.

"And that the following nights will have a change of venue," Tanya added.

Bodder sighed. "If we extend the programming and shorten each program incrementally, we could probably bill him as——"

"The main event!" Tanya interrupted.

Krogan heard a splash of water and turned to see Bodder standing over the cigar with an empty glass of water.

"Main event?" Bodder said incredulously. "Why don't you set up a ten-thousand-dollar prize for anyone who can unseat him? See what he's *really* made of . . . see if he's all talk. I mean, isn't that what promoters did in the old days with their house champ?"

Right then, Krogan decided there would be a time to meet Bodder alone—to let him know exactly to whom he was speaking so sarcastically.

"I *like* that idea," Tanya said, her eyes bright with enthusiasm. "Only it should be more than ten thousand. Make it a half million and we'll have half the country watching."

"I was only joking," Bodder spat.

Grossman stood up from behind his seat. "Make it a million and the whole country will watch."

Bodder plopped into his seat, his open hand dragging down slowly from his forehead to chin.

"Yes!" Tanya yelled. "It'll be a full-page ad in tomorrow's paper. A million dollars for anyone who can complete a three-minute one-round bout with King Krogan. If that doesn't make the action real enough for you, nothing will. It will be the biggest open prize and the biggest show on earth."

Bodder stood up. "And what about when he loses in the first bout? What do we do with the rest of Armageddon?"

"The winner continues, whoever it is. If they don't agree to that, they can't get in the ring," Grossman said emphatically. "But if Krogan here continues to win, we'll make billions."

"See that it's done," Krogan ordered, then left.

19

Gavin anxiously paced the vinyl-floored hallway of North Shore Hospital's trauma center. He had been asked numerous times to sit in the waiting room, but he simply couldn't sit. On the other side of the double doors an emergency operation was being performed on Amy to remove her ruptured spleen, a fairly routine operation had she not been eight months' pregnant. She also had three broken ribs and a concussion, but the spleen had to be taken out now or she would bleed to death. This was the good news. The doctors had told him that it didn't look good for both the mother and the baby making it. Something about the possibility of a detached placenta.

He turned quickly at the sound of a door opening. Chris was walking toward him with his palms up.

"So what's going on?" he said.

"Splenectomy, for starters."

"What's that?"

"They're taking out her spleen."

Chris frowned. "What's a spleen do?"

"I don't know. *They* don't even know. It has something to do with cleaning your blood."

"I thought the liver does that."

"It doesn't matter. Whatever it does she can live without it. The problem is the pregnancy. It complicates everything. They . . ." He had to pause to fight back tears. ". . . they said they don't know if the baby will make it because the placenta may have been detached from the impact, and they don't want to do a C-section unless they absolutely have to because of the trauma Amy's been through."

Chris cursed under his breath but didn't have anything to say.

"How could this have happened?" Gavin said to the ceiling, then looked Chris in the eye. "Can you tell me how something like this can happen? A cement truck, for crying out loud? *A cement truck?* What, did I have a sign out that said, 'Drive-in House'?"

Chris sighed. "We need to talk a minute about what happened."

Gavin shook his head in disbelief. "Sure, why not?"

"Okay, why don't you start by telling me what you saw and who the dead guy in the backyard was."

"Larry . . . Larry Larson. He was the decorator Amy hired."

"Decorator? You?"

Gavin shrugged. "She said the house was too masculine."

"Whatever. Go on."

"He was going over colors with her," Gavin said, then paused to reflect. "I think I was talking to him when you called me. The next thing I know I'm driving up the block and this cement truck runs me off the road and plows into my house. What am I—a magnet for this kinda crap?"

"Is that it?"

"That's all I can think of at the moment. Tell you the truth, my mind hasn't been there. It's been here . . . just here."

Chris nodded, but then sighed. "There's more. It gets weird. I'd tell you to sit down, but there're no chairs here."

"What gets weird?"

"Did you see the driver?"

Gavin remembered the driver laughing as he passed. "Not really. Just a glimpse. Why?"

"Did you know the truck had a passenger?"

"Yes! I remember that. And I remember thinking that was strange."

"It gets stranger, Gav. The passenger was the operator. He's dead. The driver's missing," Chris said, nodding, as if what wasn't said was what Gavin needed to sit down for.

Gavin's first thoughts didn't seem to come from his mind so much as from his chest, where two drills were busy boring holes—one of anger and the other of fear. When his brain finally caught up to his heart, he said, "A copycat? Someone trying to gain instant recognition?"

"That was the second thing I thought of," Chris said.

"What was the first?"

"That Karl Dengler had escaped."

In that instant Gavin wondered why he hadn't thought of that. Did he really believe, deep down, that the Krogan demon did in fact exist and Dengler was no longer a threat? "Dengler's in solitary, Chris. To escape would be impossible."

"That's what I thought, too, until I saw this." Chris reached inside his jacket and pulled out a plastic bag, handing it to Gavin.

"What's this?" Gavin looked at Chris and then the bag, which had enough gray dust inside to obscure the lightweight but hard object inside.

"Go on. Open it."

Gavin opened the bag and looked in. *What the . . .* "Where did you get this?"

"The, uh, ashtray . . . of the cement truck."

Gavin's eyes were paralyzed, staring, staring. "Forensics. One of the sickos who were at the marina when the boat went off the ramp into that sailboat. One of those guys knew about the lobster-claw roach clip. One of them handed it to me. One of them could have planted it."

Chris shook his head. "Not possible. I found it, Gav. I checked the ashtray for drugs and there it was, just like then. Forensics hadn't even been there yet."

"Is this some kind of sick joke?" Gavin said angrily.

Chris shrugged his shoulders. "If it is, it's a pretty damn good one. I can only think of a handful of people who know the punch line . . . and Dengler's one of 'em."

"Did you . . . ?"

"Of course. It was the first thing I did. He's locked up snug as a bug."

"Then who else c—"

"I don't know. I was hoping you might be able to shed a little light on this."

Gavin could only think of one thing, and he wasn't about to talk about it with Chris. He looked at his watch. 8:05. He wondered when the Bronx Zoo closed. He had to find out. As insane the notion that any of what Buck had told him was actually true, he had to call the zoo—now. "I don't have a clue. I've got to make a call."

"Who?"

Gavin pulled out his cell phone. "Great. It's off. Can't use a cell phone in a hospital . . . have to use the one in the waiting room," he said and left Chris, who followed him down the hall.

"Does this have something to do with the lobster claw?"

Think, think. "Maybe Buck knows something."

"The guy who just had the heart attack? You're going to call him *now?*"

"I'll leave him a message to call me as soon as he can," Gavin lied. The last person he wanted to tell was the Reverend Buchanan. "Did you get anything from the cement company?"

"Not much, but we did talk to the crew at the construction site."

"What construction site?"

"Where the truck was stolen. All anybody could tell us was that someone, whom no one saw, called the operator to the passenger side of the truck while the foundation was being poured. The next thing they knew, the truck was driving away with the cement still pouring out. There was a cement trail four blocks long. If that doesn't sound like Krogan . . . uh, I mean Dengler, I don't know what does."

"But you said—"

"He is, he is. Snug—"

"As a bug in a rug. I know. You need a better analogy with this one," Gavin said, pushing through the waiting room door. His eyes darted around the room until he saw the phone in an alcove across from a few vending machines. Actually, two phones. Both were occupied.

"Looks like we've got a minute," Chris said. "Want a coffee?"

"No," Gavin said. "I'll go outside and use the cell."

Chris nodded and headed for the vending machines. Gavin pressed the on button and hurried through the emergency room's airlock to the warm outside air while it booted up. The signal was poor, but he managed to get through to information and a moment later was connected to the Bronx Zoo's general information. After listening to a zoo advertisement about their new jungle world and Asian rain forest exhibits, he was offered five choices that each led to several other choices before he settled for "hours and rates, press one." The zoo was open daily from 10:00 A.M. to 4:30 P.M. He cursed. Before he shut off the phone, he thought of calling Buck. A ridiculous thought. Why would he want to do that? If the tortoise was dead and Buck knew it, he would have already called. *More likely the tortoise is still alive,* he said to himself. On second thought, Buck was in a hospital recovering from a heart attack and probably could not be reached easily. Why was he even thinking this? He shut off the cell and went back inside.

"Here," Chris said, handing Gavin a steaming cup of coffee.

"I told you I didn't want any."

"Decaf. Milk, no sugar."

Gavin sighed and took it.

"Did you reach him?"

"Who?"

Chris stared at him for a moment. "Buck?"

"No."

"Hmm. So where're you staying tonight?"

"Staying?"

"Look, I know it's hard to think now about anything else but Amy, but you don't have a house anymore. I think you should stay with Pat and me. We've got the bedroom in the basement and a bath. You could have your privacy and use the basement door."

Gavin shook his head the whole time Chris was talking. "I'm staying here."

Chris looked as if he was about to say something but didn't.

"Thanks Chris. Maybe later. I'll let you know."

Chris nodded. "Fine. Just don't be bashful. I'll leave the basement door open. You can come whenever you want. Up to you."

20

"All that is needed for evil to prosper is for good men to do nothing,'" Walter Hess said aloud to himself as he sat on the edge of his small cabin boat, his back to the water, scuba gear on. His pastor had preached those very words again just Sunday, quoting some important person—maybe FDR.

He checked his watch. 11:34 P.M. The *Sachacus,* America's fastest ferry, had been docked for over two hours now. If the maintenance tech was on his usual schedule, he would soon take his lunch break at the table near the coffee machine one hundred feet from the ferry in the ticket sales building. If Hess's calculations were correct, this little breach of company procedure should take just over an hour, and would cost one boat and over two hundred lives. But not just any lives. Gamblers. Diseased lives supporting alcoholic Indians running a casino. Only a government run by Jews would encourage such a thing. His lip curled as he thought of those who were polluting the nation's blood and heart. The crescent moon kept the cover of darkness secure in the waters just off Sea Cliff Beach. The small chop was calm enough to operate easily in but disruptive enough to camouflage bubbles and the headlamp. His boat was anchored among many other moored boats in front of the Sea Cliff Yacht Club. When a jumbo jet flew over, headed toward La Guardia Airport, he pointed his finger at it and said, "Bang."

Hess decided to check his equipment list one more time before taking the plunge. Headlamp . . . already on his head with fresh batteries. Air . . . not for breathing, but an extra tank of compressed air on his back to supply his pneumatic tools. He had already checked the additional air-line from the tank and tested the easy-connect with both the drill and grinder, the next items on his list. With his free hand, he tapped the tools clipped onto his weight-belt: first the drill, which had a three-quarter-inch steel bit and then the grinder, complete with a four-inch diamond blade and a gauge to set the blade depth at three millimeters. Next: the grappling hook and cable in a small black gym bag. Red crayon in the right sleeve of his wetsuit: check. And finally, his knife, just in case. The tool had proved invaluable the day before.

Hess was doing his best to stay focused and humble, but he couldn't help but be proud of himself. Pride was the root of all sin, but after all, he was only human. Last night he hadn't gotten to sleep until one in the morning, instead watching the train wreck on every news channel his boat's little television would pick up. He had seen the experts hypothesize on everything from al-Qaeda to Salafi to neo-Nazi cults.

And then the news of the Bible Scripture carved into the chest of the dead jock was released, creating new theories and demolishing some old ones. Pictures of the wreck were splashed across the front pages of every newspaper at the newsstand, though he had bought only one, and even then, just to read about the business end of his work. He constantly reminded himself not to get puffed up. After all, the real credit belonged to God—Hess was just a servant, a specialist servant.

It appeared that the experts had no idea who was responsible. The Nassau police department issued a toll-free tip line. He wanted to call it, but not before God gave him the exact words to say. Which He would, of course . . . when the time was right.

He thought about the senator whose picture emblazoned the

newspapers and TV news reports. Hess remembered the politician promising to do everything in his power to see justice done. Justice. People like Sweeney had so little understanding of justice. If he'd open his eyes instead of kissing ethnically inferior babies for votes, he'd see what justice was being done. Sweeney also had other choice words—insults. It was because of people like Senator Sweeney that God needed a soldier like Hess.

With yesterday's success came a new boldness. Hess remembered how nervous he'd been waiting for the train to come, telling himself over and over to relax, clumsily trying to set the jacks and work the torch with shaking hands. What a difference a day made! He felt like a new person. The papers labeled him as an "expert technician." He smiled at the thought. If that was all he was, he would still have reason to be anxious. An expert technician? Yes. A specialist? Definitely. Destined? Now therein lay the difference. His anointing from God paved the path before him and gave him true peace . . . the peace that passed all understanding, as his pastor would say.

A movement caught his eye.

"A man of habit," he muttered as he watched the maintenance tech step off the *Sachacus* and walk toward the ticket building, carrying his lunch bag. After the man disappeared through the door, Hess took one final look around, pulled his mask on, bit into the mouthpiece of his regulator, and fell backward into the channel's cool dark waters. Moments later he was some twenty-five feet below, following the channel's bottom to the superfast catamaran passenger ferry.

The meaning of the Indian name *Sachacus* was not lost on Hess as he approached the rear of the vessel. The literal translation was, "He is fierce." Sachacus had been the chief sachem of the Pequot Indians from 1634 until his death in August 1637. During Sachacus' brief tenure as chief sachem, he presided over the most powerful tribe in southern New England. Now, almost four hundred years later, thanks to the U.S. government, the tribe was back, and in his estimation, more powerful than ever. But they were about to be served notice to scurry back to their reservation and close the door behind them.

With the powerful waterjet thrusters in view, Hess began his ascent to the catamaran's one-hundred-forty-eight-foot-long starboard hull. Long and white, it penetrated five feet from the water's surface. Impressed as he was with the turbines, they were not his mark. He continued on. What he was after was at the other end of the hull. He checked his watch. 11:52. The maintenance man would be gone for another fifty or so minutes.

He passed the stabilizing fin that extended three feet below the hull. In unsteady seas the onboard computer worked the fin to steady the vessel for the passengers' maximum comfort and safety. The thought made Hess smile as he continued on toward the end of the hull. Once there, he ran his right hand along the front edge until he broke the water's surface. With his left hand he took the crayon from his right sleeve and dragged a short red line where his elbow hit, approximately nineteen inches from the surface. About six inches above that, he dragged another line and tucked the crayon back into his sleeve for later.

Hess held his breath and quietly surfaced, making sure no one was around before starting up the drill. A careful scan of the dock and the channel satisfied him. As he descended back to his working level, just below the surface, he unclipped the drill from his weight-belt and attached it to the extra black hose line he had so proudly crafted, then briefly pulled the trigger. A roar of bubbles gushed out of the drill's side and the three-quarter-inch bit spun at three thousand RPMs. *So far so good,* he told himself. He brought the sharp bit to bear on the lower red line, two inches from the front edge, pulled the trigger, and pushed. The flood of air and whine of the drill was loud underwater, but above the surface there would be no sound but the boil of the bubbles, and that would blend with the choppy waves and not be noticeable to anyone farther away than the dock.

12:14. The drill bit broke though the other side. The hole was about two and a half inches deep through solid aluminum, as expected. He detached the drill from the hose, clipped the tool back to his belt, and took hold of the grinder. He knew the rest of the hull beyond the leading edge was five millimeters thick . . . a fact he'd gleaned from the ship's captain during a friendly conversation. The gauge on his grinder had been preset for three millimeters and welded in place to eliminate any slippage under pressure. He quickly attached the air hose to the grinder and set the diamond blade on the higher red line. Staying parallel to the surface, he cut a channel along the hull from the leading edge to a point approximately eight feet back. As with the drill, the underwater squeal was loud and the gush of bubbles scary. He constantly had to remind himself that the sound could not be heard above the water . . . but inside the boat the metal hull would send a drone throughout the vessel. Even worse than the sound was the visibility. He didn't have to see while drilling the hole, but cutting a channel in a straight parallel line one foot below the surface with a steady stream of forced bubbles exploding against his mask was a different story.

Kicking his feet hard to keep pressure on the grinder, he completed the desired distance. Upon inspection, his line was a bit wavy, but not enough to cause a problem, he thought. The captain had mentioned also that the ferry would not rise out of the water as its speed increased; hence his cut line would be at the same depth blazing along at forty-seven knots as it was now while docked.

Hess turned his back to the leading edge and started cutting the three-millimeter channel on the other side of the right hull, again pushing against the tool to keep it flat as he cut. He didn't want any variation in channel depth. Just a few more minutes and . . . He cursed. The grinder was slowing, visibility improving, the whine not as loud. He was running out of air to run the grinder. He tried slowing down, but it was no use. There wasn't enough. He pulled the emergency reserve and then the trigger on the grinder. Back in action . . . but a foot later the grinder slowed to another halt.

He looked at his watch—12:31—and cursed again. He had hoped to be safely on his way back to his own boat by now. He looked at his progress. About four feet. Not enough. He needed the other four feet to be sure. Thinking, thinking. He still needed to attach the grappling hook to the drilled hole. He reattached the dead grinder to his belt and reached for the bag with the hook . . . then froze, staring at the light beam from his headlamp. He knew where he could get some air.

As fast as he could, he unbuckled his breathing tanks, wiggled them off his shoulders, and switched the regulator hoses. He might not be able to breathe, but he could cut.

Hess exhaled as he ascended to keep his lungs from exploding. He broke surface and looked in the direction of the ticket building. All clear. 12:39. He had about three minutes. He breathed in and out deeply three times, then took a last breath and went back to work. The grinder came to life with a surge of new air. After the first foot his lungs could no longer hold out. When he came up for air, he looked again at the dock and the building. 12:41. The tech should be out any moment. He had completed five feet and wondered if he should quit. If he were spotted, all would be for nothing. He took a deep breath and went back to work.

Hess worked the grinder for the next fifteen seconds before he noticed a familiar sluggishness. His second air tank was running out. He cursed, came up for another breath, and pulled the reserve. 12:43.

Don't be stupid, he told himself, staring at the closed door. He could feel the anxiety swirling around his chest and abdomen. He was about to look at his watch again but instead took a breath and went under. One more foot was all he needed. Six and a half feet should be enough. He started in again but stopped after six inches, remembering something else he wanted to do back at the leading edge. He broke surface slowly, watching the door as he rose. While easing his way to the front, he worked off the wing nut holding the grinder's guide. Pulling off the guide, he put the grinder back in the three-millimeter channel at the tip of the edge and pulled the trigger. The diamond blade sunk in easily.

The lunchroom door began to open. Hess instantly took his finger off the trigger.

The maintenance tech took a few steps onto the dock, then stopped. Hess allowed himself to sink, then swam under the hull and resurfaced on the other side, out of sight. He hadn't cut as much as he wanted to, but his time was up. He clipped the grinder back to his belt and found the bag with the grappling hook. He peeked around the hull and saw the tech enjoying a cigarette. Great, he thought sarcastically. He slowly eased out the hook, which had a cable and U-bolt attached. He slid the U-bolt through the hole he'd drilled and tightened it up, all the while watching the tech.

With the grappling hook hanging from his drilled hole on a two-foot cable, Hess took his red crayon, wrote on the hull's bottom, then started toward his own boat, swimming on his back so he could watch the tech safely onto the *Sachacus.*

1:54. Hess started his engine and left the mooring area at five miles per hour. Once past the no-wake buoy, he eased the throttle forward until he was cruising out of the harbor and into Long Island Sound. Following the exact path with his GPS that he had traced on a recent ride on the *Sachacus,* he veered east. One more chore to tend to before calling it a night.

21

The sudden movement of Amy's fingers jolted Gavin from his light sleep. He had spent the night in a chair by her side, holding her hand, occasionally using the edge of her hospital bed as his pillow.

"Gavin?" she whispered.

"I'm right here, baby," he said, rising to his feet.

Her eyes opened slightly in his direction, then her gaze began to take in her surroundings—the intravenous tubes, the half-drawn pink curtain, the beeping heart monitor. "What happened?" She cleared her throat and winced slightly.

Gavin had prepared himself for this very question. He wanted to tell her everything he knew. Who else could assure him he wasn't going insane? Who else could help him figure out what to do next? "There was an accident, baby. You ruptured your spleen . . . they had to remove it. It's a useless organ anyway. You'll be fine. You just need to rest up for a bit."

"Spleen?" she said, her eyes opening wider. "Where's my baby?" She pulled her hand away from Gavin's and grabbed for her abdomen.

Gavin drew her hand back. "Hey, hey, calm down. The baby's going to be okay. The doctor will be in later to tell you she'll be fine as long as you relax and keep mostly horizontal. At first they were afraid the placenta had detached, but now they say everything's normal."

Amy paused again. "She?"

Gavin smiled and nodded. He had suspected that Amy was hoping for a girl, and this bit of news was just what he needed to distract her from the nightmare they were in. "Yeah, the doctor thought I knew and just blurted it out to me last night." The tear forming in the corner of Amy's eye told Gavin his suspicions were correct. He squeezed her hand.

"A girl," Amy said, as if to tell herself with her own words.

"That's right, sweetie . . . and remember the most important thing for *her* is that *you* rest." That part was true but was delivered with all the emotional deception Gavin could muster. What the doctor had actually told him was that the baby had nearly died and would have little chance of surviving if Amy didn't spend the rest of her pregnancy like a mummy. The doctor had also ordered him not to tell her anything that would cause fear and anxiety.

Amy looked at him without a blink. "Are you sure the baby's all right?"

"Perfectly. She's got her mother's stubbornness."

"Tell me you're not lying."

"I wouldn't lie to you at a time like this."

Amy closed her eyes. "Yes, you would . . . if you thought you were protecting me."

Gavin didn't answer. He would quit while ahead and hope his expression wasn't giving him away as it usually did.

"So what happened? My head hurts. My whole body hurts."

"Like I said, there was an accident."

"Where? How? I don't remember anything."

"You hit your head. The doctor said the facts might seem fuzzy to you at first."

"Fuzzy would be an improvement. Hit my head where?"

"Right over—"

"Not where on my head, Gavin. Where *on earth?*"

"The house."

"Our *house?*"

Gavin nodded.

"What did I do, fall down the stairs?"

"You didn't do anything. A driver lost his brakes coming down the block, couldn't make the turn, drove right through the front door. Next time we buy a house we don't buy one in the middle of a *T*," Gavin said, wondering if he should be smiling or not. Amy was looking at him suspiciously, as if there was a lot missing from his story . . . as if she knew what was missing from the story but wanted him to tell her anyway. Why did she have to be so smart?

"And what was I doing when the car hit—answering the door?"

"Uh, no. I found you in the hall near the bathroom. You were almost . . . killed," Gavin said, choking on the word. He hadn't planned on adding that last part, it just came out. He felt his eyes welling up. Great. "I'm sorry, but when I saw you on the floor I thought the worst. As it turns out . . . I was wrong."

"How bad is it?" she said, alarmed.

"It?"

"The house. Why do I get the feeling we're having two different conversations?"

"Don't worry. The house can be fixed."

Amy's eyes widened. "That bad?"

Gavin shrugged. *Don't elaborate,* he told himself.

Her face paled. "*Larry.* I was with Larry Larson. Is Larry all right?"

"He got lucky. Didn't even have to go the hospital."

Amy sighed with relief and then had another disturbing thought. "And Cedar?"

"Fine. In fact, he's the one who found you," Gavin said, then immediately wished he hadn't.

"Found me? You couldn't find me? Didn't Larry know where I was?"

Gavin shook his head, hoping to get out of this alive. "I mean Cedar was standing over you when I got there. He was concerned. He loves his mommy."

"Oh. And the driver?"

"Fine, fine. He didn't go to the hospital either. Okay, no more questions," he said, waving his hand. "You need your rest and I need to check on a few things back at the house. The truck left quite a hole. I need to make sure the house is . . . secure."

Amy frowned. "Truck? It was a truck?"

"Trucklike. You know cars today. They're either small or like trucks."

Amy nodded slowly. "Like mine."

"Yours?"

She frowned. "Wasn't my car parked—"

"Yes. That's good . . . your memory's coming back." *No thanks to me,* he thought sarcastically. "The guy just missed it. That was a close one."

"Hmm. Are you sure the driver's not hurt? I mean, how could he hit the house enough to—"

"He didn't voice any complaints and he's not here in the hospital. Look, I was too focused on you to care about anyone else."

"What am I, just unlucky? Everyone's fine except me?"

"That's enough, you need to stop talking and rest. You're healthy and so is the baby. That's all you need to know right now, okay?"

"I don't feel healthy, Gavin."

"Well you are," he said, angry and scared but determined not to show it.

Amy stared at him for a long moment, then shrugged her eyebrows and resigned herself to her pillow. Gavin gave her a heartfelt kiss and told her he would see her soon. On his way out the door, he told the nurse that Amy was awake but not to mention anything about the actual accident. He also made it clear to her there were to be no newspapers or TV in Amy's room. In the meantime, Gavin had a mental "to do" list he'd been waiting to attack. First stop, the Bronx Zoo.

22

Sachacus: 9:41 AM.

Captain Rick, as his crew fondly called him, picked up the black telephone next to his plush control seat to address the passengers. Though he couldn't hear it from the bridge, he knew a bell had just sounded, alerting his guests to either pay attention or, in the case of the regular customers, tune him out.

"Good morning. This is Captain Richard Crane. I'd like to welcome you all aboard the *Sachacus,* America's fastest ferry. Please note that the life preservers are under each seat and that your seat cushion can also be used as a floatation device in an emergency. As a courtesy to other smaller boats, we will motor through the harbor at no-wake speed, but thereafter reach a cruising speed of fifty-two knots, or about sixty miles per hour. We've been blessed with clear, friendly weather and anticipate our arrival in New London, Connecticut, to be on schedule. So make yourselves comfortable and feel free to help yourselves to our complimentary continental breakfast at the concession stand."

He returned the receiver to its cradle and inspected the monitor screens and indicator lights surrounding him and his first mate. He made his routine check of the live-water-currents screen at his left, the depth monitor to his right, and the global-positioning-system screen that would help keep the ship on the exact path it had traveled every voyage since the ferry had begun shuttling casino customers from Long Island to New London, two hours away.

Behind Captain Rick was another control center manned by the navigator, who kept a constant read on another set of security-related monitors and a special eye on a radar screen for lobster buoys and small floating debris that would escape the captain at such high speeds.

With the effortless push of the "combinator," a small joystick just larger than a Tootsie-Pop, the hundred-forty-eight-foot jet ferry surged forward and rapidly but smoothly accelerated.

"Jet-Ski coming fast on the starboard," said Mark Donovan, the twenty-seven-year-old first mate, craning his neck until he was out of his seat and facing the stern. "Coming up on the wake there, Cap—ohhh, he lost it."

Captain Rick smiled. "Maybe next time."

"Maybe not," Mark said, picking up his seven-by-fifty binoculars. "The wake never seems as big as it really is until you're on it. He's getting back on. I think he wants another try."

"You had your chance, son," Captain Rick said, giving the combinator a final push. Another smooth surge forward. "He'll just have to be content with foam."

The door behind opened and closed, allowing a momentary leak of passenger noise. The chief engineer, Randy Trayor, entered the wheelhouse and began checking his gauges.

"How's it going, Chief?" Mark asked.

"Not bad. Not bad at all," he replied, giving Mark a wry smile. "Just thought I'd stop by to let you deck officers see who's really in control of this vessel."

They all laughed while still keeping a close watch for other craft entering their space—a stressful chore, not unlike air-traffic control. The actual maneuvering of the vessel could be accomplished with the strength of a single finger. What took work—indeed, the combined skills of a highly educated and focused crew—was operating the fastest ferry in the country without damaging other vessels in the ship's huge wake. Captain Rick and his crew were highly paid to keep their passengers on a tight schedule without endangering other slower craft, and without inciting smaller boat owners to sue the giant ferry company for alleged damage. A public-relations tightrope, to be sure.

"Small cluster of fishing boats over there, Cap. One of them tied to buoy thirty-two. Don't they know that's one of our landmarks?"

"The nerve," Rick said as he watched his first mate record the landmark and the time in the ship's log. The phone rang. "Bridge."

"You guys care for anything up there?"

"Diet Pepsi sounds good for me. Anyone else? Chief?"

"I'm good."

"Mark?"

"Coffee, black."

"Heard that, Cap. One diet Pepsi and a black coffee coming up."

"Tug and barge ahead, Cap," Mark said, lowering his binoculars. "Looks like the *Earl Grey*."

"Oh, wonderful," Captain Rick said, checking his watch. 9:55. He unclipped the radio receiver and spoke. "*Earl Grey . . . Sachacus. Earl Grey . . . Sachacus* here."

"*Earl Grey* here. I see you coming, *Sachacus*," said an elderly voice.

"Uh, yeah, we'll be coming by on two," Rick said, meaning he wanted to pass by on the port, or right, side of the tug, rather than on one, meaning starboard or left. "Want us to slow?" he asked, already knowing the answer.

"That would be appreciated."

"You got it, *Earl Grey*," Rick said as courteously as he could, watching Mark roll his eyes. Most tugs would have told him to bring it on full speed, knowing that a fast Tricat like the *Sachacus* puts out a smaller wake at full speed. But not the *Earl Grey*.

A diet Pepsi appeared next to him as the phone rang again. He nodded a thank you.

"Bridge."

"One hundred eighty-two passengers, Cap."

"Okay, thanks," Rick said, making his log entry.

"One eighty-two? Not bad for a weekday," Mark said as they passed the tug at half speed.

"Yeah," Rick agreed. "Now all we have to do is get them to the blackjack table on time."

A few minutes later they were past the *Earl Grey* and flying along at full speed.

23

Walter Hess was startled out of sound sleep by the buzz of his alarm clock. He quickly shut it off. 10:08 A.M. He had fallen asleep only four or five hours ago. As a precaution, he had set his alarm clock and was now very glad he did. The *Sachacus* would be by in a few minutes.

His boat was rocking gently. He sat up, stood, felt woozy, like a bad case of jet lag. Whatever. It would all be worth it. He had done a good job and was about to see the fruit of his labors. He braced himself by grabbing a lightly pitted chrome handrail and stepped into bright daylight. He yawned. "What a beautiful day for judgment." He immediately thought of the Scripture he'd written on the bottom of the hull and how he'd been reading it just the day before. *So appropriate,* he thought. *So . . . God.*

He took a moment to look around. First south, in the direction of Long Island. About five hundred yards away, far enough so as not to disturb the speed or path of the jet ferry, he had anchored the telephone pole, horizontally, with an anchor at either end. Actually, not just an anchor but a mooring, cupped into the bottom and pointing east, the direction the *Sachacus* would be traveling, and the faster the better. According to his tide calculations, the forty-foot-long pole he'd borrowed from the Army Corps of Engineers, who were building a dock near the shore, would be about a foot and a half below the surface right now. Perfect height for the channel he'd cut in the starboard hull and for the grappling hook that would rip open the bottom like a banana peel.

He could envision the water gushing into the gash. The object wasn't to sink the boat. He knew better than to think he could accomplish that. The vessel was virtually unsinkable unless blown apart. No, the gaping hole would snow-cone the water in, driving the bow underwater while the jets, unlike a propeller drive, would continue propulsion even out of the water, driving the bow even deeper. Like throwing a pipe into the spokes of a bicycle's front wheel, the full-speed momentum would cartwheel the vessel, flipping it onto its back. Survivors would be few if any, and he would deal with them personally.

He continued to survey his position. His boat, safely and strategically placed just north of the ferry's path, looked like any other boat out fishing for the day. The two fishing rods mounted on the rail were kept in place with weights on the ends of the lines to keep them taut.

Hess saw boats in the west, but not the one he was waiting for. He looked at his watch, then west again. After a long moment of squinting, he remembered his binoculars, shaking his head at his slow thinking. He fetched a pair of olive-green Steiners he had last used for hunting and scanned the horizon. They weren't marine glasses, but they would do the trick with the sun still behind him. The rocking of the boat made it harder to still the images. He bent his knees to absorb the motion and—there, he saw it. *Sachacus.* Five to ten times the size of any other boat. Without the glasses, a white dot on the horizon, but traveling forty to fifty knots, it would be here soon.

Hess had been calm up to this point, but now he was getting nervous, just as he had when the train was bearing down on the split rail. Only then he'd had the jock to occupy his mind. He looked east, then north for anyone that could interfere with the

Sachacus' path. A couple of potential candidates were in view, but none imminent. Just then a boat, named the *Grady White*—a twenty-four, maybe twenty-six-footer—appeared within fifty feet, seemingly from nowhere. Two men, one setting fishing rods, the other, a guy with a gray beard and ponytail, walking back from the bow, apparently having just set the anchor. Before joining his friend on the deck, he stared right at Hess and gave a friendly wave.

Hess slipped on a pair of dark sunglasses and waved back, then glanced to his left toward the cabin, where his twelve-gauge Mossberg pistol-grip pump was loaded with double-aught buckshot. Economic but effective. How did they manage to sneak up on him like that? Killing them could disrupt the *Sachacus.* They would be glassing him any minute, as well as the *Grady White.* But they, or at least one of them, had clearly seen his face. This would probably mean nothing, but he didn't want to deal with *probably.*

"Any luck?" the man with the beard called out.

Hess shook his head, said nothing.

"Got two stripers. No keepers."

Hess nodded. He couldn't tell the guy to leave and didn't want to speak. He walked to one of his rods and reeled in the line, as if checking it, then lowered it and picked up the second rod. Maybe the guy would take the hint that he wanted to be alone and that the fishing was bad here. Hess glanced up toward the *Sachacus.* He could clearly make out the Tricat's unique design. He glanced inconspicuously at his watch. Right on time.

"What kind of bait you using?"

Hess cursed. "Eels," he said.

"Really? And no luck? Weird, this is a great spot. Caught a— whoa!" he yelled, grabbing for his singing rod, the tip bowing and jerking frantically. His friend set his rod in a holder and found a net while the bearded guy fought with the reel.

Hess, hoping it would be a small bluefish, kept one eye on the approaching *Sachacus*.

"Oooo, baby," the man hooted as the net slipped under the fish. Once it was aboard, he held up a huge striped bass with both arms. "Now *that's* a keeper!" he yelled.

Hess smiled nervously, cursed under his breath, gave the guy a thumb's-up, and then feigned attention to his own rods again. But his attention was focused on the view over the rim of his black glasses. The *Sachacus*. His hands shook with fear, anticipation, and excitement.

"Hey, buddy boy!" the bearded guy called out.

Hess turned, wondering if it might be worth shooting him just to shut him up.

"See that?" the guy said, pointing southwest.

Hess looked, as if he didn't know he was pointing at the ferry, then looked back at the guy.

"That sleek-looking angel in white is the boat from hell."

I know, Hess thought.

"The wake from that thing will crash over the back of your transom. Seriously. You're gonna need to reel in your lines and swing your bow around. Caught me once; never again. I remember one time . . . there must have been . . ."

Hess heard the bearded guy babble on and on, but it was just background noise. The hundred-fifty-foot Tricat had arrived and was blazing along at better than fifty knots. He unconsciously began a countdown in his mind. *Ten . . . nine . . . eight . . .*

". . . we all had eels, except for Fred, my brother-in-law. He had a fly rod. So we're just . . ."

. . . six . . . five . . . four . . .

". . . and Fred snags another one, this one bigger than the . . ."

. . . three . . . two . . .

". . . next thing ya know, the eel bucket gets knocked over and—What the— Oh, my God!"

Hess could no longer hear the bearded guy, but didn't know if it was because he was silent or if he himself didn't have the mental capacity to take in human words *and* what he was seeing before him. What transpired in less than ten seconds seemed to take much, much longer. All the research, all the math, all the preparation, and still he could not believe what he was seeing. The nose of the *Sachacus* appeared to fall into the water as if it had just gone off a cliff. The momentum drove it in deep, heaving the rear up into the air. The jets continued shooting water out like a giant fire hose as it rose higher, higher, sending the bow deeper until the jets pointed straight into the air. The vessel, a geyser, a colossal fountain, trembled there for an instant, as if a decision couldn't easily be made.

"C'mon . . . c'mon," Hess said through gritted teeth, feeling the need to combat the combined wills of the passengers for it to settle back down.

"Noooo!" screamed the bearded old fisherman and his friend.

"Goooo!" Hess countered, praying with all his might for God's kingdom to come through mightily and prevail against the forces of darkness. He closed his eyes tightly, in his mind's eye seeing the *Sachacus* give way and fall on its back. He held the vision as firmly as he could, remembering how strong faith could move a mountain. When he opened his eyes, he couldn't account for what he actually saw. The *Sachacus* was falling over, but much slower than he would have thought possible. Apparently, the crew had managed to maneuver the jets in the direction of the fall. Gravity was winning the battle, but he had hoped the ferry would slam the water's surface, not settle into it as if a crane had lowered it. He wondered how the captain had been able to think and respond so quickly.

His awe of the crew was quickly followed by an awe of his own work. When the ferry finally came to rest, the exposed hull re-

vealed the gash he had planned for. A moment of silence was followed by a clamor of activity from the *Grady White*. The bearded guy
was pulling the anchor while his friend revved the engines. Their
boat was quickly under way, flying toward the capsized ship, fishing
lines still out with bait skipping on the water's surface, rods bending.

Hess reached for his binoculars and quickly focused. A couple
of swimmers, a few more. Survivors. There shouldn't have been
any. Why would God have allowed anyone to survive? Maybe some
weren't meant to die. Maybe it was just a test to see if he would
leave or stay to . . . help.

Hess threw his rods overboard, hoisted anchor, and took off to
join the rescue. After all, the *Grady White* guys might think of him
as suspicious if he simply left. On his way he encountered the rip-
ple wake from the capsize. The wave engulfed his bow, and water
flooded back to the cabin area. If he had stayed where he was and
been caught by it coming over his transom, his boat might have
been sunk.

Up close, the flipped catamaran looked like a pair of dead
whales, their white bellies to the sun. More people in the water
now, most clinging to flotation devices. They all seemed to be getting out through the front and rear doors. Many of them were
bleeding from the head. The fishing guys were heroically hauling as
many aboard as they could fit. Hess put his engine in neutral and
drifted toward the ferry.

"Help!" called a male voice to his right. He turned to see a sur-
vivor holding a bluish cushion, kicking his way toward him.

Hess took hold of his knife, slipping his fingers through the
spiked rings that had subdued the jock at the train wreck. He
leaned over the beam and reached his left hand to the man. The man
weakly stretched out his arm. They clasped and Hess drew him
near.

"What's your name?" Hess asked, glancing around to see if anyone was looking his way. He couldn't be certain he wasn't being watched, but the man was touching the boat now and on the side away from the ferry.

The man frowned, but finding his breath, answered, "Mark."

"What's your last name, Mark?"

"Levine."

A moment later Hess was watching the man's surprised expression slowly disappear in the murky darkness below. He watched the face sink out of sight until other cries for help distracted him. He looked up and scanned the area. Maybe two dozen people were thrashing about or floating with the aid of a life preserver. The fisherman heroes were still at it, hauling survivors aboard their small vessel. Other boats were on their way; he saw only bows, no sterns. A helicopter . . . two helicopters.

A good soldier knows when it's time to slowly back away and disappear.

24

Gavin checked his watch for the tenth time as he endured an interminable wait, along with the usual zoo visitors, in the admission-ticket line. He considered flashing his badge to get to the front of the line but wasn't sure what explanation he'd give for his pushiness. Telling the truth would be the first step toward an early retirement and a padded room. Half an hour of fidgeting in line and eleven dollars later he had a ticket and a special-events bulletin about the new Congo gorilla forest. He hurried up the long, winding blacktop path through the African plains and baboon reserve, and was nearly out of breath by the time he reached the Reptile House.

Some two years had passed since his last visit to the Reptile House, but it felt like only a week. He stopped at the entrance briefly before going in at a brisk pace.

Samantha the python was in her usual spot, the first glass cage on the right as he entered the eerily dark corridor. Gavin continued a few more feet before slowing and then coming to a complete stop. The corridor was eerie all right, but not quite eerie enough. He wasn't cold. He should have been trying to shake off a deep shiver about now. Over the last year he'd convinced himself that the cold he and Amy used to feel had all been psychosomatic. He'd even made fun of himself for believing in such child's tales. Now he would welcome the cold. He wanted it so badly, he was trying to *think* cold. To will it into being with the same brain that couldn't make it go away the last time he was here. Shaking his head in frustration, he continued on.

The hallway emptied into the large room where two life-size bronze tortoises faced each other, something Jeremy would never allow another tortoise to do with him without attacking it. The attendant spotted him staring at the statue. It was the same elderly guy who had been there the last time. The man waved an abbreviated salute as Gavin walked by him.

"Been a while, but I see you couldn't stay away forever," the man said, surprising Gavin that he'd chosen to speak to him.

"I came to see the tortoise," Gavin said in passing.

"That's right. You were Jeremy's biggest fan."

"Is it still in the same cage?" Gavin asked, half looking back as he rounded the corner to the tortoise's hallway.

"Nope."

Gavin stopped, gave the attendant a puzzled glance, then hurried the rest of the way down the hall to the cage Jeremy had been in. Maybe the old man had misunderstood the question.

Empty! But why? Maybe Jeremy was simply someplace else.

A moment later Gavin was back asking the attendant, "Where is it?"

The elderly man frowned, probably confused by Gavin's intensity. "It . . . it died. I'm sorry."

"Died? Are you sure?"

The attendant nodded slowly. "Sure, I'm sure."

"When?"

"Why, just the other day."

"How?" The answers were coming way too slowly.

The old man looked at him narrowly. "Are you sure you're all right, mister?"

Gavin pulled out his badge and held it open for the old man to examine. "I *need* to know how the tortoise died."

The attendant found a pair of glasses and frowned as he carefully read the badge. "Detective . . . Nassau County. Why do the Nassau County police care how a tortoise at the Bronx Zoo dies?" He chuckled. "Was Jeremy under some kind of house arrest?"

"All I can tell you is that a crime has been committed in Nassau that could possibly connect with this tortoise. More information than that could jeopardize the investigation." Gavin knew he was way out on a limb here, but he wasn't very good at lying, and the truth was more unbelievable than any lie.

The attendant massaged his chin, and then returned his glasses to his pocket. "I used to watch you come in here every Sunday and go straight to Jeremy's cage with a woman who had no more desire to be in here than the rats they feed ol' Samantha over there. Now you tell me Jeremy was under investigation. I don't understand what this is all about, but I'll tell you what happened . . . not because I believe a word you're saying, but because you could've read it for yourself in the newspaper."

"Newspaper?" Gavin couldn't remember reading a paper since the day before the train wreck.

"*Daily Post,* in the middle somewhere."

"When?"

"Day before yesterday. Or was it the day before that? Not sure."

"So how, then? How did Jeremy die?"

"Strangest thing. That's why it was in the paper. Lester kidnapped him, and then got into a car accident. They were both killed."

"Lester?"

"Lester Davis. Wildlife keeper of tortoises. Jeremy's daddy. A good man. Gave Jeremy a lot of attention."

Gavin looked toward the ground for a moment, then back up to the attendant. "Was anyone else involved in the accident?"

He shook his head. "Don't know. The road was wet. He skidded off and flipped over a rail going from the Cross Bronx Expressway to the Major Deegan. It's a bad turn there. Looks like he was heading upstate."

"Buck's?" Gavin wondered aloud.

"Excuse me?"

"Nothing."

An hour later Gavin was heading north on his way upstate to see Buck, hoping to wake up from his nightmare. He stuffed in the last bite of a salted pretzel he'd bought from an outdoor vendor at the zoo. *Breakfast and lunch,* he thought. He'd been in too much of a hurry to find something to drink. Now water sounded good—a cool, clear glass with ice. But even his tugging thirst couldn't keep his mind occupied for more than a few moments.

"Coincidence?" he said into the high winds sweeping around his convertible. "Coincidence?" he repeated. "How many coincidences does one have to experience before one decides one is not experiencing a coincidence?" He wanted to sit down with the HBO producers and ask them to explain what he was going through. They seemed to have all the answers. Right. He might as well add Chris and the lieutenant to that list while he was at it. How was he going to explain his theories to them?

His beeper vibrated. He arched his back, dug the beeper out of his pocket, read the number. Chris. He slowed down to where the winds were just less than the usual roar and called Chris on his cell phone.

"Gav? Where are you? I called the hospital, but they told me you'd left."

"Were your ears burning? I was just thinking about you."

"Did you hear?" Chris said urgently.

"What?"

"Where are you, in a cave? There's been another attack."

Gavin's throat tightened with fear. Did something else happen to Amy?

"The ferry flipped."

"What ferry?"

"It's been on every radio station for the last hour."

"What ferry?"

"The *Sachacus*."

"Chris . . . I don't know what the *Sachacus* is."

"The high-speed ferry that goes from Glen Cove to New London, Connecticut. The casino ferry."

"The jet boat?"

"Bingo."

"My God! Any survivors?"

"More than you might think looking at it, but the casualties are high. Most of the crew lived, and thanks to them, what could have been a total disaster was minimized."

"What do you mean?"

"I'll explain when I see you. It's complicated."

"How did it flip?"

"I don't exactly know yet, but it looks like our boy again."

"What makes you think so?"

"The same blue-collar, hardware-store workmanship we saw at the train wreck. No explosives. And guess what else?"

"He left a business card."

"Minus the phone number. This one written with red crayon on the bottom of the hull. Easy to read with the boat on its back."

"What does it say?"

"Micah five-fifteen. Another Bible verse."

"I figured that, but what does the verse say?" Gavin said, amazed that the Bible had a book called Micah.

"'I will execute vengeance and wrath on the nations which have not obeyed.'"

Gavin took a moment to let the words sink in. "And this ferry brought who to where?"

"Exactly. It's hard to believe this garbage found its way to Long Island. Guess he feels there's a lot of targets here."

"Like a shark in a swimming pool."

"Oh, by the way, the Feds wanted the prints we found on the Camel pack."

"Just make sure someone stays on them. You know how they can be. We'll find out who this guy is in the newspaper before they call us back."

"Hey, speaking of the newspaper, guess who showed up with the media?"

"Senator Bruce Sweeney, giving blood, promising to fight terrorism and pointing to the debris as an example of how the current administration isn't doing enough."

"How'd you know?"

"I can read your squeaky mind."

Chris chuckled. "Right. Say, how's Amy doing?"

"She's moment to moment right now. She needs to stay put and listen to the doctors. Otherwise . . ."

"What about you, Gav?"

"I'm fine."

"Sure you are. Do you have a place to sleep tonight, or are you going to move into the hospital permanently?"

"Don't worry about me."

"Uh-huh. Okay, I won't. But we need to get together ASAP. We've got a few leads to follow up on, and the clock's a-tickin'. Who knows what he's got planned next. Where are you now?"

"Driving."

"I figured *that*. Where? I'll come to you."

Gavin closed his eyes for a moment and exhaled. "That won't work, Chris. I'm headed . . . north."

"North? What the heck does north mean? I'm on the North Shore right now."

"I'm going upstate."

"Upstate?"

"I'm going to see Buck. You know, the black preacher. I thought he might know something about the crash," he lied.

There was a moment of silence. "What would he know about the crash? Isn't he in the hospital with a bad heart?"

Gavin didn't know what to say. He was thinking hard, but like Amy, Chris always knew when he was lying. "Just a thought, Chris."

"Just a *thought?*" Chris's tone was one Gavin had rarely heard directed at him. "Your house gets mowed down by some diabolical copycat, your wife was almost killed and is in the hospital, and you're driving four hours away to see a guy who you know hasn't left the hospital in almost a week and—"

"Chris, stop. There's more, but I can't get into it over the phone. I'll be back soon. See you tonight at your house. If Amy's still stable, I'll spend the night in your basement apartment." It was all he could think of to calm his partner, whom he often referred to as his Saint Bernard. Chris always felt better when he was saving someone.

"Okay, okay, just get back here as soon as you can."

Gavin hung up the phone and hit the gas, knowing Chris thought he was either crazy or lying. Then he wondered the same about himself. *Was* he crazy? He remembered Buck's words to him over two years ago when he had told the old man he needed to see in order to believe. He'd never forgotten the deliverance minister's response: "In my business, Detective, you often have to *believe* in order to *see*." Gavin contemplated those words afresh for the next two hours.

25

When Gavin peeked into Buck's hospital room, the reverend appeared to be asleep. He was propped up by pillows, his bed cranked up at a forty-five-degree angle, oxygen tubes in his nose, intravenous bag dripping clear liquid, a monitor beeping slowly. Thank God it was still beeping.

Before going any further, Gavin ducked into the room's lavatory to relieve himself, then downed six paper cupfuls of water. It wasn't very cold and had a weird taste that lingered on his tongue, but at least it was wet. He caught a glimpse of himself in the mirror and sighed. He was wearing the same clothes he'd put on before the visit from the cement truck the day before. He wondered if he owned any others or if they were now just part of the rubble. He could definitely use a shower and a shave. He sniffed under his arm and frowned before leaving.

He was glad to find that Buck had been moved out of the coronary care unit into a room. He was, however, not thrilled to see that Buck shared the room with another patient, another old man with a tracheotomy tube in his neck. He was wide awake and waved as Gavin walked back to Buck's bed.

Gavin nodded at him, then stood over Buck. He reached to nudge his shoulder but felt awkward about waking the old preacher. Behind him was a chair, but he instantly rejected the idea of sitting down. He had to talk to Buck now and get back.

"He had a bad night," said the other patient in a strange voice, holding the hole in his neck closed in order to speak. "I think they gave him something to make him sleep."

Not answering, Gavin looked up at the intravenous bag. Drip, drip, drip. He considered how wrong it would be to mess with whatever they were giving him.

"Buck," Gavin heard himself say. The other patient gave him a frown. "Buck." This time a little louder.

"Did I mention he had a bad night?"

Gavin ignored the other patient and was reaching for Buck's privacy curtain when he heard . . .

"Detective?" Buck's voice was dry and weak.

"Yes," Gavin said, quickly back at his side. "I'm right here."

"Are you alone?" His eyelids were cracking open.

Gavin took a quick glance at the other patient. "Yes."

"Hmm. Have you been praying for Jeremy?"

Gavin searched for words, then finally said, "That wouldn't have mattered."

Buck's eyes opened with alarm.

"The guy taking care of Jeremy kidnapped him."

"Lester?"

"Yes. He's dead," Gavin said, then leaned closer. "A car wreck. What else is new? Happened on the entrance ramp to the thruway. Looks like he might have been coming up to see you with the tortoise. Probably the fault of Krogan's demon friends, right?"

Buck's eyes closed. "Krogan will be back. You will be contacted."

"You might say I've already been contacted," Gavin said, and then told him about the cement truck, the decorator, and Amy in the hospital. He noticed the other patient staring at them, unblinking, and said to him, "You didn't know demons drove cars, did you?"

The old man's expression was a cross between astonishment and irritation as Gavin grabbed for the privacy curtain and closed him off from view.

"This time it's you who must stop him, Detective," Buck urged Gavin under his breath. "You must get to him before he gets to you."

"Me? You must be kidding. How am I supposed to do that? He knows me and I don't know him. Besides, I don't even believe this demon stuff is real half the time. Buck, is this really happening? Please tell me there is a chance you're wrong."

"You know it's real when it's happening, Detective, or you wouldn't be here with me."

"Yeah, I know, there are no atheists in foxholes. But at least they know who's shooting at them. Agghhh, I can't do what you do . . . I don't know what you know . . . and frankly, I don't want to."

"This is not about 'want,' Detective. We're dealing with life and death, light and darkness. You must call on God and learn from Him in the light," Buck said, opening his eyes wider, "and never doubt in the darkness what God has given you in the light."

"I'll try to remember that."

"You *have* to remember that."

"Can't you just give a name of someone already involved in this stuff?"

"Yes. His name is Detective Gavin Pierce."

Before Gavin could answer, his beeper vibrated. Chris again.

"You don't mind?" Gavin picked up Buck's room phone.

"Dial nine first," Buck said.

Gavin nodded and dialed. "What's up?"

"You didn't, by any chance, read today's *Daily Post?*" Chris asked.

"No."

"I didn't think so."

"Why?"

"You follow wrestling?"

"The WWX?"

"Yeah."

"Of course not."

"Well, there's a full-page ad about a thing there starting tonight called Armageddon."

Gavin rolled his eyes. "Chris, I'm here in the hospital with Buck. We're in the middle of—"

"Fine, fine, I'll chat with you later about the main attraction of the show, who just happens to be a guy named Krogan."

"What?"

"Thought you might be interested. And get this . . ." Chris laughed. "The WWX is offering a million dollars to anyone who beats him in a five-minute bout. Not *our* Krogan, of course, but quite a coincidence, wouldn't you say?"

"Why do you say he's not our guy?" Gavin demanded, then immediately realized what Chris's answer would be.

"Hello? Our guy's in the big house, remember?"

"Right. I keep forgetting."

"Ever hear of Jackhammer Hoban?"

"Well, yeah, who hasn't? But like I said—"

"You don't follow, I know, I know," Chris finished for him. "Anyway, it seems this guy Hoban has had a sudden resurgence. He won a title fight on Monday, and the ad claims he started calling himself Krogan after Monday night's fight."

After the tortoise died, Gavin thought, a shudder trickling down his back.

"Anyway, I'll see you later. Sooner the better. We've got a lot to go over."

"Later," Gavin said, hanging up the phone and turning back to Buck. The old man's eyes were closed again. Again, Gavin was tempted to turn off the IV. How was he ever going to get Buck to help him in this condition?

"Buck."

"Yes?" The old preacher opened his eyes.

"I guess at this point we can consider the tortoise route a failure."

Buck sighed and nodded slowly. "Lester could never tell the zoo the truth . . . and now he's dead. It's my fault. I should never have asked him to even consider such a task."

"Hmm. So let's say we find that Krogan lives inside . . . a professional wrestler, for example. What would be the first thing to do?"

"The first thing is always the same as the last thing."

"Dial nine-one-one?"

"I guess you could say that—only, a heavenly emergency line. It's prayer, young man! The first thing to do is pray for Krogan's host."

"Krogan's host? You mean the guy that drove through my house with a cement truck and put my wife in the hospital! *You* pray for him! Pray I don't kill him!"

"Detective, when are you going to realize that your fight is not against flesh and blood, but against the spirit that influences its decisions and, in Krogan's case, possesses his life?"

"So what kind of prayer do you pray for someone like Krogan's host?"

"Mercy, forgiveness, and ultimately, surrender. And then you need to pray for Krogan to be bound. You must understand that God's heart is for the man and against the demon. When the demon is bound, the man will be weak. That's when the man must be seized or the demon cast out."

"If I recall, Buck, this is a battle you almost lost against Krogan on Ellis Island. I was there, remember? We were fortunate to get out of there with our lives. How am I supposed to do this alone?"

"You won't be alone, Detective. When you pray you are never alone. And to come against the likes of Krogan you must also fast."

"What good does that do?"

"It helps you become weak, surrender to God. It is when you are weak that you will be strongest."

"I want you to know that nothing you say makes any sense to me."

"Pray first, then understanding will come, Detective."

"I know who Krogan is."

"That is why you must know who God is."

"No, I mean I know *who* Krogan is."

Buck reflexively lifted his head off his pillow. "You do?"

"I think so. A drugged-out alcoholic WWX wrestler has just reappeared on the scene big-time, and he's changed his name to Krogan. This all happened just after our tortoise died. Can a repossession happen that fast?" Gavin said, wondering if *repossession* was the correct word. It was all so out of this world.

"When a demon leaves a host it reenters the spirit world it was originally born into. Jesus called it 'the waterless place,' a desert-like wilderness, if you will, because demons can no longer nourish themselves there. Ever since the resurrection, it has been a place saturated with the light of God, and the demons cannot hide. They are exposed to the light, tortured by it, and want to leave as quickly as possible. In agony, they search in haste for their next home, usually human. In our time, this can happen very quickly. Once in its new home, the demon seeks to control, dominate. In Krogan's case, the overpowering of the new host can be swift. He gives them more of what they already want, then destroys them with it."

"Buck . . . do you think Krogan will come up here . . . for you?"

"Not if you stop him first," the old man said with a weak smile.

Gavin glanced at his watch. 2:44. If he left now he could be back on the Island by six—oh, but then there was rush hour. Make that seven or seven-thirty.

"Gotta go, Buck. Sorry for being the bearer of bad news, but I didn't know where else to turn."

"What will you do now?"

"Krogan sent me a message. I think it's about time I sent him one."

26

Krogan pushed open the glass door of the Harley Davidson dealer and went directly to the bike displayed in the window. He had never seen anything like it, ever. The seat was cut low like other Harleys, but that was where the similarities ended. The entire bike was a raw, anodized aluminum—not a metallic silver paint but real metal, like a stainless-steel knife. He envisioned himself riding it at a hundred-sixty or more. The vision excited him.

"Help ya?" said a deep voice from behind.

"I want this," Krogan said, focused on his own reflection in the glistening alloy gas tank.

"Yeah, well, who doesn't? The V-Rod's the hottest bike on the market. It's just awesome."

Krogan turned to face the man, middle-aged, long gray beard, tattoos on his forearms, black Harley T-shirt over a gut, black pants over black boots. He reminded Krogan of so many others he had killed, usually for their bikes. "I wanna ride this."

"Hey, wait a minute . . . aren't you Jackhammer Hoban? Yeah, yeah . . . I read about you in today's paper. Full-page ad. You're gonna fight in that Armageddon thing tonight, and you're gonna challenge anyone. A million dollars to anyone who can beat you. That's wild, man. Wild." The man shook his head. "Also read you changed your name to Krogan, like that psycho. Sweet move . . . I like that. But, hey, looking at you in person, I think it'll be a hard million to earn. I saw you on Monday night's title fight. Man, oh man, did you whip Tyrant's butt! And I heard it was real, that you threw the script out. Is that true?"

"The bike," Krogan growled, his glare removing the salesman's grin.

"Oh, right. What did you want, a test ride? In your case I'll waive the usual formalities and hook you right up. Not like we don't know where to find ya," he said with a laugh. "Just take it down Peninsula Boulevard a little ways. There's an open area a half mile down for you to check it out. If you like it, are you thinking of buying one today?"

"I want it now."

"Uh, yeah . . . sure . . . great. I can do that. I'll, uh, have one brought around front and—"

"Now."

The salesman stepped backward, almost tripping over his feet as he hurried away. A moment later he reappeared with a few other salespeople behind him, all looking at Krogan.

"Here we go, Mister, uh, Krogan," the salesman said, pointing through the glass where a V-Rod was standing, another employee at its side.

Krogan exited and straddled the bike, the bright alloy finish flashing in the sunlight.

"Okay, now," the salesman said, all chummy-like. "The key goes right here and, uh, you're gonna need a helmet. I'll be back in one second."

Krogan kicked the shifter into neutral and turned the key. The engine started instantly. He pulled in the hand clutch, kicked the gearshift down to first, and revved the engine. A moment later he was gone.

* * *

Two hours passed before Krogan blazed into Nassau Coliseum's parking lot on the V-Rod. The odometer read one hundred sixty-eight miles—eighty-seven more than when he had left the showroom, five of those miles collected off the road. The once pristine machine was scratched and soiled with sand, straw, grass, and mud.

Krogan passed a gaggle of fans who had gathered early to see their heroes arrive. They pointed and screamed at him as he turned down the ramp to the coliseum's massive lower level. Coliseum security recognized him and waved him in as he downshifted. Once inside, he screeched to a skidding stop and then stepped off the bike, letting it fall to the ground like a child would an old bicycle at a playground.

He didn't know what time it was and didn't care. It was still light out and the fight wouldn't start until dusk.

"Hey, Hoban!" called a loud voice as he passed by the weight room. "Oh, I'm sorry. I meant Krogan," the voice said sarcastically, then laughed.

Krogan stopped in his tracks and turned back, stepping into the room, where a dozen wrestlers were pumping up for the event. That is, until he walked in. Most of them stopped and looked up at him. The scene reminded him of another time long ago.

"A million freaking dollars . . . and no script to protect you?" a belligerent voice hollered, the same voice that had called his host's name a moment ago. Krogan's host knew the man as Malcolm "The Mountain" Murchison. The WWX had hired him six months ago after he'd won the World's Strongest Man contest, where the contestants carry cars and boulders. The WWX was bringing him along and had plans to make him one of their new superstars. In the weight room, Murchison was a giant among giants. "When we fight, I will not need three minutes against a has-been like you. Tyrant wasn't expecting you to—"

Murchison continued his ranting, but Krogan's attention went to one of three television sets suspended from the ceiling. All were tuned to different stations, but all were showing the same event, albeit from different angles. With music coming over the weight room's sound system, the TV volume had been turned off and close captioning scrolled at the bottom of each set's picture of what looked like a capsized boat. Krogan read the captions just long enough to realize the same guy who had derailed the train was being blamed for flipping the boat. He marveled at how such a feat could have been accomplished and again found himself envious of a host with such creativity.

"Agggghhhhh," roared another wrestler working out on the bench press. Hoban had known him as Kamehameha, a powerful Hawaiian wrestler who'd named himself after the first Hawaiian king. The Olympic steel bar was bending under the dunnage of four plates per side totaling four hundred five pounds. Once, twice, three times. Veins popping, muscles bulging, eyes screaming, the Hawaiian finally allowed the hefty bar clang to rest in the forks.

Suddenly Krogan wanted to feel the blood flow and the muscles harden . . . something he had missed while imprisoned in the cursed tortoise. He walked over to the bench, where the wrestler had sat up, resting for his next set.

"Leave," Krogan commanded.

Kamehameha looked at him indignantly. "Say what?"

Krogan locked onto his eyes, holding him motionless with his gaze. *"Hele, hemu lapuwale,"* he said, in the wrestler's ancient native language calling him a fool and telling him to leave at once.

Kamehameha's eyes widened with surprise. "How do you know—"

"Hemu!" Krogan ordered.

The Hawaiian wrestler turned pale and slowly moved away without a word.

Krogan settled under the bar. Without the usual ritual of

stretching, warming up with lesser weights, and making sure of balanced hand placement, he lifted the load off the rest with a grunt and lowered it to within an inch of his chest. Krogan tested Hoban's natural strength and enjoyed the pain of the straining muscles along with the increased heart rate. Breathing and surging adrenaline from his host's fear of not being able to get the weight back up if he held it to his chest any longer was a problem his host would soon learn not to concern himself with. He would teach Hoban to expect supernatural strength. Then someday, in all likelihood, Krogan would use his host's newfound confidence to kill him. In the meantime, he would burn him out physically and mentally like spiritual LSD and when—

"Nobody walks away from me while I'm talking to them and lives to tell about it," Malcolm "The Mountain" Murchison said, straddling Krogan as he lay on the bench, Murchison's massive hands gripping the bar, pushing downward. "Whether I kill you now or in the ring makes no difference to me."

Krogan cursed at him, which made Murchison push harder.

"I . . . can't . . . breathe," Krogan gasped, the bar now deeply creasing his chest.

"So then don't," Murchison said, grinning.

Krogan's panicked expression transformed slowly, eerily into a smile. Murchison leaned into him until he was pushing with all his weight. Krogan continued to smile until he finally puckered his lips and threw him a mock kiss and said, "I'm sorry I wasn't paying attention to you." He then thrust the barbell away, sending both the weight and Murchison backward to the floor. In a flash Krogan was on him, their roles completely reversed. Murchison cried out in pain as Krogan shoved the barbell into his chest. "Now, what is it you were saying?"

A moment later, Krogan walked out of the weight room, leaving Malcolm "The Mountain" Murchison curled in fetal position on the floor, coughing spasmodically, while the other wrestlers looked on, stunned. He walked through a rising hallway that emptied into the arena. The festivities would not start for another few hours. WWX stage crews were setting up microphones, tables, and cameras, testing sound levels and checking light switches. Spurts of heavy-metal music were coming on and off. WWX security personnel in black-and-white shirts wandered about with walkie-talkies.

"Hoban the man!" said one of the stagehands to Krogan, holding up his hand for a high-five.

Krogan ignored the man as he walked by. He did not want to be liked, much less engage in some ritual with a menial drone. His audience would be unseen to human eyes. He would give an exhibition for all those who despised the creator and his precious creation. He would be an example to some of his less-than-ruthless comrades of how easily darkness can dominate. He would take and enjoy. Play with the creation like a cat would a bird with a broken wing.

He climbed to the upper seats of the coliseum, sat down, and gazed into the empty arena. In the center of the ceiling was a circle of twelve large lights focused only on the ring below. He stared at the lights, like glowing numbers on a giant clock, until his mind started to drift to another time. The intermittent music and the voices of stagehands fell to the background, then into silence. The workers' motions slowed until he saw no movement at all. Downward light beams formed from the twelve lights, stretching until they reached the floor surrounding the ring. Out of the quiet he heard faint cheers that grew louder and louder. The twelve beams of light became solid stone pillars topped with robust flames spewing thick black smoke. The pillars moved farther apart, separating, until they encompassed the entire floor before the seats.

The vision became clear. The ring was gone. He saw the crowds and their attire. The torchlit floor of battle was muddy and sticky, almost waxy, and he remembered its being called a *keroma*. A dozen or more naked men stood with him at one side of the arena while two men fought in the middle. The fight would continue without break until one of the men surrendered by raising a right hand with a pointed index finger. There were no other rules, no weight distinctions. The men would battle in any way they wanted, without clothes or weapons. Meanwhile, Krogan waited impatiently for his turn. The fighting was fierce by their standards, but he would change the standards.

The crowd cheered as one of the naked men overpowered the other, choking and punching until the sign of surrender was finally given.

A man in white, draping clothes entered the *keroma*, holding a parchment list of names at his side as the two fighters, soiled and bloody, were helped away by guards, one walking, the other carried. The man in white called for the next two contestants. "Talus. Krogan."

Krogan and his opponent stepped forward. Krogan's host was not as big as the seasoned Talus, and had never been in the *keroma* before. His only reputation was as a soldier who liked to drink and fight with anyone, anytime. The crowd knew him well, hated him, and wanted him soundly beaten. Two other men, also draped in white, hurried over, sprinkled olive oil on the contestants' bodies as an anointing, dusted them with white powder to make them easier to grasp, then scurried away. The man with the name list ordered Krogan and Talus to face each other in the center of the *keroma*, then signaled them to commence.

At the signal, Krogan smiled and Talus attacked. Talus's initial surge and grasp sent the crowd wild with anticipation. A moment later, Talus lay facedown in the mud, dead, his neck broken. *Too easy,* Krogan thought. After the limp body was carried away, he remained, demanding to fight again. The crowd agreed and the moderator complied. He allowed the next fight to last longer. Krogan enjoyed the pain of the ensuing fights, and by day's end, he had defeated all his opponents, leaving most of them dead.

As Krogan enjoyed his vision of that first day in the *keroma,* he remembered how he ruled the games for the next year and a half, until finally he was ambushed and killed in his sleep by a small mob of previously defeated opponents. He also remembered coming back in a new host and slaughtering each of his murderers in *their* sleep before leaving Athens for a newly founded city called Rome.

His vision moved ahead in time, nearly two hundred years. He was back in Athens again with a new host, this time as a spectator. The arena looked exactly the same, but the fighting was much different. Now it was part of the Olympic games, and rules had been implemented for safety.

As the Olympic battles began to fade out in Krogan's vision, the world of the WWX reappeared. The music sound levels were still being tested, stagehands were still adjusting microphones and wheeling in equipment, and men in business suits were standing by the ring talking.

Krogan closed his eyes and thought again about the way he had repaid the ones who had ambushed him in his sleep. Even though they didn't realize whom they were really dealing with, he had needed to avenge himself. Now he considered how much more he should repay Pierce and Buchanan for casting him into that blasted tortoise. They did indeed know what they were dealing with, which would make their terror all the more enjoyable.

27

Gavin hammered the elevator's "Close Door" button with his index finger. He would have preferred the stairs, but he didn't know where they were. Amy's room was on the third floor. Her new room. He had tried calling her directly as soon as he left Buck at Delhi Hospital, but there had been no answer. He eventually found out they had changed her room and were keeping the phone off, hoping she would get rest. They were unable to give her painkillers because of the baby.

The elevator door finally closed. On the way up he thought again of how he had wanted to stop off at Buck's neighbor's house to see how Samantha was faring with the Quinns, but quickly reminded himself he couldn't possibly do that. He simply didn't have the time . . . again.

The elevator stopped at the second floor. Two doctors casually entered, then alertly held the door as it started to close.

"Thank you," said an orderly in green hospital garb.

They all seemed to be moving at half speed. Gavin pressed the "Close Door" button again. Was everyone in the hospital on drugs? He watched for the third-floor button to light up. *Ding.* While the door was still opening, Gavin was already out, searching for room numbers. Three-ten, three-twelve . . . there it was, three-sixteen. He went inside without hesitation.

Amy's closed eyes opened as Gavin approached the bed.

"Where have you been?" she said weakly. "We were worried," she said, holding her belly.

"Don't ever worry about me. How are you feeling? How's the baby?"

"We're okay. My muscles are sore . . . everywhere, but they don't seem very concerned about that, so I'm not. They gave us some Tylenol, but no codeine. I'll be fine, but you were gone all day. Where were you?"

"Working. The same terrorist that derailed the train has capsized the ferry out of Glen Cove. I called the hospital and they told me they wanted you to rest."

"I heard about the ferry. Chris came by earlier, looking for you."

"He found me."

Amy paused for a moment, staring straight into his eyes. "What did Buck say?"

Gavin was speechless. He would have to yell at Chris first, then kill him. "How did you know I saw Buck?"

"I didn't."

The room suddenly felt much smaller. "I wanted to tell him about the truck going into the house before he heard it from someone else."

"Like who?"

"Like you."

"You couldn't call him?"

"I had promised him I'd look in on Samantha and thought I'd kill two birds with one stone. I wanted to make sure—"

"Don't," Amy interrupted.

"Don't what?"

"Don't lie to me. You don't want me to worry, so you're only telling me what you think I want to hear."

Gavin paused, then shook his finger at her and kissed her gently on the lips. "Nice try. But I'm only telling you the truth. Buck doesn't need any more stress and neither do you."

Amy gave him a long look. "And Jeremy?"

Two birds flew by the window. If it were springtime, the male would probably be the one chasing the female, but now that the courtship was over, eggs hatched, and the kids out of the nest, Gavin figured the female was chasing the male. "What about Jeremy?"

"Did you check up on him? Is Jeremy still . . . with us?"

Gavin rolled his eyes. "No, I did not check up on the tortoise. The first thing Buck told me was not to worry, that Jeremy was fine. If anything happened, he would be the first to know and he would call us immediately."

Amy's expression didn't change.

"But——" He held up his hands in surrender. "——if it will make you feel better, I'll try to get to the zoo tomorrow."

"Try?"

"If I knew the terrorist's schedule, I could be more definite."

Amy smiled and Gavin relaxed. He was home free . . . for now. "When do I get a phone?" she wanted to know.

"They don't want you to be disturbed."

"Well, then, they'd better get me a phone soon, or I'll be plenty disturbed."

"Fine, I'll tell them on my way out. Is there someone you want me to contact?"

"Yes. Larry. I'd like to make sure he's okay and find out what he thinks about the damage."

Great, Gavin thought as he nodded. "Okay, Larry. Anyone else?"

"Yes, *everyone* else. Please, Gavin. Just tell them to get me a phone or I'll go down there myself."

Gavin agreed, then gave her a good-bye kiss and left. On the way out he told the nurse to order the phone. "Starting tomorrow . . . as late as possible."

When Gavin drove out of the hospital parking lot, he surprised himself by remembering to turn his cell phone back on and then looked at his watch. 5:46. He called the Nassau Coliseum and found out the WWX Armageddon show would start at seven-thirty. He considered the errands he needed to run and figured he would get there a little late if he hurried. What else was new?

On his way down Old Country Road to police headquarters he passed a Sports Authority. A quarter mile later he pulled a U-turn and went in. Sneakers, tennis rackets, footballs, golf clubs, women's sportswear, baseball jerseys . . . *Where are they?* Bicycles, guns, fishing poles, pogo sticks, swimwear, beach balls . . . *Ahh.*

Ten minutes later he was back on the road again with four orange Frisbees. With any luck the homicide department would be empty.

Gavin turned on the radio to find every station updating the ferry sabotage. The unofficial report on one station from an anonymous source claimed police were looking for a member of a neo-Nazi religious cult. He wondered where they'd gotten that from. He could just picture the lieutenant with a phone on each ear, his beeper and cell phone both ringing, wondering where his man Pierce was. He would just have to remind him that Amy was in the hospital because his house had been run over by a cement truck. Now there was an excuse he'd never used before. He fished for his phone to call Chris, but then thought better of it. At this point Chris would have some new questions he wouldn't be able to answer, at least not truthfully, and he didn't know how much longer he could keep lying to people. It was not something he was very practiced in.

A few minutes later Gavin was behind his desk at Homicide waiting for his computer to boot up. The red number light on his voice mail was blinking. Forty-two messages. He imagined ten belonging to the lieutenant and Chris—hopefully nine from the lieutenant and only one from Chris. The rest would be split between the media, FBI, and false leads on the terrorist. He paused for a moment with the notion that one of the leads could be true . . . or that the terrorist *himself* might have called . . . Oh, well. Later.

He looked around and was relieved to be alone. He figured everyone was on the North Shore combing for evidence. The new computer he had received from the department, along with everyone else in Homicide, looked out of place on his World War I vintage desk. To the detectives in Homicide the new computers fanned the flame of new hopes . . . two of which were high above all others. One, that maybe within the next decade or so they'd be networked with other counties, even states, to share records without the help of the Feds. Two, and more important, that the next money spent might go to fix the air conditioning.

He jumped as the phone rang. He reflexively reached for the receiver, but then withdrew his hand. How much more important would message forty-three be than all the others compared with how awkward it would be to talk to either the lieutenant or Chris. He watched the computer continue to boot up, loading the antivirus program. He drummed his fingers, listening to his own voice answer with the promise to get back as soon as possible. He turned the volume down.

But what if it was Amy trying to somehow reach him. His cell phone never had good reception in this place. "Aghhh," he said aloud. He turned the volume back up.

"Hello, Detective Pierce? This is Father Lauer. I was the priest at the train derailment. Please call me at six-seven-four-HOPE. I need to talk to you about the subject matter you asked about the other night."

Gavin paused, then grabbed the receiver. "Hello!"

Nothing. Gone.

He replayed the message, scribbled down the number on a Post-It pad, and pocketed it, wondering why the priest needed to talk to him. If anything, he needed to talk to the priest.

Computer ready, Gavin typed in "www.galapagos.com," not knowing where the screen would take him but hoping for a picture of a tortoise. A moment later he was listening to jungle music at a travel site. There was a picture of a cruise ship, a bird, a seal, and yes . . . a tortoise. In fact, the tortoise looked so much like Jeremy that Gavin stared at it longer than he'd planned. Perfect. He brought the cursor arrow to the tortoise, right-clicked to zoom, and then clicked again on print. After retrieving the print, he cut out the tortoise, enlarged it on the copy machine, and made six copies.

"This ought to do," he said aloud, holding up a piece of his work.

"Do what?" came a voice from behind.

"Chris!"

"Oh, you remember me," Chris said as he took a moment to examine the immediate area Gavin had littered with paper snippings and a pair of scissors. He then picked up the other five copies of the tortoise picture. "You know, Gav, I normally wouldn't ask. You've always been a bit of a mystery and that's fine. But when we have one maniac on the loose terrorizing the country with tools he probably bought at garage sales and another who drove a truck through your house . . . and with your wife in the hospital . . . I find *you* visiting a sick preacher upstate and then making copies of turtle pictures. I figure, being your partner and all, that it's time we had a talk."

"Not now, Chris. I don't have time," Gavin said, plucking the pictures out of Chris's hand and walking to his desk.

"Don't have time? Why? Now where are you going?" Chris followed Gavin to his desk and then looked at the monitor screen. "The Galapagos Islands?" He laughed. "Don't tell me—your cruise ship leaves in fifteen minutes, but you'll tell me all about it when you get back."

"I know this looks crazy, but I don't have time now to explain."

"No need to worry there, pal. I already think you're nuts . . . or haven't you been listening."

"Believe me. You haven't seen anything yet. Or rather, you've seen but don't know what you're seeing. Or something like that. I don't remember anymore."

"You're scaring me, Gav."

"Forget it. Let's just say I *am* crazy and leave it at that. Leave your basement door open. I'll see you in the morning." Gavin started quickly for the door.

"Whoa!" Chris said, keeping pace a step back. "I was serious when I said we had to talk. We've got some solid leads to go over before the soldier moves on to his next project."

Gavin hurried down the hall with Chris right behind him. A nightmare. "I can't do this now, Chris. We'll meet tonight when I get back," he said, flying down the wide marble stairs.

"Not good enough, Gav. I'm coming with you."

Gavin allowed a mock laugh as he hit the outside air, shaking his head with determination. "No, you're not!"

"I'm sorry, Gav, but I have to," Chris insisted, a half step behind, the same way Superman would have said it to a twelve-year-old. "There's too much happening and you're a part of it all."

"Your older brothers must have tied you up a lot when they went to their friends, didn't they? You can't come!"

"I always got free. We'll talk about it in the car."

Gavin looked at Chris without saying another word. The Boy Scout, Saint Bernard, Canadian Mountie, and Nun-of-the-Month qualities had dug in their heels. There was no way of getting rid of him when he got this way, and time was running out. "I don't have time to argue. Fine, we'll talk about the case on the way, but you're staying in the car when we get there."

"Where?"

"Nassau Coliseum," Gavin said, sliding into his seat. He turned the ignition key, hoping the car would start and rev before Chris could respond. He pumped his foot and cranked and cranked and cranked. Why did this always happen when Chris was around?

"That WWX thing I told you about?"

"Yes."

"You mean this is *my* fault?"

"Yes, it's all your fault." The car started.

"This can't be happening now. I can't be letting this happen now."

"Try to stop me."

28

You need a bigger car," Chris said just loud enough to overcome the wind and the Tiger's throaty engine.

Gavin shifted into fourth as he glanced to his right. Chris's knees were touching the glove compartment. Good. "I like it just fine, thank you."

"I feel like I'm in a freakin' go-cart . . . and without an airbag."

"We've had this conversation before."

"Did you know you're almost out of gas?" Chris's eyes were on the dashboard.

"Don't worry about it."

"But you're on *E*."

Gavin sighed. "It's been on *E* for the last four months. Like I said, don't worry about it."

Chris giggled like a schoolboy, the way he always did when something didn't work with the Tiger. "Who's worried? The best thing about this car is if we run out of gas, I can push from where I sit without opening the door. Look, I can touch the road with my fingernails."

"Then file your nails, stop your whining, and tell me about the soldier guy before I unload my gun into you."

"Okay, okay. For starters, the soldier guy has a name."

Gavin's brow rose. "Really, other than 'Soldier Guy'?"

"According to the Feds, that pack of Camels you found had the prints of a Walter Hess."

"Those cigarettes will get you one way or another," Gavin said, coming to a light, six cars back in a crowded intersection with multiple arrows for turning traffic.

"Yup, he should have heeded the surgeon general's warning."

Nervously, Gavin looked at his watch. The WWX show would start any minute. He thought about putting his police light on the dashboard, but he knew Chris would remove it. How was it possible that Chris was in the car with him?

"How did you get the Feds to give that information up so fast?"

"I told them you had a lead on a cult he belongs to."

"So you lied to the FBI?"

"Well, you told me you were going to see that Reverend Buck character and thought he might possibly know about some white supremacist religious group."

"So basically . . . you lied to the FBI."

"Basically."

"And I guess the bad news is that we don't have a clue as to where he is."

"Correct."

"What else?"

"Lots. The Feds provided us with a decent profile of this guy."

"You're kidding. Are we both talking about the same FBI? This really isn't like them. Why are they being so generous?" Gavin beeped his horn the second the light turned green.

"One word: terrorism. They've gotten a little shell-shocked over so much blame the last couple of years. They actually *have* regrouped their antiterrorism efforts. We just haven't seen it until now because we haven't needed to deal with them lately on this level." Chris raised his voice again, leaning toward Gavin to be heard over the surrounding elements. "Consequently, they're being more cooperative in the hope others will be more cooperative."

Gavin nodded, shifted into third, and weaved wherever he could. "How novel. That's what they've been saying all along, but didn't believe it before."

"Personally, I think they're just finally willing to give up a little of the glory to disperse more potential blame. By the way, did you ever hear of road rage? Isn't it weird the way everyone around you seems to always have it?"

"Shut up and tell me about Hess."

"He's a local . . . from Long Island, that is. Out east."

"Where out east?"

"Tauppauge."

"Tauppauge?"

"Yeah, something like that. I'm pretty sure that's what the report said."

"I've never heard of it."

"Small town. Never been there."

"How do you spell it? You're probably pronouncing it wrong."

"Pronouncing it wrong?" Chris laughed. "Give me a break. How does anyone really know anymore how any of those Long Island Indian tribes pronounced the names of these towns? Every other town on this island has a name we're pronouncing wrong and have no freakin' idea of the meaning. Some Indian told the first white settler of Tauppauge that the name meant 'sun setting over beautiful lake' when it actually meant 'moron lives here.'"

Gavin took his eyes off the road to give Chris a blank stare. "Do you think that's why Hess went after the *Sachacus*?"

"You scoff."

Gavin rolled his eyes.

"Anyway, we caught a break with the fingerprints. Hess had applied for a pistol permit and was denied because he failed to report an arrest from ten and a half years ago. Even though the judge reduced the crime to loitering, the FBI wound up with his file and . . . prints."

"What did he do?"

"Stole a piece of cheese from a supermarket. Claimed he was hungry and broke."

"A piece of freaking cheese because he was hungry? No other priors? That's it?"

"As far as arrests go. But there's more. The FBI also provided us with a few photos of him," Chris said, then began opening a manila envelope.

Gavin nodded, but he was having a hard time concentrating on anything Chris was saying. His mind kept drifting to Krogan and the message he was going to send him.

"This is him," Chris said, holding a photo in front of Gavin's radio. "The picture taken at the arrest."

"*This* is Soldier?" Gavin said, taking brief glances at the photo.

"Adorable, isn't he?"

"He looks about ten."

"Eighteen."

"They fingerprinted and photographed him for shoplifting a piece of cheese?"

"Must have been a slow night. When his name popped up, the Feds were quick to find this photo," Chris said, replacing the first photo with a second.

"Does the media have a copy of these?"

"Not yet, but they will tomorrow morning."

"Why wait?"

"I just got these before I saw you. We want our guys to know who this guy is before anyone else. And this will give us time to double- and triple-check our information. If the public gets hold of him before we do, they'll drag him to the nearest tree."

"Works for me," Gavin said under his breath.

"And if he's the wrong guy . . . or has a partner we don't know about?"

"Easy, Big Dog. Just kidding," Gavin said as he glanced long enough at the photo to see a medium-built, boyish-looking blond man smiling while talking to another man in a crowded place. He frowned. "Where was this photo taken? He doesn't seem to be aware that anyone was taking his picture."

"He wasn't. The Feds took this photo at a private gun show in Georgia last year."

"Private gun show?"

"Invitation only. A religious group calling themselves 'The Chosen.' Very secretive. Very dangerous. Growing. The gun show and everyone involved vanished overnight. They hope Hess might lead them to their new hideaway."

"What have The Chosen done to draw FBI crosshairs?"

"They're suspected of numerous bank robberies to fund their operations."

"I'd like to hear how they rationalize that to their followers."

"Simple. The government is the enemy of God and run by Jews who rejected and crucified the true Messiah. Their recruits usually have histories of being short on cash, out of patience, and looking for someone to blame for it all. All they need is a leader to deliver them as they get ready for the end of the world."

"With automatic weapons, no doubt."

"That, too. So they don't pay any taxes, rob from federal institutions, and pocket any government grants they can get their hands on."

"Sounds like the Mob," Gavin said, then crushed the gas pedal to get through a yellow light. He wasn't even close. A horn blared.

Chris paused to sigh, then continued. "Worse. They believe what they're doing is right; their plans are God's plans, which makes them braver. The Feds have been trying to infiltrate the group but have mysteriously lost a couple of agents in the effort. What they do know is that some of the group's leaders, called 'missionaries,' have been 'sent' out to start churches around the country, slowly influencing the congregants into their way of thinking. Occasionally, a special congregant will be selected and funneled back to the mother group to become one of 'The Chosen.'"

"Where does Hess fit in?"

"The Feds aren't sure. He isn't a missionary, but his pastor might be. The best way to infiltrate the core group would be as a selected congregant. They don't know yet who his pastor is, but the prospect of finding him has them very excited. They smell blood."

"Excited? A train gets wrecked, a ferry sinks, and they're excited because Hess might lead them to a missionary?"

"Hey, I said they were being more cooperative, I didn't say the leopard changed its spots. And by the way, with Hess having this type of background, everyone's more than a little concerned about the Fourth of July. It's just two days away."

Gavin nodded. "Any leads on his whereabouts?"

"He moved out of an apartment over a garage about a month ago. Disappeared. According to his landlady, he was a bit of a recluse. Paid his rent on time with cash and was quiet. The perfect tenant."

"Yeah, perfect. Where did he work?"

"Here and there. He was a handyman. Did odd jobs for cash."

"He's handy, all right. Relatives?"

"Parents are divorced and gone. One in Florida, the other in Massachusetts."

"Telephone?"

"He had one and we're working on his calls in and out. So far nothing, but we've just started. He also had a computer. We're checking his IP for e-mails and websites. Can't wait to see what turns up there."

"Sounds like we got a lot of work ahead between handyman clients, phone calls, friends, neighbors, suppliers, and e-mails."

"Yes, which brings up the question."

"What question?"

"How much time are we going to spend at the coliseum watching a freakin' WWX show?"

"Not long. Did we get any prints from the cement truck?"

"Yes, but they all belonged to the passenger. The driver apparently wore gloves. Which, by the way, was not the case with Krogan. His prints were everywhere, remember?"

"I remember. But that was before he was a celebrity."

Chris paused.

Gavin felt his partner's gaze and was waiting for a lecture he had no believable comeback for. He thought about how Buck must have felt two years ago when Gavin first questioned him about spiritual beliefs that were impossible to prove, yet had to be true. "What about forensics?" Gavin went on. "Any hair? Blood? There had to be blood."

"Well, of course. Not as much as you might think, but enough to make a match. But we're saving it for a suspect. A real one."

"We've got one."

"We can't just get a blood sample or pluck the hair out of someone just because they changed their stage name. And if you try getting it yourself . . . the old-fashioned way, I'll be locking you up."

"If you can guarantee me Amy will be in the same cell, I'll take it. At least we'll have a roof over our heads, and Krogan will be on the other side of the bars."

"Let me get this straight. You think this Jackhammer Hoban wrestler not only changed his name to Krogan but became so enamored with the real Krogan, the one *in jail,* that he drove through your house with a cement truck because you're the one who arrested Dengler?"

Gavin took another moment to think. "Not exactly, but you're getting closer." Maybe he was going about this all wrong. He was worried about what Chris would think if he just came out and told him Krogan was a demon. What if he allowed Chris to be the detective and get closer himself to what would have to be the inevitable conclusion?

"Explain."

"The lobster-claw roach clip presents a major problem with Jackhammer Hoban. He wouldn't have had any way of ever knowing about it. The claw was never made public and wasn't needed at trial. There's no way anyone but you, me, Amy, Buck, and Krogan would have known to leave it in the ashtray."

"So then I'm also a suspect," Chris said.

Gavin gave him a glance. "You're always my first suspect. But I ruled you out early."

"Oh . . . thank you. I guess our partnership counts for something."

"Actually, no. I figured you wouldn't have driven over Amy's new minivan when you had the chance to crush this car instead."

"This is true. But then if you don't think Hoban drove through your house, why are we going to the coliseum?"

"I think he's . . . connected."

"How?"

Gavin exhaled. "Look, all I can tell you right now is that there's more to this Krogan thing than Karl Dengler."

"You sound certain of that."

"Fairly certain, but I'll know for sure very soon. And hopefully so will you."

"At the WWX?"

"Yes."

"What are you going to do, ask him?"

"I won't have to ask."

Chris sighed. "You've lost your mind and I'm along for the ride. Meanwhile, the guy we're supposed to be chasing is probably preparing for his next casualty."

"Sorry, Chris, but I can only be in one place at a time and at the moment, Krogan tops my list."

"You know," Chris said. "I've known you for a long time, and in that time I've known you to be stubborn, brave, persistent, loyal, obstinate, spontaneous, inflexible, a lousy driver, mulish, a decent detective—at times—pigheaded, a below-average carpenter—"

"Okay, enough, or I'll make you walk," Gavin said, and then looked Chris dead in the eye. "And you know I'll do it."

"Did I say 'stubborn'?"

"You said all you're going to say."

"Sorry, Gav. I know you're under a lot of stress, but I've never seen you irrational . . . or at least not *this* irrational. You know full well that Krogan is locked up pushin' life without parole. I admit, the lobster claw and the WWX guy naming himself Krogan is weird. But not as weird as him coming after you. Makes no sense. Very irrational. Not you."

"Okay, you've made your point."

"That wasn't my point," Chris said soberly.

Gavin rolled his eyes. "There's more?"

"My point is . . . you're lying to me."

"Lying? What did I say that was a lie?"

"It's what you didn't say, Gav. You can't fool me. I know you too well—not that you're that tough to figure. This WWX guy doesn't know you from Adam, and you know it. So what's the deal here? I don't like walking into places when I don't know why I'm there."

Gavin took a moment to think. Chris was right. Being his partner and not knowing the truth could be very dangerous. But this wasn't something he could just come out and say. Chris wouldn't believe it and would only cause more trouble by getting in the way. But then again, there comes a time when there's so much trouble that more trouble doesn't mean anything. Chris had always been a voice of reason, and a little reason could go a long way right now. Maybe he was selling him short. Maybe he would understand. He could use someone to confide in, and Chris was always one he could trust.

"Chris," Gavin said as he drove into the Nassau Coliseum parking lot.

"I'm listening."

"There is more. But when I was first told what I'm going to tell you, I didn't believe him."

"Who?"

"Buck."

Chris smiled. "I knew he had something to do with this. You've been acting strange ever since you got his call."

Gavin nodded. "Yeah, well you were wrong when you said Jackhammer 'Krogan' Hoban doesn't know me from Adam. In fact, you couldn't have been more wrong."

"He *does* know you?"

Gavin nodded. "The truth is . . . he not only knows me, he probably knew Adam."

29

Krogan was hungry. He threw opened the door to the concession booth and looked past the startled faces to the hot-dog machine. None of the workers in their blue uniforms said a word as he made his way to the glistening wieners rolling under the hot lights. The fans waiting in line were enthralled. Krogan's name rippled outward from the counter like a tremor. Soon a crowd was clamoring, with children being propped on shoulders to see their hero . . . or villain.

"Where are the buns?" Krogan snarled, his eyes darting.

A young girl with a ponytail and blue cap pointed fretfully at a drawer under the stainless-steel rollers. "There."

Krogan snapped open the drawer, tore open a plastic bag, produced a white hot-dog roll, picked off a turning frankfurter, then ate it in two bites. "Mmmm," he said, oblivious to the staring crowd. He heard the fans yelling out his name, pleading for an autograph or at least his attention, but he was only interested in another hot dog on a bun . . . and then another and another.

"Hey, Tiger," said a familiar female voice from behind. "I've been looking all over for you."

Krogan turned. Tanya the Terrible. She had on more makeup than when he'd last seen her at her father's office and was dressed in her customary skin-tight black leathers and low-cut top. "I was hungry," Krogan said.

"I . . . can see that. It's great that you have a healthy appetite, but don't you think you should take it easy? You act like you've never had a hot dog before."

Krogan took a final bite and smiled. "Eighteen-seventy-one. Coney Island."

Tanya tilted her head like a confused dog. "Eighteen-seventy-one? Coney Island? What does that mean?"

"First hot dog on a milk roll."

Tanya raised her brow. "I didn't realize you were such a history buff. Or frankfurter, uh, expert. Anyway, you're late for makeup. You need to get down there pronto. You're on soon . . . and I really hope for everyone's sake you don't get sick," she said, looking at the ravaged frankfurter machine.

"I don't want makeup."

"Since when?"

Krogan ignored her question and strode away, out of the concession booth and into the main lobby. Fans parted before him like water around a boat. Tanya, also crowded by fans, asked people around for some of their makeup for Krogan. They willingly rummaged though purses and backpacks and handed her what they could as she hurried after him. "Okay, Tiger. I need you to slow down for a minute," she said. "You're about to go on national television and we need to make sure you're on the same page—I mean, that we're in sync with your, er . . . performance. Just give me one minute, in there," she said, motioning to a nearby men's room door. "And I promise to give you my undivided personal attention."

Krogan stopped. He looked at Tanya, taking her in. He then turned and went into the men's room with Tanya hurrying after him. As the door closed behind them the background music coming from the arena increased in both volume and intensity.

"Out," he ordered two men at the urinals, who quickly obeyed, their faces filled with surprise and confusion at the sight of the two celebrities.

Tanya produced the makeup she'd collected and began to organize it as she said, "The preliminary bouts will be over soon. Then you'll be introduced as——"

"Preliminaries?" Krogan growled.

"Of course, baby. We want to warm them up for you," Tanya said, reaching toward his face with a powder pad.

"There will be no preliminaries."

"Don't worry. It's just the two new guys, Fire and Mace Murdock. You're the main event."

"I am the *only* event." He scowled, pushing her hand away, then knocking a man down who'd entered the lavatory just as Krogan was exiting.

Krogan ignored the stir of the crowd as he walked down the dark aisle toward the lighted ring. He could hear Tanya calling from behind. He would deal with her later. The air was cloudy, pungent with the smell of the fireworks that should have introduced him rather than the two clowns in the ring. *Idiots!* As he neared the ring the buzz in the audience grew.

When he was about to climb into the ring, Tanya caught up to him and grabbed him by the arm.

"You can't go in there now. You need—I mean, don't you want to be properly introduced?"

Krogan paused as he heard his name being called out like a drum beat, instantly reminding him of ancient Athens. With each second the chant took on new voices, louder, louder. He looked at Tanya the Terrible and laughed at what he saw. Confusion in her face. Fear in her eyes. The emptiness of her soul. Pathetic human. She needed to be occupied, empowered, dominated, possessed . . . and then taken down like all the rest. "I am the only one who can properly introduce me," he said, then paused again to look deeply into her eyes. "Find me later and I will introduce you to some old friends. If you please them, they will be with you the rest of your life."

Krogan left Tanya unblinking and speechless as he climbed through the ropes. The two wrestlers, Fire and Mace Murdock, were locked up with each other in a corner, apparently unaware of his presence. Fire, who wore only red briefs, had long red hair flowing over his sculpted muscles, shiny from oil. Murdock sported a shaved head and black beard. He was huge but fat. Krogan heard the announcer enthusiastically speaking to the crowd, heard him mention his name along with the two clowns. The announcer was a fool.

One of the wrestlers, Fire, threw Murdock backward in Krogan's direction. Krogan stuck out his foot and tripped the corpulent wrestler. There was a thud and a groan, but Krogan had already turned to face Fire, who was looking very confused.

It was time for their routine to come to an end.

"Your pain will introduce me," Krogan said in a deep whisper. "All will bow down."

Fire looked angry. "What's up with this? You don't just come in here and mess with us. I don't care who you are."

"You will."

Fire paused, then laughed. "Hey, fine, you want to go with me . . . here . . . now . . . no rules? We can do that. All that means is I get the million before someone else does."

Krogan didn't have to glance over his shoulder to know that Mace Murdock was on his feet and about to charge. Fire had his hands up, moving cautiously forward. He lunged, leading with a right fist aimed at Krogan's head. Cat quick, Krogan caught Fire's fist with his left hand and in one motion turned the fighter's palm inward and pressed hard against the back of Fire's hand with his thumb, bending the wrist acutely so it appeared as though Fire was pointing his fingers at his own face. The redheaded wrestler's scream silenced the crowd as he dropped to his knees, Krogan controlling his position effortlessly with one hand.

Mace Murdock's right fist was about to crush Krogan's right ear when he found that Krogan had likewise caught his punch with his free hand.

"Aggghhhhh," Murdock shrieked in the highest pitch to leave his mouth since his circumcision. In an instant he was on his knees alongside Fire, the two wrestlers agonized, unable to lift their heads.

Krogan jerked his chin toward the shocked audience. "All will bow," he roared. "All will bow down to Krogan. *Shadahd!*" He then applied thumb pressure on the back of the wrestlers' hands until he heard two snaps. The wrestlers screamed and rolled on the mat. Krogan lifted his arms in the air. A moment later, the four corner posts of the ring ignited like giant Roman candles, shooting colorful sparks high into the air, a dazzling effect the WWX had originally planned on for Krogan's introduction. The audience exploded in cheers and boos, just as the producers had hoped they would.

"Ladies and gentlemen." The crazed announcer excitedly proclaimed the contest for a million dollars that had been megahyped through television, radio, newspapers, posters, and flying banners along the South Shore beaches. A giant digital clock was lowered from the ceiling above the ring to display the three-minute countdown.

Krogan stood motionless in the center of the ring staring out at the audience. He knew many of his comrades were looking on. Outside the boundaries of the ring a line of contestants had formed. The WWX had arranged things so that street contestants would split time with their own wrestlers in alternating bouts. Anyone willing to sign an injury waiver was eligible to try the three minutes for one million. Since Krogan had entered the ring early with Fire and Murdock, the organizers decided the next competition would be against a walk-on.

Two WWX girls escorted the first challenger, a hooded man in a black Ninja suit, up a steel staircase to the ropes, then held them open for him to climb through. The announcer introduced the man as Johnny "The Phantom" Bromante. Some of the crowd began chanting, "Krogan, Krogan, Krogan."

At the sound of the bell, The Phantom quickly ran to a corner and climbed up until he was standing on the top rope, his feet wide apart. "Before you beat me you first have to catch me, Big Man."

Krogan looked up at the man and was about to move toward him when his attention was distracted by a flying object that broke through the outer darkness of the audience into the strong show lights above the ring. A Frisbee! The toy flew a few feet over his head, then landed behind him near the ropes. He was about to turn back to his opponent when he noticed an image taped to the Frisbee with some words written under it.

"Krogan. Krogan, Krogan."

The chants became louder and louder, drawing his attention back again to the man on the ropes. Suddenly Krogan was hit in the chest by another Frisbee, which fell at his feet, twirled on end, and finally came to rest faceup. His eyes widened as he clearly saw the picture of a Galapagos Island tortoise and "*Shadahd* This!" written underneath. His gaze snapped up, looking in the direction the Frisbee had come from. How dare he! *How dare he!* Who is this human that he should taunt? Mock! *Threaten!*

"Two minutes remaining," called the announcer.

Krogan angrily picked up the Frisbee and threw it back into the darkness and yelled, "Down, Pierce! I'm going to take you down—Uuuhhhh."

Johnny "The Phantom" Bromante had taken advantage of Krogan's lack of focus and had jumped off the ropes and onto his shoulders. The surprise lunge took Krogan off his feet and landed him hard, face first, onto the mat. The Phantom, with his arm around Krogan's neck, pulled with all his might.

Krogan, his neck stretching back, saw Tanya at ringside. She was frowning, the first Frisbee in her hand. He could think of nothing he wanted more in all the world than to have Pierce in his hands. He hadn't felt this kind of humiliation and rage since, since . . . since he'd first found himself in the tortoise over two years ago. And that was also Pierce's fault.

Tanya's face was becoming hazy. His host wasn't breathing and hadn't been for some time, with The Phantom's tightening choke-hold. He was losing consciousness. He quickly thought about death and a new host, but then just as quickly thought of the further humiliation of having been defeated by Pierce and the man on his back in the black Ninja pajamas in front of both the earthly and spiritual arenas watching him. *Never!*

"Thirty seconds," called the announcer.

Krogan rose to his feet with The Phantom pulling tightly on his neck. He grabbed the man's arm with both hands, pulled it away from his neck, then threw the shocked challenger over his shoulder and hard to the mat. The Phantom immediately tried to scramble away on his hands and knees, but Krogan grabbed his ankle, then swung him around once before throwing him out of the ring, where he crashed onto the television commentators' table some twenty feet away with five seconds left on the clock.

Krogan paced the mat, looking in the direction he thought Pierce might be as medics rushed to Johnny "The Phantom" Bromante's unconscious body.

30

Gavin flashed his badge, and the two coliseum security guards with flashlights looked at each other, shrugged their shoulders, and walked away.

"You throw any more of those Frisbees of yours and I'll be the one flashing the badge. And it will be at *you* while I'm reading you your rights."

"Relax, Chris. I got my point across."

"Apparently, though I'm not exactly sure what that point was, except to infuriate the Krogan clone and almost get that Phantom Johnny guy killed."

"I needed to prove to myself that Jackhammer Hoban is harboring the same Krogan entity that Karl Dengler was harboring two and a half years ago and to let him know that I know and that his days are numbered . . . again."

Chris paused. "You can't be serious. This is a joke, right? Entity? You mean you think there was some kind of spirit inside Dengler, and it left him and is now in this guy?" Chris motioned toward the ring.

"You heard me right."

"This is what Buck told you?"

Gavin was about to answer but then winced along with Chris at what Krogan had just done to another wrestler. The fans' response was passionate, albeit mixed. A fight broke out just three rows away.

Chris started to get up, but the security guards were on it immediately.

Chris settled back down in his seat, keeping an eye on the source of the disturbance. "Can we leave now?" he said. "You did what you came for . . . unless you plan on getting in line to fight him while you're at it. You can use a million bucks right about now."

"It's not the money I want. It's him."

"I was only kidding. Forgive me for forgetting who I was with. Come on, let's get out of here."

"Wait," Gavin said, rearranging himself in his seat. "Remember Karianne Stordal?"

"The airline stewardess who was a passenger in the car when the *real* Krogan crashed into and killed John Garrity and put me in the hospital? Of course I remember. How could I ever forget?"

"Okay, remember when we hypnotized her because she couldn't remember the driver?"

"Yeah, and then she remembered his name was Krogan."

"Right. And what happened when she was asked to recall the first time she met Krogan?"

Chris rolled his eyes. "She started speaking Hebrew. Something tells me we're getting back to the entity thing."

"Ancient Hebrew."

"Okay, ancient Hebrew. Dr. Katz said she was probably experiencing a past-life event."

"And you believe that?"

"My mother does. And so does Pat. They say that kind of stuff happens all the time. Hey, half the world believes in reincarnation. Tell you what: if it's true, I wouldn't want to know what you're coming back as. Probably a bulldog. Here, Gavin! Here, boy!"

"Are you finished?"

"Sorry."

Heavy-metal music blared with more fireworks as the next challenger was introduced. All the fighters were beginning to look the same to Gavin, as were all the results of fighting Krogan. The cloud of smoke drifted from the ring area, out over the seats, and hung there like a mist. After the music stopped and the bout started, Gavin focused back on his conversation with his partner.

"So what if it wasn't reincarnation, Chris? I mean, we can't remember conversations we had last week, or even yesterday, most of the time. How can someone remember what someone else said to them in another lifetime . . . many other lifetimes . . . thousands and thousands of years ago? Human memories can't do that."

"I don't know, Gav. Maybe the soul remembers better than the brain."

"You're grabbing for straws. The past lives of Krogan and Karianne were meeting constantly through the centuries, and she remembered every one of them in perfect detail. How does reincarnation explain that?"

"If I remember correctly, Dr. Katz was pretty excited about them meeting in other lives. He said it was 'unprecedented.'"

"Yeah. You should talk to Katz now. I'm sure he's singing a different tune after Karianne kicked the stuffing out of him."

"Karianne did what? Why? How?"

"With her past life."

"What are you talking about?"

"You heard me. Karianne's past life—"

"The one that was speaking ancient Hebrew?" Chris said sarcastically.

"That one, yes. And the one that spoke French, Hun, Mongolian, Japanese, Norse, Roman, and who knows how many other languages."

"I don't know what you're talking about. I think you've completely lost your mind."

"Chris, what I'm trying to tell you is that it wasn't reincarnation, at least not human reincarnation. The past lives existed, yes. But they weren't Karianne's."

"So what's your answer? And I hope you didn't dance me around this crap without having an answer of your own."

"You bet I do."

"So what is it already? Say it!"

Gavin leaned close. "Demons," he said quietly, as if to soften the impact of his words. "All kinds of demons. Demons that like drunks. Fear demons, lazy demons, weak demons. And," Gavin went on, turning his gaze in the direction of the lighted ring, "very, very strong demons that want to get together and party with other demons and celebrate the end of the party with a wild crash for no better reason than because they hate God's creation and want to see it taken down piece by piece. And some carry a grudge from one life to the next, because to them . . . it's all one lifetime. Theirs."

Chris was silent. The kind of silent that made Gavin think his partner was cautiously afraid he actually *had* lost his mind. Together they had arrested countless EDPs whose alibis sounded frighteningly similar to Gavin's explanation.

"Don't do this to me, Chris," Gavin said angrily.

"Do what?"

"Act like I need to be handled carefully, like a cracked egg filled with nitro."

"Is that how you see yourself?"

"I swear, Chris, if you don't start arguing with me soon, I do to you what Krogan did to Johnny 'The Phantom' Bromante."

Chris frowned. "This is no joke. The demons, I mean. You really believe this?"

"You missed a lot while you were in the hospital, Chris."

"Well, how come you didn't fill me in?"

Gavin sighed, then went for it. "Because the tortoise wasn't supposed to die, and Krogan wasn't supposed to get free and come after us."

Chris looked at him blankly. "You mean the tortoise on the Frisbee?"

"No. That was just a picture. I wanted to see what kind of response I would get. Anyone else wouldn't have cared, but as you noticed . . ."

"Maybe you'd better start at the beginning."

"Gladly, but not here. I need something to eat," Gavin said, his body reminding him the only thing he'd eaten all day was a salted pretzel from the zoo and a lone chocolate-chip cookie he'd found at the coffee machine back at Homicide.

"I'm for that. My treat. I'll call Pat and tell her we're on our way."

"Sounds good, but I need to stop at my house first to try to find some clothes."

"You can wear mine," Chris said with a smile, getting up to leave.

"Yeah, right," Gavin said as he followed, but then stopped in the aisle and turned for a last look at Krogan. The monster had just started another match. Could anyone in the ring with him possibly know what he or she was up against? Gavin thought again about Amy in the hospital with the baby clinging to life inside her. He thought about the demolished house. He thought about the dead decorator and cement truck driver. Buck's advice to take Krogan on himself seemed ridiculous in light of what was happening in the ring before him. Even if he killed the man, the demon would be back. He needed help. What could he possibly do? Nothing. Almost nothing. He opened the plastic bag he'd brought with him. He still had another two Frisbees. He threw both of them. One went wide, but the other landed in the ring. Krogan picked it up and yelled something, but without a microphone it was impossible to hear him over the crowd.

"I'll be back," Gavin said, quietly, weakly.

31

Walter Hess put down his fork, leaned over the small tabletop, stretched and adjusted the rabbit-ear antennas on his boat's little television until the picture cleared. For some reason channel seven had the best news and worst reception. For the second day in a row he found himself the center of attention on every major network news channel. Such recognition. The time would come when he would speak up and give God the credit He was due. In the meantime, he should be humble. He looked around the cabin. Small cabin, small boat, old but reliable engine, hand tools, small bunk, one blanket, a pillow that doubled as a life preserver, an old television, and modest food. Humility was key to the success he was having. His simplicity had made him invisible to the world that was hunting him. He considered how Jesus had walked through angry crowds without being touched and then disappeared. *God resists the proud but gives grace to the humble,* he thought. Why else would they have the whole world talking about him and looking for him without a clue as to who he was, where he was, or what he would do next?

"Thank you, Jesus," he said, then plopped back into his seat, picked up a slice of white bread, and gathered another forkful of baked beans and freshly caught flounder. A few moments later the plate was clean and he considered himself satisfied physically, mentally, and, more important, spiritually. He looked at his watch. High tide in about two hours. It would be dark. Good. He needed to get some fresh supplies and could only do it when the tide was high and the sky was dark enough for him to go unnoticed.

Hess was about to get up when Senator Bruce Sweeney's face filled the screen. As the camera panned back, he could see the senator was on a rescue boat with an orange life preserver donned over a white button-down shirt. His hair was neatly combed, and several other official-type personnel surrounded him. The capsized *Sachacus* was in the background. A channel seven microphone was just visible. Hess reached over the table to turn the volume up, wondering if the rescue boat was even in the water.

". . . and as I said yesterday at a similar disaster, the focus needs to be on tighter security. If it takes getting people out from behind their comfortable little desks in their comfortable little offices to roll up their sleeves and help the cause, then that's what we need to do. If I can do it . . . we all can do it. We all need to join in and get dirty."

"Then your rally against terror is still scheduled for the Fourth?"

Sweeney nodded. "Whether it's the Fourth of July or the fourth of March, the message to stay focused and attack the problems— terror being one of them—is what I'm giving my life to. The date doesn't matter, but if we expect to keep our freedom and our ability to celebrate it freely, then we need to get to work and follow a leadership that is willing to work."

Hess turned down the volume and went over to his bunk. He lifted the thin mattress, opened the storage hatch under it, and pulled out an aluminum gun case. He unlatched the case and opened it. The gun inside was a sharp contrast to the rest of the cabin's modest decor. A 50 BMG Barrett rifle. Model 99. Single shot. He would have preferred a semiautomatic but couldn't afford it. The single shot alone had cost him over three grand.

He feathered his fingers along the cold, olive-green metal stock in proud admiration. Just over fifty inches in overall length. His gaze moved to the fifty-caliber rounds in their clear plastic case. Seven-hundred-fifty-grain bullets. Seven times the size of his hunting rifle's ammo.

Hess carefully took the premier sniper rifle out of its case, shouldered it, and pointed it toward the TV. At twenty-five pounds, the rifle was better than three and a half times the weight of his hunting rifle. He flipped up the protective lids on the Leupold 10X scope and peered in, hoping to put Sweeney in the crosshairs. Too close . . . way too close for a rifle capable of exploding the pompous senator's head from a mile away.

"God resists the proud," Hess said as he brought the fluted muzzle around to the hinged-open front window of the cabin. The boat was completely still, anchored in glass-calm waters near the Roslyn Marsh. He rested the bipod feet on the window ledge and took a quick peek through the scope. Much better. About three-quarters of a mile away was a peninsula known to the locals as Bar Beach. He took his baseball cap off and slid his eye behind the ten-power scope and focused. The bold optics snatched every bit of light from the air. In the vast parking lot a second shift of workers was putting the finishing touches on the rally platform the senator would be speaking from. Hess smiled at the detail he could make out from such a distance. He focused on the tattooed Asian letters, or whatever they were, on the arm of one worker who was operating a drill. He imagined for a moment what he would see in the scope if he took the shot.

"And gives grace to the humble."

Hess squatted down as he continued to look through the scope. The crosshairs lifted over the heads of the workers and into the trees beyond the parking lot and higher, higher, higher, until the high-tension wires from the power plant on the other side of the harbor came into view. He followed one of the wires to the right until he came to a ceramic insulator that kept the two-hundred-thousand-volt current passing through the bare cable wire from electrifying the giant steel stanchions. He set the crosshair in the middle of the large ceramic insulator. *The weakest link,* he thought. He now imagined what would happen to the insulator if he took the shot. In his mind's eye he saw the power cable fall on the platform and then sweep across a parking lot full of Sweeney supporters.

Hess smiled contentedly and recited a verse from his morning reading: "Then the Lord spoke to Moses saying, 'Take full vengeance on the sons of Israel and on the Midianites. Afterward you will be gathered to your people.'"

Hess carefully returned his prized weapon to its cushioned case and snuggled it back into the hatch under his bunk. He then shut off the television, peeked through his cabin windows to make sure there were no surprise visitors, and went out onto the aft deck. He looked at his watch again. The water was probably high enough, but the sun hadn't set yet. He would wait. No sense in getting sloppy or impatient. For the next two days he had to be more careful than ever to measure his movements. He was at a new level now. Soon his immediate mission would be over, and he could return to The Chosen with news that would undoubtedly gain him a secure position within the trusted leadership. But this was not a time to dwell on dreams, even if they had been prophesied. God would take care of his future as long as he continued to be true to his calling.

Two hours later Hess idled into the shallow creek that ran under the Roslyn Viaduct. Hess was alerted to a small orange light to his left. A cigarette. Closer, the moonlight revealed an old black man sitting on a wooden bulkhead with a line in the water. He appeared to be alone and gave Hess a nod as he passed. Hess returned the nod but not the sentiment. How easy it would be for him to sneak around and slit the man's old, black throat. Who knew how many more the man was still capable of breeding.

But, no. He was called to bigger things now. Such spontaneous acts were to be forever in his past. Besides, the old man would be looked for and the search could impede the greater plan.

A couple hundred feet later he was directly under the bridge and tying the boat up to an old, wooden ladder. His storage container was a hundred or so yards away. He climbed up the ladder and turned to see which way the boat would drift. It stayed pointed in the direction he'd come from, and then backed away from the ladder until the rope was taut. The tide was already on the way out. He couldn't waste any time. He hurried along a narrow path through weeds and dirt mounds until he came to commercial equipment parked by various contractors. The way was dark, but he'd become very accustomed to the route over the last few months. Finally he arrived at his forty-foot shipping container, one among many under the long viaduct.

Around the rear of the container he found his hidden key under a flat rock, then hurried back around and opened both large padlocks. The hinges were well oiled and the door opened quickly and quietly. He took a quick look around, then entered and turned on a small battery-powered fluorescent lamp offering just enough light for him to see halfway into the container. The first and most important item was a fresh scuba tank to replace the empty one he'd used up working on the *Sachacus*. He found the spare where he'd left it, squatted down, and lifted the black tank onto his shoulder. Hopefully he wouldn't need it.

He started out the door and was startled by a figure walking by just twenty feet away. The figure was startled also.

"You scared me," said the figure. It was the old man with a bucket and a pole in his hands.

"Sorry," Hess said, setting down the scuba tank. He suddenly realized the thoughts he'd had before about killing the old man were not his own. God was warning him and was now granting the opportunity plainly and logically. The chance of the old man reporting him to someone and leading them back here was too much to risk. He thanked God once again for giving grace to the humble. "Did you catch anything?"

"Bunch of eels. Couple of 'em pretty big."

"Really," Hess said, feeling for the knife strapped to his side. He found it, slipped his fingers through the cold metal grip. "I guess your family's going to have eels for dinner tomorrow. Sounds tasty."

"You like eels?"

"Who doesn't?" Hess said.

The old man chuckled. "Well, take one, then."

"But your family."

"They're gone . . . been gone," the old man said. "I'm just gonna freeze the big ones. Use the little ones for striper bait tomorrow."

"Tomorrow, huh?"

"Yup. Stripers love eels. And there ain't nothin' better tastin' than striped bass in these or any other waters. Some big ones always sittin' in the reeds just waitin' for an eel to happen by. My eel, heh, heh."

Hess moved closer. "Well, sure then. Let me have a look at them."

32

Gavin sat across from Chris at the Grellas' kitchen table with a phone to his ear, barefoot in a pair of Chris's pajamas and a bathrobe. Showered and shaven. Most of his clothes had been destroyed in the crash, but a few remained. Fortunately, Amy had been so preoccupied with the decorating, and Gavin with the construction and train derailment, that clothes had piled up in their basement laundry room—enough to fill three loads in Chris's machine.

"Hello."

"Hi. This is Detective P—"

"You've reached Quinn Ranch. There's no one available to answer your call right now, but if you leave your name, number, and reason for your call at the tone, either Mary, Michele, or Jackie will get back to you as soon as possible." *Beep.*

"Hi, Mary. This is Detective Pierce. I hope all is going well for you up there. I was calling to see how Samantha was and to give you a new phone number to call me at in an emergency." Gavin left Chris's house number and hung up.

"Guests first," Pat said as she placed a healthy plate of steak and potatoes in front of him with an ear of fresh-picked corn on the side. Gavin knew he was hungry, but he hadn't known how hungry until now. He dug right in.

Chris wasted no time, either. He sliced through a tender piece of red meat, stabbed it with his fork, and then paused to display it proudly. "Barbequed skirt steak, medium rare . . . my favorite cut."

"Mmm," Gavin agreed, his mouth full, chewing passionately. He paused to take a gulp from a tall glass of iced tea. "A roll?" Pat asked, extending a plate of freshly baked dinner rolls. Somehow, everything smelled so intensely good.

"Mmm," said Gavin and Chris simultaneously, each taking one.

"Well, I hope you two gentlemen will excuse me. I'm going to bed," Pat said.

" 'Night, hon."

" 'Night, Pat. And thanks," Gavin said, buttering a steamy hot roll.

Chris watched Pat go up the stairs, and then pointed his knife in Gavin's direction as if it were his finger, paused to swallow, and said, "So when did you first become convinced that Buck was right and Krogan was actually a demon?"

Gavin took a wash of tea to clear his mouth before speaking. "There wasn't any one instance. More like mounting evidence. I guess I first started to consider Buck's explanation when Karianne attacked. There she was, all five and a half feet of her, a hundred and ten soaking wet, tossing us grown men around the room like rag dolls."

"I didn't hear about this."

"No . . . you weren't about to. She would have killed us for sure if I hadn't managed to stab her in the leg with Katz's tranquilizer."

"Why did she attack?"

"Well, according to Buck, it wasn't really her attacking, but some demon inside her named Sabah. Katz had her hypnotized, and I called the demon by name. The next thing I knew, Karianne was off the couch and we were looking to save our lives."

"How did he know this demon's name?"

"That's his business. Or was. These deliverance ministers tend to run across the same demons from time to time."

"Why's that?"

"I don't know." Gavin shrugged. "I guess because we're all stuck on the same planet and there's a finite number of them. Anyway, he had told me not to mention the demon's name without him around. I thought it was all nonsense, like you probably do right now, but on the one percent chance there could be something to it . . ."

"You did exactly what you were told not to do."

"Wouldn't you have?"

Chris didn't answer.

"Well, the experience left me with more than a hunch that there was more to what he was saying than met the eye. And apparently you need to have a working knowledge and faith to speak to demons if you want to survive the conversation."

"Does this sound a little weird to you?"

"It is weird," Gavin admitted.

"You don't have to tell me, Gav. I know it's weird. I just wanted to know if you think so," Chris said, then pointed his knife in the direction of Gavin's plate. "Want some more?"

"Uh, no. This was great, but I usually have strange dreams when I eat too much too late, and the way conscious life has been going lately, I don't want to give my nightmares any more fuel than they already have."

"Refill on the tea?"

"Sure."

Chris topped off their glasses, then led Gavin outside to the backyard patio, where Gavin flopped into a cushioned lounge chair. Chris took a chair next to him at the table and lit a large citronella candle in a glass vase. Behind Chris, hanging from the limb of a tree, a blue light was zapping bugs. The sky was clear; no moon, but the stars were bright enough to beg off the need for any additional light. Behind Gavin a built-in pool was gurgling.

"So what else, Gav?" Chris asked.

"Huh?"

"You said there were a few things that convinced you, and as of yet, I'm not convinced that a little girl throwing around adult men, even guys the size of Katz and his interpreter . . . what was his name?"

"Steinman."

"Right, Steinman. Just because she was throwing you guys around doesn't mean she was possessed by demons."

"You had to be there."

"Maybe, but I wasn't. And women have been known to do amazing things under the right set of circumstances, like lifting trucks off their children. And you said yourself she was under hypnosis."

"Well, Karianne got my attention. But that wound up being the warm-up for what I saw with Krogan himself at Ellis Island. He was about to bury a rock into my forehead when Buck showed up. You should have seen the look on his face when he saw Buck. I'll never forget it. It didn't last long, but for a moment, there was no denying that Krogan was afraid."

"So what did little old Buck do?"

"He ordered him to cease."

"Cease?"

"Yeah, that's what he said. Cease. After he said cease, Krogan couldn't move his arm. He was like a statue. The rock fell out of his hand and I got out from underneath him as fast as I could."

"And then what?"

"That's when Buck opened the chest and pulled out Jeremy."

"Jeremy?"

"The tortoise."

Even in the dark Gavin could see Chris roll his eyes. "I know, I know. Believe me, when I saw that the secret weapon Buck was tot-ing around was a tortoise, I thought we were all dead for sure. But that's when the next unexplainable thing happened."

"The tortoise beat up Krogan?" Chris mocked.

"I will make you pay for this someday. No, Buck commanded the demon inside Dengler to go into the tortoise. When he did that——" Gavin sat up on the lounger. "——I swear on my grandfather's grave . . . Dengler collapsed and the tortoise started freaking out."

"Freaking out?"

"Big-time. This young tortoise was as docile as a loaf of bread . . . and just like that, the thing's climbing out of its shell, eyes bulging, trying to get away, and when we run after and grab it, it's snapping at us like a rabid dog. Meanwhile, Karl Dengler, who just moments before was exhibiting hydraulic-type strength, is down and out like a beat-up sack of potatoes."

Chris shook his head. "I don't get it. What's with the tortoise and the magician? Why didn't you just shoot him?" He laughed. "Just imagine cops everywhere having to hand their guns in because the department decides they'd be better off with turtles."

Gavin almost smiled and probably would have if he weren't so beat. What he hated the most right now was that his response was going to make him sound like Buck. "You can't *kill* a demon, Chris. They're eternal. All you can do is imprison them. If I'd shot Den-gler, Krogan would have escaped and come back after me and Amy and Buck, like he's doing now."

"The demon can't just leave a human on its own?"

"Apparently not."

"Why not?"

"I don't know. Buck told me to read in the Bible where Jesus cast the demons into the pigs and they killed themselves to escape."

"Did you read it?"

"No."

Chris smiled, shaking his head. "So then what happened?"

"In short, Dengler goes to jail, the tortoise goes to the zoo, where Buck has a—quote—'brother in the Lord' taking care of it until less than a week ago, when both the caretaker and tortoise are killed in a car accident."

Chris pointed his glass at Gavin and said, "About the same time Jackhammer Hoban decides to call himself Krogan and your house gets run over."

"Not about . . . exactly the same time. And don't forget the lobster claw."

"God forbid."

Gavin stopped . . . stared at Chris in silence. "You don't believe any of this, do you?"

"I believe I'm going to say good-bye to iced tea and hello to Tylenol PM. If I have any dreams tonight, I don't want to remember them in the morning."

"I know the feeling. But come on, Chris. Don't you think what I've told you *proves* Hoban *is* Krogan? How else could a Frisbee with a tortoise on it get anyone that mad?"

"Proves? You're a cop, Gav. Do I have to remind you what proof is? Forget a judge and jury, just think about handing this kind of proof to the lieutenant."

"I'll settle for *you* at the moment."

"I'm not your problem. You don't think the Lieu is going to want some answers when Walter Hess makes his next move and you're out trying to arrest a WWX wrestler for sharing the nickname of a guy we already have in jail? You'll be fired, Gav . . . and I don't want to be enjoying my next meal feeding you in a straightjacket."

"But, Chris, how did Hoban know it was me? How did he know I was the one who threw the Frisbee at him? You heard him yell my name when he threw it back at the crowd," Gavin pleaded.

Chris paused for a moment, then waved his hands. "Ah, I don't even know if it *was* your name he yelled, with the screaming and all. You just heard what you wanted to hear. With all that noise, he could've been yelling something else. And why shouldn't he be mad? He's in there fightin' for his life and he gets hit with a Frisbee from the crowd. The thing could've said, 'I love you' and he would've been screamin'."

"The problem with you, Chris, is that you don't want to believe."

Chris pointed his glass again. "And the problem with you is you *do* believe. Take my advice and forget this demon crap before you get yourself—and probably me too—in deep trouble. And try to remember what the day after tomorrow is."

Gavin shrugged. "What's the day after tomorrow?"

"God help us," Chris said. "It's the Fourth of July."

"Right. I knew that."

Chris just shook his head.

Gavin had hoped with all his heart that he wasn't wasting his time . . . but he was. The day, the late dinner, the stress had all caught up to him and tomorrow was going to be another busy day. Chris was right about one thing, though: Walter Hess would be back, and if Gavin were found to be chasing a WWX wrestler when he could be stopping another terrorist attack, he'd lose his job . . . and probably for the price of a padded room.

33

Krogan lay facedown on a massage table while two "house ther-apists," with names that sounded more like those of pets than people, worked on his cable-tight muscles. Tight, but not from the fighting. He had been looking forward to this session even before the competition had begun, but now he could think only of the taunting he'd suffered from that sniveling insect. The same one who had taunted him in the zoo two years ago. The insolence! To battle his human form like the others would be one thing, but to know what lived behind the flesh and still mock was quite another . . . es-pecially in the arena of the unseen. He was surprised at himself for miscalculating. The destruction of his home and the finding of the lobster claw should have sent Pierce shivering into a hole of fear. Better this way. More pleasure from seeing him suffer.

There was a knock at the door. One of the therapists opened the door a crack to answer, then stepped back to let Tanya the Terrible enter. She was still in her painted-on black leathers and looked con-cerned about something. *Her problem,* he thought.

"Sorry to interrupt, but there are a couple of police officers outside asking about a Harley Davidson motorcycle that someone took for a test drive earlier today. Apparently, Hempstead Harley thinks that someone was you. I told them they had to be mistaken, but they insist—"

"I haven't finished the test. Tell them to leave," Krogan said, his face still in the face-hole of the table.

"You haven't finished the . . . but you can't just take . . . . Never mind," she finally said, then left. A few minutes later she returned, pulled up a chair and sat down next to his head. He could see her black shoes. Her feet looked uncomfortable, trapped, cramped, strangled . . . just like he had been in the tortoise . . . just like the insect detective would be soon.

"They're gone, but only because I spoke to the owner and told him the WWX would buy it."

Krogan didn't answer. He didn't care what she was saying. There was only one thing on his mind.

"So in the future, if there's anything . . . well, enough of that. What I really wanted to tell you was how great you did tonight. I mean, I have never . . . no one has ever seen anything like that . . . ever. You were amazing. But I was wondering about this Frisbee that landed in the ring. I mean, it seemed to get you upset and I couldn't figure . . ."

While she went on about the Frisbee and the fight, Krogan lifted his head and saw her holding one of them. In his time, Krogan had had to deal with many "men of God" who had thought themselves up to the task only to end up wishing they had never interfered. Even Jesus had mentioned to his precious band of misfits that it would take prayer and fasting to deal with him. But never had someone with so little faith and so little knowledge given him so much trouble. How was he supposed to enjoy this newly stolen life with such humiliation lurking in his shadows? No. The pleasure of business had to come before the pleasure of pleasure. He had to get to the root of the problem. He knew *what* the root was, but he didn't know *where* it was.

"Anyway, enough about this stupid thing," Tanya said, tossing the Frisbee away. "Let's talk about the Krogan phenomenon. When you first came up with the idea for . . ."

Krogan considered the problem at hand. There were basically three ways to find his prey—not the insect detective, but the root. The first was from the waterless place between worlds. From there he could communicate to his comrades at will, regardless of their location. But—and there was a big but—he wasn't *in* the waterless place, and his comrades wouldn't be anywhere near his prey because of those pesky angels. So for the moment, suicide wouldn't help.

The second way was similar. He could call out to others already in the waterless place. They could look for him and then show him his prey in a vision. But those angels again. Nothing was harder than dealing with angels in the waterless place. It was painful enough just being in that blasted, constant light, much less engaged in battle. That left him with his final option.

". . . ratings were the highest ever and every indication points to a . . ."

"Tell them to leave," Krogan ordered in a deep whisper.

Tanya paused, her face confused. "Them?" she asked, motioning toward the therapists.

"Now."

Tanya gave them a look, hitched her chin toward the door, and they disappeared. She looked at Krogan and smiled. "So you got me . . . alone. If you like, I can pick up where they left off."

Krogan returned the smile and then held her gaze without blinking. "Come closer," he said.

She did, slowly. He sat up, locked her eye to eye. She came closer, closer. He gently slid his right hand over and up her arm, across the top of her shoulder . . . and around her neck. Her smile vanished as her eyes grew wide with surprise as he tightened his grip. But while his grasp was strong enough to hold her rigidly in place, it was not tight enough to restrict the airflow.

"I require your assistance," Krogan whispered.

Tanya nodded slowly.

"Look into my eyes. See behind them."

She stared, unblinking.

"My words will be your thoughts."

Her eyes returned to their normal size, still transfixed on his, as he knew they would be . . . no longer having a choice . . . blank . . . available.

"You will diligently seek out and find someone for me, then tell me where he is. Do you understand?"

She repeated his instruction.

"You will speak of me to no one about this."

"I will do as you say."

"I will now say his name and you will remember it, but speak the name to no one."

". . . speak the name to no one."

"Reverend Jesse J. Buchanan," he said, wanting to spit as the words left his mouth.

She repeated the name perfectly.

"When you find him you will report back to me. Do not let him know who you are or what your instructions are."

"I will find him," Tanya said.

Krogan smiled, confident her subconscious was deeply branded with his instructions. "Yes, you will find him," he said assuredly. "If the insect could find him . . . so will you."

34

Gavin had skipped breakfast, wanting to be at Amy's bedside when she awoke. He was wearing jeans, a white polo shirt, and sneakers. Not exactly the department standard, but at least the clothes were clean. He slowly pushed open the hospital room door enough to peek inside.

"Hi, you!" Amy sang cheerfully from her bed.

"I didn't think you'd be awake yet," Gavin said, then checked his watch again, wondering if he'd made a mistake. 7:14. "What are you doing awake?"

"Please, all I've been doing for the last two days is sleeping. My eyes popped open about an hour ago, and I'm feeling pretty good today . . . thank you for asking," she said with a smile. "And look." She waved her arms. "No more tubes or wires!"

"I can see that. Great." Gavin smiled with an inner trepidation. Her energy was encouraging and scary at the same time. He could hear the doctor's voice telling him it was absolutely necessary for her to stay in bed and rest if they were going to have any shot at having a safe delivery. With her feeling as well as she looked and sounded, he might need to use his handcuffs.

His eye went to the black telephone that sat on the bedside table. He picked up the receiver and heard a dial tone. He saw the wire leading away and wanted to snip it.

"Come to me," Amy said, reaching out for Gavin as he drew near.

"Easy now," he said when she locked her arms around his neck and kissed him passionately on the lips. He went with it but then broke for air and said, "I miss you terribly, but—"

"Shut up and kiss me," she said.

Gavin eased himself next to her on the bed before she had a chance to climb out. He wanted to close his eyes and pretend they were home in their own bed. A home and a bed Amy still believed existed, with a little renovating to do around the front door. How was he going to tell her . . . and when? Definitely after the birth.

"It's so good to hold you," she whispered. "Why don't you take me out of here and bring me—"

"We can't! There's nothing I would love more, baby, but the doctor made it crystal clear that leaving here before the birth is not an option. We're just going to have to deal with it."

Amy paused silently, then nodded. "Hey!" she said with another sudden burst of enthusiasm and a bright smile. "I have to test your brain . . . see if you're normal."

"What?"

"Just get me that magazine," Amy said, motioning to a magazine on a tabletop to his left. "And don't look at it."

Gavin retrieved it. "*Get Away?*" he said, reading the title of what looked like an airline travel mag.

"I said don't look."

"Sorry."

Amy flipped through a few pages. "Ah, here it is. Okay, think of a number from one to ten."

Gavin smiled slightly, then shook his head. "I know this," he said.

"No you don't. Just do it. Think of a number."

"Nine."

"Think!" Amy said loudly. "I didn't say 'tell me.' You *can* think?"

"Okay, I thought of one . . . I mean, I thought of a number . . . not one . . . I mean, it might be one but . . ."

"Just shut up. None of this requires speaking. If you have a number from one to ten in your head, just nod."

Gavin nodded.

"Congratulations. Now multiply it by nine."

"Go on."

"If the number is a two-digit number, add the digits together."

"Okay."

"All right, now subtract five."

"Subtract five . . . done."

"Okay, now listen," she said, reading. "Determine which letter in the alphabet corresponds to the number you ended up with . . . like one equals *A*, two equals *B*, three equals *C*, etcetera."

"Is that it?"

"Of course not. Did you do it?"

"Yeah."

"Good, now think of a country that starts with that letter."

Gavin rolled his eyes. "Go on."

"Remember the last letter of the name of that country."

"All right."

"Think of the name of an animal that starts with that letter."

"Done. How much longer?"

"Shut up. Now remember the last letter in the name of that animal."

"Last letter remembered, boss."

"Okay, now think of a fruit that begins with that letter."

Gavin sighed. "Should I have been writing this down?"

Amy gave him a look.

"Name of a fruit. Got it."

"So tell me, Gavin. . . . Are you thinking of a kangaroo in Denmark eating an orange?"

Gavin's eyes widened. "How did you know that?"

Amy laughed. "According to this, ninety-eight percent of people will give that answer. The other two percent will come up with a koala in Denmark eating an apple or a cat in the Dominican Republic eating a tangerine or tomato, or a few other unlikely possibilities."

"But a tomato is a vegetable."

Amy sighed. "It doesn't matter, darling dearest. Some people think it's a fruit. Like some people think you're a detective when actually you're a fruit."

Gavin was about to reply, but she put her index finger on his mouth and said, "But you're my fruit, and that's what makes you important." She kissed him. "And sometimes you can be a very sweet fruit," she said, then kissed him some more.

Gavin felt a familiar tingling sensation. He reached into his pocket for his pager and looked at Chris's cell phone number followed by a 9-1-1. He sighed and showed Amy.

"Gotta go?" she said.

Gavin nodded. "Chris wouldn't use that number lightly," he said, then gave her another long kiss before putting the pager back in his pocket.

Amy frowned. "You don't seem overly concerned."

Gavin didn't reply for a moment, then smiled thinly and said, "You're here, the emergency is out there. How bad can it be?"

On his way out, he glanced again at the telephone. The last thing he wanted was for her to find out on her own. But how long could he hide the truth from her? Maybe it would be better to just tell her. At least he would be here to comfort her. At least he could keep her imagination from thinking the worst. But what could be worse than what had actually happened? The pager vibrated again. Chris . . . 9-1-1.

Outside the temperature had climbed to the mid-eighties, and

it wasn't even nine o'clock yet. The news had called for a three-day
heat wave that would bring temperatures up over a hundred, with
Long Island's typically high humidity. *Great,* Gavin thought, considering the Fourth of July was tomorrow. When he arrived at the
Tiger, he found his cell phone plugged into the cigarette lighter,
charging, just where he'd left it. The black leather seats were hot
from the sunlight, a disadvantage with the top off. He dialed Chris.

"Detective Grella," Chris answered.

"It's me, Detective Grella," Gavin said, wondering when Chris
would ever recognize his phone number.

"I know. I just wanted to remind you that one of us is working."

"My hero. What's happening?"

"How fast can you be in Old Roslyn?"

"Fast. Five minutes."

"Good. Then I'll see you under the viaduct in five."

"What's going on?" Gavin said, but Chris was gone. He started
the car, but before he pulled away, he dug and dug through his wallet for that . . . found it. He punched in the number on the card,
set the flashing red light on the dashboard, and drove away, no
siren. Ringing, ringing . . . then finally . . . *Aghhh* . . . a machine.

"Hello, you've reached Father Lauer's answering machine.
Sorry I could not be there to answer your call personally but if—
Hello? Hello?"

"Hello," Gavin said as cars pulled over to the shoulder to let him
by. "This is Detective Pierce. I'm looking for Father—"

"Detective! Hi. Thank you for returning my call. I was afraid we
might have gotten off on the wrong foot the other night. You had
your hands full—literally—and under all the stress, I may have
misunderstood your—"

"Don't worry about it," Gavin said, not wanting to hear an apol-
ogy but not knowing exactly what to say next. Was this someone he
could talk to without wasting more precious time? He had this

awful feeling that he was going to be placated by someone who should know about these things but didn't really, or worse, didn't believe demons were really anything more than some sort of conglomerated cosmic *Star Wars* dark-side Force that pinned a soul's good luck against some bad luck. But he needed to talk to someone, and he wasn't likely to find a booklet on "How to Get Rid of Your Demon" on the rotating bookrack at the local supermarket checkout.

"Well, fine, but I believe the question you asked me the other night was a sincere one, and I was hoping we could get together and talk a little more about it."

"When?"

"Hmm, let's take a look at the calendar," the priest replied. Gavin listened to breathing as the man checked. "How about next Thursday sometime?"

"How about today?"

"Today! I'm sorry, but I'm booked all morning and then I have a Salt meeting with four pastors at lunch and then immediately after that I—"

"Where's the pastors' lunch?" Gavin interrupted.

There was a moment of silence. "In Glen Head, at a Pastor Benjamin's house, but—"

"Tell the boys to brush up on their demonology and then buckle your seat belts, Father. I'll see you at lunch." Gavin hung up, wondering what a salt meeting was. He imagined he might be crashing some kind of sanctimonious religious ritual, but then again, the priest had said it was at lunchtime. Maybe the salt had to do with food.

Gavin buried the gas pedal as he came down the hill on Northern Boulevard, then flew across the half-mile-long Roslyn Viaduct at over a hundred. The off-ramp curled around and quickly dumped him in front of a uniformed cop, who was detouring traffic to the left. Gavin gave him a nod and went right.

Under the middle of the bridge, a good quarter mile away, lights were flashing from several squad cars, an ambulance, and a fire truck. *Busy, busy,* he thought as he pulled the Tiger off the road, deciding not to add to the congestion. He hurried out of the car, pausing only long enough to warn the pigeons in the bridge's understructure to mind their manners or be shot. The sound of radios, diesel engines, and voices echoed about the tall concrete arches that supported the green steel girders above. An aromatic bouquet of low tide rode on a light breeze.

The Roslyn Viaduct was apparently being used as a roof to keep the weather off all manner of junk below. A tree removal guy was using a section to dump logs and store equipment in two steel storage containers that looked as if they belonged on the back of a truck. Farther down were a couple of parked landscaper trucks with another steel container. Gavin wondered just who owned the land under the bridge. He would have thought it belonged to the county or state. Maybe it did. Maybe these were just squatters who needed a place to dump their respective loads.

"Gavin," called Chris from the crowd, waving him over anxiously. He was standing by another steel container. Battleship gray, apparently painted over rust in some spots. What in the world was going on? He had expected to see another Soldier Guy work of art. Nearer, he could see the doors had two massive padlocks.

"You should have told me we were playing the firemen in softball; I would have brought my glove," Gavin said as he walked up to Chris.

"We suspect this is his," Chris said, motioning toward the container.

Gavin looked around at the assemblage of manpower and then back at Chris. "You're suspicions must be pretty strong. Everyone's here but the media and Feds. I assume you purposely left them un-invited. We may find them a bit disgruntled at our next picnic."

"There wasn't time to notify everyone. Anything useful we find will be made available to them."

"Uh-huh. How'd you find it?"

"Combination of a website visit and a phone call on a discontin-ued cell phone. He found the container on Ebay and then worked out a cash deal on the phone with a company called B S Martin in California."

"And . . . they delivered it here."

"Exactly," Chris said, his attention drifting to the activity around him as he spoke. "He might be a genius with hand tools, but he's no computer wiz."

"Maybe he just didn't plan on losing a fingerprint on a pack of cigarettes when he bought the shipping container."

A voice crackled over Chris's radio. "No, one's enough," Chris said in the radio. "We're pretty tight in here as it is."

"So why haven't you opened it?"

"What?"

"*It.*"

"Oh. We're waiting for the bomb squad, just in case it's booby-trapped. The last thing I want is to explain to the lieutenant why the proper precautions weren't taken after someone gets blown up," Chris said, then motioned over Gavin's shoulder. "Speaking of the devils . . . I mean, demons."

"Very funny," Gavin answered as he turned to see the bomb squad approach. "So this was your idea?"

"What?"

"The bomb squad . . . the standby ambulance . . . the fire truck . . . the catering truck."

"What catering truck?" Chris said with alarm.

"Just kidding. Although I could use a coffee and a buttered roll."

Chris sighed. "Yeah, like I told ya, I just wanted to follow proper procedure. Why?"

"Nothin'. I just hope for your sake something blows up."

"You're so sure it won't?"

"I'd bet my house on it," Gavin said.

Chris snorted. "Fine, all the change in my pocket against what's left of your house."

"Ah, I don't want to take your money. But think about it. He doesn't like bombs. He hasn't used one yet. Whoever opens that door is more likely to get a suction-cup arrow in the forehead . . . or a boxing glove in the nose."

"Then maybe you should open the door, tough guy. I'll send the bomb squad home."

"Good idea, but may be too late. He could be watching us right now," Gavin said, looking around.

"I've got eyes on all roads leading to here looking for him. If he gets within a mile in any direction, he's ours."

"Suppose he puts on glasses, a fake nose, and a mustache?"

"Ah," Chris said as he waved Gavin off and left to address the bomb-squad team.

Gavin backed away, glad to not be making the decisions right now. *Bomb squad,* he thought and shook his head. On a day like today. These guys made him feel fortunate to be in homicide. The temperature had climbed to around ninety, maybe more, and these brave men were dressed in black, insulated, modern-day versions of knights in armor. Black helmets with thick face shields. The only thing going for them was that the viaduct provided shade. In the sun they would probably pop like black ants under a magnifying glass.

A few moments later the immediate area was cleared and the perimeter was widened. The two sizeable locks were cut with hydraulic bolt cutters and then the latches were cabled and uneventfully pulled open from a safe distance. Everyone stayed put as the black knights tiptoed inside. A few minutes later they walked out and took their helmets off.

"All clear," yelled one member of the squad.

"May I make a suggestion?" Gavin said to Chris as they came out from behind a patrol car.

"No," Chris said.

"Send everyone away but forensics and spread the word that all we found were lawnmowers and rakes. Let everyone know we were wrong. False alarm. Otherwise, by tonight the word will be out about the container and we'll lose any chance of him ever showing up here again. Also, break off any visible spot checks down the road, and keep one pair of eyes on anyone coming in here."

Chris tugged on his chin in thought. "I hate to say it, but you might be right. But I still think I was right to bring everyone on board to open it. If something were to go wrong . . ."

"You did the right thing, Big Dog. Get ahold of your bomb squad and tell them the plan before they hit the perimeter."

Chris nodded and started off to cut off the squad.

"I'll see you inside the box," Gavin called, then started toward the container. He had only gone a few yards when he slowed to a stop, frowned, and then looked left. Some excavating equipment, several fifty-five-gallon drums, beyond that some dirt hills with tall grass on top blowing in the breeze, an old steel fence with a gate that was cracked open, a weed field, and beyond that . . . low tide.

Gavin strolled the length of a football field and found himself standing atop a bulkhead at the edge of a canal, the only water being a foot-wide stream cutting through the muck, bottom fed from a cement culvert about fifty yards away, behind the stores on Main Street. The water was probably coming from the spring-fed duck pond across the street. Definitely low tide. Gavin looked at the bulkhead on the other side. The high-tide mark was about three and a half feet above the muck. To his right he saw the stream widen until it reached the bay's low-water mark, about a quarter mile away. By his feet was an old wooden ladder thick with barnacles and seaweed . . . except for the middle of the rungs. He turned and looked back in the direction of the storage container. . . .

"Where were *you?* Taking a leak?"

"When's high tide?"

Chris shrugged. "About six hours from dead to peak. Smells pretty low right now."

Gavin nodded. "We might have caught a break for once."

"How?"

"He's got maybe an hour, possibly a two-hour window twice a day that he can get in that creek with a small boat," Gavin said, pointing his head toward the old bulkhead a hundred yards away. "So far everything he's done has been by or on the water. I don't think he drives here. I think he gets here by boat at high tide . . . and probably only at night."

Chris nodded. "That's what I would do," he said as he looked at his watch. "It's time."

"What?"

"His face is being spread across every channel as we speak."

"All the more reason to come at night," Gavin said.

"If he does, we'll be ready for him. Come on, let's have a look in here."

35

Krogan sat at the kitchen table of his host's Jamaica Queens apartment, roaches scurrying around his bare feet, dressed only in the boxer shorts he'd put on to go outside and get the newspaper. Light passed over his left arm through an open barred window. The sounds of people, horns, and trains went unheard as he stared at the front page. "More Terror," he said, reading the headline over a strange-looking picture of a flipped boat. The paper said the capsized ferry was the fastest in the world and belonged to some casino. He smiled. *Fastest in the world,* he thought.

Krogan turned the paper over and saw a picture of himself on the back page throwing the Ninja guy out of the ring. He read the title: "Resurrected From The Dead." He cringed after the words left his mouth and had to shake off a shiver. He read a little farther and found the article was about his host and how he had revived his career. "Fools!" Krogan laughed. "He did nothing."

He turned back to the front page and then back to the last page. He did this several times. He didn't care that the front page would get more attention from humans. He didn't need their attention. But he did like what he saw on the front. "More terror," he quoted again, looking at the flipped ferry. He no longer wanted to look at the back page. He didn't even want to see the title again, but he paused a moment to picture the detective reading the title and laughing . . . knowing. He thought about the Frisbees again.

"Agghhh," he yelled, then threw the paper across the room, where it came apart and floated to the floor.

Krogan clenched his fists and closed his eyes, seeking a vision. Communicating between worlds was not as difficult for him as it was for others. While he was comfortable in the darkness of his host, his view was limited to human eyes and he needed the eyes of comrades in the waterless place. They might be in pain from the light, but their view was vast and none would deny his request, lest they pay the consequences of his wrath. He would not bother asking them to find Buchanan. Wherever that man was, demons in the other world were not likely to get close. No, the preacher would be inside one of thousands of angel clusters. But the one responsible for the capsized ferry—now there was someone with potential. Influencing someone with a brain could be a welcome change of pace.

The vision Krogan saw came fast but was not what he expected. He opened his eyes, pushed a kitchen chair over on his way across the room, and turned on a small television with rabbit-ear antennas. He waited impatiently as a fuzzy version of the image he saw in his vision appeared on the TV. No wonder the vision had come so quickly, with so many eyes watching televisions.

At a knock at the door, Krogan turned and, after a moment, smiled and nodded knowingly. He opened the door and pulled Tanya in by the arm. Her glassy, distant gaze confirmed what he already assumed.

"Tell me what you've found," he said.

"Reverend Jesse J. Buchanan lives in Hamden, New York, at Samantha's Dairy Farm," she said in a monotone, expressionless.

"Hamden? Where's Hamden?"

"Just west of the Catskills. Take the Clearview Expressway to the Throgs Neck Brid—"

"Enough. I'll find it," he interrupted. She immediately stopped speaking.

He thought for a moment, piecing together answers to questions he had wondered about over the last couple of years at the zoo while eating leaves. Samantha was Buchanan's granddaughter. She had died in the Norway crash with her parents. Buchanan, unfortunately, had survived the crash and had been hiding from him upstate before he got brave enough to hunt him down with that stupid tortoise. He'd named a dairy farm after the girl. As a memorial? Or . . .

"Do you have the phone number for this . . . this farm?"

She handed him a piece of paper from her small, black purse.

He left her standing where she was while he went to his bedside and dialed the number. An answering machine picked up. The voice was a young girl's. He wanted to leave a message but instead slammed the phone down. Buchanan would know in an instant he had been found . . . and he would run off again with his granddaughter . . . *who was still alive!*

Krogan went back to Tanya, who was staring into space, her purse in hand. He looked deeply into her eyes. "When I snap my finger you will not remember any of your assignment or research regarding Buchanan. It never happened. You've been here with me the whole time," he said, then thought a moment, smiled mischievously, and said, "You will also develop a headache and be irritable to everyone but me. The only time you will have relief is when you think of me fondly." He snapped his fingers.

Tanya blinked slowly, then frowned as she became aware of her surroundings. "I . . . I feel . . . strange."

"A pity," Krogan said, then walked away to get dressed.

Tanya followed unsteadily, looking about the apartment. "Where are we? What happened to this place?"

"We had a wild time. You were an animal. Don't you remember?"

"I did this?" she said, pointing at herself as she looked around the messy apartment in amazement. "I tried to stop you," he said, pulling his pants on. "You hit me and started throwing things. You said you were better than any wrestler."

"Me?"

"You were drunk. You drank half of that bottle of tequila on the counter."

She looked at the counter. "Me?"

"You. Why do you think you have that headache?"

Tanya frowned, then winced and palmed her forehead. "I'm . . . sorry," she said.

"Don't apologize. Just clean up your mess."

"Where are you going?"

"To visit a friend. What are you driving?"

Tanya thought a moment. "My Ferrari, I think."

Krogan smiled. "Give me the keys . . . and your money."

Tanya did as she was told and said, "What time are you coming back?"

"I'm not."

She didn't reply at first, watching him pull his boots on. "How will I get home? I . . . I don't think I even know where I am."

"You're in hell, baby. Call a cab."

"I have no money."

"Then take my bike."

"Where is it?"

"You just walked past it on your way up."

She frowned. "But I've been here all night," she said, then winced again, harder.

Krogan didn't reply, just grabbed the tequila and laughed on his way out the door.

Outside, he found the Ferrari parked in front. A convertible-black like everything else Tanya owned. He noticed the license plate: WWX-3. He shoved the seat all the way back and squeezed in. The black leather interior had that new smell, but was already very hot. That would change soon at the speeds he had in mind. He inserted the key and started the engine. He loved the sound of it. *What a toy,* he thought. He guzzled down some tequila and then looked at the dashboard, noticing a monitor under the stereo. He pressed the power button. "GPS," he said aloud, remembering the one he'd had on the lobster boat in his last human life. He pressed the menu and scanned down the options until he saw "phone number." He smiled, took another swig of tequila, then pressed in the phone number. After a brief moment of calculating, "Samantha's Dairy Farm" appeared on the screen. He pressed, "OK to proceed."

"Please proceed to the highlighted route," said a woman's voice. A road map with a red arrowhead indicating Tanya's car filled the screen.

Krogan drained the rest of the tequila and threw the bottle into the side of a passing car. He shifted into first and crushed the gas pedal. Horns blared and tires screeched as the Ferrari fishtailed into the traffic, leaving a cloud of burnt tire behind him. He heard one crash and then another as the female voice of the GPS said, "Make right turn ahead."

36

Gavin stood with Chris before the half-open doors of the storage container under the Roslyn Viaduct with a couple of forensic techs—two women who had introduced themselves as Sasha and Jenny. Sasha was a pretty brunette and Jenny was just as pretty, but strawberry blonde and a little shorter. Chris "Big Dog" Grella had told them to stand behind him in case something went wrong. They both tried to keep a straight face but couldn't.

The scent of low tide was still lingering in the late-morning heat. The fire truck, ambulance, bomb squad, patrol cars, traffic cops, and crowds of people wondering what in the world was happening had all left. A few plain-clothed spies had been strategically placed near and far to give a no-profile heads-up in case anyone, especially Walter Hess, were to show up unannounced.

"Gloves on now. And please be careful," begged Sasha.

"We'll be all right," Chris said.

"She means with what we touch, genius," Gavin said to Chris and then turned to the techs. "You'll have to excuse him. He's really a kindergarten crossing guard, and we're all mindless toddlers walking into traffic."

The women now looked at Chris with benevolent smiles, obviously thinking him adorable. Gavin shook his head, stuck his hands into the stretchy latex gloves, and pushed open the door. "Night visits," Gavin said, motioning at the hinges.

"Greased." Chris nodded. "Why would he care if the door squeaked during the day?"

"Exactly." Gavin took a few steps in and stopped to take in the view.

"Wow!" Chris scanned the interior. "This looks more like a contractor's workshop than a terrorist's ammo dump."

"It's both," Gavin said, proceeding very carefully. He didn't care that the bomb squad deemed the container safe. They had their own definitions as to what a bomb was: something that explodes. But Hess was rewriting the book on how to derail trains and capsize ferries and who knows what else. He was as out-of-the-box a thinker as one could get, and he'd made the art of the unconventional seem easy.

Along the left wall were shelves and bins holding supplies of wood, steel, plastic, rubber, and some scuba gear. Along the entire right wall of the container was a forty-foot workbench, half of it mounted with a grinding wheel, chop box, radial-arm saw, drill press, lathe, and vertical belt sander. The very end seemed to be a small section with books and magazines. Fluorescent lights ran along the ceiling over the length of the counter, but there didn't appear to be a switch anywhere to turn them on.

Gavin wondered for a moment where the electricity came from, then saw a small generator under the counter. He didn't remember anyone mentioning an exhaust pipe on the outside, but there had to be one.

The rest of the counter was sparsely littered with bits and pieces and some partially assembled objects that made no immediate sense. Mounted on the wall behind the work counter were all manner of hand tools and a six- or seven-foot-wide plastic laminated map of Long Island Sound. On a shelf under the map were erasable markers of various colors. There were no marks on the map, but semi-erased tints and hints of where marks had been.

"Here," Chris said, pointing to a reddish area in the light blue water where the ferry had flipped.

"Didn't you say the ferry hit something anchored in the water just under the surface?"

Chris rolled his eyes. "A minor fact that's been in every newspaper and news channel, and yeah, I may have mentioned it a few times. Glad to see you're paying attention."

Gavin sensed the techs glancing in their direction. "Then you might want to put this in your scrapbook," Gavin said, handing Chris a small photo he noticed among the counter debris. "Bet you dinner this was taken on the *Sachacus*."

Chris looked at the photo of a monitor that showed a map from Glen Cove to New London, Connecticut, where the ferry would dock for the waiting casino bus. The two locations were connected by a dotted line with a little boat image showing the exact location the ferry was at any given moment.

"Their monitor would have helped him confirm that his own, probably handheld, GPS readings were in line with their regular route."

Chris nodded. "We had wondered whether he followed the *Sachacus* with another boat to get the readings, or actually went on as a passenger."

"Probably both," Gavin said, looking at another tinted smudge mark on the map. "And this would be the Long Island Railroad."

There was something very eerie about reading the pre-strike map of terror.

"This looks familiar," called Jenny.

Gavin turned to see a hydraulic jack like the one used to spread the train rails apart.

"He put it all together right here with the help of that welding equipment," Chris said, pointing to a couple of tanks of acetylene and oxygen, some coiled rubber hose, and a small selection of torches against the wall. "You know, Gav, you could use a container like this at your house. You'd have everything you need to put your home back together. All we need is a fraction of this stuff for evidence. Why don't you just impound it and have it dragged over?"

"Great idea, Big Dog. And while we're at it, we could build one of these and keep it in your backyard," Gavin said after rolling open a blueprint on the counter.

Chris came to his side. "Yeah, baby. We can play with it in the pool . . . Where do you suppose he found blueprints to the *Sachacus?*"

"I don't know. *Popular Mechanics?*" Gavin pointed to hand calculations written near the bow. "This guy is in serious need of a hobby."

"Yeah, like writing programs for video games."

Gavin sighed and let go of the blueprint. The drawing rolled up on the counter, exposing even more debris. "There's so much here, but how much of it is from past projects and how much of it has to do with his next target?"

"Has he used one of these yet?" Sasha asked, holding up a shiny brass tube that was quickly recognized as a very large caliber cartridge.

Gavin raised his brow. "Nope. Let me see that."

"Uh-oh," Chris said. "BMC fifty-caliber. Looks like he brought a souvenir back from the gun show. What do you think the chances are that he just collects the ammo?"

"Zero," said Jenny, turning the pages of some kind of magazine. "Ever hear of a Barrett's rifle?"

Chris cursed. "Tell me you've found an owner's manual."

"Complete with cash receipt on page . . . four," she said, holding up a yellow paper. "Bought three months ago, if we can believe the date. Your boy has a new toy."

"Our terrorist just turned sniper," Chris said.

"Unless he's got other plans for it." Gavin stared closely at the cartridge.

"Like?" Chris said.

"I don't know. He's a run-a-muck racist with a flair for the spectacular, with a gun that could hit a head-sized target from a mile away."

"Are you thinking who or what?"

"Both with this guy. The first thing is to check if any visitors are coming to town, starting with the president. Check both official and unofficial trips."

Gavin looked at the map again. "There are natural gas tanks along this coastline. What thickness steel is safe against one of these rounds?"

Jenny's brow rose. "We'll let you know. Those rounds come in quite a variety, including explosive."

"Great," Gavin said. "He can aim, fire, and explode from a mile away. And a gas tank is bigger than the broad side of a barn, so he doesn't even have to be a good shot."

"You know," Chris said thoughtfully. "He might be thinking of Senator Sweeney."

"Sweeney? Why? I mean, I know why I would want to shoot him, but what are you thinking?"

Sasha was nodding her head. "He's having a rally tomorrow at Bar Beach."

"It's been in all the news, Gav. And he's made terrorism—and specifically Hess—his whipping boy. And that thing could go right through standard protection."

"Then Sweeney should call it off," Gavin said.

"Yeah, right. He's going for the glory in the next election. If he backs down from this rally, the media will be all over him."

"Then we'll use him for bait."

"What do you think he is, a worm?"

"Yes, but one we have to protect. If our soldier guy is after Sweeney with a BMC fifty, he'll be shooting from within a mile radius. The only clear shot would be from the harbor or the power plant on the other side. It would be easy enough to stake out and screen the power plant."

"The plant, yes, but what about the harbor?"

"Harbor patrol."

"There'll be thousands of boats camped out in this and every other harbor all day tomorrow for the fireworks," Chris pointed out. "If he doesn't want to be found, he won't be."

"Well, the harbor will take some thinking," Gavin agreed, "but if he takes a shot, we'll have him. The mouth of the harbor can be sealed. He'll be surrounded."

"But remember, tomorrow's the Fourth—even a bomb wouldn't be noticed with all the competition. He can take a shot and we won't know where it came from."

"Interesting reading," Jenny said from the back of the container. "Some gun magazines I've never heard of, some military stuff, a copy of *The Turner Diaries*, and a well-used Bible."

"Bible?" Gavin said. He looked at his watch. 12:47. The pastor's Salt lunch meeting, or whatever the thing was called, would probably be over soon.

"Yeah. complete with highlighting and underlined verses."

"Chris, I hate to say this, but you're going to have to call the Feds and let them know what we got here. We can't automatically assume Sweeney's the target. If not, we still need to know what he plans on doing with these fifties. Before the Feds get here, we need to get this place dissected and labeled. Let's go through those books and magazines and look for any underlines or dog-eared pages. Any newspapers or magazines stuffed under tools or buckets might have articles he saved and got tired of reading," Gavin said, handing the cartridge to Chris.

"Where are you going?"

"I've got a lunch date. I'll be back."

"Lunch . . . with who?"

"Some pastors."

"Pastors! We back to this Krogan crap again? Look, I know you just think you're protecting your family, but this is going to get you in trouble. Big trouble. And what pastors do you know? You don't know any pastors."

"Maybe not, but Father Lauer does, and we're going to chat a bit. It'll keep me out of trouble."

"Father Lauer. A priest? Who is this guy? What kind of craziness are you getting yourself into now? What's he, an exorcist? He's an exorcist, right? God help us, Gav, you're off the deep end."

"Father Lauer was the priest at the train wreck."

"Him? The one giving last rites? He's an exorcist?"

"There was only one priest there. And he called me. He wanted to meet. And to tell you the truth, I don't know what he is."

"Bull. You're going too far, Gav. You can't do this now . . . *not now!* I know you, man. You'll hook up with these guys and I won't see you again. You'll drag them over to see Jackhammer Hoban, embarrass yourself down to your toenails, and waste the most valuable time you've ever been needed for. You see all the work we have here," Chris said angrily.

"I have to go, Chris. I'm late. The sooner I get out of here, the sooner I'll be back."

"You're nuts, man. We need you here. If the lieutenant calls, you're on your own. I'm done covering for you."

"*Don't* cover for me. This is my fight, not yours."

"Yeah, right. Go on. Get out of here. Wacko."

37

Gavin turned onto Prospect Avenue and immediately began looking for house numbers. When he thought of some of the doors he had walked through over the years, it was weird this one should make him feel so nervous. He was familiar with criminals. He knew the crime business inside out. He was comfortable with crime. There, he was the expert. He pressed the gas when he realized number eight was at least another block farther down.

There it was. Two cars in the driveway and a few in the street. Conservative cars. The kind of car you would never be able to find in a parking lot without first putting your key in someone else's door. Nothing like the Tiger he was driving. Already he felt out of place. He found a parking spot a couple of houses down.

A small Tudor-style house with a well-manicured winding brick walkway. At the front door he stood on a baseball home plate with "You're Safe" written on it in black letters. Not seeing a doorbell, he knocked.

"Come on in. The door's open," called an unfamiliar voice from inside.

Gavin entered a small foyer that immediately led into a living room where Father Lauer and three other men were sitting on an L-shaped couch. A ceiling fan above was going full tilt, and several half-full glasses of seltzer with ice sat on a coffee table in front of the couch. No air conditioning. Hot. Smelled like cookies but he didn't see any. Father Lauer, wearing black slacks and a white T-shirt, stood up and extended his hand.

"Hi, Detective. We were beginning to think you wouldn't make it."

"Sorry. Something came up and I was having a hard time getting away. Goes with the territory." A territory he was completely ignoring at the moment, he thought. Maybe he *had* lost his mind.

"Well, let me introduce you to my friends. Detective Gavin Pierce . . . this is Pastor David Benjamin, Pastor Jim Hartington, and Pastor Robbie Mullens," Lauer said, moving from left to right along the couch. By the time the last person was introduced, Gavin had already forgotten most of the names. This scared him. As a highly trained detective, he was considered an expert in remembering details, especially names.

Lauer continued. "All three are local pastors and this is David's house. We meet here once a week and talk and pray about the needs and visions of our separate and very different congregations."

Gavin nodded. *What am I doing here?* he thought. Aloud, he said, "You told me this was a 'salt' meeting? I thought maybe that meant you were just having lunch."

"Salt speaks of covenant," Benjamin explained in a serious tone. The pastor was about fifty, moderately heavy, brown hair with a white goatee. "We find the reference in the fourth verse of the first chapter of Acts. The Greek word *sunalizomai,* from which I am taking an inductive leap, is translated into English, 'Gathering them together.'"

Mullens laughed warmly. "Is *that* why we call these Salt meetings?" he said in a deep, booming voice with a southern accent. He had a red, round face and even sitting he looked tall, and probably had a cowboy hat stashed somewhere to go with his boots.

"Yes . . . let me finish," Benjamin went on. "Arab societies to this day retain such expressions as 'there is salt between us' and 'I love you as I love salt.'"

"I love you as I love salt?" Mullens asked incredulously, then looked at Gavin and explained, "No one on earth researches like our friend David here."

Benjamin shrugged with a smile. "I'm not making this stuff up. Anyway, Gavin, we have determined not to let our obvious denominational differences get between us as we keep Jesus as our focus and common denominator. For example," he said, reintroducing everyone with their church affiliations. Gavin nodded but wanted to run. Chris was right. He *had* lost his mind.

Mullens smiled. "In other words, we aren't here to major in the minors. We're all in the same boat, and we'll do a whole lot better if we'd all try rowing in the same direction."

"I'm with you, Gavin," Hartington said with an English accent. He was older, seventy to seventy-five, shorter, and looked, Gavin thought, like a happy Hobbit in a business suit. "I thought we were just here to thank the Lord Jesus for a bit of lunch."

"More seltzer?" said a female voice.

"Thank you, sweetheart," Benjamin said. "Gavin, this is my wife, Rachel."

Gavin turned to see an attractive woman about ten years younger than her husband. She placed a tray down with fresh ice and seltzer. "Hi," Gavin said.

She smiled. "Can I get you something else, Gavin?"

"No thanks. Seltzer's fine."

She smiled again and left.

Benjamin now leaned forward, his thick brows furrowed together. "How is it that we can help you, Gavin?" he said with concern in his voice.

"And *sit down* before you give us all stiff necks." Mullens motioned behind Gavin.

Gavin turned to find only a baby grand piano filling up the rest of the room. He sat on the bench. "This is hard for me to talk about . . . because I find it difficult to believe any of it. I need someone—a specialist, if you will—to do a job for me, or at least tell where I can go to get help."

"What kind of a job?" Hartington asked.

Gavin looked at Hartington. Another face of concern. Gentle men. A circle of gentle men. What he needed was a Howitzer, and here he was sitting with men who seemed likely to want to *counsel* Krogan.

"That day we met at the accident, you mentioned demons," Lauer said, apparently trying to help.

Gavin nodded. "Some of you might remember a serial killer we arrested a couple years ago named Karl Dengler?"

"Krogan?" Mullens blurted in a loud voice, which appeared to be his normal volume. "Yup. Remember him well. He was a real animal."

Gavin nodded. "As real as they get."

"Oh yeah," Mullens said. "A member of my congregation was at the New York Aquarium when he drove into the whale tank with a truck. She's all right now, but she spent a week in the hospital at the time."

"A very scary week," Benjamin said to Mullens. All heads nodded with frowns of concern and interest.

"Go on, Detective," Lauer said.

"Wait a minute!" Mullens interjected before Gavin could start. "Detective Gavin Pierce. Homicide. You were there, too . . . at the aquarium."

"That's right." There was something about this loud guy knowing Gavin's business that helped ease the nerves a little.

"I knew your name sounded familiar. Your father was killed?"

"My grandfather, yes," Gavin said, then proceeded to speak

through the *I'm sorries.* "What you might also remember was that the passenger in the truck Krogan was driving was killed in the crash. And this wasn't his first or last crash. But with every crash on record, the passenger owned the vehicle and died, so we never had a witness to question. That is, every other passenger but one. Who she was and how she survived isn't important, but what *was* important was that we were now going to find out who this mystery driver was. At least that's what we thought. After interrogating her thoroughly, we found she had zero memory of the driver. We then decided to use hypnosis."

"I don't remember the hypnosis part," Mullens said. "And I read everything written on the case."

"We never let the media know about the hypnosis. For that matter, we never let the department know about it either. Anyway, under hypnosis she remembered the driver and told us his name was Krogan. That's when it got weird. When we asked her to go back to the first time she met Krogan, she started speaking to us in ancient Hebrew."

Mullens was about to say something, but Benjamin motioned for him to let Gavin continue.

"The psychologist thought she was having past-life experiences. We went with that for a while but later found out that the psychologist had somehow tapped into a demon who was reminiscing over old times with another demon named Krogan."

Hartington grinned and pointed at Gavin with a short, shaking finger. "So you think this Karl Dengler chap you have buttoned up in the clinker is possessed by this Krogan?"

"Not exactly," Gavin said, then exhaled, surprised they had followed him so far, but knowing they would never believe the next part. "When we arrested Dengler, Krogan, the demon, was sent into a giant tortoise and then held captive at the Bronx Zoo for the last two and a half years. And now the tortoise is dead and Krogan is on the loose again in the body of a WWX wrestler named Jack-hammer Hoban, who recently changed his name to—"

"Krogan," Mullens said. The others looked at him. "Excuse me, but this is all over the news now. And, yes . . . I do check in on the WWX once in a while."

Benjamin rolled his eyes. Hartington said something to Mullens about the WWX, probably interested in what channel it was on, Gavin thought. Lauer was looking straight at Gavin. Nobody was laughing at him. They hadn't told him to leave. They looked as though they wanted to hear more. But they were ministers, Gavin figured, so they were probably just being polite now and would laugh about him later.

"Could we back up a little to the tortoise?" Hartington asked.

Gavin nodded, hoping he wouldn't have to repeat everything he had said.

"You said the demon was in a tortoise and the tortoise was in the Bronx Zoo?"

"I don't believe I read *that* in the newspaper *either,*" Mullens said, then laughed loud and easy.

"Yes," Gavin said.

"Why didn't the demon leave the tortoise while it was at the zoo?" Hartington asked.

"Because the tortoise was still alive. The tortoise was chosen because they live longer than humans . . . but not when they're killed. As soon as the tortoise died, the demon left and found Hoban and took him."

Hartington frowned. "Demons can't leave things that are alive?"

"It's a theory," Benjamin said. "For the demons to get out of the swine herd that Jesus cast them into, the entire herd committed suicide. And though demons were afraid of Jesus, there is no account of them fleeing people to avoid an inevitable clash."

"What is it you want us to do, Detective?" Lauer said.

"I need someone who knows what to do with this thing," Gavin said, then went on to describe what happened to his house and how Krogan would keep coming back. Mullens remembered reading about the house crash in the paper. "I was hoping you might be able to tell me what to do."

The pastors looked at each other with concern, none of them saying a word.

"May I ask another tortoise question, Gavin?" Hartington said.

"Sure."

"How did you get Krogan in the tortoise? What did you say? And if you could do it the first time, why don't you just do it again?"

"Me? I did nothing. I don't know anything about this stuff. Buck did it."

"Buck?" Benjamin said.

"Who's Buck, Detective?" Lauer said.

"Buchanan . . . Reverend Buchanan. He just likes to be called Buck."

The room fell silent. Everyone looked at one another as if Gavin had just told them he was James Bond. Finally Benjamin said, "The Reverend Jesse J. Buchanan?"

"You know Reverend Buchanan?" Mullens was without a smile for the first time since Gavin had walked in.

"Yes, but he can't help right now. He had a heart attack and he's fighting for his life in the hospital."

"I thought he was dead," Benjamin said.

"So did Krogan, which was what Buck wanted. After he lost his wife, son, and daughter-in-law in a Krogan crash, he took his granddaughter and vanished. He said enough was enough and it was time for a change of occupations. But I wanted Krogan bad and convinced him to return to action one more time. I kind of wish now that I'd left well enough alone."

"Buchanan burned out," Benjamin said, as if talking to himself. "Sometimes I think I'm burning out."

Mullens laughed. "You already are, my friend. Charred through and through. But that's okay. We still love you."

"It's so nice to be cared for by those who aren't afraid to speak the truth in love," Benjamin said sarcastically but then added a wink.

"You did the right thing, Gavin," Hartington said while the other two continued. "I'm sure Jesse Buchanan told you there's a war going on. If we're not attacking, we're being attacked."

Gavin nodded. "Buck has told me that. I just don't know how. That's why I'm here."

"How much do you know about spiritual warfare, Detective?" Father Lauer asked.

"I feel like a baby walking through a jungle. Can you guys help me or not?"

Mullens stood up and walked over to Gavin, putting his hand on his shoulder. "Son, before you mentioned Buchanan, your story sounded mighty wild, and I for one thought we had a loon on our hands. Meet them all the time. I want to apologize. Reverend Buchanan came through our church once, and that meeting lasted sixteen hours. People came from all over and were delivered of everything from alcoholism to acrophobia."

"What's acrophobia?" Gavin said.

"Fear of heights," Benjamin answered.

"Fear of heights?" Gavin said incredulously. "I have fear of heights and Buck knew that. Why didn't he fix it?"

Hartington giggled. "Just because you're afraid of heights doesn't mean you have demon problems. Most of the time our problems have nothing to do with demons. But when they do—"

"Buchanan's the man," Mullens interjected.

"He's a legend," Benjamin said. "He has a powerful anointing, like no one I've ever seen."

"What Jim's sayin' here is true," Mullens said. "You can go through a hundred problems before you find one with a demon attached, but when they're attached to the problem, ooooh, baby. And this Krogan fella doesn't sound like your basic demon."

"According to Buck, he's anything but basic. During the hypnosis, he was described as being at Jesus' crucifixion, laughing. And Buck said he thought Jesus spoke about Krogan when saying a demon like him would require prayer and fasting."

"We're *on* a fast," Mullens said. "That seltzer's our lunch," he pointed out.

"Do you want us to cast him into another tortoise?" Hartington asked, apparently serious, possibly even excited about the idea.

"Been there, done that. This time I want him in a real jail with real guards on a suicide watch. The only problem is that I can't arrest him."

"I thought you said he drove through your house with a cement truck and killed your decorator," Lauer said.

"He did, but I can't prove it. At least not yet. There's blood in the cement truck that will prove to be his, but we can't place him at the scene, and we're not allowed to just force a blood test on someone. I mean, what am I supposed to do, stab him with a knife and then test the knife? Not that the thought hasn't been entertained. Obviously, if I did anything like that and it proved a positive match, even a bad lawyer could have it thrown out of court for improper procedure. Enjoyable, but improper."

"I say we kick his butt," Mullens said. "Spiritually speaking, of course."

"What if he were to *confess* to the crime?" Benjamin wondered aloud. "If he were to admit to you that he did it, wouldn't that be just reason to arrest him and take a blood test?"

Gavin shrugged. "Sure, but how would I get him to confess . . . especially to me?"

"You beat him in the wrestling ring," Benjamin suggested. "Isn't tonight one of those Armageddon challenges?"

"How did you know that?" Mullens asked.

"I watch the WWX once in a while . . . purely to see who I should be praying for, of course."

"Of course," Mullens muttered.

"Let me get this straight," Gavin said. "You're talking about me going in the ring with Krogan and beating him into a confession, and then arresting him based on that confession?" *I'll be killed,* Gavin thought.

"Yes," Benjamin said. "We wrestle not against flesh and blood, but against principalities, against powers, against the rulers of the darkness of this world, against spiritual wickedness in high places."

"Buck told me that. And it doesn't make any more sense hearing it from you."

"Getting him to confess shouldn't be any harder than casting him into a tortoise, and you've already done that," Lauer reasoned.

"I just got done telling you, I didn't do anything. Buck did all the work."

"That's where you're wrong, Gavin," Hartington spoke up. Other heads were nodding, as if they knew what Hartington was going to say. "Buck may have been an instrument, but it was God's will and power channeling through him, and it will be God's will and power channeling through you."

Gavin said nothing, but at that moment he felt a chill run up his spine.

"We're ready to stand by you, Detective," Lauer offered boldly. "We're all prayed up and fasted up. We're ready to go."

"Go?" Gavin looked around at the intent faces of the ministers. All appeared confident.

"Absolutely. We'll stand in the upper four corners of the Nassau Coliseum . . . north, south, east and west."

"I've got the south," Mullens said with a wink.

"You can count me in," Hartington said.

"We'll be your prayer support," Benjamin said. "Jesus said 'Where two or more are gathered in my name, there I am in their midst.' With the four of us, I would imagine Krogan will be seeing enough angels to beg you for mercy."

"I somehow doubt that," Gavin said.

"Then that's the next order of business," Hartington declared. "Your faith."

"Now you sound like Buck again."

"We'll take that as a compliment," Benjamin said. "Do you know God, Gavin?"

"I don't usually get to know the good guys as well as the bad guys. But if the bad guys exist, I guess He does also."

Benjamin shook his head dramatically. "We've been called not to just believe He's there but to *know* Him. Are we to be content to know about God intellectually when we've been created to know Him spiritually?"

"Are you asking *me*?" Gavin said, feeling intimidated.

"You're a logical man, Detective," Lauer said. "So I'll give you an analogy. Think of your faith as a telescope. All this time you've been wondering about it—how it fits into your life, its size, its shape, its color, how it works, how it doesn't work. You examine it for what it is, but you never look through it. The time has come for you to look through it."

"Yes," Mullens agreed. "Then we can go to the coliseum, get you a good spot in line, and start claiming some ground. Gentlemen, we're going to war."

While the ministers nodded and smiled at one another in confident agreement, Gavin felt a gnawing in the pit of his stomach. For all their enthusiasm about "going to war," Gavin still couldn't picture himself as the guy to be leading the charge.

38

Krogan zoomed down Main Street, Hamden, in a flash. The police car that had taken off after him in that speed trap never had a chance, but it had added to the thrill of the ride. He'd have to take that route on the way back to Long Island, he decided.

"Make the next right," said the female voice of the Ferrari's navigation system.

Krogan had spent the ride up thinking about Buchanan—the humiliation the old man had caused him in both worlds, and conversely, the most humiliating way he could kill him, and how much better the world was going to be for Krogan without him. Yes, this would be the third and last time they would meet. There would not be a fourth. Every human runs out of luck. This one had just taken a little longer to come up empty.

Krogan downshifted and made his turn. Time to slow it down.

"Your destination is ahead on the left. Your route guidance is complete."

Krogan's excitement was abruptly tempered with caution. If he were between worlds, in the waterless place, he would right now be under heavy attack from more angels than even he could handle. Just knowing that gave him pause, a rare reaction on his part. Even in the flesh, he couldn't think of another demon that would tread this close to the likes of Buchanan. But Krogan wasn't just any demon. Those in the waterless place would see him and know his glory.

Just ahead Krogan could see a white mailbox with small lavender letters that read *Samantha's Dairy Farm. Very cute,* he thought sardonically. He turned into the gravel driveway and stopped. A wire fence, probably electrified, bordered the driveway on either side. To his right, several brown cows with pink bows around their necks stopped grazing to stare at him. *How disgustingly adorable,* he thought. If he had the time, he would brand his name into their sides and then slit their throats.

His gaze turned to the house at the top of the driveway. A white two-story with pink shutters and a wraparound porch. Looked like a little girl's dollhouse. There was little doubt who the decorator was. To the right of the house was the broad side of a long, white barn with about two dozen small windows running the length of it, all with pink shutters. Between the shutters were large detailed paintings of multicolored butterflies.

Krogan drove slowly up the tree-lined driveway. Near the top of the hill, the driveway emerged into the open and he pulled over. Surprise would be important. Buchanan, with help from his suck-up celestial bodyguards, might realize who he was even in a host he'd never seen before. He had to admit Buchanan was special in that regard. But even Buchanan could be surprised . . . like in Norway, when—*Surprise!*—he and his family were gone. Almost, anyway.

Behind the white barn stood two other structures, a smaller barn and a chicken coop. The old preacher had to be here somewhere. First Krogan checked the house. He walked up onto the porch and peeped in through the white lace draperies. He saw nothing. He tried the front door. It was open. He pushed it open slowly and listened carefully. He walked inside, leaving the door open behind him. If someone came by to check on why the door was open, it would be their bad luck. Curiosity kills.

The house was immaculate. He looked into the living room. Swords of sunlight stabbed through the curtains and cut amber lines across an old, wide-plank pine floor. He paused to look at some family photos on the wall. A picture of Buchanan and his wife on their wedding day, looking happy, in love. *Too bad.* He sneered. The only picture he had ever seen was in the newspaper after the crash.

Krogan quickly lost interest in people who were dead and gone. He went into the next room. The kitchen. Again, incredibly neat and clean. No dishes in the sink. No boots on the floor. Did anybody live here? He checked the refrigerator. It was almost empty. A tub of butter, an assortment of jelly jars, salad dressing, some eggs, but no real food. Not even milk. What kind of dairy farm was this?

Krogan went upstairs and checked the bedrooms, just in case Buchanan was upstairs sick or taking a nap. Beds were made and there were no clothes on the floor. The old man was an utter neat freak. *Disgusting.*

He went back out on the porch and looked toward the barns. The closest appeared to have farm equipment in it, probably tractors and stuff. He stepped off the porch and started toward it. Leaning against a fence post was a pitchfork. He grabbed it. He'd always wanted to throw a pitchfork through someone. He could probably nail Buchanan from a hundred feet away. He eased up to the first of four garage doors, took a quick look, then ducked inside. He was right about the tractors. There was also some kind of forklift with *LULL* written on the side. He wondered how far he could throw a cow with it. Beyond that was a flatbed truck on lifts, the front wheel off. But no Buchanan.

Krogan felt anger bubbling up through his veins, tightening his jaw, clenching his teeth. Had those blasted angels seen him coming? Did they warn Buchanan, hide him, take him away? He raised the pitchfork to throw it into the rear wall of the barn. Then he heard a noise outside. He stepped out the door and peered around, his eyes darting about. Nothing. Another noise. It was coming from behind the barn. He went back in and ran around the tractor to the rear of the barn, then looked out one of four small windows along the wall. Horses. Three girls on three horses. He recognized one from a picture in the house. "Samantha," he whispered with a smile. He looked at the pitchfork and then back at Buchanan's granddaughter. He quietly slid open the window with the sharp tips of the fork. The girls were letting the horses drink from a white bathtub in the field just thirty or so feet away. An easy target. She was dead. He listened as the girls spoke to each other and the horses. Useless chatter about a horse trial she would never get to see. He didn't know where Buck was, but his granddaughter would make a good appetizer.

A door shut behind him. He spun, cat quick, pitchfork raised, ready to throw. He saw nothing. A different door. He ran to the front of the barn. An elderly black man with white hair had just entered the chicken coop. He must have been in the smaller white barn, tending cows or something. The door of the coop shut closed. Buchanan! Got him. He would have Samantha for dessert.

Krogan went back in the garage and hurried across each bay until he reached the far end. The chicken coop was just next door, almost attached. He was about to step out when a thought came to mind. He smiled, almost laughed. He turned around and gazed at the *LULL*. The all-terrain forklift had an extending boom. Krogan hurried to it. Just as he expected, the key was in the ignition. He quickly and quietly opened the well-greased garage door. How considerate of the preacher to maintain his farm so well. He hopped aboard the *LULL* and placed the pitchfork next to his seat.

The *LULL* started after a few cranks. Excellent. If the old preacher saw him and came running, he would get a pitchfork in the neck. Krogan played with the simple controls. No sweat. He stepped on the gas, drove out through the garage door, unable to stop himself from laughing. The chicken coop was small. How much fun can a demon have in one day? He would remember this forever. He drove around to the front door of the chicken coop, blocking any possible way of escape. Through the glass door he could see Buchanan, tending to his chickens. The old man must have gone deaf. Whatever. Krogan lowered the forks. The chicken coop was raised off the ground, probably to allow the chicken crap to fall out through the floor. A fatal flaw in the design. He eased the *LULL* forward, the forks finding the space under the coop. He raised the forks slowly, very slowly, until they touched the floor. Buchanan still hadn't noticed, his attention still focused on his stupid chickens.

Krogan yanked back on the fork lever, instantly lifting the front of the coop off its foundation. He stopped and laughed, as white chicken feathers exploded inside the coop. The frenzied clucking sounded as if the chickens thought this was as funny as he did. The old preacher turned and raced toward the door, waving frantically at the feather cloud. A pity Krogan could not make out Buchanan's face clearly enough to see the fear.

"Where are your bodyguards now, Preach?" Krogan yelled. He yanked on the lever again. The coop rose, angled effortlessly upward. Buchanan fell away from the door. Krogan pressed the throttle as he continued to pull on the lever. With the chicken coop tottering at a steep angle, Krogan found another lever that extended the boom. He pushed the lever till the chicken coop was completely vertical. He heard Buchanan scream in pain as feathers billowed through window openings. He laughed heartily.

Krogan saw movement in his peripheral vision, followed immediately by the sound of horse hoofs and whinnying. The three girls that galloped around the barn were approaching him from behind. He extended the boom farther while stepping on the gas. Creaking, glass cracking, feathers flying, he continued to push.

"No! What are you doing? Stop!" screamed the voices behind him as the chicken coop teetered. He pulled back on the boom lever, put the *LULL* in reverse, backed away, lowered the forks, and rammed the bottom of the chicken coop. Again he raised the forks and drove forward until the chicken coop flipped completely onto its roof. Buchanan's screaming had stopped. The frantic clucking had quieted. Feathers were floating to the ground.

"Yes!" Krogan proclaimed victoriously, stretching his arms to the sky for the unseen world to see. "You're dead. I've won!" He took a moment to bathe in his glory before his attention was drawn to the next task. Time for dessert.

He threw the *LULL* into reverse and stood on the gas pedal. He cranked the steering wheel to the left, spinning the machine a hundred eighty degrees.

39

"Amy! My God!"

Amy was snatched from her light sleep by a voice more familiar to her than any other. She opened her eyes to see her twin sister, Amber, rushing to her bedside.

"Oh, hi, Amber," Amy sang sleepily. "How was the Mediterranean?"

Amber had been away on a cruise with the new love of her life, Eric. Amy had seen no reason to interrupt her sister's vacation with news of the accident.

"Never mind my vacation. Yes, it was great. But somebody should have called me about you."

"I'm fine," Amy said with her best reassuring smile, as if no one else knew what they were talking about. "And besides, there was nothing you could have done. I felt better thinking you were having a good time with Eric. And you did, so perfect."

"How fine can you be, Amy?" Amber said incredulously. "You're in the hospital, your house is destroyed, and your decorator's dead . . . and from what I heard from your neighbor, you're lucky you weren't killed with him."

In the instant before Amy's conscious mind was able to register the meaning of Amber's words, her chest tightened and neck cramped as if all oxygen had just been sucked out of the room. "That's impossible," she heard her voice say reflexively, but even her primeval denial could not black out fears she had harbored from the beginning. Fears that penetrated her heart with all the sensitivity of cannon blast.

"Impossible?" Amber said.

"Whoever you spoke to is wrong. The house looks much worse than it is and Larry's fine. Gavin saw him. He didn't even need to go to the hospital."

Amber was about to speak but paused. For an instant, Amy saw her sister's expression change from bewilderment to awareness and then back again. It didn't take much guesswork for Amy to figure out that she'd been purposely kept in the dark.

Amber tried to cover. "You know, the plane lands, I get a change of clothes, and drive over to surprise you and see what I thought would be a perfect, perfect, house. Instead I see . . . some damage. Look, Amy, who am I to tell you? Maybe it did look a lot worse than it really is. What do I know? I'm a computer geek, not a carpenter. And your neighbor was probably exaggerating. Just some nosey old lady from up the block."

Amy stared at Amber for all of five seconds before reaching for the phone.

"Who are you calling?"

"A friend," Amy said. If she was right, there were only three people on the planet who really knew what was going on. One was Gavin, and she couldn't believe anything he told her anymore. Maybe she would have done the same thing if she were him, but she wanted truth, and at this point his truth would continue to be whatever was best for her and the baby. Another would be whatever poor slob Krogan was controlling. Whatever was happening had to involve the demon, otherwise Gavin would have been more honest. That left only one person she could count on to speak the truth . . . assuming Gavin hadn't lied about him, too, and he was still alive.

"Delhi Hospital. Can I help you?"

"Mr. Jesse Buchanan, please," Amy said, her voice quivering, fearful of what she might hear.

"One moment, please . . . transferring you to room two-oh-three."

Thank you, God! Amy thought as the phone rang.

"Hello?" The voice was weak and scratchy, but it was there.

"Buck?"

There was a moment of silence, and Amy wondered if she might have reached the wrong number.

"I was hoping you would call, my dear. I . . . I haven't been my-self lately. I'm deeply sorry for what you're going through. I feel re-sponsible, but there is nothing I can do about it. Are you well?"

"I'm fine, Buck," Amy said, glancing at her sister, who was lis-tening to every word with severe concern. "You are not responsi-ble for anything. You only did what we asked and helped more than anyone else could or would have . . . Buck?"

"Yes."

"What has Gavin told you about our situation down here?"

Amber closed her eyes. She apparently felt terrible, but Amy could not concern herself with that now. She listened with forced patience as Buck spoke. As she suspected, Krogan had destroyed the house. Tears fell as he told her about the cement truck and Larry's death, as well as the deaths of the tortoise and the zookeeper Lester Davis. What shocked her even more was to hear that Krogan was now a WWX wrestler, taking on all comers at the coliseum.

When Buck had finished she asked, "How is Samantha doing?"

"Samantha's fine, my dear. She's in very good hands."

Amy wrapped up the call by talking briefly about Buck's health and wishing him well. She promised to call back soon and hung up.

"What do you think you're doing?" Amber said.

"I'm getting out of here," Amy replied as she slowly and unsteadily slid her feet from under the covers to the cold floor.

"I don't think so," Amber said. "You get right back in that bed or I'll call a nurse."

Amy stared Amber in the eye. "Gavin needs me, Amber. Don't you dare keep me from him."

"Then I'm coming, too. Where is he?"

"I don't know where he is, but I know where he'll be."

40

God was angry, Gavin thought. David Benjamin had said that on their way over to the Nassau Coliseum, riding shotgun in the Tiger while the others followed in Mullens's van. He had also given all kinds of analogies and spoken a lot about his own past experiences, but Gavin only half listened, his main thoughts centered on the fact that God was angry. As He should be! Gavin wondered if God had as hard a time smiling as he did. Amy would chide him, tell him he needed to stop and smell God's roses.

Which made him wonder why he'd never wanted to. How was he supposed to enjoy the roses with all the pain he saw . . . experienced? There was just too much going wrong. The only fragrance he wanted to breathe was Amy's and his little baby-girl-to-be; his only thoughts were of death to all who tried to stop him. Maybe God could be equally loving and angry with the rest of the world, but for the moment, Gavin would go with what he thought he was best at: the angry part.

Now, Gavin looked out Mullens's van window. They were in the parking lot with thousands of other cars. His own Tiger was just outside the window in the next space.

"Before we go in we should pray for Gavin again," Benjamin said, his expression aggressively steeled.

"If God is angry, then why doesn't He step in and change

things?" a quiet Gavin said, drawing all eyes. "I mean . . . He is God, isn't He?"

Lauer spoke up first. "He does step in, but mostly through us."

Benjamin, who never seemed to be short of an analogy, said, "Try to think of God as a judge and you as a cop. The judge gets angry but works in a system that requires teamwork."

"If God did everything, there would be no relationship," Hartington added. "There comes a time when He calls on *us* to get involved."

Gavin studied all the faces looking at him in the van. Strangers, really, though he felt a growing camaraderie. "Do you guys honestly believe Krogan's going to confess to murder just because I tell him to in the ring?" he said, remembering how Krogan had thrown the Ninja guy into the audience like a rag doll.

"You have to remember Ephesians 6:12," Mullens said. "'We wrestle not against flesh and blood.' This is a spiritual fight and Krogan's body will submit."

"We? *I'm* the one in the ring. All you guys are doing is praying like sports fans for their home team," Gavin grumbled, watching out the window at the people pouring through the coliseum doors. Armageddon would soon begin.

"Would you mind if I read you something about prayer?" Hartington asked in his comforting English accent.

Gavin motioned for him to continue.

Hartington pulled a small, leather-bound book from his suit jacket. The book appeared well worn, softly cracked and frayed around the edges, much like its owner. He arranged himself in his seat, put on a pair of reading glasses, licked his thumb, and fingered through the thin pages, then cleared his throat and read.

"'And another angel came and stood at the altar, holding a golden censer, and much incense was given to him that he might add it to the prayers of the saints upon the golden altar which was before the throne. And the smoke of the incense, along with the prayers of the saints went up before God out of the angel's hand. And the angel took the censer and he filled it with the fire of the altar and threw it to earth . . . and there followed peals of thunder and sounds and flashes of lightning and an earthquake.'"

Hartington stopped and looked up. "Chapter eight continues to describe a scene that would give even Krogan the shivers. With the right type of prayer, God delivers. And when He delivers, Krogan and the rest of his kind are but insects."

Gavin nodded. "Insects have been around a lot longer than we have, and probably will be around long after we're gone."

Gavin was met with frowns all around. "Look, I know you guys are bewildered at how God could choose someone like me to go up against the likes of Krogan, but it's simple from where I stand."

The frowns turned to raised brows.

"He either didn't choose me or He made a mistake."

The frowns returned, and Benjamin spoke up. "God has chosen the weak to confound the strong and the foolish to confound the wise."

"So you're saying I'm weak and foolish?"

"No. Contrarily, if you haven't noticed," Benjamin said with a warm smile, "we're the weak and foolish. Apparently, it is us who've been chosen to confound you."

Gavin produced a rare smile. "Hopefully, you've been chosen for more than that. I'm already confounded."

They all nodded in agreement, then gathered around him, laid their hands on his head and shoulders, and prayed for his faith and safety. By the time they were done, Gavin was sure he was making a huge mistake.

*   *   *

Inside the coliseum, Gavin followed Father Lauer to his designated prayer position. The three other ministers were already at their chosen stations, strategically—at least in their minds, Gavin thought—at the north, south, and east points of the upper rows. Lauer was to occupy the west.

"Listen," Gavin said to Lauer over the pounding music. "Whatever happens, thanks for helping . . . all of you."

"Just be confident. Remember the verses from the book of Revelation Jim read you. This is a spiritual fight, where you have the decided advantage. When the time comes, we'll stand at the top of our aisles and pray like there's no tomorrow," Lauer promised.

"Thanks," Gavin said, then left, mulling over Lauer's choice of words.

Gavin worked his way down the stairs and through the aisles. On the big screen were clips from Krogan's earlier fights . . . if you could call them that. Gavin tried not to watch. He wasn't even dressed for a fight. Everyone else who planned to fight had some sort of costumed gym attire. In his jeans and white polo shirt he'd scavenged from his laundry last night, he looked and felt more like a bartender than a serious contender. At least the ski mask he'd borrowed from Benjamin's son would add a little mystique. But then again, maybe not.

Everyone seemed to be talking about what Krogan was going to do tonight. He heard one skinny, green-haired teenaged girl talk about how Krogan was definitely going to kill someone, and how it wouldn't be against the law, because stuff happens in sports.

"Gavin Pierce," a voice said as Gavin was passing by.

Gavin stopped and turned to see a young black man, twenty at most, with penetratingly clear white eyes, wearing worn but clean jeans and a white T-shirt. He was sitting back with his hands crossed over one knee, smiling.

"Do I know you?" Gavin asked, wondering if he was even talking to the correct person.

"You have many friends here tonight, Gavin Pierce," the young man said. His teeth were perfectly straight, pearl white.

"Who are you?"

"One of your friends. I'm here for the fight . . . your fight with Krogan."

Gavin was shocked. "What fight? Who told you I was going to fight Krogan?"

"You did, Gavin Pierce," said another voice on the other side of the aisle.

Gavin turned to see another man staring at him a few rows down. The man was also dressed casually. He was fair skinned with blond hair and exceptionally clear eyes, which held that same knowing look as the other guy. And that same smile.

"Me?" Gavin wondered if Chris was somehow messing with him for leaving him today and not coming back. "Very funny. I've never seen or spoken to you in my life."

"But we know you . . . and we're here to help. Do not fear. You will be safe."

"Help?" Gavin said.

"Yes." He heard yet another voice. Gavin turned again to see a young but completely bald man with piercing blue eyes standing in the aisle behind him. "Ask and you will receive according to your faith. Do not surrender to the adversary . . . surrender instead to God."

Gavin said nothing, momentarily focused on the words being spoken instead of who the men were surrounding him. He turned to look back at the first man and found the seat empty. He quickly turned back to the blond man, but he was also gone . . . and then so was the man in the aisle, much faster than Gavin believed possible.

"What the—does anyone *else* around here know me?" he asked the people immediately around him.

"Yeah, aren't you my social studies teacher?" some teenager said, causing his friends to laugh.

"No, he's my private health teacher," said the girl next to him. The laughs grew louder.

Gavin left. He didn't know what to make of what just happened, but he needed to get down to the challengers' line.

41

Krogan was furious as he drove the WWX Ferrari down the ramp to the underworld of the coliseum. Fans lined the ramp walls, chanting his name as they recognized him. He noticed the guard in the security booth wave and then pick up the telephone as he passed him.

The pleasure of finally killing Buck fled with the escape of his granddaughter and her friends on horseback. Why the *LULL* had stalled just before he was about to sweep her horse's feet out from underneath it with the forks, he could only guess. She didn't know him like her grandfather and her death would have only added to a glorious day, but the fact that she had slipped through his fingers was humiliating—and that it had probably happened from unseen intervention was irritating. He couldn't wait to get his hands on someone . . . tear his head off.

He screeched to a stop and heard the female voice of the navigation system telling him for the third time that he had arrived at his destination.

"Shut up," he growled as he punched a hole in the Ferrari's monitor, cutting his knuckles. When that failed to stop the voice, which was now repeating itself over and over in a robotic-like monotone, he got out of the car, grabbed the rocker panel under the door with both hands, and with a loud roar, lifted the side of the car up and pushed it over on its back, crushing the windshield. With the engine still running and exhaust pipes vibrating, he could still hear the skipping techno-voice of the navigator.

"What are you doing!" screamed Tanya as she ran toward him. Apparently it was she whom the guard had alerted with the phone call.

"Parking."

"This is how you treat my car!" she cried, her voice about three octaves higher than usual, staring at the upside-down WWX-3 license plate.

"Like you, it didn't know when to shut up," Krogan snarled as he passed her by, starting toward the arena.

Tanya sputtered, staring at her mangled car, then back at Krogan. "You're late!" she yelled, running after him. "Where have you been?"

"I'm never late." Krogan stopped, staring into the vacuum of space. He spun around quickly and looked . . . searched . . . his eyes darting. He felt something . . . and didn't like it. An intrusion? He heard the heavy-metal music coming from the arena. *This is my house,* he thought, annoyed that such a twinge in his senses would happen here. He grabbed the blabbering Tanya by the arm and whirled her into his gaze.

"Hey, that hurt," was the last thing she said before Krogan called her mind back into submission.

"You will keep your mind as an open channel to me tonight. Stay near while I fight. Stay focused on me . . . you will hear my thoughts for you and you will obey my will."

Tanya nodded and fell into step with his gait as he marched up to the introduction chamber unannounced. Stage coordinators and crew, startled by his sudden appearance, were scrambling about, calling instructions on headsets, pointing and pushing. Krogan paused momentarily at the stage opening below the giant screen, not to wait for the stage crews to catch up, but to search for unseen intrusions. He couldn't see them, but he sensed their presence. They were here. Why? He also sensed his own comrades, watching as they always were . . . as they should be.

The spotlights found him with Tanya by his side. The crowd erupted in applause and then with chants of his name.

"*Shadahd,*" he yelled, then ripped off his shirt and his shoes and threw them into the audience, leaving torn jeans shorts that he had put on before he left his apartment. A moment later fireworks exploded at his side, in sync with the pounding bass rhythms. He started toward the ring.

42

Gavin walked up to a reception desk two hundred feet back from the ring. Beyond the desk was the challenger line, considerably smaller in numbers than the night before, when the probability of an extended hospital stay or possibly a funeral became a stark reality.

"Can I help you?" said a man with black spiked hair and pierced eyebrows wearing a WWX T-shirt with a button showing only a hand with an extended middle finger.

"I'm here to fight Krogan," Gavin said.

"You?"

"Yeah, me."

"Like that?"

"Is there a dress code?" Gavin said sarcastically.

"Uh, no, but—"

"You have a problem with the way other people dress?"

"Huh?"

"Good, then sign me up."

The man shrugged and handed Gavin a few sheets of paper. Gavin didn't bother to read any of the fine print that occupied most of the three sheets. He filled in the usual information about who he was and where he lived in bold print. As he wrote in his address, his pen almost tore through under the weight of his anger, underlining the number of his house. He wrote Chris's name for whom to contact in case of an emergency, signed everywhere he could find, and then handed back the papers.

The man's pierced brows rose at the sight of Gavin's lettering. He then shrugged and said, "What do you want to be called?"

"What?"

"Your stage name? Every challenger has to have a stage name for the announcer to announce. That's what he does."

"I don't care. He can call me whatever he wants."

"Uh-uh. He doesn't get paid to do that."

Gavin rolled his eyes. "Call me . . . I don't know . . . . Call me The Challenger."

"Excuse me?"

"The Challenger."

"Are you sure?"

"Write it down."

"Okay," he said, then started to write. "Does challenger have one *L* or two?"

"It doesn't matter, just write it. . . . I think two."

"Can I see some ID?"

Gavin opened his badge wallet, showing his shield and a photo. "Will this do?" he said.

The man's eyes widened. "You're a cop."

"I know."

"Do you have a gun with you?"

"Why?"

"Because that would be against the rules. Shooting him before the three minutes are up would probably void the prize."

"I'll try to be patient."

The man's eyes widened further. "Do . . . do you have a driver's license?" he said weakly. "I'm supposed to ask for a driver's license."

"No. Do you have any other stupid questions?"

"N-no. You're in."

Gavin took only a couple of steps before the man called back to him.

"Say, uh, Gavin," he said, reading from the signed papers. "What's this all about?"

Gavin turned and said, "I've been asking myself the same question for the last two and a half years, pal. Same *wrong* question. What I'm being told is that it ain't *what* . . . it's *who* . . . Understand?"

"Uh, yeah. I think so."

"Good. Later you can explain it to me," Gavin said, then left.

The line consisted of a row of seats behind the announcers' table, about twenty of the seats filled with hopeful challengers. Yesterday there had been a dozen rows. The challengers, dressed in various battle outfits, all looked at Gavin as he approached. He put on the ski mask. He felt stupid, but he didn't want Krogan to recognize him before he got into the ring. The contestants stared at him, all with that same quizzical expression on their faces the receptionist had had. Gavin ignored them and sat down, wondering how he would ever get in the ring without cutting in front of someone.

The outer lights of the coliseum darkened as Krogan came down the entrance ramp with a woman at his side. She seemed to be dressed in black spray paint. Gavin closed his eyes, trying to shut out all the hype that was making him sick—the cheers, explosions, music—and focus on what had been spoken to him by Lauer's team and by the strangers in the crowd. Who were those guys? He knew the pastors would tell him they were angels, but he refused to be caught up in some religious notion brought on by circumstance. Sure, he wanted to believe there were angels out there to help him, but not at the expense of creating them himself. Never. There had to be another reason why these guys all knew what they knew and looked like they did and disappeared that way . . . God, he hoped they were angels.

Krogan climbed into the ring and was announced again, but this time in the terms and conditions of the Armageddon contest. Three minutes for a million didn't sound easy anymore. Didn't sound possible anymore. When the announcer finished his sickeningly enthusiastic promo, he introduced the first challenger—Mammoth. Fifty zillion watts' worth of spotlights bore down on the biggest WWX wrestler Gavin had ever seen. The contender was easily twice Krogan's size. Abnormally sized everything, without looking fat. Definitely the circus strong man's much bigger brother.

Mammoth strutted down the ramp and up to the ring in an outfit that could have passed for Fred Flintstone's clothes. A cable with a hook at the bottom was lowered from the ceiling like a crane looking for an I-beam. Mammoth slipped one foot into the hook, and the cable lifted him high in the air over the ring. Finally, after displaying that Krogan would be fighting the human equivalent of a Kodiak bear, Mammoth was lowered into the ring. The cable was retracted back into the ceiling and a giant cage lowered around the ring. Gavin wondered if this was more drama from the WWX or the result of a new clause in their insurance policy to keep the audience from being injured from flying challengers.

✳   ✳   ✳

Krogan sized up his towering opponent. Did they think mass mattered to him . . . or numbers? This was exactly what he wanted after losing Buchanan's granddaughter. His only consolation was that she would feel the pain of grief for the grandfather who had cared for her. The thought made him smile. He looked in Tanya's direction. She was focused on him just as she was supposed to be. He looked at the challengers and started to feel as if he were wasting his time with helpless children.

The announcer started the countdown of Armageddon's second day of contests. *Armageddon,* Krogan thought with a wry grin. If they only knew. He thought of the terrorist in the news. How much more satisfying would it be to destroy trains and ferries and instruct Christians to kill in the name of their cursed creator? How much more fun would it be to lead misguided sheep down—

There it was again. He looked out into the crowd. *There!* For an instant he saw a few vertical bars of light, but then they were gone . . . or at least hidden. Were his human eyes failing him? He quickly discarded the notion. No human sense could confuse what he had perceived. But why were they here? What did they want of him?

"Three, two, one," the announcer said.

Mammoth charged. Krogan had no intention of making this challenge interesting. He didn't want to take his eyes off the audience, but he would for a moment. Mammoth raised his right arm high, then brought it down in a powerful tomahawk chop. But to Krogan, it was child's play. Like lightning, he swung his right arm high and over Mammoth's oncoming hammer-fist, crushing the giant's exposed jaw with an elbow and continuing the movement through until their arms locked below their biceps. Mammoth's feet left the ground as Krogan continued to drive the giant's arm forward, bending it back and dislocating it at the shoulder. Mammoth was on his back, his jaw bleeding and broken . . . unconscious. The fight was over. The crowd was stunned into silence.

Krogan looked back in the direction of the audience. He could feel his inner agitation at the unseen presence. He looked toward the amateur challenger line. Several of the would-be contenders were leaving.

Suddenly two bars of light appeared as if turned on by a switch. Boldly. Defiantly. He knew he had sensed something. But what was this? Between them was a contestant. Was that what this was about?

Protection for a contestant? Krogan snorted. What, were they here to battle? Didn't they know who he was? A mere two angels of guardian magnitude were no match for him. He had walked through larger opposition without a scratch. Regardless, he hoped they would engage him so he could send them limping back to their master. Krogan laughed. *Bring it on,* he thought. Why not? The notion of boredom and wasted time was a universe away. Here was a fight the unseen would be more interested in.

The cage was lifting.

*   *   *

While the cage disappeared into the ceiling, several stagehands dragged Mammoth off like a dead whale. Gavin was in shock along with the rest of the coliseum. There could be no doubt in the eyes and minds of the next challengers that they were all dead men. The announcer then explained to the audience that the next challenger would come from the amateur line.

"No thanks," said the next contestant loudly, standing up and telling Gavin, "Good luck, man" on his way out. Several others in succession also got up, shaking their heads as they made their way up the aisle to the scornful boos of the crowd.

Gavin felt the sweat coursing down his sides as he looked at Krogan. The demon's unblinking eyes were staring only at him. Why? Could he see through the mask? Maybe. Gavin knew little about what limitations or powers Krogan had, but what he did know was that the guy in the ring, demon or not, was responsible for a lot of pain and sorrow. And somehow the monster was going to pay for it all . . . tonight.

Fear and anger bore through Gavin's chest as he imagined his grandfather talking to him, and his friend and neighbor John Garrity, both of whom had been carelessly killed for Krogan's enjoyment. Buck's family. And now Amy in the hospital nursing her pregnancy after having their home blown apart and her decorator killed. Enough was enough.

As the music cranked up, the big screen displayed Mammoth's defeat from every angle. The remaining contestants grimaced at the dislocation of the shoulder and the slam to the ground. Was he out his mind for trying this? Gavin asked himself. Other contestants seemed to share that thought as more stood up and left. But he wasn't about to leave. Out of his mind was exactly where he needed to be right now.

"Him," Krogan yelled, pointing at Gavin. "He's next."

There was a pause as the announcer tried to figure out what was happening and whom Krogan was pointing at. The few remaining contestants looked at him in disbelief. No one complained.

Gavin started to get up. The ski mask felt hot and scratchy around his face and neck. A hand from the seat next to him pushed him back down. Another contestant? Through the eyeholes of the mask, Gavin could see a man with fair skin, long red hair, and crystal blue eyes. He said, "Do not try to fight him with your natural strength, Gavin. He cannot be beaten if your focus is on the flesh."

"Do not raise a hand against him," said another voice on his other side.

Another man . . . no . . . the same man. Gavin quickly looked back, expecting to see that the first man had vanished, but he was still there. Twins?

"He will try to draw you in, but your focus must be on your mission, not on damaging his host. You will be given understanding and the words to say. Do not be anxious."

"Yes, you must leave the battle to us. He is powerful, but we are many . . . and most of his followers have already fled, sick from our presence," the second one said with a thin smile, then laid his hand on Gavin's thigh.

Gavin felt strange. Good but strange. His mind started to clear from the many thoughts that had been pressing in on it. New thoughts were emerging. The conversations he'd had with Buck and with the Salt guys were coming to him. He remembered the verse Benjamin and Buck had both quoted about not wrestling with flesh and blood but against spirits. Why hadn't it dawned on him that he was going into a wrestling ring to actually wrestle with a spirit? How weird.

The driving music calmed and the announcer finally declared, "The next challenger to take on the champion is . . . The Challenger!"

Spotlights blasted Gavin from all sides. The reassuring hands were gone, yet he felt strong, at peace. He stood up, legs steady, chin high, and walked up to the ring. Krogan stood in one corner, watching.

"Krogan . . . Krogan . . . Krogan . . ." chanted the crowd.

A smiling WWX girl stepped on the bottom rope and lifted the top for Gavin to enter. "Are you sure you want to do this?" she said nonchalantly while smiling for the camera.

Gavin figured he must look pretty pathetic for her to say that. But then again, maybe it was her job to say that to every amateur climbing in, just to get them a little more nervous about their fate. He adjusted the ski mask, which kept drooping over his eyes. How did people ever rob banks with these things?

"What's a nice boy like you doing in a place like this? Short on cash?" Krogan said with a crooked smile while strutting toward the center, his deep, whispery voice sounding animal-like.

"I'm here for you, pal, not the money."

"Oh, really?" Krogan said, surprised. "I would think a guy like you would be here to raise money for your church."

He was probing . . . and somehow Gavin knew it. The demon had apparently seen the angels and was wondering why they were here. "Guess again, slimeball. What, did my friends make you nervous?"

Krogan's smile evaporated. "What friends?"

"You and I both know who I'm talking about, hotshot. And there's plenty more where they came from," Gavin said, his confidence building with every word. He felt a tingling he'd never experienced before. He couldn't believe it, but he actually felt like laughing. *Imagine that,* he thought. *Laughing . . . me!*

Krogan's eyes started darting around the audience. Gavin didn't look, because he knew he would see nothing, but Krogan was seeing things. That was obvious. He wished he could see what Krogan was seeing. His expression had changed from smug to alert, turning around, looking to either side. Whatever was out there, they certainly had his attention.

Krogan spun back around to Gavin. "Who are you?"

Gavin pulled off his mask and stared him straight in the eye. "I'm the guy who's going to take you down, Krogan."

Shock swept across Krogan's face, his eyes huge. "Pierce!"

"I thought you might remember me . . . after all we've been through."

The announcer started the countdown for the match to begin.

Krogan smiled, his smugness returning. "I suppose I should thank you. This was my second most gratifying day ever, second only to *The Day,* when the son was crucified. This is better than I'd hoped . . . much better."

"Three . . . two . . . one . . ."

43

The bell rang to start the contest. Gavin had seen enough of Krogan's other matches to know that the beast would first wait to be attacked, probably as a show of unconcerned dominance and willingness to take on all strategies. Gavin found it hard not to take Krogan up on his postural offer. Every natural cell in his body was screaming for him to throw the first punch, second punch, and anything else he could throw from his well-trained arsenal of hand-to-hand experience. But that wasn't the game plan. As the demon stood tall and still, Gavin neared him, hands down . . . forced to his sides.

"What's the matter, Krogan? Feel like we're ganging up on you?" Gavin bluffed. He couldn't see any of the "many friends" he was supposed to have helping him and wondered if Krogan could.

Krogan smiled nonchalantly. "Gang up? Those two weaklings who were at your side are long gone, bozo. You are alone, Pierce. Just you and me. And soon there will just be me."

"That's not what I see," Gavin lied, gambling that Krogan was unable to know what he could see. "You're surrounded and they're closing in. Nervous?"

Krogan frowned, then started to circle around to Gavin's side. The crowd, which had been stunned by Mammoth's defeat, was now beginning to boo at the lack of action in the ring.

Gavin ignored the distraction and stayed focused on the task at hand. He counter-circled, keeping Krogan in front of him. He could sense the confusion. But he wasn't sure if Krogan was confused over Gavin's talking about things that weren't there, or because Gavin was speaking about things he wasn't supposed to know.

"Are you here to talk or fight?" Krogan snarled.

"I already told you . . . I'm here to take you down."

"Then do it. You came to me. Here I am."

"And what do you expect me to do? Drive into you like you drove into my house?" Gavin said, hoping for an admission that would end the fight before it started.

Krogan was about to speak but stopped himself. His chin rose as he looked down on Gavin suspiciously, then after a long moment smiled thinly. "Very crafty, Pierce. But your friends should have informed you that I'm better at this than you are. They should know."

So much for Plan A. Gavin tried not to show disappointment. "Did you drive through my house with a cement truck?" he demanded.

Krogan laughed and shook his head. "Why do you ask me a question you know the answer to?"

"I command you to tell me," Gavin said, as the Salt guys had instructed him to.

"By whose authority?" Krogan laughed. "The Nassau County police?"

"Not this time, you filthy beast." Gavin remembered how well that had worked two and a half years ago. "Answer me in the name of Jesus . . . now!"

Krogan winced and buckled, pulling his arms in as if he'd been punched in the abdomen, veins swelling in his neck and face. He looked up at Gavin in total surprise. Sweat framed his face. "Not bad, Pierce. Not bad. This will be more satisfying than I thought."

The audience was growing more impatient at the inactivity, chanting Krogan's name now and booing louder. Their champion wasn't killing someone yet, and a minute had already passed. Meanwhile, Gavin felt incredibly focused. He understood his job, and he wasn't allowing the crowd or Krogan's obvious physical advantage to distract him.

"Confess, Krogan. Did you drive—"

Krogan lunged and Gavin instinctively darted, sidestepping the charge . . . or at least he at first thought he had. But he'd never reacted that quickly before, and after a moment, he realized he'd somehow been moved from Krogan's path like a matador sweeps a cape. Krogan couldn't stop before hitting the ropes off-balance, but quickly regained his footing and spun around.

Gavin smiled in admiration and relief. He had been promised, and the angels—or whatever they were—were delivering. "What's the matter, Krogan? Have a real fight on your hands?" he said, suddenly in no hurry to get the confession. He could enjoy watching this all day.

"You're gonna need more help than that, Pierce. They can only keep you from me for so long. When I get you, I'll have no mercy."

"You're the one who's going to need the mercy. But I hate to tell you that's not my strong point."

"Gavin!" called a distressed voice from behind, causing him to snap his head around.

"Amy!" he cried. There she was, Amber at her side, hands cradling her beach-ball abdomen.

What is she doing here!

How could he pay attention to Krogan, God, the angels, his new Salt friends, or anybody else with Amy here, about to have a baby where she stood? He couldn't care about anything else. He dashed to the ropes, but took only a couple of steps before falling on his face, his right leg anchored by the ankle. He turned to see Krogan on his hands and knees, holding him fast but unable to do much else. Apparently, the angels weren't here to do the work without his participation. *Just great!*

"Let him go, Krogan," Amy screamed.

To Gavin's surprise, he immediately felt Krogan's grip loosen. But any appreciation for Krogan's being dealt another blow was lost on the fact that Amy was stressed and angry. All he could remember was her doctor telling him that she needed to spend the rest of her pregnancy mummylike in bed. He turned toward Krogan, but for the sake of the counsel everyone had given him today, he restrained from kicking him in the head with his heel. *Really* restrained. He didn't understand how Krogan could be hurt more by not physically hitting him, but the surrender to the spirit-world approach seemed to be working. "Release me and confess," Gavin ordered.

Krogan cried out, as if in pain as his fingers sprung open from Gavin's ankle. Gavin didn't understand how any of this speak-respond dynamic worked, but he had a strong feeling Krogan understood it well.

Gavin heard a woman's scream and he whirled about. This time it was Amber. She was standing over a kneeling Amy. *Praying,* Gavin thought. *Amy's praying for me.*

"Her water broke!" Amber yelled at Gavin, as if he would know what to do. For a moment Gavin was furious with Amber for having brought Amy. She should have known better. But then again, nobody could tell Amy not to do something once she was determined to do it. "Jesus!" Gavin cried. "Not now . . . not here!" He sprang to his feet, but again before he could get out of the ring, he was stopped, his shirt grabbed from behind. He continued forward, his shirt ripping off his back. He had to get to Amy. He had to get her to a hospital. He had to get her there now.

Krogan's arm was around Gavin's waist, pulling him off the ropes and throwing him hard to the mat in the middle of the ring, knocking the wind out of him. After a moment of respiratory paralysis, he gasped, stunned and sucking hard for air. This wasn't working. The more attention he paid to Amy, the more strength Krogan gained. And apparently Krogan was not interested in anything less than a fight to the death. Gavin's death. But how could he focus on both Amy and Krogan? Clearly, the fastest way out of the ring was through Krogan, who was now dropping like a rock through midair, right at him.

"Cease," Gavin ordered, remembering the word Buck had used in their last battle. He rolled and sprung away from the slam as quick as a cat.

Krogan, writhing in pain, managed to get to his hands and knees. Gavin was beginning to understand that his words brought more pain than physical impact ever could.

Now what!

Beyond Krogan, Gavin could see uniformed police streaming down the aisles toward the ring. The announcer was speaking, but Gavin couldn't catch what he was saying. A horn blared. The crowd erupted. Police surrounded the ring. Gavin yelled desperately to one of them, pointing, "She's having a baby! Help her! Help her!"

Krogan was on him again, and Gavin was on his back, his head slamming on the mat. He felt dazed. He heard the cops yelling to Krogan but couldn't understand what they were saying with the loud ringing in his ears. Krogan had three heads . . . then two. The world was coming back into focus, but before he could utter another word, cops were grabbing Krogan's arms. He shook one of the officers off like a toy.

"Stop!" Gavin tried to yell but could only whisper as two more cops were on Krogan's free arm.

"Hold it right there, big guy. You're under arrest," said a familiar voice.

Gavin turned to see Chris standing in the ring. "Arrest?"

"Easy, Gav. We'll take it from here. He's under arrest for the attempted murder of Gregory Robertson, this morning in Hamden, New York," Chris said, not taking his eyes off Krogan.

Krogan frowned, then looked to the side of the ring, probably assessing the situation. Even by his standards, he was vastly outnumbered. Angels, cops, the Salt guys, and who knows who or what else?

"Gregory?" Gavin said incredulously, realizing Krogan had found Buck's farm. He'd probably—

"She's got my gun!" shouted one of the uniformed cops outside the ring. All heads turned to see the woman in black who had entered with Krogan now pointing the officer's gun at those standing around her.

"Easy, now," one of the cops said. "No one has to get hurt here."

"There're a lot of people around you, lady," another cop said.

Without warning, she threw the gun into the ring. In the same instant, Krogan shucked the four cops holding him as if they were Styrofoam mannequins and grabbed the gun. Everyone immediately froze and backed off.

Krogan smiled. "You lose, Pierce," he said, pointing the nine-millimeter's deadly barrel between Gavin's eyes.

"Cease," Gavin ordered.

Krogan was straining to hold the gun outstretched and steady. The veins in his arms and hands swelled, his face deep red, his eyes growing, growing.

The gun fired. There were screams. The audience gasped, then hushed eerily.

Unable to pull the trigger on Gavin, Krogan had turned the gun on himself. The gun fell from his fingers, blood dripping from a hole in his chest. Krogan stared into Gavin's eyes and with a crooked smile, repeated, "Like I said, Pierce . . . you lose."

44

. . . Pierce, you lose . . . ."

Krogan's words were still echoing in Gavin's ears as he stared at the dead body of Jackhammer Hoban.

"What did he mean by that?"

"Huh?" Gavin said to Chris, who was standing next to him, also staring at the body.

"What did he mean by 'you lose'?"

"I already explained this to you, Big Dog. He's gone. He's escaped. The murderer's gotten away," Gavin said, looking Chris in the eye.

Chris sighed, shaking his head. "I knew you were gonna tell me this. I have to admit that none of this makes any sense. When I got the call from the state that this guy was at Buchanan's farm, I got an ice pick in my spine. I couldn't believe it. But how can your explanation be true? Last I looked, I wasn't a character in a horror movie or something. I mean, a real demon? Next you'll be telling me about ghosts, aliens, and angels."

Gavin just stared at him, then said, "Do the DNA on him. You'll find he's the guy who drove through my house. I gotta go." Gavin turned and started walking away.

"Go! Now where are you going?"

"I don't know, but somewhere my wife's having a baby."

Just then a cop came running up to the ring. Gavin recognized him as Officer John Kelly, whom he'd see at the train wreck. He was sweating and breathing hard. He caught Gavin's stare and said, "Detective . . . your wife . . . she's calling for you."

Gavin ran to Kelly and grabbed him by the shoulders. "Where is she?"

"We couldn't get her to the hospital . . . too late . . . . She's . . . she's in a dressing room. Come on . . . I'll show you."

Moments later Gavin was running in Kelly's wake through a rubbernecking crowd and then backstage, Chris right behind him. Another crowd in a curving hallway, mostly cops and WWX staff, parted as Gavin approached. He tried to read their faces but couldn't since most of them were busy looking at his ripped clothes and scratched body. Kelly opened a door and went in.

The first thing Gavin saw was the back of a woman paramedic standing over an ambulance stretcher.

"Here he is!" Kelly said, sucking in air.

The paramedic turned and stepped away, letting his searching gaze find its mark quickly. Amy's eyes met his. She looked exhausted, eyes at half mast, but she had a glow not unlike that of the angels.

"You okay?" she said weakly.

"What's happening?" Gavin said desperately, unsure of what kind of attention she needed.

"The question isn't what, Gavin . . . it's who," she said with a sly smile. Gavin frowned. Was the whole universe in on some kind of joke where he was the punch line? "What do you mean?" He drew close to her.

"Easy, Gavin. You don't want to disturb your daughter's first meal, do you?" Amy smiled at him, peeling back the white blanket just enough for him to see the newborn infant enjoying nourishment from her mother's breast.

Gavin couldn't move . . . couldn't breathe . . . couldn't blink.

Tears welled up in his eyes as he felt the need to swallow. "Is . . . is . . ."

"She's perfect," Amy said with a broad smile, her own eyes glazing. "Do you want to hold her?"

"No . . . I mean, yes . . . not yet. She looks so . . ."

"She's yours, Gavin. And she's got your appetite."

"I . . . I can't believe it."

"Well, you can thank Barbara over here." Amy motioned toward the paramedic. "She's a real pro."

"Thanks," Gavin said to the paramedic, a thirty-something black woman with a beaming smile.

Barbara shook her head. "Mom's the hero. I was just here to catch. And I'm sorry to break this up, but we need to get to the hospital. This room gave us some privacy in a pinch, but it's not exactly where we'd like to set up shop, if you know what I mean."

Gavin nodded as he looked around the dressing room for the first time. The place was a wreck, and he was just now realizing it smelled of liquor. He held Amy's hand as Barbara gave instructions to start clearing the path for the move to the ambulance.

"Congratulations, Pop! And you too, Mrs. Pierce," Chris said, slapping Gavin on the back. "There'll be plenty of time to see baby, so I won't ask you to disturb her meal. Having just been born, right now she probably looks like you, Gav, but don't worry, that'll change in time. With any luck, she'll look like her mom."

"Thanks, Chris," Gavin said, still looking about the room. "Whose dressing room is this, anyway?"

"I don't think you want to know," Officer Kelly spoke up, standing guard by the doorway.

Gavin looked at Amy, who didn't seem to hear what Kelly had said, then at Barbara as he whispered to her calmly, "Get them to the hospital now. I *don't* want them in here."

Catching the seriousness in his demeanor, Barbara nodded and began wheeling Amy out.

But not before Gavin could give Amy a kiss and tell her he'd be riding behind the ambulance. They kissed again and then both gave the baby a little kiss on her head. He just couldn't believe it. He was a father, Amy was fine, and the baby was thriving. He thanked God in his heart, gave another little kiss, and let them leave.

As the room emptied, Gavin fell back and kept Chris with him. "This was Krogan's dressing room," he said, looking around.

Chris nodded. "I heard."

"You mentioned to Krogan that he was under arrest for attempted murder."

"Yeah, he flipped over and crushed a chicken coop this guy Gregory Robertson was in."

"Gregory is Buck's farmhand. He's deaf. From the back, he'd look a little like Buck, and Krogan must have mistaken him. You said he lived?"

"Yes. From what I understand, he wasn't even hurt, just scared."

Gavin nodded. *Wow! I guess the angels had more than just his bases covered today,* he thought. "Now he knows Buck is still alive."

"Who?" Chris looked startled. "The demon?"

"Yes, the demon. Who else?" Gavin sounded a bit agitated.

"Sorry, Gav, but this whole business takes a bit of getting used to."

"Tell me about it."

"So you think Buck is in danger?"

Gavin stared at Chris, trying to keep in mind that he was new to this. "Nothing's changed, Big Dog. He'll be back . . . and he doesn't seem to waste much time." Gavin picked up a newspaper off the makeup table that was open to page three, with a picture of the capsized ferry. He turned the paper over to confirm it had a picture of Krogan on the back, then laid the paper down.

"Where did Hoban live?" Gavin asked.

"I don't know. I'm new here, remember?"

Gavin nodded. "Let's find out where and take a ride."

"I can't, Gav. I've got to get back on the Hess case. I don't want to remind you after all you've been through today, but tomorrow's the Fourth and this guy's still out there."

"This *is* the Hess case, Big Dog. Trust me."

As Gavin and Chris were about to leave the room, the door opened and a balding man in a blue business suit entered. He looked as if he'd lost his way to a deposition, with his power tie, ring, watch, and cologne.

"Detective Pierce?" the man said.

"Yes."

"Mark Bodder. I'm Michael Grossman's attorney." He extended his hand.

Gavin took it tentatively. "We're in a hurry, Mr. Bodder. What's up?"

Bodder cleared his throat. "As you might imagine, what happened here tonight came as a complete surprise to us, and quite frankly, we're not looking for any further trouble. Especially from you."

"I don't understand what this has to do with me."

"Well, you were the challenger. And despite the unorthodox bout and the eventual outcome, you lasted beyond the required three minutes while the bout was still under way. Didn't you hear the horn sound and the announcer declare you the winner?"

Gavin just stared, saying nothing.

Bodder reached into his suit jacket and produced a piece of paper. "This was supposed to be presented to the winner in the ring, but under the circumstances . . ."

"Are you telling us he won a million dollars?" Chris said, incredulous.

"Well, yes. Congratulations," Bodder said, then handed Gavin a check. Gavin just stared at it.

"Well, Gav," Chris said, giving him another pat on the back. "Looks like you won't need me to rebuild your house." He laughed.

Gavin pocketed the check and looked at Bodder. "Where did Hoban live?"

45

Walter Hess had seen enough. *More* than enough. His abdomen felt like he had eaten a brick and he wanted to vomit. He got up from his seat, picked up his small television, ripped the plug out of its socket while the pretty young newscaster was still speaking, walked out on the deck of his small cabin boat, and with a loud scream, threw the TV into the middle of Long Island Sound. He raised his fist toward the sunny blue sky and yelled angrily, "I did everything you told me to do! I thought you were protecting me!"

Hess fell to his knees and dropped his forehead to the hard fiberglass deck, the hot sun cooking his naked back. What had he done wrong? What clue had he left behind that led them to him? His face was everywhere . . . *everywhere.* He'd been betrayed. Forsaken.

He put all his weight onto his forehead, rocking, allowing the coarse, nonskid surface of the deck to dig in . . . hurt. He needed to feel the pain. In tears, he prayed, "Why did you allow my clients and neighbors to lie about me the way they did? All I did was speak your truth to them. Even the people in my own church sold me out. The church you brought me to. Why didn't the pastor speak up . . . defend me? Where was he? Where were you? I'm your soldier. Your tool. Now they know my name, my face, my family . . . and they'll hunt me down like a dog. Why have you forsaken me this way?" he repeated over and over.

An unexpected icy breeze blew over his back and lingered, cooling the sun and causing goose bumps to rise. More discomfort, he thought. Good. He welcomed it. *Bring it on. Why not?*

"What!" He snapped his head up and swung around. "Who's there?" he shouted, suddenly paranoid. He didn't understand why he thought someone was there, but he definitely did. Strange. Like a commercial jingle that wouldn't leave, he heard words in his head. Not just words, but sentences. And not just sentences, but dialogue. *Voices.* Was he losing his mind? Was the stress of having his name and face publicized as a terrorist causing him to crack?

"Krogan?" he heard a voice say in his mind. He recognized the voice as being familiar, even his own. But why would he be saying that word, that name? The name of a serial killer, and more recently a name taken on by the wrestler who'd killed himself yesterday, according to the news. That must be it. The news had just mentioned his name and his mind was regurgitating useless information . . . just like one of those jingles.

"I have come to stay," said a voice. A different voice this time, definitely not familiar. Not his own. Stronger . . . more dominant. *But, hey, the mind gets weird stuff stuck in it all the time.*

"He's mine."

"No longer. You will both serve me."

The voices were becoming confrontational . . . territorial . . . like two animals vying for a piece of meat. Like two—

"Ughh," Hess gasped as icy cold shot through his body like voltage. He flipped onto his back and began to shake violently, his eyes rolling back and his teeth locking down on his tongue. He grabbed the sides of his head as a thousand thoughts rushed by like faces staring out the windows of a speeding train from two feet away. He was no longer in his boat, his natural senses ripped away to what seemed like other times and places. His ears heard screams, and his eyes saw flames engulfing everything from straw huts to modern jets. He saw bare, bleeding knuckles gripping the reins of a horse as it galloped through smoke and pain. He *inhaled* pain. It had a taste that was strangely pleasurable.

Hess bolted upright. He was back in his boat . . . and no longer shaking. Froth and drool and blood from his bitten tongue dripped from his chin. But before he could gather his thoughts, another wave of cold energy washed through him, the same energy, but this time not as violent, as if he had somehow adapted to it. An image appeared before him. An image so vivid, a vision so real, that he could not see his boat or even the deck he was sitting on. Indeed, he felt as if he were sitting on dirt, feeling the grit between his fingers. Before him were three crucifixes. He knew the man in the middle was Jesus. There was no question. He was at Golgotha. There was weeping and laughing. He heard mocking. Jesus lifted His head, His face swollen and bruised. Lines of dark blood carved His face from the crown of thorns digging into His head. He yelled with a loud voice, "*Eli, Eli, lama sabachthani.*"

Hess knew the words. He understood the meaning. He also understood that he had just spoken the same words in English while complaining to God on his boat. Jesus had had the same complaint just before He died. And after the complaint, He was resurrected into a new life . . . just as now he was being resurrected into a new life. As the vision continued he heard another word he understood.

"*Shadahd,*" yelled a voice next to him. No, not next to him . . . his own voice. The vision faded. He felt different . . . new . . . energized. God had given him a new gift—a new power to continue as never before. He jumped to his feet and looked toward the harbor a few miles away. He stretched and breathed deeply, then laughed heartily. He couldn't remember the last time he'd laughed so loud. He was now excited to continue his mission. He quickly found his field scope and clamped it to his transom mount.

The shock of having seen his face on network news was gone.

The ensuing panic that had torn through his mind after hearing his life history lied about and misrepresented by past neighbors and clients had miraculously subsided. Anger, fear, and hate had been replaced by a determination and strength that could only come from one place. What more confirmation did he need that he was doing God's holy work?

From the middle of Long Island Sound, Hess peered through his field scope. Boats were filling historic Hempstead Harbor for the fireworks show scheduled for that evening. Senator Bruce Sweeney would be speaking in a half hour. The authorities certainly had their hands full. Their job was virtually impossible: allow everyone to enjoy their constitutional right to celebrate the Fourth of July while keeping an eye open for a terrorist that might be anywhere and capable of doing the unexpected.

Hess imagined every harbor to be on the same high alert, but he was surprised at the number of patrol boats and even a helicopter overhead. He could remember how just days earlier he'd been tentative before derailing the train. Now he was fearless . . . in fact, excited at the prospect. So excited he could hardly contain himself, as if he were his own newest toy.

Working quickly, he readied his scuba gear and kept it convenient for escape. He then found a baseball cap, put it on backward, and slid on a large pair of dark sunglasses. So much for a disguise. He now looked like half the other people tooling around in their boats. He even had fireworks. The only difference between his and theirs was that his were bigger . . . and way more fun.

Moments later he was cruising full throttle into the harbor.

✳   ✳   ✳

Gavin lowered the marine binoculars and rubbed his tired eyes as he and Chris motored slowly through Hempstead Harbor in— what else?—a Chris-Craft. It was a white twenty-footer that, according to Chris, he used mostly for . . . well, boating, whatever that was. Gavin was not a boat enthusiast. In fact, he didn't like boats. And he especially didn't like being on them. The last time he'd been on a boat, two and a half years ago, was the most memorable and stressful hour in his life. But none of that mattered. Not today. Not as long as Amy and his little baby girl, Violet Lynn, named after Gavin's grandmother, were both safe in the hospital . . . resting finally.

"Anything?" Chris said.

"He'll be here. I know I would."

"You mean, Sweeney?"

"Can you think of anyone you'd rather shoot with a fifty BMG?"

"No comment. And besides, he'd need an antitank missile to get through the steel podium he's standing behind."

Gavin nodded and said, "That's what bothers me. He's planned everything else down to the smallest detail, and by my scorecard, the only two mistakes he's made were the pack of cigarettes and underestimating the captain of the *Sachacus'* ability to think on his feet. I figure Hess knows everything we do and has figured an out-of-the-box solution for it."

"Let's hope you're wrong."

Gavin pointed as he saw the *Millennium,* another jet ferry similar to the *Sachacus,* leave the dock. "They check the hull of this one?"

Chris snorted. "As a matter of fact, they checked the hulls of every ferry within fifty miles of here and who knows where else? And they also instituted random route changes between destinations."

Gavin heard a loud explosion and turned quickly toward it.

"Another M-eighty," Chris said. "How will we ever know which one is really the Barrett rifle?"

"Sweeny will let us know," Gavin said, glassing an ocean racer headed toward the peninsula where Sweeney was. He picked up the

radio and notified the harbor patrol, which had already been notified by the helicopter.

Chris shook his head. "Somehow, I doubt Hess will come blazing in here with an ocean racer after his face has been plastered on
every screen and this place is crawling with police and Feds. If I was
him, I'd drift in with the high tide while sitting back with a beer and
a fishing line tied around my big toe."

"A line around your big toe?" Gavin said, still glassing boats and
people at a distance as Chris looked at the closer ones.

"Yeah. This way you know if you got one if you fall asleep.
Didn't you ever read Huck Finn?"

"Hmm . . . what happens to Huck Finn's big toe when a bluefish grabs the line?"

"They don't have bluefish in the Mississippi."

"Uh-huh. Let me know the next time you go fishing." Gavin saw
the harbor patrol quickly corral the ocean racer once the boat
passed the "No Wake" buoy near the peninsula. Around the other
side of the peninsula was a two-mile stretch of mirror-calm water
coveted by water skiers at high tide and clam diggers at low tide.
Beyond *that* was the Roslyn Viaduct and Hess's storage container.
Hess had not returned to the container and at this point probably
never would.

The *Millennium* exited the harbor to the thrill of Jet-Skis and
Wave Runners. Gavin figured Chris wanted a piece of the wake
also. A ride with Vinny Randone would cure him of that, Gavin
mused, flashing back to when the crazy man had helped him chase
down Krogan the last time. The thought brought him to Amy and
Violet. In fact, every thought was bringing him to Amy and Violet.
He wanted to be with them right now. It occurred to him he didn't
even have a picture. He needed to get—

"Look," Chris said, slapping Gavin on the arm.

"Where?"

"There." Chris pointed to a small cabin boat that had passed the no-wake line without slowing down.

Gavin was instantly there in his binoculars. He could see two harbor patrol boats leaving the ocean racer. The cabin boat still wasn't slowing but was actually veering toward the patrol at what appeared to be full tilt. Not an action that they were expecting from the stealthy Hess, but to Gavin, eerily reminiscent of another scene he remembered all too well.

"Go!" Gavin said, lowering the glasses.

"Us?"

The surprise in Chris's face and tone was justified. They were supposed to slowly nudge around as one of a growing number of spectators and simply look for Hess, who was expected to do the same thing, and be in a position to assist if needed *in their assigned area.*

"Yes, us . . . now . . . go!"

"But what if—"

"It's him, Chris . . . I saw him," Gavin lied, knowing what he had to say to get Chris to act.

The Chris-Craft responded with authority. Chris had told him many a time about its powerful engine, but Gavin had never paid attention. Whatever, he couldn't dispute the thing was fast, and in moments, Gavin was digging for his sunglasses to keep his eyes from tearing up.

"Goes pretty good, doesn't it?" Chris yelled proudly.

"Very nice," Gavin replied, acting unimpressed.

"I love this boat. Turns on a dime, too."

"That's great."

"You should come out more. Bring Amy and Violet. I'll let you take the helm."

"Good idea."

"Or now that you have some money, you should get one, too."

"Look!" Gavin pointed. The cabin boat, heading dead on to the larger harbor patrol vessels, had managed to juke and outmaneuver one patrol boat while rounding the peninsula near the power plant. The helicopter flew over Gavin's head on a straight course to the disturbance but would have to respect the high-tension wires to avoid being zapped like a bug on a blue insect light.

Maybe *that* was the plan, Gavin briefly thought. Get the helicopter to fly into the wires and crash itself and a tower onto Sweeny and his rally crowd. *Not very Hesslike, though. Too much left to chance. No way. Keep thinking.*

Moments later the Chris-Craft was rounding the peninsula. The first thing Gavin noticed was that the harbor patrol boats had backed off the chase. The tide was coming in, but it was still too low for the larger boats. The helicopter had smartly steered clear of the power lines and was flying two or three hundred feet over the cabin boat, which was following the channel markers.

"He's still speaking," Gavin yelled, noticing all the cars still in the parking lot at Bar Beach.

"Sweeney?" Chris yelled back as he blew past the harbor patrol boats with an acknowledging wave.

"Yeah," Gavin said, then picked up the radio and called the ground ops, informing them the confirmation was high on Hess driving the small cabin boat toward Roslyn, and that they'd better get Sweeney wrapped up. They promptly informed him the senator had no intention of stepping away from the podium, and the plan was now to contain and capture at a safe distance from the senator. And not to shoot unless being shot at. The guy in the boat, who had not been identified except at high speed with binoculars, was at the moment a suspect, nothing more.

"He thinks he's going to seize the moment," Gavin said.

Chris nodded and yelled back, "He's got to prove he's the man. What's he gonna do, run away because a powerboat cruises by and keeps going? With all the Feds, secret service, and police around him on the land and sea, he's in good hands . . . and what could be better for him than for Hess to finally be nailed with Sweeney standing right there, pointing the finger. Votes, baby, votes. Besides, how's he gonna fire that fifty BMG from the water while being chased?"

"What's he doing?" Gavin said as the cabin boat veered right and beyond the channel buoys toward the tall swamp grass and muck. Within seconds the white boat was sliding on the shiny-wet surface, carving a shallow hull-shaped groove until it came to rest in the tall grass.

Chris cursed. "I hope you don't think I'm bringing my boat in *there?*"

Gavin frowned. Containment didn't seem to be a problem. The boat was grounded and would stay that way for at least the next couple of hours, until the tide was high enough to float it out. Capture, in the meantime, was less certain. Most of the boat wasn't visible through the grass.

The good news for the moment was that there was no clear shot from the boat to the podium over a half mile away through the tall grass. The road beyond the shoreline was lined with police and federal vehicles. The harbor patrol had sealed off the channel from behind, and in the distance Gavin could see more flashing lights on the viaduct. There didn't appear to be a way out for Hess, but there also didn't appear to be any easy way in. Anyone trying to get through to him on the muck would sink in and be easy targets. Two more helicopters had arrived, but with the threat of the Barrett rifle, they were also keeping a cautious distance.

Chris had slowed and was approaching the spot where the cabin boat had turned out of the deeper channel, which would soon be deep enough for the harbor patrol to creep in. The radio crackled with a helicopter sighting of a gun barrel sticking out the front window of the cabin.

Chris looked at Gavin. "What's this guy think he's going to do . . . shoot at someone he can't even see, a half mile away, through grass?"

"Maybe he just wants to let us know to stay away," Gavin said as he pocketed his sunglasses and picked up the binoculars. As he adjusted for the closer distance, blades of grass came into focus, and just beyond that the front of the boat, and then, yes, the rifle barrel, as reported by the helicopter. But what the copter didn't report, apparently because of its elevated view, was that the barrel was angled upward.

"Big Dog, tell them the barrel is angled up. He's looking to shoot a bird," Gavin said as he followed the angle of the gun to see what it was pointing at. Nothing. The gun was pointed far above the political rally and under the helicopters. Gavin considered that if Hess shot the gun at that angle, he'd hit nothing until Connecticut. He lowered the binoculars and rubbed his eyes.

Chris radioed Gavin's message and then asked if Senator Sweeny was still speaking. He put the radio down and said to Gavin, "The good senator is loving this. Like I said . . . votes, baby, votes."

Gavin looked at Chris. "Volts!"

"Votes . . . I said. Not volts. What sense does—"

Gavin wasn't listening as he fumbled to get the binoculars back to his eyes. He turned and focused on the high-voltage power lines coming from the Long Island Power Authority plant. He lowered his view to the podium where Sweeny was speaking. "Get him out of there, Chris. Get them all out of there. He's aiming for the power lines," Gavin yelled.

Chris screamed into the radio while Gavin followed the deadly wire with the glasses until he came to the stanchion. Then he saw it. The insulator. Not an easy shot from a half mile, but definitely doable, given the time needed to aim a Barrett rifle. *Given the time.*

"Rev this thing up, Big Dog . . . and get us over there," Gavin yelled.

"Are you crazy?"

"He's not going to shoot us. He's got bigger fish to fry . . . literally."

"But my—"

"So it'll get a little dirty. Go!"

Chris cursed as he threw the throttle forward, made a small circle, and went through the buoys. The shallow path the cabin boat had carved out had filled in with water. The Chris-Craft was faster and lighter and—

A deafening blast was followed by a flash flame that lit up the front of the cabin boat. Gavin turned to see an explosion where the insulator had been. The huge tension wire dropped but then caught, sparks gushing from it like a Roman candle. The wire was shaking, but apparently, the hit wasn't direct.

"He's gonna take another shot," Gavin yelled. "Keep the throttle pinned."

"We'll hit him!" Chris shouted.

"I know," Gavin yelled, then motioned to Chris and jumped overboard.

He heard Chris scream, "My boat!" just before he hit the slimy muck at about forty miles an hour. As he skimmed across the top of the slippery black clay, the Chris-Craft stayed on course and crashed into the cabin boat. Gavin continued his slide through tall grass as if on ice, and then splashed into another water channel—a vein not large enough for a boat but deep enough to have to swim to keep from drowning. A second later, Chris, completely black, shot off the top of the muck and landed right next to him in the drink. Gavin grabbed him.

"Chris?" he said, trying to keep Chris's head above water. "You okay?"

Chris was gasping, his eyes white, the entire rest of him caked black. "I hate you," was all Gavin heard before another explosion sent both him and Chris under the water, swimming for their lives. When they resurfaced, the two boats, some hundred feet away, were in flames and small debris was falling from the sky around them.

Gavin started swimming toward the flames and Chris followed. The channel led to within a few yards of the boat and kept going behind the grass. The heat of the flames kept him back. Nothing could have survived the explosion, but maybe nothing had to, he thought, seeing tracks in the muck leading to the water.

"You owe me a boat," Chris muttered.

"Don't be ridiculous . . . you're a hero. You saved Sweeney and his rally."

"Hess?"

Gavin jerked his chin toward the tracks.

By the time they climbed their way out and were picked up by a harbor cop in a small boat that looked borrowed, the tide was substantially up, the flames were out, and Gavin had agreed to buy Chris a new Chris-Craft. And though a search was under way, Hess was still missing.

46

One month later

I'll be at the house," Gavin called into the kitchen, then took his hot cup of morning java and newspaper and stepped out the front door of his new home—the old Johnson place that used to be next door. A short walk took him to his old home, where he found a small patio table and chair on the front lawn, in the midst of a major construction project, mostly paid for by his reluctant homeowner's insurance company.

He walked around an orange plastic construction fence that surrounded a huge hole, twenty feet deep, filled with eight-foot-diameter precast concrete septic rings. This would become a dry-well for the leaders and foundation drainage for the water that had plagued him in years past. If he was going to do it, he was going to do it right, especially now that he had a little money, compliments of the WWX. Taxes had taken almost half, and his newly acquired residence took most of the rest, but he would owe nothing to a bank, and his old house would bring in rent, which would help nicely with the new expenses that came with parenthood. And Amy could be the mother she was capable of being . . . a new job she loved.

Gavin sat down at the round table, arranged himself comfortably, and took a shallow slurp of his hot coffee. "Mmmm." Without the sound, there was not as much taste. Nothing like the first half of the first cup. He opened his paper, just as he had been doing every day for the last month. Today was Saturday and the framers—not Chris and him, thank goodness—were off and the place was quiet. He felt for the alert device under his shirt, and of course, the necklace was still on him. Just checking. "Giant Asteroid Just Misses Moon," was the news heading that first caught his eye. It was nice to see normal headlines again. The article went on to describe what would happen to the earth if the moon were suddenly gone. Nothing was mentioned about the increase of arrests and births that occur during a full moon. He wondered for a moment if—

Gavin's attention was grabbed by the sound of a truck coming down the block. The first thing he noticed was that it wasn't a cement truck . . . but it was a carting truck with a Dumpster on the back. He couldn't think of anyone doing construction in the immediate neighborhood besides himself, and he already had a Dumpster that wasn't even half full. He set the paper down and stared at the truck, which was going faster than it should on a residential block. He strained to see into the windshield, but the glare of the sun made it impossible to see the driver. Just then, the throttle let up and the truck began to break for the corner. He watched it come to a stop, then turn and drive away.

"Looking for someone in particular?" said a voice next to him.

Gavin startled, snapping his gaze to the right. A man with a shaved head and small dark sunglasses stood with a crowbar in his right hand. He looked different than in his pictures . . . older, stronger, more ragged. He'd also grown a scruffy goatee and picked up a scar on his cheekbone. But he didn't look different enough for Gavin not to recognize him.

"You should consider a new barber," Gavin said, trying to keep his composure, thinking about the emergency alert.

Hess smiled eerily and pointed the crowbar at him. "You saw through my disguise," he said, then tossed aside the sunglasses.

Gavin exhaled quietly. The man's eyes had changed, too. Deeper, grabbing, like Dengler, like the tortoise, like Hoban. "On vacation from 'The Chosen'? Have they taught you any new tricks?"

"As usual, you're full of surprises, Detective. But if you knew me better, you would know that I teach the lessons."

Gavin felt a surge of courage that reminded him of when he went into the ring. "I know you better than I want to, Krogan. Has your new toy asked for your autograph yet?"

"Very good, Pierce. As a matter of fact, he has. But as you might imagine, I'm pressed for time."

"Time? I would think someone that's been around as long as you wouldn't be in such a rush. How old are you anyway?"

The eerie smile returned. "Years have no meaning to me, Detective. But I do have a few minutes to pick up on our last conversation. Only this time, I don't see any of your friends around to help you. What a pity."

"My friends?" Gavin said, poking himself in the chest and activating the emergency alert necklace. "You mean the ones who ended your wrestling career? Have you ever considered a job placement agency?"

"Enough talk," Krogan said, suddenly irritated. "You have caused me far more trouble than you're worth . . . which will be nothing after I return this tool you so carelessly left lying around."

"You forgot one thing, Krogan."

"I've forgotten nothing, especially you."

"Oh, that's right—you guys don't forget things . . . not needing to rely on human memories and all that. But that didn't seem to help you remember that I'm a cop."

"You're going to give me a ticket?"

Gavin ignored the comment. "You made the mistake of letting

me get to know you. You were so busy enjoying your revenge thing that you didn't bother to consider how predictable you were becoming to me. I was in your dressing room . . . and your apartment. Your being too arrogant to clean up after yourself leaves clues that anyone but a blind man could find. And I'm not blind. Not anymore that is. You see, I knew you would be here, and I even knew *who* you would be this time. And if you don't think I'm ready for you . . . guess again."

Krogan started looking around him.

"For the last month I've spent a lot of time thinking about you, Krogan, and you might be flattered to know that you've been a topic of conversation with a friend of mine whom I think you know."

Krogan's eyes were like flames. "Enough!" he roared as he wielded back and swung the crowbar at Gavin's head.

"Cease! Be still," demanded a voice from the walkway on the other side of the drainage hole.

The crowbar came to a halt just inches away from Gavin's flinching face.

Gavin opened his eyes. "I love the way you say that."

The shock in Krogan's eyes made Gavin wish he had a camera.

Buck, who had been more than willing to spend the last three weeks convalescing with Gavin, Amy, and Violet, had been looking healthier every day. For this occasion, he had apparently decided to leave the cane in the house. "Deal quickly with him, Gavin. He is not to be toyed with."

"Since you're right here . . . why don't you just . . ."

Buck shook his head. "Remember what we talked about. He's come to see you, and he must understand what a mistake that was. Let him see what you've been given. He must learn the cost of coming to you."

Gavin nodded. He understood the principle well enough; it was just the application that was foreign to him. He turned to Krogan, who was as still as a statue. *Deal with him quickly,* he thought. That would normally mean grabbing the crowbar, using the tool to break a bone or something that would require his total attention, and then punching, flipping, or tripping him into the twenty-foot hole that had been waiting for him for almost a month now. But that would be exactly what Krogan would want, and there was something about giving him what he wanted *and* expected that steeled Gavin's decision to lay down his usual arsenal for a weapon designed specifically for the likes of this dangerous beast. A weapon that, ironically, Krogan had helped to form in him. A weapon of the heart, an organ that in this business surpasses the mind. A weapon of surrender and trust. The weapon of faith.

"Into the hole, Krogan," Gavin ordered. He heard cars racing down the street but wouldn't turn.

Krogan laughed and, struggling, raised the crowbar slowly. For an invisible force, this spiritual warfare, as the pastors called it, sure had enough visual evidence. "Do you think I am a common spirit, that can be ordered about with your common faith?"

Gavin glanced at Buck, not interested in this being a training session.

"Drop your weapon, Krogan," Buck said.

"Yeah, now," Gavin quickly added, hoping to add whatever he could.

The crowbar dropped from Krogan's fingers. Gavin felt like picking it up and whacking him in the back with it, but he didn't and resisted even the thought of it. A car screeched to a stop and then another and another. Footsteps running. More cars screeching.

"You lose again," Krogan said through a locked jaw.

"Shut up," Gavin ordered. Not quite the way Buck would speak, he thought, but the result seemed be the same, as Krogan didn't say another word.

"Freeze!" someone yelled. Gavin turned to see police and Feds two and three deep with guns drawn. Buck's glare was on Krogan, and Gavin wondered if that was why the demon was still motionless. His faith was slipping again. He could feel it.

"Gavin," called Chris as he ran up.

"Stop . . . everyone," Gavin ordered. "Someone give me their cuffs. And don't come near him with a weapon."

"Take mine," Chris said, tossing them.

Gavin caught them with a clink and walked around Krogan. "Hands behind your back . . . now."

The arms moved slowly but they came. Gavin cuffed him and then asked for shackles to be tossed over. A few moments later, chained like the Frankenstein monster, Krogan was dragged away with suicide-watch instructions. A half hour later, everyone was gone but Buck, who was sitting patiently at the patio table. Gavin took a seat next to him.

"Will we ever have to deal with Krogan again?" Gavin thought aloud.

"It's in God's hands, Gavin. Someday he'll be out again. Time is on his side, for now. I've learned that you're never too old to look over your shoulder."

Gavin nodded, staring into space.

"What else, Gavin? You seem troubled."

"Ahh, I don't know. There's so much that just doesn't make sense. I mean, I know there's a God and I know there are demons and angels and that there's this war going on."

"But you're confused about all the pain and suffering?"

"Well, there's that. But . . ."

"Concerned that you don't measure up to God's standards?"

Gavin looked him in the eye. "I've heard about the mercy and the grace and I'm all for it. And I figure there's a lot more to life than correcting my faults, no matter who's doing it."

"But there's something else."

Gavin nodded.

"What then?"

"I couldn't get him in the hole," Gavin said somberly.

Buck looked at the hole for a long moment before answering. "It doesn't matter."

"But I told him to go in and he didn't. He should have. According to everything you and the Salt guys told me . . . he should have. But he didn't."

Buck smiled and patted Gavin's folded hands on the table. "The end result is the same. God's will was done, and that's what we are to work toward."

"He said I lose."

"He lied. He lied to you and to himself. He lost before time began. Don't let his lies darken your life, Gavin. You dug a hole, had it all prepared, looked at it every day for the last month. Now it's time to put a lid on it, and in the end you'll have a dryer basement. There are many such holes in life. Sometimes you just have to be satisfied not knowing the answer. Hess is another hole: Hess thought he was serving God, but just because he and others like him are wrong doesn't mean there is no true way or true God."

Gavin looked at the hole. Buck made it sound so simple. Why did he have to think so much?

"You've come a long way and have been given much. More dark times will come—they always do—but never doubt in the darkness what God has given you in the light."

Gavin nodded and understood. He wished Buck could stay longer, but he knew the old man would be leaving now. He left Buck and went to the house, where he knew Amy and Violet would be waiting for him. Suddenly that was the only thought in his head. He smiled.

DRIVEN

by W. G. Griffiths

Gavin Pierce is a Long Island detective who loses his grandfather in a horrific drunk driving accident. As he probes the case, he discovers it's only one in a string of bizarre vehicular homicides in which the "drunk" in question always disappears . . . even though he leaves the same sinister calling cards in his wake. As Gavin desperately searches for the one piece of evidence *never* left behind—a living eyewitness—what he does find chills his soul to the bone.

"Subtly creepy . . . read this with the lights on and the doors locked!"
—Nelson DeMille

THE CHRIST CLONE TRILOGY: IN HIS IMAGE

by James BeauSeigneur

Appearing in a world that faces plagues and nuclear war, Christopher Goodman is a boy with miraculous powers and visions who was cloned from the cells of Jesus Christ. Who is this youth and is he truly the Messiah? Can an impure being arise from the sacred living flesh of Jesus? All that's clear is that mankind is staggering toward a final apocalyptic conflict, and humanity's salvation or damnation may depend on the Christ Clone. Combining the visionary power of Tim LaHaye and Jerry B. Jenkins with the global suspense of Michael Crichton and Tom Clancy, James BeauSeigneur presents a brilliantly researched and vividly imagined epic that explores the astonishing future of Man . . . and the true nature of God.

"Powerful . . . an engrossing and ingenious story . . . a fine mix of scientific, political, and religious knowledge."

—Charles Sheffield, Hugo and Nebula Award-winning author

"Intelligent, well-researched, and flawlessly executed. . . . By far the most exciting, true-to-life portrayal of End Time events I've ever read."
—John Terry, *PropheZine*